THE ORPHANS

by

Matthew Sullivan

WET BANDIT

Copyright © 2015 by Matthew Sullivan

All rights reserved. Published in the United States
by Wet Bandit, Inc., Virginia.
Visit us on the web at wetbanditbooks.com

Cover illustration by Kristie Minke
Editing by Lauren Leibowitz

ISBN 978-0-9963020-0-5 (intl. trd. pbk.)
ISBN 978-0-9963020-1-2 (ebook)

The text was set in 12-point Minion Pro

10 9 8 7 6 5 4 3 2 1

WET BANDIT

First Edition

For my family and friends.
Thank you for all of your support.

CHAPTER
ONE

CHARLIE KIM NEVER PLANNED on becoming an orphan. He planned on being the valedictorian of his high school class; making the varsity soccer, basketball, and baseball teams; and attending Stanford University, just like his parents did. He planned on majoring in Finance and minoring in Computer Science, landing an analyst job at a top private equity firm, and earning his first million before his twenty-fifth birthday. He planned when he would start his own investment fund, the number of corporate boards he would sit on, and when he would retire, which would mostly be a formality since he had already decided that he would never completely retire. He even planned when he would marry, how many kids he would have, the schools they would attend, and so on.

For all intents and purposes, Charlie Kim had planned his entire life, the details of which were laid out in perfect cursive and chronological order on the pages of a pocket-size

Moleskine notebook that Charlie carried with him everywhere he went. Absent from those pages was any mention of becoming an orphan.

Five exhausting days after the policeman showed up at his house and delivered the news about his parents, Charlie stood before two sealed mahogany caskets, both suspended side-by-side over their burial plots. He subconsciously used his thumb to bend the corner of the notebook, which rested in his suit pants pocket, before letting the pages snap back like a flipbook animation. He repeated this motion—a nervous tic that he'd picked up a year earlier, during his first week of high school—over and over.

A small sea of people was gathered behind Charlie. Most of their faces would've been unfamiliar to him if he'd even bothered to note their presence. He hadn't. He was too wrapped up in his own thoughts to be mindful of anything existing around him. Whether it was the other attendees, the birds chirping in the distance, or the sweet natural perfume from the freshly trimmed cemetery grass, the rest of the world slipped past his senses unnoticed.

Charlie's lack of awareness wasn't limited to his surroundings. He was even oblivious to the signals that his own body was sending, including the aching in his chest, a side effect of the many hours he'd spent spastically clenching and heaving, and how his bloodshot eyes, unable to lubricate themselves after pouring a bathtub's worth of tears and pushing him to the brink of dehydration, were as sticky as newly paved asphalt. His eyelids twitched, refusing to blink, as he continued to stare at the caskets.

The caskets had remained closed throughout the wake and funeral mass. During the wake, Charlie had attempted to open his mother's casket. At no point since he was told of their passing had Charlie actually seen his parents' bodies, and part of him held out hope that when he opened the casket it'd be empty.

Charlie had gotten as far as unfastening the first of the many casket locks, and was about to go for the second, when the funeral director stopped him. He let Charlie know that it wasn't a wise idea. Charlie relayed his doubts, but the funeral director assured him that his parents were, in fact, inside each of the caskets. The somber look on the funeral director's face let Charlie know that he was telling the truth. What the funeral director didn't tell Charlie, with either words or expression, was that even if he'd managed to open the caskets, he wouldn't have recognized his parents.

A car accident had claimed the lives of Alan and Mary Kim. Partners in life and business, they'd been driving down the 101 freeway, on their way back to their Atherton home after a meeting in San Francisco, and were less than a mile from their Woodside Road exit when they crashed.

Nothing about the single-car accident made any sense to Charlie. It happened on a stretch of highway that his parents had traveled multiple times daily over the past twenty-plus years. Charlie had even made sure to check the traffic on his cell phone before his parents left, and if anything, there was less congestion than usual. There were no work crews with orange cones and caution signs to disrupt the traffic flow. On top of that, it'd been a beautiful, cloudless day, just like the day of their funeral. There hadn't been even a single drop of rain or anything that might explain why Alan lost control of the vehicle and slammed into the overpass support pillar.

Their SUV was crushed like a recycled can of Coke. Alan and Mary died instantly. The policeman who broke the news to Charlie had made sure to let him know just how quick and painless their deaths had been. It was a misguided attempt—by someone who had clearly never endured a similar grief—to make Charlie feel marginally better. That and much more replayed in Charlie's mind as his eyes stayed locked on the caskets and his thumb continued to cycle through the notebook pages.

It wasn't until a hand clamped down on his shoulder that Charlie finally snapped from his trance. He whipped his gaze toward the hand's owner, his grandfather, and glared.

Kyung-soo Kim looked back at his grandson and nodded sternly. Grandpa Kim was Charlie's last surviving family member, but to say that they were actually "family" would invoke the loosest application of the word.

Charlie had first sensed the rift between his grandfather and the rest of his family at an early age. But it wasn't until that night six months prior, when he eavesdropped on his parents discussing whether or not they should encourage the newly widowed Grandpa Kim to move in with the family, that Charlie became aware of the exact history. He overheard how Grandpa Kim had disowned Charlie's father when he chose to leave Korea for college, and doubled down on his position when Alan married Charlie's Irish-American mother.

Charlie returned the favor by disowning his grandfather on the spot. He wanted nothing to do with the man who wanted nothing to do with them. Charlie had crossed his fingers that his parents would decide to withhold their invitation, but his parents—frequent travelers of the high road that they were—elected otherwise, and opened their arms and household to the man who had pushed them away.

While Grandpa Kim reluctantly accepted their offer, he did nothing to endear himself to his gracious hosts, skipping family meals and spending nearly all of his time alone in his room. Charlie met his grandfather's cold shoulder with a frigid one of his own, leading Mary to conclude that Charlie and Grandpa Kim must have shared some sort of genetic stubbornness.

Channeling that stubbornness, Charlie went to yank himself free from his grandfather's grasp, but stopped when he discerned a tear forming in the corner of the old man's crow's-footed eye. It caught him completely off-guard. It was the first breach that he'd ever detected in his grandfather's hardened exterior—a lifetime's worth of fatherly regret condensed into one tiny drop.

Grandpa Kim withdrew his hand from Charlie's shoulder on his own accord. He cleared the drop with his index finger and nodded once more; this time, in the direction of the priest, who was waiting to recite the final blessing.

Charlie nodded back. He let out a long sigh, and then he and Grandpa Kim stepped forward and laid their hands on the caskets.

"Eternal rest grant unto Alan and Mary Kim, O Lord," the priest said, "and let perpetual light shine upon them. May their souls, and the souls of all of the faithful departed, through the mercy of God, rest in peace. Amen." The priest gave one last splash of holy water, and then two portly cemetery workers lowered the caskets into the ground.

Once the caskets had reached their final resting spot, the workers offered shovels to Charlie and Grandpa Kim, who accepted the tools. Charlie and Grandpa Kim took turns collecting piles of loose soil and scattering them across Alan's grave. They did the same for Mary's, and then handed the shovels back to the cemetery workers.

Charlie took a couple steps back, returned his hands to his pockets—and his notebook pages—and drifted off into his own thoughts. As he watched the cemetery workers continue to fill in the plots, he wondered what would happen next. Would his life ever be the same? Could it ever be the same? The questions were complex, but the answers were simple: no way, no how. As far as he was concerned, his parents weren't the only ones in a hole; he might as well have been right in there with them. With each shovelful of soil, Charlie came up with a new way in which his own life was over now that he was, and forever would be, an orphan.

One by one, the attendees began to casually make their way from the gravesite. Only Charlie stayed behind. His feet remained planted, his eyes didn't waver, and his thumb just kept flipping the pages of his notebook.

After a few more flicks, Charlie's thumb abruptly halted. For the first time, he actually felt the pages with his fingers. A thought flashed across his mind. His cheek muscles tugged at the corner of his mouth, some tiny fraction of a smile: He'd discovered his way out.

CHAPTER TWO

CHARLIE WAS BESIDE HIMSELF with disbelief. How had he not come up with his solution sooner? It was so obvious. It was literally right in the palm of his hand. All he had to do was stick to his plan.

While Charlie had been dead set on achieving his long list of goals before his parents' passing, he was even more determined now. He knew that it was his only hope for success and, in return, happiness. He clutched the notebook, still in his pocket, careful not to squeeze too tight and risk damaging the prized pages. For the first time in five days, he felt a sense of normalcy. A sense of confidence.

His disbelief having turned to determination, Charlie took off from the gravesite. He cut through the dispersing congregation, weaving in and out of narrow and rapidly disappearing lanes like an NFL running back with a nose for the end zone. He knew that he needed to get home as soon as possible, to the stacks of assignments—the accumulation of close to a week's worth of absences, during which he made no effort to keep up—that demanded completing.

Charlie mashed his teeth, angry for letting himself fall behind like he had, especially with midterms right around the corner. Now he'd have to cram harder than ever before to catch up and make sure his grades didn't slip. He knew that there was little margin for error: Just one A- on his transcript could be enough to prevent him from making valedictorian and getting accepted to Stanford, which would then prevent the rest of his plan. Like dominoes lined up in a row, each needed to fall for the next one to tumble. Charlie tried—in vain—to block out any thoughts of failure as he surged toward the cemetery exit.

Most of the other attendees weren't in as much of a rush as Charlie. It wasn't heavy hearts that slowed them down, but instead, the rarity of having so many of Silicon Valley's finest in the same spot at once. Funeral or not, if there were networking or business opportunities to be had, they'd be had. And so, start-ups were pitched, power lunches were scheduled, and deals were negotiated.

Even worse than the opportunists were those who thought it fit to share their own take on the rumors that were already swirling around town. Charlie wasn't alone in questioning the circumstances of his parents' crash; just about everyone with knowledge of the accident had. However, unlike Charlie, they didn't only have questions—they also had answers.

"Trust me, it wasn't an accident," insisted one confident attendee to his fellow gossipers. "I saw him last week.

Something was definitely off. He didn't seem like his usual self at all."

"I heard their prototype stopped running," another member of the group added. "After how everyone was hyping it up as the biggest breakthrough since the airplane, that's gotta be a crushing blow. It had to have taken its toll. I mean, I don't know what I would've done."

"Maybe the same thing he did?"

"Yeah, maybe."

The "thing" that they agreed Alan had done was intentionally crashing his Jeep. They had more than just hearsay to support their conclusion. The medical examiner had found no trace of alcohol or drugs in Alan's body. The police detective confirmed that their car had no mechanical flaws. And, as the local news reporter pointed out, the lack of skid marks on the highway showed that no attempt had been made to stop the car from crashing.

That left just two possibilities: Either Alan had fallen asleep at the wheel, at eight o'clock in the evening; or, as the funeral attendee noted, it wasn't an accident. Those who had worked with Alan knew he could pull an all-nighter without so much as a yawn, which meant there was really just one possibility.

The gossipers slammed the brakes on their untimely conversation as Charlie darted in between them. Uneasy looks bounced around the group like pinballs. Thankfully for all parties involved, Charlie hadn't heard one word of their discussion. The group let out sighs in succession as Charlie continued on his way, undeterred.

Charlie had moved on from chiding himself and was focused on determining the order in which he was going to tackle his heap of homework, a task much easier said than done. While he knew that he had several hours' worth of reading and problems for AP Biology and Precalculus, he also had to factor in the four-page paper that was due in his sophomore Language Arts class and could presumably take even longer, as writing was definitely not his strong suit.

Charlie was heavily debating the merits of each of his strategic options when a voice outside of his own head managed to sneak its way into his consciousness. It was both the familiarity of the voice and the combination of the words it spoke—two of which were his father's name—that allowed it to tiptoe past his eardrum blockade, override all of his thoughts of homework, and stop him in his tracks.

"It's a huge loss," continued the booming voice. "He could have been the next Tesla."

Charlie turned to the source, a hulking man with thick, dark hair, a chiseled jaw, and deep-set eyes so penetrating they could double for lie detectors.

Two bodyguards in black suits and aviators flanked the man. The older of the bodyguards was nearly as big as the man he was charged with protecting and had a faint scar on his weathered cheek that resembled an N. The younger bodyguard was at least a half-foot shorter than his partner, slight of build, and while he was clearly in his mid-30s, his slicked, gray hair attempted to indicate otherwise.

Charlie didn't even notice the guards; his eyes remained locked on—as if pulled by tractor beams—the other man.

"Terry Heins," he said as he offered his hand for a shake.

There was no need for the introduction. Charlie not only knew who Terry Heins was, he knew everything about him. Charlie had watched every interview and read every newspaper clipping and magazine article he could find on the man the media had dubbed "The Billionaire Maker of Silicon Valley." Charlie knew that Terry had gotten his start in currency speculation before transitioning to private equity, where his company, Abbadon Capital, had been early investors in hundreds of start-ups, including every major social media site. He knew that depending on the day and the stock market, Terry was either the wealthiest or second-wealthiest person in all of California. He also knew that he wanted to be just like Terry.

While Charlie had always admired his parents' integrity and passion, it was Terry's business acumen that he intended to emulate with his own career. Terry was a force to be reckoned with. He didn't just play the game, he dominated it. Terry also had a plan of his own. It was only after reading about how Terry had meticulously mapped out his own life that Charlie had decided to do the same, borrowing from the successes of both his parents and Terry.

Charlie considered telling Terry how influential he'd been and how much he'd learned from him before deciding that it would be much more prudent to just play it cool. He straightened his spine and his suit coat. "Charlie Kim," he said matter-of-factly as he completed the handshake. "And just so you know"—he tightened his grip as best he could, an act made nearly impossible given the fact that his tiny hands were dwarfed by Terry's baseball mitts—"my dad's engine was way better than the Tesla engine."

Terry smirked, amused by the show while also impressed with the young Kim's poise. "You're preaching to the choir, kid. Why do you think I invested a hundred million in your parents' company?"

"Uh, what?" Charlie stuttered. His shoulders slunk, his eyes lost focus, and his grip loosened to the point of letting go, as his mind was too busy racing—trying to figure out why his parents had never told him about Terry's investment—to remind his body to keep up all of the nonverbal cues that he'd learned to project confidence.

"It was a private deal," Terry said, noting Charlie's bewilderment. "Just like all of my deals. At least until the companies go public; then it's all over the news. But as you can imagine, we take our confidentiality agreements very seriously. And I respect the fact that your parents clearly did, too."

"Yeah, of course," Charlie said, still coming to terms with Terry's explanation.

"And just so you know, I wasn't referring to Tesla Motors. I was referring to Nikola Tesla. The inventor. He was a visionary. Just like your father. Just like I'm sure you are." Terry put his hand on Charlie's shoulder. "I can tell you're going to do great things. Your parents would've been proud."

Charlie instantly forgot that his parents had ever kept anything from him. All of his focus went to absorbing what he'd just heard. He couldn't believe Terry Heins had just implied that he was a visionary. His body was overcome with lightness, like his blood had been replaced with helium or laughing gas, and it all rushed straight to his head.

While Charlie continued to revel in Terry's praise, Terry's attention shifted to his older bodyguard, who tapped his watch. Terry nodded. He turned back to Charlie, gave his shoulder a gentle squeeze to get his attention, and then let go. "I'm sorry, but it looks like I need to get going."

"Wait! Are you sure?" Charlie blurted out, not wanting the conversation—or the compliments—to end.

"Unfortunately, I am," Terry said. "But don't worry. We can pick this up later."

Charlie's eyebrows arched in excitement. "Yeah! Totally. I mean, I know you're super busy, but I'm free whenever."

Terry retrieved a business card from his jacket pocket and handed it to Charlie. "That has all of my contact info."

Charlie examined the card. It was considerably nicer than any other business card that he'd ever seen, most of which had been his father's. Every time his parents started a new company, Charlie would get a new business card for his collection. But Terry's card wasn't like the cost-conscious cards his father had given him. It was a slick, jet-black with crisp red letters. It wasn't the typical flimsy cardstock, either. There was a noticeable heft to it.

Terry continued, "If you ever need anything, big or small, you just let me know."

Charlie wasted no time taking Terry up on the offer. "How about a summer internship?" he said. "If given the chance, I know that I could excel and more than prove my worth." The words rolled off his tongue naturally, like they'd been rehearsed, because they had been. Charlie had decided long ago that if he ever crossed paths with Terry, it'd be one of the first things they'd discuss and had even practiced his lines in front of his mirror many times over.

"That sure was quick," Terry said with a chuckle.

"I can email you my résumé as soon as I get home," Charlie added, maintaining his strict professional demeanor.

Terry's smirk faded as he realized the deadpan look on Charlie's face wasn't going anywhere. "Oh, you're serious."

Charlie answered with a firm nod.

"How old are you, thirteen?" Terry asked.

Charlie was accustomed to being mistaken for younger. He'd yet to sprout a single whisker, and even after the added boost from a summertime growth spurt, he was still one of the shorter sophomore boys at Atherton Prep. At five and a half feet, he was also well shy of his overall goal of becoming six feet tall, a height he'd decided on after reading a study that claimed taller people are more successful.

"I'll be sixteen in a couple months," Charlie said.

"You don't say," Terry said, seemingly intrigued. "You might not actually believe this, but I was about the same size as you when I was your age. Maybe even a tiny bit smaller."

"Really?" Charlie couldn't believe it. Not only did it mean that he and Terry Heins had something in common, it meant that maybe his six-foot goal, which he'd been close to writing off, wasn't out of reach after all.

"I swear." Terry took a moment to himself. "I actually see a lot of myself in you. I don't see why we couldn't figure something out for the summer."

Charlie flexed the muscles in his throat to keep himself from screaming. He swallowed his excitement and calmly replied, "I look forward to the opportunity to work with you."

"So do I," Terry said. He went to leave, but stopped short. "One last thing: If you happen to see Walter Sowell, let him know that he can take as much time off as he needs. My guys will be working around the clock to make sure we can get your father's engine up and running."

"Yeah, of course," Charlie said, too consumed with thoughts of his summer employment opportunity and how it'd set him up going forward to really process what he'd agreed to.

Terry patted Charlie on the back, shot him a wink, and then he and his bodyguards headed for the exit.

Charlie watched as Terry and his men hopped into a Bentley, its windows completely blacked out, and drove away. As soon as they were gone, Charlie's attention returned to the business card. He ran his fingers over the embossed lettering and imagined having his own business card just like it: CHARLIE KIM, PRESIDENT/CEO. It was only a matter of time before his vision would become reality. He just needed to hurry home and get cracking on his homework. He slipped the card in his pocket and made it one step before Terry's message for Walter Sowell finally registered.

Walter Sowell was Alan's old college roommate, best friend, and one third of every company that Alan and Mary had ever started. The setup was always the same: Alan was the creator, Mary handled the strategy and finances, and Walter, a technology whiz in his own right, handled a little bit of everything else. Walter was also the closest thing to an uncle that Charlie had ever known, and yet he'd been absent from the wake, the funeral, and the burial—a fact that Charlie had only just realized. As Charlie thought about it more, he determined that he hadn't seen Walter since the day before his parents' deaths.

Charlie retrieved his cell phone and called Walter. Anger and anxiety wrestled for control of his emotions while the phone rang. It kept ringing until it was cut off by Walter's voice mail recording and a notification that his inbox was full.

Charlie's heart fluttered as anxiety claimed victory. He knew it was unlike Walter to let his mailbox fill up, let alone leave a single message unheard. Charlie chewed on the corner of his mouth while he attempted to answer the questions swirling through his mind. Why hadn't Walter picked up? Where could he be? Had something happened to him?

Charlie sent Walter a text message asking him where he was and if he was all right. He stared at his phone for a minute. It'd never taken Walter more than thirty seconds to respond to one of his messages.

Another minute passed. No reply came.

CHAPTER
THREE

THE SUN HAD SET by the time Charlie and his grandfather returned home. While it'd be considered nice by most anyone's standards, the Kim's three-story Victorian was decidedly outdated compared to the rest of the affluent community, which had undergone a full architectural face-lift over the past decade. Almost all of the old Victorians that had previously dominated the area had been leveled and replaced by Tuscan villas, French chateaus, and the occasional concrete compound.

The Jameses across the street had opted for the latter, sparing no expense on their 15,000-square-foot compound, which even sported a rooftop pool and tennis court. Charlie had encouraged his parents to do the same with their property, but it wasn't in Alan and Mary's DNA. They preferred the charm of their home and had never concerned themselves with keeping up with the Joneses or the Jameses, anyway.

As Grandpa Kim pulled their car into the driveway, Charlie found relief not only in the fact that he was finally home and could get started on his work but that Walter's sedan was parked just ahead of them. Before the car could even come to a complete stop, Charlie threw open his door, leapt from the car, and dashed for the house.

Charlie fruitlessly scoured the downstairs before finding Walter passed out on the back patio, his scrawny body sprawled across a lounge chair. An empty six-pack of beer bottles rested on the adjacent side table; however, Walter gave the appearance of someone who had polished off at least twice as much. His face was flush and his hair was wildly unkempt, even by the low standards he'd established for himself.

Walter had frequently insisted to Charlie, or to anyone who would listen, that the average human, over the course of their lifetime, wasted approximately one hundred days fixing their hair. By cutting out the comb, Walter reasoned that he afforded himself more time than everyone else to do the things that he enjoyed, like working on any of his and Alan's projects. He also had a similar theory about sleep, which made finding him in such a deep slumber that much more surprising to Charlie.

Charlie gave Walter a nudge.

Walter jolted awake, nearly falling out of his chair before catching himself. "You trying to start a fight, tough guy," he said as he slowly gathered his bearings. He had called Charlie "tough guy" ever since Charlie was a little kid. Charlie did the same. A friendly joke between two decidedly not tough guys.

"Maybe," Charlie said. "Were you here the whole time?"

"Yeah," Walter said, momentarily averting his eyes. "I'm sorry I skipped out on everything. I just couldn't stand to see your dad and mom like that."

"You wouldn't have seen them, anyway. They kept the caskets closed the whole time."

"Even still. I'm not good with that kind of stuff."

It wasn't just the pain of seeing his friends being buried that had kept Walter away; he also had no desire to see the other attendees. Everywhere Walter went, he was asked for his take on the rumors. Just the day before, he'd come close to fighting a former colleague outside of a coffee shop for suggesting that Alan had purposely crashed his car.

"Listen," Walter said gently, "there's a chance you might hear some stuff about your parents. But I just want you to know that none of it's true."

"What kind of stuff?" Charlie asked.

"I don't want to say. But you'll know when you hear it."

"Well, Terry Heins said—"

Before Charlie could finish, Walter snapped, "Don't believe one damn word he has to say!"

It was the first time Charlie had ever seen Walter fly completely off the rails, or even get rattled at all. He was so taken aback by Walter's sudden display of emotion that every muscle in his body reflexively tightened, and for a split second, he actually forgot where he was.

Walter took a moment to calm himself. He apologized for his outburst and then asked what Terry had said.

Charlie told Walter what Terry had said about Alan being the next Nikola Tesla. Walter agreed with the assessment.

Charlie also mentioned the investment Terry had made in their company.

"He did a lot more than invest," Walter replied.

"Like what?" Charlie asked.

"It's not for you to worry about," Walter said. It wasn't just that he didn't want to cause Charlie any concern. The truth was that Walter wasn't quite sure himself.

"Well, he seems like a great guy to me," Charlie said. "He gave me his business card and told me to call him if I need anything. He even said he'd give me a summer internship."

"Let me see the business card."

Charlie went to retrieve the card but stopped, thinking better of it. "No way. You're just gonna take it."

"Just let me see it."

"Fine," Charlie said. He reluctantly dug the card from his pocket, gave it one last hard glance, and then handed it over.

Walter grabbed the card, crumpling it as soon as it met his palm. "The last thing you need is help from Terry Heins. You just have to trust me when I say to avoid him. All right?"

"Whatever." Charlie rolled his eyes. He had better things to do than get lectured. "Anyway, I have a ton of homework to catch up on, so I'm gonna get moving on that." He started toward the back door.

"Hey!" Walter called out, halting Charlie. "If you ever need anything, you come to me first. Okay? Of course, that's assuming it doesn't have anything to do with girls or sports. In which case, you're on your own."

Normally, that would've gotten a solid laugh or at the very least a chuckle out of Charlie, but not this time. He showed no signs of amusement. He just glared at Walter: Is that it? Charlie didn't receive the reaction he'd wanted, or any reaction at all. Walter's attention had already shifted to something else. He watched as Walter considered the business card that was still cupped in his palm, the wheels in Walter's head clearly turning.

After a moment, Walter slipped Terry's business card into his pocket. "All right, well, I actually need to take care of some work myself. Gotta get the engine running. For your dad."

Charlie remembered what Terry had said about telling Walter to take as much time off as he needed, but Charlie knew that the suggestion wouldn't be well received and might just lead to more arguing. So, instead of passing the information along, Charlie said nothing.

Walter continued, "But why don't you and me grab dinner tomorrow? That is, unless you already have something planned." Walter smirked. He liked to give Charlie a hard time about his planning, always in good fun.

"I don't know," Charlie said, still putting up his front. "It depends on how much of my homework I get done."

"How about I just bring something over, then? We gotta eat, right? These massive physiques don't fuel themselves." Walter flexed his pipe-cleaner arms for effect.

Charlie's mouth turned up ever so slightly.

"Come on. Let it out," Walter urged, knowing that he'd finally broken through Charlie's façade.

Charlie shook his head, releasing a wide grin in the process. "Fine. That works for me. Just put those guns away."

"Good call. This is California, after all. And I don't exactly have a permit." Walter tugged his sleeves to cover his puny biceps and then opened his arms wide. "Now get in here. I can't head off without a hug."

Charlie obliged.

"I love you," Walter said as he held Charlie tight.

Walter's words washed away the small amount of animosity Charlie was still harboring. After a moment, he replied, "I love you, too. But now I seriously need to get to work."

"All right, all right, all right." Walter gave Charlie one last squeeze, and then let him go. He quickly rounded up all of his empty beer bottles.

"Are you sure you're okay to drive?" Charlie asked as he gestured to the six-pack in Walter's hand. "You and Dad used to have to split that."

"Yeah, I'm fine. It took me almost eight hours to finish. Assuming I'm still tipping the scales at a massive 155 pounds"— Walter quickly did the math in his head—"My blood alcohol is about .021. Even if I lost a couple pounds, which my pants would argue otherwise, I'm still looking at .027, tops."

"Just making sure," Charlie said. He trusted Walter's math and his word, but after what had happened to his parents, he was even more sensitive to the risks of driving, not to mention driving while impaired. "Well, be careful."

"Don't worry. I will. And I appreciate you looking out for me." Walter tousled Charlie's hair, turning the teen's black mop into a mess that matched his own. "Hey! Look at that. Now you look like me."

"Awesome. That should help keep the girls away."

"Without a doubt. It's worked my whole life."

Charlie and Walter said one last goodbye, and then Walter headed off.

The very second that Walter was out of sight, Charlie rushed back inside his house. He snagged a pen that was lying on the kitchen counter, retrieved his Moleskine from his pocket, and quickly scribbled down Terry's phone number and email address from memory on the front page of the notebook. He turned to the next page, which contained the most recent version of his plan, and added the summer internship to the top of his list. There was no way he was going to let anyone, or anything, get in the way of his opportunity of a lifetime. That much he knew, or at least he thought he did.

CHAPTER
FOUR

WITH WALTER ACCOUNTED FOR and on his way, Charlie was finally able to focus on his homework backlog. Even though Terry had promised him the internship, he knew that it didn't mean he could just coast. He grabbed a glass of water from the kitchen sink to combat the dehydration that he was no longer able to ignore, and then headed upstairs to get cracking on his assignments.

Charlie's bedroom was the converted attic on the third floor of the house. He'd relocated to the room when Grandpa Kim moved in with the family, but he chose to leave most of his clothes and junk in his old room. All that was in the new room was a bed and nightstand, a desk with his computer, and a throw rug to cover the cracking laminate tile flooring.

The previous owners had failed to properly insulate the room during their partial renovations. As such, it was always warmer or cooler than the rest of the house, and usually the opposite of what one would want it to be. That particular night, it happened to be cooler.

Charlie threw on his Stanford University hoodie and took a seat at his desk. He blew into his hands for extra warmth, and then retrieved his Language Arts folder, having decided it'd be best to just get the paper out of the way first. He skimmed over the assignment sheet. His task: Write a four-page essay on the most important moment in his life.

Charlie contemplated his seemingly endless options. He knew better than to go with his first impulse: his conception. Half his class would probably pick their conception or birth, and they all would surely be docked points for their lack of originality. Many would argue that losing his parents was the most important moment in his life, but Charlie had already decided that he wasn't going to let that affect him.

Charlie turned to the pages of his Moleskine, certain that they held the answer. He read over his list of goals multiple times but still couldn't determine which moment was the most important. Arguments could be made for and against each milestone he had planned.

The harder he tried to come up with an answer for his essay, the further he felt from reaching any resolution, and the more frustrated he became. Before long, he began to sense a dull pain in his forehead. It was as if someone had his frontal lobe in a vise and was slowly cranking the handle.

Charlie knew the feeling well. He'd battled stress headaches for much of his childhood. The first one came when he was in the third grade, right before he and his classmates were tested for the Gifted and Talented program. He also knew that unless he did something, the pain would only get worse. So Charlie decided to put the essay on hold for the time being. He figured it was better to keep moving on his other assignments anyway, and he could just come back to the essay later.

◆ ◆ ◆

After only a couple of hours in the zone, Charlie had zipped through all of his accumulated math homework. The aching in his head had long since disappeared, and it was time to move on to Biology.

Before cracking his Biology book, Charlie took a quick glance at the clock on his computer screen. It was already 11:15 p.m. While he'd been successful in suppressing any thoughts of his parents and focusing on his schoolwork, he couldn't help but think of them at that moment. It was right around that time of night that his parents would call up to him and encourage him to shut it down and go to bed. They would also wish him goodnight and tell him how much they loved him. "We couldn't love you more," they would shout together. It'd become their nightly ritual ever since Charlie had moved to his third floor bedroom.

Charlie turned his attention to the stairs that led down to the second floor and the closed door at the bottom of the staircase. A faint light emanated from the crack in the door. He kept his eyes fixed on the entrance for a few moments, just in case, by some miracle, the call might come.

It didn't.

Charlie sighed and shook his head. He should've known better. Back to work. He flipped to the appropriate chapter in his Biology textbook and determinedly perused the pages.

Charlie was halfway through the second chapter of his required reading when he hit a wall. Hoping to get the blood flowing and milk some extra energy from his worn-out body, Charlie stretched his limbs so long that his joints cracked and popped like bubble wrap. A tiny boost followed, but only for a minute. After that, he was worse off than before. His eyelids started to feel more like sandbags. With every sentence that his eyes attempted to interpret, it only added more sand to the bags, until the weight had become unbearable.

Charlie decided to shut his eyes for just a second. He let out a jaw-stretching yawn, folded his arms on the top of his desk, and then rested his head in his elbow crease. He reminded himself of his one-second time limit before drifting off to sleep ...

◆ ◆ ◆

Charlie's eyes fluttered open. Immediately, he knew that much more than one second had passed. He lifted his head off of his desk and peeked at his computer clock to check how long he'd been out. Much to his surprise, the clock claimed that it was now 7:15 p.m. Charlie blinked hard to reset his pupils and checked the clock again—same time. It didn't make any sense. He'd either magically lost over four hours or slept for nearly twenty, neither of which seemed plausible.

The clock wasn't the only thing off. Charlie realized that he was no longer wearing his hooded sweatshirt. In fact, he wasn't wearing any of his clothes from before. He'd somehow switched to athletic shorts and a loose-fitting T-shirt. Before he could contemplate the possible reasons for the time difference and his wardrobe change, he was stopped by the sound of rustling and voices coming from downstairs.

"We need to hurry," a female voice insisted. "We're going to be late."

"I'm in no rush," a male voice responded. "He can wait."

Charlie instantly recognized the voices—they belonged to his parents. More than just their voices was familiar; so were the words they spoke. Charlie was able to place everything: He'd heard them have the exact same conversation just five nights earlier. He concluded that he hadn't woken up. He was still asleep and was just having some sort of lucid-dream-memory hybrid. Charlie knew how to tell if it was, in fact, a memory. If it was, his mother would be calling his name any second.

"Charles Kim," Mary hailed from the foyer, just as expected, "can you please come down here? We're about to leave."

Charlie smiled. Hearing her speak his name sent a warm rush through his entire body that gave him a sudden and powerful burst of life. He sprung from his desk and sprinted downstairs.

Charlie beamed as he made his way down the steps toward Alan and Mary, who waited in the foyer. Everything felt so real, like he was living it all over again. The only difference—a dire one, at that—was that he knew what would happen when they left. His thoughts jumped to the crash. He knew he had to convince them to stay home, or at the very least, to make sure that they took a different route—only he couldn't.

As soon as his parents acknowledged his presence, all Charlie could say or think were the same things he'd said and thought that night. "Where are you going?" he asked his mother.

"Your father and I have a meeting in the city," Mary said.

"I'll check the traffic." Charlie pulled up the traffic report on his cell phone and showed his parents that the roads were clear, nothing but green on the digital map. Mary thanked her son.

Alan, who was much more reserved than his usual self, chimed in, "Can you do me a favor, Charlie?"

"Of course, Dad," Charlie said. "Whatever you need."

"Take a break. At least ten minutes. Heck, go crazy and watch a whole TV show or play a video game."

"I don't know if I can handle anything that crazy," Charlie said, half joking.

"I'm serious," Alan said. "I've noticed you've been pushing yourself really hard lately. I don't want your headaches coming back."

Charlie had told his parents that his headaches had gone away for good a couple years earlier, and they seemed to have. But Charlie had hidden from his parents the fact that they'd come back stronger after he'd started following his plan. The same list of goals that boosted Charlie's confidence and sense of purpose had also boosted his anxiety. But for Charlie, it was a small price to pay, and the pros far outweighed the cons.

"Your father's right," Mary agreed. "You need to find a balance. You need to enjoy being a teen. You'll have more than enough time to be an adult later."

Charlie was used to his parents encouraging him to "enjoy being young" and always found their suggestion to be equal parts amusing and ridiculous. He couldn't imagine many other parents actually advised their kids to do less schoolwork.

Charlie figured it was easier for his parents to say; they didn't know what it was like being a teenager these days. When they were in high school, they didn't even have AP classes, and most of their classmates only took the SATs once, if at all. Charlie had taken his first practice SAT when he was in seventh grade and had read daily vocabulary sheets ever since. One of his words from that morning had been "appeasement," and that was the exact strategy he decided to employ.

"I'll throw on *Jeopardy* or something later," Charlie sighed.

"Good," Alan said. He nodded to Mary. "All right, let's get this over with."

Alan and Mary took turns hugging Charlie.

"We should be back by ten at the latest," Mary said as she let go of her son. "But hopefully earlier."

Alan put a hand on Charlie's shoulder and nodded. "And don't forget—"

"To take a break," Charlie sighed, cutting him off. "Don't worry. I will."

Alan smiled. "More important, don't forget that—"

Alan's reminder ended abruptly; however, he wasn't interrupted by anyone. His words simply stopped short when Charlie blinked. Charlie would've obstructed the basic autonomic action if he'd known what would happen afterwards. In the short amount of time that it'd taken for his eyes to reopen, his parents disappeared from the foyer.

Charlie's thoughts scrambled like eggs in a pan. That wasn't how their conversation had ended. His parents hadn't pulled off some sort of mid-sentence David Copperfield disappearing act. He knew for a fact that they'd both given him hugs, and then he'd watched them drive away. This vision he was reliving was all wrong.

As Charlie attempted to figure out what was going on, he realized that he was no longer bound by the constraints of his memory and could finally think and speak for himself.

"Mom! Dad!" Charlie shouted, but there was no response. "Don't go! Stay!"

Charlie's body went stiff as he struggled to come up with a solution. Then it dawned on him: the garage. That was where they had to be, and he might still be able to cut them off. If he got there in time, he could tell them why they couldn't leave. He could tell them what would happen. Maybe, just maybe, he could save them, if only in his dreams.

Charlie sprinted for the garage and ripped open the door. But he was too late. His father's SUV was already gone. Even in his dream, there was nothing he could do. Charlie started to hyperventilate. His vision blurred, and his whole world began to spin.

◆ ◆ ◆

Charlie shot up from his desk, wide-awake and gasping for air. His sweat-drenched clothes were stuck to his body.

Charlie was no stranger to nightmares or sleeping problems. Most nights, he'd spend at least an hour staring at the ceiling, his mind racing, before his body would finally shut down. Many of those nights, a nightmare would follow. His experience provided him no ease, only the knowledge that of all the terrible dreams his mind had ever conjured, the one that he'd just woken from was the worst by far.

It took a minute for Charlie to regain his breath and composure. Once his mind was finally clear, Charlie did his best to remember what his father had told him before they left. But no matter how hard he tried, he was unable to summon Alan's last five words: We couldn't love you more.

"We couldn't love you more," Alan had said to him before he and Mary had left for their meeting. The same thing they said every night before bed, and had told Charlie multiple times each day, ever since he was a baby. And yet, Charlie had no recollection of his parents ever saying it to him.

Charlie was so focused on trying to remember his father's words that it was a moment before it hit him that he'd actually forgotten the conversation altogether. He remembered that it'd happened, that they were in the foyer, and that Alan and Mary had left for something, but he couldn't recall where his parents were going, their demeanor, or a single word they'd said. It was the last time he'd seen them, it'd taken place just days ago, and it was seemingly wiped from his memory.

Charlie's eyes darted frantically about his bedroom. How was this possible? He almost never forgot anything. He even remembered the combination for his fifth-grade gym lock, which he hadn't used in years. He wasn't sure what was wrong with him, but he figured something had to be. The more he considered the cause, the more his thoughts kept pointing in the worst possible direction: He was losing his mind.

CHAPTER
FIVE

FOR CHARLIE, THE PROSPECT of losing his mind was exponentially more frightening than losing any particular memory itself. His eyes nervously searched for anything that might offer proof that what he was experiencing was an isolated incident and not the onset of a much larger problem. They quickly found their shot at salvation: his Biology textbook.

Charlie snagged the book from his desktop and tore it open. He flew through all of the chapter review quizzes; testing himself on cellular structure and reproduction, plant and animal life cycles, photosynthesis, natural selection, and so on.

After he recited his response to the final quiz question, Charlie sighed his lungs empty. He'd nailed every single answer. He still remembered it all. Soothed by the fact that it appeared to be just the one specific event that had escaped his memory, Charlie convinced himself it wasn't as big a deal as he'd initially thought. He reasoned that it was most likely some natural coping mechanism and, if anything, holding onto the memory of his parents' last night would only serve as a distraction. It was better to save his brain space for something else, like the last Biology chapter that he still needed to read.

Charlie checked the time on his computer. It was 1:23 a.m. He'd been asleep for less than two hours, but thanks to the adrenaline rush, he felt like he'd slept a solid eight. Charlie knew that if there was one good thing about nightmares, it was the resulting jolt to the system. It was comparable to drinking a pot of coffee and chasing it with a couple energy drinks. Charlie wiped the nightmare from his thoughts, turned to the page where he'd left off in his textbook, and got back to business.

◆ ◆ ◆

By seven o'clock the next morning, Charlie had plowed through nearly all of his homework, including multiple assignments for Civics and French. Only his four-page paper remained incomplete.

Charlie stared at the blank Word document on his computer screen. The flashing cursor was both taunting him and lulling him into a hypnotic state at the same time. He'd been trying to start his draft for the past hour, but the furthest he'd progressed was an opening sentence, which he deleted almost immediately after he finished typing.

Charlie's blaring alarm clock roused him from his trance. It was time to get ready for school. He'd have to put his paper on the back burner once more and hope that the answer would come to him later, maybe when he least expected it. The odds of that happening, as rare as they were, seemed better to Charlie than his odds of figuring it out on his own.

Charlie silenced his alarm and then headed to the second-floor bathroom. He studied his face in the bathroom mirror: Dark, heavy bags had started to form under his bloodshot eyes. It was nothing a piping-hot shower couldn't fix.

Charlie took a quick shower, got dressed, grabbed a bowl of cereal, and made it to the curb outside of his house just in time to catch the chartered bus that Atherton Prep provided for its privileged student body.

◆ ◆ ◆

Twenty minutes later, Charlie joined the throngs of students as they flooded the gates of their elite institution. While short on close friends—he didn't have the time to cultivate such relationships—Charlie did have many acquaintances, which he maintained as a necessary exercise in networking. All of his acquaintances, and even his non-acquaintances, were surprised to see him back at school so soon. But their astonishment paled in comparison to the confusion of his teachers, who didn't even get the chance to inform Charlie that he'd have all the time he needed to turn in his assignments before he was already handing them his completed work.

Only Charlie's Language Arts teacher, Mrs. Gamlen, was able to offer the extension, which Charlie eagerly accepted while still attempting to explain his reasons for not having his paper completed. Mrs. Gamlen stopped him and told him it wasn't necessary. She understood.

Any feeling of relief Charlie received from Mrs. Gamlen's empathy was exhausted when she handed him his most recently graded writing assignment. At the top of the paper, in bright red ink, was a big, fat B. There was no plus, either, just the miserable, lonesome B. It was the first grade below an A that Charlie had received all year, and the first grade below an A- since three years before. For the rest of class, it was also the only thing on Charlie's mind.

Once the period ended, Charlie approached his teacher with the intention of arguing his way to a better grade. While he didn't feel great about doing it, he knew his best bet was to play the emotional card. Charlie cited his parents' deaths and the enormous stress that he was under, and how it'd clearly affected his writing.

"I couldn't be more sorry about your parents," Mrs. Gamlen said, "and I will definitely take that into consideration on your next paper. But you do realize the paper I handed back was turned in over two weeks ago, right?"

Charlie froze, busted. He'd been so confident in what he considered his ace in the hole that he never imagined his teacher would challenge the timeline. He attempted to free himself from the bind he'd tied. "Uh, I know," he stuttered. "But, like, I had other things going on, too. Other problems at home." Charlie couldn't believe he just attempted to cover his lie with another lie, but his mouth had just said the words without ever asking his mind to sign off on them.

Mrs. Gamlen had heard the rumors about what might have "caused" the Kim's crash, and took Charlie's words as confirmation of their truth. "I see," she said.

Charlie, meanwhile, took Mrs. Gamlen's noticeable softening as an opportunity to close the deal. "I just really need an A in this class," he said, unknowingly overplaying his hand by switching the topic from his paper grade to his class grade.

"You don't need to worry about that," Mrs. Gamlen said. "There's still plenty of time to pull your overall grade up. Just make sure to put your maximum effort into the next paper."

That was the last thing Charlie wanted to hear. He was struggling with his assignment enough. Extension or not, he didn't need the added pressure. Before Charlie could respond, students began pouring into the room for the next period.

"I need to get ready for class," Mrs. Gamlen said. "But if you ever want to talk about anything besides your paper grade, I'm always available."

"Great. Thanks," Charlie said, but he was really thinking the opposite. His little plan had failed miserably, and he was stuck with the damn B.

As Charlie exited the classroom, he could feel his forehead beginning to throb again. He went to his locker and popped a couple ibuprofen tablets. He closed his locker, and then retrieved his Moleskine from his pocket and turned to the back page.

Charlie had a secret that he hadn't divulged to anyone. While his notebook full of goals was common knowledge, what wasn't known was that his notebook recorded more than just that. Starting on the last page and working backwards, Charlie had documented all of the failures that he'd accumulated.

So far, his defeats had only been minor. Just stumbles here and there. Never big enough to curtail his overall plans, but they all left their own little scars. Every time Charlie was reminded of one of his failures, he'd get angry. He used that anger as added motivation. He believed that it helped him refocus and gave him the edge that he needed.

The most recent notation on Charlie's list of failures was getting cut from the junior-varsity soccer team. It was one more thing—on the growing list of things—that he'd hidden from his parents. He'd even gone as far as staying after school and making up stories to keep up the guise of being on the team. When his parents inquired about attending a game, he just told them that they were playing a weak opponent and it'd be a blowout, but that he'd let them know when there was actually a good matchup that was worth attending.

Charlie jotted down his disappointing paper grade and then pocketed the notebook. He started toward his next class, but stopped when he heard his name blasted over the loudspeaker. His presence was requested at the principal's office.

Charlie reluctantly made his way down the locker-lined hallways. He'd never been called to the principal's office before, and had no idea what to expect. When he arrived at the office, Principal Salner was waiting in the doorway. Standing behind her was a stout police officer.

Charlie immediately recognized the officer. His name was Lieutenant Carter. He was the same policeman who had informed Charlie of his parents' accident. Charlie also recognized the pensive look on Lieutenant Carter's face—it was the same pained expression that the officer had worn the night that he stopped by his house.

CHAPTER SIX

AFTER A FEW UNCOMFORTABLE seconds, it was already apparent that neither the principal nor the policeman were interested in being the first to speak. Charlie did them the favor of breaking the silence. "What's going on?" he asked.

"I am so sorry," Principal Salner said, her sympathetic eyes attempting to comfort her student in addition to her words.

The principal's pity provided no answer to Charlie's question, only the confirmation that what he was about to hear wasn't going to be good. "For what?" he demanded.

Principal Salner glanced at Lieutenant Carter; it was his turn to speak, whether he wanted to or not.

Lieutenant Carter swallowed hard before breaking the news to Charlie. "Walter Sowell suffered a massive heart attack last night. By the time the paramedics arrived, it was too late."

Charlie's face stayed blank as thoughts shot across his mind like bullets on a battlefield, with similar results. He couldn't believe that Walter was really gone, and to a heart attack, of all things. Sure, Walter wasn't exactly the epitome of good health—he'd never heard of an exercise he liked, much less tolerated—but he was just forty years old. And he'd been at Charlie's house only hours before, and had seemed perfectly fine.

Charlie felt the opposite of fine. He felt similar to how he'd felt when he found out that he'd lost his parents, except worse. All of the feelings that he'd worked so hard to repress resurfaced as his emotional recall pulled him back to that night. He was hit with the loss of his parents and the loss of Walter all at once, like a tsunami of suffering. His lungs grew heavier by the second, as though they were filling up with mercury instead of oxygen, and his tear ducts continued to swell as Lieutenant Carter filled in the rest of the details.

The officer explained that around midnight, a neighbor had noticed that Walter's car lights were left on. When the neighbor stopped by to inform Walter of his oversight, they found the front door cracked open and Walter lying on his living-room floor, unconscious. The coroner estimated that he'd been deceased for close to an hour before his body was discovered.

This time, Lieutenant Carter spared Charlie any details pertaining to the speed and pain associated with Walter's passing. Maybe it was because he'd learned his lesson, or maybe it was just because he couldn't make the assertion with any real certainty. Whatever his reason, he left it out. Instead, he simply reaffirmed the principal's sentiment and then waited for Charlie to acknowledge what he'd told him.

Charlie was close to giving the confirmation the officer required in the form of a full-on emotional explosion. But just when Charlie's chest and eyes felt like they might burst like water balloons filled beyond capacity, Charlie's fingers found his trusty notebook, and his focus shifted back to his plan. Instantly, the pressure in Charlie's chest disappeared, and he regained his breath. He wiped the yet-to-pop tears from the corners of his eyes with his shirtsleeve and swallowed the mucus that had pooled in the back of his throat.

"Is that it?" Charlie asked, seemingly unaffected.

"Uh, yeah," Lieutenant Carter stammered, not expecting Charlie to respond in such a manner or to be so casual in doing so. He shared a look with Principal Salner, who was equally perplexed.

"All right," Charlie said. "Then I guess I should probably get back to class."

"Are you sure?" Lieutenant Carter said. "I told Principal Salner that I could give you a ride home if you need it."

"Thanks for the offer, but I've already missed enough class as it is. Plus, midterms are coming up." He nodded to Principal Salner. "But I will take a pass from you."

"Huh?" Principal Salner said, still too confused by the situation to process what Charlie was requesting.

"I've never done this before, but I'm assuming I'll need some kind of pass, since I'm gonna be late to class. Mrs. Hasbrouck is pretty strict about tardiness."

"Yes. Of course. I'll, uh, get that for you right now. Just hold on a second." Principal Salner fumbled with her pen as she filled out Charlie's excuse slip.

◆ ◆ ◆

Throughout the rest of the school day, whenever Charlie's thoughts began to drift toward Walter or his parents, he'd reopen his notebook and skim over his list of goals, and then his failures. The thoughts would cease, and his concentration would refocus the very second his eyes landed on his paper grade.

The grade was still on the top of his mind when he returned home. He kicked pebbles and muttered words that started with the letter B while he trudged up the concrete driveway. "Bull blank. Butt bag. Bass bucket—" He cut off his little rant as his feet came to a stop just before a manila shipping envelope that had been left on the front porch welcome mat.

Charlie reluctantly retrieved the envelope. It was the first package that had been delivered to their house in months, maybe years. Alan and Mary had always made sure to send everything to their office; it was the only way they could sign for things. But this package left on the doorstep had required no signature, and much to his surprise, it wasn't addressed to his parents—it was addressed to him. Even more shocking than that was who had sent it.

Charlie's eyes practically stretched out of their sockets when he read the black return-address label. Abbadon Capital was printed in dark red letters, just like it was on Terry's business card. Adrenaline shot through his body and washed away any thoughts of his paper grade.

Charlie knew there was only one thing the package could be. It had to be an offer letter for his summer internship.

While that would've required a much faster response time than the average person could have ever expected, Charlie knew that successful people like Terry didn't become successful by operating like the average person, or by resting on their laurels. They acted quickly, decisively, and frequently. Charlie remembered that Terry had said so himself in one of his newspaper interviews. He was so fond of the quote that he not only highlighted it, he also did his best to live by it. But as much as he'd liked the quote when he first read it, he appreciated it even more now that he was on the receiving end of its application.

Charlie swelled with pride, knowing that he must have impressed Terry so much that Terry considered it imperative to get his offer in writing before someone else beat him to it. Even before he ripped open the envelope and plunged his hand inside, Charlie was already plotting his next move. It was the obvious play: He'd have to counter Terry's offer. He was well aware that you must always counter any first offer, especially if it's a good offer. That was another Terry quote. Terry would have to expect him to do the same, to counter regardless. He might even rescind his offer if Charlie didn't.

Charlie's visions of advanced negotiations vanished—along with most of the wind in his sails—when his fingers failed to find an offer letter or even any type of letter. All he came up with was a nondescript flash drive. While it wouldn't have been out of the realm of possibility that Terry would put his offer on a flash drive, Charlie had a feeling that wasn't the case, as the drive didn't have the slightest hint of Abbadon's company colors. It was royal blue with splashes of yellow.

Charlie examined the drive in his palm. The color scheme seemed vaguely familiar to him. He flipped the drive over. On the other side, was a wordmark logo: PEGA SYSTEMS.

Charlie realized why it looked so familiar. It was from a company that his parents and Walter had created and sold no more than five years ago. Charlie even had the matching business card in his bedroom desk. He never kept the flash drives, though. That was all Walter. Walter loved to pilfer all of the old promotional electronics, particularly the flash drives. "You can never have too many flash drives," Walter would always tell him. Charlie had heard the line so many times that it was still as fresh as the day Walter had first said it.

Charlie repeated the line to himself. That's when the truth hit him like a Mike Tyson uppercut. The package wasn't from Terry—it was from Walter.

CHAPTER
SEVEN

CHARLIE BURST INTO his house and bolted up the stairs. He didn't have the slightest inkling as to why Walter had mailed the drive to him, why he'd sent it using an Abbadon packing label, or why, at the very least, he hadn't even bothered mentioning it the night before. Charlie had so many questions, but he knew there was only one way he might figure out the answers to any of them: He needed to find out what was on the storage device.

Charlie didn't slow down until he reached his bedroom. Even then, his momentum almost carried him out of his desk chair as he slid into the seat. He steadied himself and then hit the power button on his computer.

"Come on, come on!" he huffed and puffed, short of breath from his sudden burst of exertion. The machine made no attempt to speed up its booting process. If anything, to Charlie, it seemed to have actually slowed down. He banged the side of his desktop computer, hoping it might respond better to physical intimidation.

After a couple more smacks, the computer finally finished booting. Charlie jammed the flash drive into the USB port. The drive folder popped up on the screen. Charlie scanned the contents. There were dozens of files. Charlie recognized most of them as programs Walter had developed, programs that Walter had already shown him. Charlie was certain that Walter would've only sent him the drive if he'd wanted him to see something else, something more recent. He sorted the folder by creation date. Three files jumped to the top: an MP4 video file named WATCH ME FIRST, a spreadsheet named CONTACTS, and a PDF file named CONTRACT.

The video file was the obvious first choice, not just because of its name, but also because it was the most recent of the three files. It'd been created around eleven o'clock the night before, only a little more than an hour before Walter's neighbor discovered his body. Charlie double-clicked the video file, which immediately began playing upon opening. Much like the neighbor, nothing could've prepared him for what he saw.

On the screen was a poorly lit webcam shot of Walter. The darkness not only made Walter's exact location impossible to determine, but also accentuated the whiteness of his eyes, which darted back and forth from the webcam lens to something offscreen—presumably another computer monitor—as he delivered a panicked message.

"Hey, tough guy," Walter said. "I don't have a lot of time, but I'm sending you this because you need to know the truth.

Your parents didn't die from the car crash. They were killed. And Terry Heins was behind it all."

Charlie slapped the space bar on his keyboard, pausing the video. He buried his head in his hands. "You gotta be kidding me," he said as he tugged his hair so hard it sent tingles throughout his scalp and down his spine.

The news wasn't just the last thing Charlie had expected to hear, it was the last thing he had wanted to hear. But now, it was all that he heard. Walter's words played on a loop in his mind like a scratched CD that kept skipping back to the worst part of the song.

After a minute, the words finally stopped and Charlie lifted his head. "No way. No way. No way! This can't be real. It can't be," he moaned.

Charlie desperately wanted to remove the drive, throw it away, and never think of it again. He got incredibly close to doing that much. But just as his fingers gripped the flash drive and began to pull, another voice popped inside his head. The voice told him to stop. It told him that he needed to let the video play out. The voice was right. Regardless of whether he wanted to or not, he needed to hear more. He took a deep breath, sighed, and then tapped the space bar again, restarting the video.

Walter continued, "If I'm right, he's killed a lot more people than just your parents, like hundreds. I don't know exactly how he does it. He must drug them or something. I don't know. I just know that they all had heart attacks. That's what really killed your parents. They were on their way back from meeting with Terry when they crashed. I was supposed to be there with them, but I—" Walter stopped. His eyes turned to saucers as he spotted something on his second screen.

Walter turned back to the camera and wrapped up the video as fast as he could. "I've included a couple files on this flash drive. One's a list. I think it might be of all the people Terry is working with. The other looks like some kind of contract. I'm not sure what it's for or what it says. I think it's in Hebrew, but I'm not positive. It didn't register with any of the web translators I tried. I gotta go. But you need to be very careful. There are a lot of powerful people on that list. I don't know how high up this goes, or even where it goes. Just be careful, okay? I love you."

The video cut out, returning to the beginning image of Walter, his face frozen like he'd just seen a ghost.

Charlie peered deep into Walter's eyes. The manic urgency they conveyed was a stark contrast to what he was used to—to the man he'd known his whole life. He barely even recognized the version of Walter that he was staring at.

As hard as it was for Charlie to reconcile the image of Walter that was stuck on his monitor, the information that he'd imparted was an even greater challenge. Charlie knew that he should believe Walter without question. Walter had never lied to him before, no matter how small the stakes were. And these stakes were anything but small.

But while Charlie inched his way toward accepting everything Walter had said as fact, there was still one thing holding him back: the reality of what it meant for him and his life if it were actually true. With all the doubt swirling on both sides of his mind, there was no doubt when it came to the most important fact—he didn't want that reality. He didn't want his parents' deaths to be anything more than an accident, or Walter's to be anything more than some combination of genetics and poor dietary choices. He wanted to take the summer internship with Terry. He wanted that to be the big launching pad for achieving all of the goals that he'd laid out in his notebook. And so, he did what he'd done many times before when caught between the pull of the universe and his own worldly desires: He became his very own devil's advocate.

Charlie rattled off every possible explanation he could think of for not believing Walter. He told himself that Walter was just acting crazy in the video because he'd clearly broken into Abbadon's headquarters—that had to be why the package was sent from their office—and, well, because Walter was kind of crazy. He always had a thing for conspiracy theories. Whether it was the government or just competing companies, he was usually suspicious of someone and rarely trusted anyone outside of his very small circle.

Charlie also noted that Walter had said in the video, "If I'm right," which meant that even he wasn't 100 percent sure that he was right. He was basically guessing. He had no concrete proof that Charlie's parents had died of heart attacks. If that had been the case, the police would've said something. It'd have shown up in the autopsy. As for Walter's heart attack, it was just a coincidence, or maybe brought on by his own mania.

As persuading as each rebuttal Charlie had conceived was, the most compelling piece of evidence that he presented to himself was the lack of motive. There was no feasible reason why Terry would want to kill his parents after investing in their business. If their company failed, something that was almost certain to happen now, he stood to take a huge financial hit. No one as successful as Terry, or really even anyone who had ever had the slightest hint of success whatsoever, would ever intentionally sabotage their own investment. It went against everything Charlie had ever learned about business, as well as everything he'd ever read about Terry.

"Maximizing profit is the most important objective, the second most important objective, and the third most important objective in business," was the line Charlie recalled Terry saying in an interview on Bloomberg Television.

By the time he'd finished his closing arguments, Charlie had successfully swayed his internal jury. Not guilty would be the verdict they would return, without any need for further deliberations. That is, if not for the lone dissenter, the voice in his head that was still causing a stir. It refused to go away. It needed more evidence before it could reach any judgment.

Charlie pleaded to the little doubt left in him.

It responded with Walter's words, "Your parents died of heart attacks. That's why they crashed." The words kept repeating, turning jurors with each iteration until the jurors in Charlie's court were split down the middle.

Frustrated, Charlie chewed on his lip with such force he nearly broke skin. He'd been so close to putting it all behind him, but in the end, he'd come up short. There would be no quick and easy way out. He was forced to come to terms with the fact that there was only one way that he could close the case and move on.

CHAPTER
EIGHT

BEFORE SETTING OFF for the San Mateo County Coroner's Office, Charlie did a quick scan over the contact spreadsheet on Walter's flash drive. He surmised that in his worst-case scenario—the one where Walter was correct about Terry—it'd be much better to be safe than sorry and know for a fact that the coroner wasn't secretly a member of this alleged conspiracy prior to asking for his assistance.

Charlie didn't find the coroner's name on the contact list; however, there were a handful of the names in the spreadsheet that he did recognize. He'd heard some of them in his Civics class, and a few others were prominent business leaders that he'd come across while doing his own research. Of all the names he skimmed, there was one in particular that stood out among the others: James Podesky.

It wasn't the name itself that caught Charlie's eye. It was the first time he'd seen it. It was James's age that had jumped out at him; he was just sixteen years old. Charlie counted this information as another strike against Walter's theory. As far as he was concerned, there was no way any truly evil organization, no matter how small in size or ambition, could possibly include someone who was barely eight months older than him.

Charlie told his grandfather that he was going to hang out with a friend. He probably could've gotten away without saying anything to Grandpa Kim before he left—the old man most likely would have never even noticed that he was gone—but he was used to telling his parents where he was going, so it was more a matter of habit.

From his bed, Grandpa Kim just nodded like he'd heard and understood Charlie. His eyes never left the TV screen at the foot of the bed.

"All right … great talk," Charlie said, and then continued on his way.

◆ ◆ ◆

Charlie arrived at the Coroner's Office shortly after five o'clock. He'd feverishly pedaled his old Mongoose BMX for ten miles—a combination of bike trails and city streets—before skidding to a stop just as the last car was leaving the parking lot.

"Wait!" Charlie shouted as he waved his arms, attempting to catch the attention of the driver.

The SUV lurched forward a couple feet before slamming on the brakes. The driver backed up to Charlie, lowered his window and asked, "Is there something I can help you with?"

Charlie immediately recognized—based off of the picture he'd seen on the web—that the man behind the wheel was not the coroner. "Uh," Charlie stammered, buying himself time as he wasn't quite sure if he should take this man up on the offer. He opted to play things safe and close to the vest. "I don't know. I was actually hoping to speak to the coroner."

"Sorry. He took off about a half hour ago, along with everyone else. That's what happens when the 49ers are on Thursday Night Football. They leave the Ravens fan to do all the work. But the good news is that anything he could've helped you with, I can help you with, too," the man said with a smile before introducing himself as Dr. Eugene Huang, the chief medical examiner.

Charlie responded with just his first name. Even though Dr. Huang had identified himself as the medical examiner, Charlie was still hesitant to divulge much else without confirming that his name wasn't on the contacts list first. If only he'd thought to copy the spreadsheet to his phone. But in his hasty exit, he hadn't thought that far ahead. He hadn't even thought to bring the flash drive with him. It sat on his desk at home, as useless as the lint in his pocket.

"What can I do for you, Charlie?" Dr. Huang asked. "Are you working on a school paper or something?"

"No," Charlie said. "I mean, yes, but that's unrelated."

"Okay, well, what did you want to ask Coroner Stevens?"

Charlie considered his options. He could let down his guard and trust this eager medical examiner, or he could come back another time. It didn't take much time or convincing for Charlie to make up his mind. He knew that he didn't want to wait until later. He wanted to get it over with right then and there. He wanted to wipe it off his books.

Charlie reminded himself that he didn't actually believe in the significance of the list, anyway. He was only there for that last piece of evidence that he needed, or lack thereof. If Dr. Huang was his only means to obtaining said evidence, so be it. "I wanted to ask him something about my parents," Charlie said.

Dr. Huang was certain he'd heard the teen correctly; he'd said "parents" and not "parent." Dr. Huang quickly put two and two together. "Your parents were Alan and Mary Kim, weren't they?"

Charlie nodded solemnly.

"I'm sorry for your loss," Dr. Huang said. "I wish I could do more for you. But at the very least, I can help you with whatever you need."

"Thanks. I just wanted to make sure that my parents didn't die of heart attacks."

Dr. Huang was clearly baffled by Charlie's request. Had nobody explained to him what happened? That didn't seem possible. "Uh, I don't know what anyone's told you," he said, treading lightly, "but your parents died in a car crash."

"Yeah, I know about the crash. I wanted to make sure they didn't have heart attacks first. Like maybe that's what could've have caused them to crash. Not that it did. I just wanna make sure it didn't."

Like everyone else, Dr. Huang had heard the rumors. More than anyone, he knew the speculation was supported by a fair amount of forensic evidence, but not so much evidence that he'd been willing to make that conclusion in his official report. Instead, he painted a rosier picture, which he repeated to Charlie. "Given the information we accumulated, it appears your father fell asleep at the wheel. That's what caused the crash."

"And from that same information, you were able to determine that he didn't have a heart attack, right?" Charlie said, eagerly awaiting the confirmation he expected to receive. He was so certain it was coming that he had already planted his foot on his bike pedal and was preparing to push off.

"No, not exactly," Dr. Huang said.

Charlie's foot slipped from the pedal and back to the pavement. "Wait. What do you mean?" he said, confused.

"We didn't perform a full autopsy. So we never actually checked to see if he did or didn't have a heart attack."

"Why wasn't there a full autopsy?"

"Taking into account your father's age, the nature of death, and probable cause, it wasn't part of the protocol. We did perform a series of toxicology exams to make sure that there was no chemical impairment. The blood alcohol and everything else, it all came back clean."

"But you never actually checked for a heart attack?"

"No. But trust me, your parents didn't die of heart attacks. That much I'm pretty sure of."

Charlie hadn't ridden all that way for just a "pretty sure." He needed more than that to put any lingering suspicion to bed and turn out the light. "So you're not 100 percent sure?"

"No, but only because we didn't run the tests. I can tell you that I am damn near 99.9 percent sure, though."

"Well, how about you run whatever test you need to run, and then we both can be 100 percent?"

"I—"

"Said you would help me," Charlie said, finishing Dr. Huang's sentence for him, albeit with different words than the medical examiner had intended. "That's what you said."

Dr. Huang looked Charlie up and down. He could tell by the desperation in Charlie's eyes that he wasn't about to give up easy. The medical examiner shook his head. "Fine."

◆ ◆ ◆

Dr. Huang led Charlie inside the forensics laboratory. A series of wash stations lined the wall by the entrance. Empty steel examining tables occupied the center of the room. Along the back wall were all of the medical examiner's technological toys, some much newer than others.

"I really shouldn't be doing this," Dr. Huang said for the fifth time.

Charlie ignored him, just as he had the previous times.

Dr. Huang continued, "Once the test is over, I'm out the door and on my way home to my wife's chicken parmigiana."

"Me, too," Charlie said. "Minus the part about your wife's chicken parm. Unless she made extras." He was confident that it'd all be over shortly. The test would come back negative and they'd both go on with their evenings: the medical examiner to his wife's home cooked meal, and Charlie to the Language Arts paper that he still hadn't made a dent in.

Dr. Huang went to the back of the lab and got to work. He readied a vial with solution, added a test strip, and then dripped a few of the leftover drops of Alan's blood. He capped the vial and gave it a couple firm shakes. "The best way to diagnose a myocardial infarction is through a full autopsy," he said.

"But since we don't have that option, we'll have to rely on a rapid test. We'll give it a minute, and then we should have the results." He set the vial in a test-tube holder.

"Is that like a litmus test or something?" Charlie asked.

"More or less. Except we obviously aren't checking the pH. When someone has a heart attack, their body releases enzymes and proteins into their bloodstream. One of those proteins is called troponin. That's what we're looking for. Since it's a rapid test, it won't reveal the exact levels. But it'll give us the approximate concentration."

"What if my dad had a heart attack a while ago?"

"That wouldn't be an issue. The body absorbs the enzymes and proteins fairly quickly. Anything over a couple weeks wouldn't register."

"Okay. Good." Charlie said.

They both turned their attention to the vial. The test strip was still as white as a brand-new Hanes undershirt.

"It should be done any second," Dr. Huang said as he checked the time on his cell phone and then started a text to his wife.

"If it turns red," Charlie inquired, "that means the test was negative, right?"

"Actually, it's—" Dr. Huang stopped himself, realizing that there was only one reason Charlie would ask such a specific question. His eyes lifted from the cell phone screen and matched Charlie's gaze, which was locked on the vial.

CHAPTER
NINE

CHARLIE AND DR. HUANG continued to stare at the vial in stunned silence, their jaws hanging from their hinges. Floating in the solution, the test strip had turned a deep maroon. Not only did Charlie and Dr. Huang share the same physical reaction, they also shared an enveloping sense of disbelief; however, their mutual feeling was actually very different applications of the same word.

Dr. Huang's reaction was one of absolute astonishment. It'd never occurred to the seasoned medical examiner that he could actually be wrong. He'd never been. It was something he didn't take lightly. "I can't believe I missed this," he said as he gently shook his head. He turned to Charlie. "I've never seen test results with such concentrated levels of troponin."

Charlie didn't respond, mostly because he'd barely registered a word that the medical examiner had said. His mind was been too busy reinforcing his own disbelief: his refusal to accept the positive test result as truth, as well as the consequences that came with that result.

Dr. Huang noted Charlie's blank look. He put his hand on Charlie's shoulder to make sure the teen heard what he said next. "There's no doubt your father had a heart attack. And given the symptoms that would typically precede a heart attack of that severity, I'm surprised he was able to drive at all."

"No!" Charlie screamed as he yanked his shoulder free and covered his ears. "That's wrong. You're wrong. That's a false positive or something. It's gotta be!" Charlie's breaths puffed short and fast like a steam engine trying to conquer the highest mountain that had ever seen tracks.

Dr. Huang waited for Charlie to calm down and lower his hands before continuing, carefully, "For you and me both, I wish it were. But if that were a false positive, we'd maybe get a hint of red. That's it. I'm sorry, but there's nothing false about those results."

"But it has to be," Charlie whimpered, his voice weighted with anguish. He'd reached the end of his long rope of excuses. But just when he was about lose his grip, he found a couple more inches of rope. "Run the test on my mom," he demanded with a sudden burst of confidence. He knew that was his last shot. If his mother didn't have a heart attack, there was still a chance that Walter was wrong. The evidence wouldn't be enough to give him the closed case that he'd originally sought, but it'd be enough to force a mistrial, and that was much better than the alternative. "Run it," he repeated.

"You realize that the odds of both of your parents having heart attacks simultaneously are slimmer than winning the

Powerball five times in a row, right?"

"I'm counting on that." Charlie said as his eyes stayed fixed on the positive test strip and his thumb began flipping the pages of his pocketed Moleskine.

"They would've had to have been drugged. But if they were, it would've shown up in the toxicology."

Charlie didn't even bother responding. He just kept staring at the strip, focusing every ounce of energy in his body in an attempt to will the strip back to its original white.

Dr. Huang sighed. He knew this was just another losing battle. Plus, as much as he wanted to get home, there was a part of him that was just as curious as Charlie. "All right, all right," he said.

Dr. Huang readied a new vial, and then added the test strip and a few drops of Mary's blood. A couple shakes and it was good to go. They both watched the vial with bated breath.

A minute—which felt more like an hour—passed, and nothing had changed. And then, in a flash, the strip turned from its porcelain white to the same dark maroon as the other strip.

"I'll. Be. Damned," Dr. Huang said, not believing his eyes. "You know what this means?"

Charlie knew what it meant for him. It meant that the jury had spoken. It meant that he had to accept that Walter was right. It meant that his parents and Walter had been murdered. And it meant that Terry Heins was responsible for it all.

Even though Dr. Huang didn't have the same information as Charlie, he had enough to know that foul play was involved. When Charlie didn't respond, Dr. Huang answered his own question. "It means I need to run more tests and find out how they were drugged. I need to change my report and open their file back up. I also need to notify the lead officer working the case."

"No!" Charlie blurted out. "You can't."

"What?" Dr. Huang said, taken aback by Charlie's extreme reluctance. "I don't understand. Isn't that what you wanted?"

"No. It isn't. None of this is what I wanted. In fact, I wanted the exact opposite. I just wanted to be sure that it was a regular accident. That's all."

"Well, it wasn't. And whoever's responsible for this needs to be found. They need to be held accountable."

"I already know who's responsible for their deaths."

"You do?" Dr. Huang said, his eyes fluttering from the shock of Charlie's admission. "Why didn't you tell me that earlier?"

"Because I didn't wanna believe it was true."

"Who killed your parents?"

"It's better for you if you don't know. The person behind their deaths is incredibly powerful. Like really, really, really powerful. All you need to know is that if you change your report, the only thing you'll accomplish is putting the both of us at risk."

Everything Charlie had just said sounded completely crazy to the medical examiner, but then again, so was everything that had led up to that moment. "I don't know," Dr. Huang said.

"Please," Charlie begged. "You gotta trust me on this."

Dr. Huang was still not quite ready to yield to Charlie's demands. "We need to do something."

"I know," Charlie said. He knew they—or more important, he—needed to do something, he just didn't know what. And then he remembered the PDF contract on the thumb drive. "Just let me handle that. At least give me a little time to see what else I can find out. To get more evidence."

Dr. Huang considered Charlie's proposal. It went against every code that he had sworn to uphold, but Charlie was both determined and persuasive. "Fine," he said, relenting once more. "I'll give you two weeks. But after that, I'm reopening the file and you're giving me the name of who you think was behind this."

"That works for me," Charlie said.

"Two weeks," Dr. Huang repeated to make sure that it was 100 percent clear. "Not three. Not four."

"Two weeks. I got it. Thank you."

"Yeah, well, whatever you're planning on doing, be careful. And good luck."

Charlie nodded appreciatively.

They both said their goodbyes and then headed their separate ways: Dr. Huang to his home-cooked dinner, and Charlie to retrieve the flash drive and decipher the cryptic contract.

◆ ◆ ◆

As soon as Charlie returned home, he went straight to his computer and opened the contract file. He tried a couple web-based translation programs, but just like Walter, he had no luck whatsoever. All reported errors.

Recalling that Walter had said it looked like it was written in Hebrew, Charlie did a quick search for any synagogues in the area and found one that was only a couple miles away. With everything that had been brought to light, Charlie knew it was even more essential that he made sure that the temple's rabbi, or anyone else he would confide in, wasn't on the contact list.

Even after he'd confirmed that the rabbi was in the clear, Charlie decided that it was best to print a copy of the contract. The drive contained too much potential evidence to risk any chance of an accidental deletion or file corruption. And that way, he could maintain possession of the contract at all times.

Charlie hit print on the file, and then made for his parents' home office to retrieve the copy. He had yet to reach the office when he first caught sight of the black fumes that had filled the room and were pouring into the hall. Without thinking, he sprinted for the office doorway.

Upon entering the smoky room, Charlie feverishly scanned for flames. He found none. While there was plenty of smoke, there was no sign of fire.

Charlie wafted away the dark gray clouds in attempt to improve his view. Slowly but surely, the room began to clear, and he discovered the source: the printer, a few plumes of smoke still billowing out of the various vents in the machine.

Charlie performed a cursory inspection of the printer. Everything appeared to be in order. Chalking it up to a fluke electrical issue, he simply unplugged the printer's power cord to prevent any further problems and retrieved his printout from the tray. He pocketed the piece of paper and then headed for the foyer.

Charlie opened the front door but didn't even get one foot outside before he was stopped in his tracks. Just ahead of him, beginning to make their way up the front porch steps, were Terry and his two bodyguards.

CHAPTER
TEN

IF TERRY HAD stopped by only a couple hours earlier, Charlie's reaction would've been drastically different. As it was, he felt his heart jump up from his chest and into the back of his throat, and his mind raced faster than the entire field on the final lap at the Indy 500. Had Terry been following him? Did Terry know that he knew? Was Terry there to kill him? Did he stand any chance if he ran? Those were just a few of the questions that shot through his head in rapid succession.

Not only did Charlie determine that his window for running had closed just as soon as he'd opened the front door, but his fear had turned his feet to cinder blocks. His mind could tell his legs to move all it wanted to, but he wasn't going anywhere. He was forced to accept whatever was coming his way, good or bad. However, he knew better than to think that good was really an option, and braced himself for the worst.

Terry stopped on the steps. The corners of his mouth sagged. "Hey," he said, his voice shockingly melancholy.

Charlie was completely caught off-guard. It wasn't the "Get him," or "Take him out," that he'd expected, and there was no sudden bum-rush attack like he'd anticipated, either.

Terry calmly continued up the porch steps. "I was in the neighborhood," he said, in the same affected tone, "and figured I'd stop by to make sure you're holding up all right after Walter's passing." He laid his hand on Charlie's shoulder.

Charlie had to fight to keep himself from cringing. He wanted to scream, "Murderer!" so the whole world could hear, but he knew that would only seal his fate. Just because Terry hadn't acted as swiftly as Charlie had predicted didn't mean his men couldn't strike in a moment's notice. Charlie doubted whether he could even get the first syllable out before Terry's sunglassed gorillas dispatched him in some fashion. No. His safest bet was to act normal, to play along, to pray that Terry and his men didn't know that he knew anything, and to do his best not to let them know that he did.

"Thanks," Charlie said. "I ... I really appreciate it."

"It's the least I could do," Terry sighed. "Walter was a good man. No, that's a lie. He was a great man."

"Yes, he was. He was an incredible person."

"Just like your parents."

"Just like you," Charlie said with a faint smile to help sell words that couldn't have been further from his heart.

"I don't know that many people would consider me an incredible person," Terry said. "I mean, an incredible businessman, yes. It's impossible to dispute that. But they most likely think much less of me as a person." He solemnly nodded, withdrew his hand, and then changed gears. "Anyway, like I said, I just wanted to make sure you were holding up all right. I'll let you get back to your grieving."

"Okay," Charlie said, with more enthusiasm than intended. He instantly regretted it as Terry honed his expecting eyes on him. Charlie quickly realized what Terry was waiting for. "Normal Charlie" would've never let him leave so easily, even given the circumstances. He quickly and clumsily added, "I mean, you don't gotta go. We can hang out or something."

Terry took a second, looking Charlie up and down, before responding, "Unfortunately, I do. As I'm sure you already know: Money never sleeps, it only takes power naps. And even those are rare." He gestured to his men. "Cain, Max, let's go."

Charlie sighed inwardly as Terry and his men turned to leave. But his relief was short-lived, and the anxiety returned tenfold when they made no effort to go. Terry just stood with his back to Charlie and tapped the toe of his Italian wingtip shoe on the porch. Each tap pounded Charlie's eardrums like a nearby thunderclap.

"Actually, there's one more thing," Terry said as he turned back around. "Did Walter happen to say anything to you?"

"About what?" Charlie said, choking on his words.

"I don't know ... anything?" A slight grin crossed Terry's mug, as if to say that "anything" didn't really mean anything, but actually something in particular.

It was apparent to Charlie that Terry knew he had information but didn't know how much or what, exactly. That was the real purpose of his visit. It was a fact-finding mission. Only after determining the facts would he respond accordingly.

Charlie went catatonic as his mind replayed all of the things that Walter had said, both the night before and in the video. He knew that he couldn't tell Terry anything, but at the same time, he needed him to believe that he was telling him everything. It was the only way he might save himself.

"No," Charlie said. "Remember, he wasn't at the funeral."

"Of course. But you saw him after the funeral, right?"

The way Terry had said it, Charlie got the sense that he wasn't asking him if he'd seen Walter as much as he was reminding him that he had. Charlie could feel every muscle in his body tightening and his carotid artery beginning to bulge from his neck. He told himself to stay calm, to stay normal, but the fact that he was continuously getting caught in his lies made it nearly impossible. "Oh. Yeah. I did," he admitted. "He was here when I got home."

"And … did he say anything?"

"Nope," Charlie asserted without thinking it through.

"That seems weird, don't you think?" Terry said, feigning confusion. "He was here, but he didn't say anything. He just left without saying a word?"

Of course that wasn't the truth. He was busted again. Charlie had dug himself into such a deep hole that he could barely see the light at the entry. He needed to give Terry something, anything that might help him climb his way out. Or else Terry might push in the excess soil and bury him alive.

"We talked," Charlie said. "He just didn't say much. That's what I meant. I, uh, told him what you said about my dad and he agreed. Then he said he had to get going."

Terry peered right into Charlie's pupils. "That's it?"

Charlie felt Terry's eyes on him like a spotlight. He swallowed hard, the air getting caught halfway down his throat. "Yep," he squeaked, desperately hoping Terry would finally buy it. Beads of sweat began to pop from the pores on his forehead while he waited for Terry to shoot down his most recent lie.

After a long moment, Terry calmly replied, "That's too bad. We've been having a lot of trouble with your father's prototype, and I was hoping he might have said something that would help me fix it. But I just don't know if that's gonna be possible now. Which is a shame. The world needs it."

"Yeah, it does," Charlie said, still uncertain if Terry was satisfied or if a whole new line of questions was about to come.

"Anyway," Terry said, finally easing up, "let me give you another one of my cards"—he dug into his pocket and pulled out a business card—"just in case you ever misplace the first one. These things are so small, it happens all the time. It never hurts to have an extra." He handed the card to Charlie.

"No, it doesn't," Charlie said. And lucky for him, he hadn't intended to say anything more, otherwise he would've definitely stopped short when he noticed that the card wasn't as crisp and clean as the one Terry that had previously given him. The corners were bent and there was a pronounced crease down the center, as if it'd been crumpled.

69

"After all," Terry said, "we still need to iron out the details on your internship."

Charlie said nothing. He just kept gazing, zombie-like, at the folds in the business card. There was no doubt in his mind that it was the same card Walter had taken from him. Charlie determined that it had to be how Terry found out that he'd spoken to Walter. Terry must have taken the business card from Walter before they did whatever they did to him. That was where he'd gotten his information, and his suspicion. It was also an admission of guilt and potentially a thinly veiled threat.

"You still want the internship, right?" Terry said. He waited a second for Charlie to respond. After he didn't, Terry added, "Do you not want the internship?"

Charlie's head shot up. "No! I mean, yes! I mean, of course I want it," he said as if his life depended on it, because as far as he knew, it did.

"Good. I was getting a little worried I was going to lose you to someone else. Just shoot me an email whenever you get a chance, and we can start the negotiations."

"Great," Charlie said, forcing a smile.

Terry smiled back and then headed down the porch steps. The younger bodyguard, Max, followed Terry, but the older guard, Cain, held back. He stood perfectly still, his sunglassed eyes never leaving Charlie.

Charlie did his best to avert his eyes from the imposing stare, focusing on Terry and Max as they made their way to the Bentley. But eventually, Charlie caved. He glanced up at Cain, staring right at the N-shaped scar on his cheek.

Cain tilted his head so their eyes were forced to meet.

Charlie saw himself in the reflection of Cain's sunglass lenses. Then, out of nowhere, he caught three faint blue sparks of light burst across the right lens like shooting stars.

Charlie had no idea what the flashes were, but he didn't need to know to be completely freaked out. He fought against every muscle in his eyelids to keep them from going wide and showing any sign of the extreme panic that was overtaking his body.

CHAPTER
ELEVEN

AFTER WHAT SEEMED like the longest thirty seconds of Charlie's life, Cain just casually turned around and rejoined his boss and partner. Charlie quickly and quietly closed the front door. He used his hand to steady himself against the door, huffing and puffing to reclaim the breath that had been scared clean out of him, while also berating himself for locking up like he had. His fear had turned him completely catatonic. At any moment, Cain could've struck him down, and he would've been unable to protect himself at all.

Charlie was certain that Terry and his men weren't through with him just yet, that they were merely deciding what to do with him. And they had to do something. As hard as he'd tried to hide it, he'd clearly tipped them off to the fact that he knew something. He knew that made him a liability. He also knew that he couldn't just freeze up again. He'd have to be stronger. He'd have to be ready for them and whatever they had planned.

Charlie took a deep breath, in and out, and then sprinted to the kitchen. He grabbed the biggest knife that he could find in the pantry, and then raced to the family room. As he approached the bay window that looked out on the front yard, he expected to find Terry and his men gritting their teeth as they stormed back toward his house. Instead, he barely caught sight of the bumper of Terry's Bentley before it disappeared down the road.

Charlie let out a long sigh, his whole body relaxing as his lungs emptied. His hand fell to his side and the knife fell to the floor. He was safe from Terry and his men, if only for the time being. He didn't know how long that time might last, but he knew that he had to make the most of it. He still had work to do. He still had a contract to translate. He waited a couple minutes before hopping on his bike and heading in the opposite direction of the Bentley.

◆ ◆ ◆

Temple Beth Israel was only a short ride from his house, but it took Charlie much longer than any mapping service might have predicted, on account of his head being on a swivel and all of the detours he took in an attempt to lose any potential followers. He was also slowed by thoughts of the blue sparks he'd seen shoot across Cain's sunglass lens. Each time he recalled the bizarre flashes and Cain's icy stare, he felt an equally icy chill course through every vein in his body.

Night had fallen by the time Charlie finally arrived at the reform temple, and the service for Simchat Torah, the end of the annual Torah cycle, was still in session. Not wanting to be out in the open, he hid with his bike in some nearby bushes.

Charlie scanned the surrounding area for anyone or anything suspicious. He saw nothing. He didn't hear anything, either. In fact, it was so quiet that the only sound he picked up was his own breathing. Against the dead silence, it seemed impossibly loud, like something that could—or would—give him away.

Charlie was in the process of trying to quiet his breaths when he spotted a man in an all-black sweatsuit approaching from the nearby sidewalk with the biggest Rottweiler he'd ever seen. The man had a build identical to that of Terry's younger bodyguard, and had his sweatshirt hood pulled over his head.

The man continued toward Charlie before stopping abruptly, no more than forty feet away. His dog let loose a ferocious snarl.

Charlie couldn't help but release a nervous yelp in return.

The hooded man shot a glance in Charlie's direction. The light of a streetlamp reflected off of his face. His eyes were hidden by the same sunglasses that Terry's men wore.

Charlie covered his mouth with his hand as the man reached into his pocket. He was going for his gun, Charlie was sure of it. Charlie closed his eyes and waited for the bang and whatever pain might follow.

After a couple seconds and no sound other than a little crinkling, Charlie lifted his eyelids. He found the man hunched over, in the process of retrieving the mess his dog had made in the grass with a small plastic baggie. The man's sweatshirt hood had fallen off and revealed his glasses were actually prescription lenses. Charlie exhaled softly as the man continued on his way.

Shortly after the man and his dog disappeared, the service ended and the attendees started to spill out of the temple. As soon as the last person had exited, Charlie crawled out of the bushes and slipped inside the synagogue.

Rabbi Samuel Klein, an older man with more gray hair than brown, was working on his next sermon when Charlie stepped through the office threshold. The rabbi looked up from his work. "Come in, my child," he said, his voice still carrying hints of a faded New York accent.

Charlie hesitated for a second. "Um. Just so you know, I'm not actually Jewish. If that matters."

"It does for some things, and not as much for others. But I assume you're here for good reason. So come in, have a seat." He motioned for Charlie to do just that.

Charlie made his way into the office and took a seat in the chair across from the rabbi. "I don't know if this is even something you can do, but I need your help translating this," he said as he retrieved the printed PDF from his pocket and handed it to the rabbi.

"I'll see what I can do," Rabbi Klein said. He grabbed his reading glasses from the desk, adjusted them on his face, and then started to peruse the paper.

Charlie watched anxiously. "I was told that it might be Hebrew, but none of the web translators recognized—" He stopped when he noted the troubled look on the rabbi's face.

Rabbi Klein skimmed a couple more lines before putting the paper down and removing his spectacles. "Where did you get this?"

Charlie didn't want to lie to the rabbi, but he also didn't want to divulge any more information than he needed to. "I found it on someone's computer."

"If I was you, I would steer clear of that person."

"So you can read it?"

"Yes, I can," Rabbi Klein said. "This is written in Hebrew, but not modern Hebrew. It is written in the original Hebrew script, which is not commonly used these days. It has not been used much over the last twenty-six hundred years, for that matter."

Charlie had no idea what to make of this information. There was no way the PDF was that old; it was a computer file, after all. Maybe someone had used the dated language to make it harder to decipher. Charlie wasn't sure, nor did he really care. In the end, he was less concerned with the age of the script or reasons for its use than he was with the actual content. "What does it say?"

"What you have here ... is a contract."

"Yeah, I know. That's what the file was named," Charlie said. He hadn't intended on coming off as rude as he had, he just wasn't sure why the rabbi had avoided answering his question. It was as if Rabbi Klein were stalling. "What does it say?" he repeated.

"It says a lot." Rabbi Klein took a deep breath, clearly not comfortable with what he was about to reveal. "This is not just any old contract. It is a contract with the Devil."

Charlie's body stiffened upon hearing the rabbi's words. He'd never really contemplated the existence of God, which meant that he'd put even less consideration into the existence of the Devil. Until the rabbi mentioned it, the prospect of the contract being between anything other than two people had never crossed Charlie's mind. Now that it had, his thoughts scattered like a pack of cockroaches scurrying for cover when the lights flash on, until there was just one little pest left out in the open. "What kind of contract with the Devil?" he asked.

"I do not feel that it is appropriate to recite it word for word," Rabbi Klein said, "but the general context is that the Devil agrees to grant the signee any assistance they require in their human life, as long as the signee pledges to serve the Devil, for eternity, in the afterlife."

"Why the hell would anyone agree to that?" Charlie said, catching his tongue after the fact. "Sorry about the language."

"It is nothing that I haven't heard before," Rabbi Klein said. "While the prospect of selling your soul might not sound appealing to you or me, the lure of fortune and power has corrupted many a man, and will no doubt continue to do so as long as man inhabits what God's hands have made."

Charlie knew that fortune and power were two things that Terry had in spades. Was it possible that Terry had signed this pledge to achieve those things, or was this was just for show? Charlie had no way of knowing for sure, other than prodding the knowledgeable rabbi for more info. "Do you think it's real?"

"Is it real?" Rabbi Klein said, holding up the paper to examine it closer. "Certainly, it is a real sheet of paper. But as far as an actual contract with the Devil, I doubt that it is, or that such a thing exists. Of course, that does not mean it should be taken lightly. So, if you do not mind, I would prefer to get rid of this."

"Sure," Charlie said, half listening to the rabbi and half trying to determine what to make of it all.

"I do not think anyone should be fooling around with things of this nature," Rabbi Klein said as he fed the contract into his shredder. "Genuine or not."

The rabbi's last words were lost in the cacophony of the shredder, which sounded like it was trying to take down a phone book instead of a single sheet of paper.

"What?" Charlie said, raising his voice over the clanging.

"I said, 'Genuine or not,'" the rabbi repeated, raising his voice as well. He turned to the shredder to see what the fuss was about. "I am not sure what is wrong with this thing?" He tapped the machine, attempting to quiet it.

But if anything, the shredder only got louder.

Rabbi Klein turned back to Charlie and shook his head. "Sorry about that." He waited for the paper to finish its journey through the metal teeth. "There," he said after the noise finally ceased. "Like I was saying, I do not think anyone should—" Rabbi Klein froze as he made what he'd intended to be a quick double check of the shredder basket.

Seeing the worry on the rabbi's face sent Charlie's fragile body and mind into a physical and emotional tailspin. What could the holy man have seen that would make his body go stiff like it had?

Rabbi Klein reached into the shredder basket and retrieved the shredded contract. Only it wasn't shredded at all—it was completely intact. The sheet of paper had traveled through the same blades that he'd used to cut over thirty sheets at a time, not to mention countless expired credit cards, and had come out the other side without so much as a scratch. "I must have accidentally changed the settings," Rabbi Klein said, refusing to attribute the problem to anything other than mechanical error. He checked the shredder. "Everything looks perfect. Maybe I should try a test run."

Trapped in his thoughts and searching for his own logical explanation—not counting the contract being authentic, which seemed entirely illogical—Charlie said nothing.

Rabbi Klein grabbed a fresh sheet of paper from his printer and fed it into the shredder. The shredder demolished the sheet with ease. "Everything appears to be in order," he said, reassuring himself. He slipped the contract back into the shredder.

Just like the time before, the machine rattled and clanged as it labored to pull the lone piece of paper though. Also like the time before, the sheet passed through the shredder's blades completely unaffected.

Rabbi Klein started to show signs of panic. He couldn't stop his mind from considering that this contract might be real. But that had to be impossible. His gaze darted about the room. What to do next?

Charlie was thinking the same thing. He zeroed in on the lit candle in the windowsill. "Burn it!" he blurted out.

"Yes!" Rabbi Klein blurted out and just as quickly offered the sheet to the much more nimble Charlie.

Charlie leapt from his chair and snagged the contract from the rabbi's outstretched hand. He rushed to the window and held the corner of the sheet over the candle's flame.

Rabbi Klein lumbered to join Charlie's side. "It is always better to burn something like that. Leave no trace," he said, attempting to sound confident but not quite concealing his underlying trepidation.

They both waited a second for the sheet to catch.

It didn't.

They waited another couple seconds.

Still nothing.

"Try the center," Rabbi Klein suggested.

Charlie obliged, hovering the sheet directly over the strongest part of the flame. Finally, the paper caught fire. "There we go," Charlie said.

"I knew that would work," Rabbi Klein said. He stared at the flames as they began to consume the contract.

But Charlie noticed there was something different about the way the fire was spreading. "I'm not so sure it is," he said.

Rabbi Klein saw what Charlie had already observed. It wasn't the paper that was ablaze—it was the ink, or more specifically, the words. They burned in bold black and red tones, keeping their shape as the radiant flames rose from the page.

Charlie removed the piece of paper from the candle. The words continued to smolder on their own for a few seconds before they extinguished. Plumes of smoke, the same color as the ones that had consumed his parents' home office, floated away from the completely intact and unaffected contract.

Without saying a word, it was evident to both Charlie and Rabbi Klein that the sheet of paper in Charlie's hand was not a fake. It was very much real.

CHAPTER
TWELVE

CHARLIE'S FEET POUNDED the pedals of his bike as he tore down the residential streets faster than he'd ever ridden before, faster than he knew he was capable of riding. He was fueled by the fear of everything he'd just learned, and by the fact that the contract was still in his possession.

Rabbi Klein had wanted nothing to do with the seemingly indestructible sheet of paper. And since they'd both agreed that they couldn't throw the contract away, thereby risking that someone might find it and unknowingly sign on the dotted line, Charlie just stuffed the contract in his pocket and took off for his house.

While the contract was on his person, more than just the piece of paper was on Charlie's mind as he zipped past his old recreational league baseball field, his parents' favorite coffee shop, and the home of his elementary school best friend, whom he'd outgrown. There was something even more chilling that kept him from daring to look over his shoulder and risk slowing down even the slightest. It was the same thing that kept his legs firing like pistons in a muscle car's engine. That something was the story that Rabbi Klein had disclosed to him after they were unable to destroy the contract. It was a story that involved similar dealings with the Devil. What Charlie had gleaned from the tale took all of his issues and multiplied them by infinity.

Charlie's mind continued to spin like the tires on his bike as he raced to get home, neither of them easing up even as his house came into view. His eyes were so focused on the front door that he didn't notice the blacked-out SUV parked across the street a couple houses down. He just flew past the truck and into his driveway.

Charlie hopped off of the back of his bike, sending it ghost-riding across the front lawn. The bike continued into the neighbor's yard, where it crashed into their perfectly planted flower garden. He didn't see or hear the collision; he was busy sprinting for the front entrance.

Charlie threw open the door and leapt inside. He slammed the door shut and then flipped the locks on the doorknob and deadbolt as fast as humanly possible. The chain lock proved to be more of a problem. His twitching hands fumbled with the bolt before finally sliding it into place. He gulped one massive breath and then took off up the stairs.

A befuddled Grandpa Kim waited in the second-floor hallway. He'd stumbled out of his room to see what all the commotion was, and was mumbling to himself in Korean.

Charlie blew by the confused old man and continued his mad dash toward his bedroom. He flung the bedroom door shut behind him as he bounded the last flight of steps to his room with haste. So much so that he lost his footing and slipped, crashing chin-first onto the edge of the wooden staircase. A gash opened and started leaking blood. He made no attempt to inspect the wound or stem the flow of tiny red droplets. He sprung up to his hands and knees and scurried on all fours to the corner of his room. He grabbed the aluminum baseball bat that was leaning against the wall and finally pushed himself up to his feet, getting into a batter's stance.

Charlie stared at the bedroom stairway, his fingers flexing as he adjusted his grip on the bat, ready to swing at whatever came his way. But nothing did. And the more time that passed, the more he realized how worthless his weapon would be anyway. He wasn't fighting fastballs.

Eventually, the weight of it all became too much for Charlie. He tossed the bat on his bed, slumped against the wall, and slid down to his seat He wrapped his arms around his bent legs and pulled them into his body, squeezing so tightly that the joints in his knees cracked. He slammed his eyes shut with equal relative force and buried his head between his legs. His toes rapidly tapped the floor like a snare drum as the story that Rabbi Klein had told him cycled through his mind.

Rabbi Klein had been hesitant to tell the old legend when Charlie initially asked him if he'd ever heard of people selling their souls. The rabbi had written the tale off as fantasy so many years ago that at first, it hadn't even registered as a legitimate response to Charlie's question.

Charlie helped shed the rabbi of his reluctance, reminding him that the contract had also seemed like a fantasy at first but had since become a very harsh reality.

Rabbi Klein conceded. He recounted the story that his grandmother had told him as a child, one that she'd heard while growing up in a small Romanian village just outside of Transylvania. It was the story of Vlad III, Prince of Wallachia, more commonly known as Vlad the Impaler.

According to the village folklore, the often-cited history of Vlad the Impaler—the inspiration behind Count Dracula—was nothing more than a consciously crafted fabrication. All of the accounts of his brutality, from bloodsucking and vampirism to mass decapitations and the flaunting of fallen soldiers' severed heads, were merely cover for his actual crimes, which, in reality, were much worse.

The true story of Vlad began with his rise to power. It was said that during his time as a hostage in the Ottoman court, a teenage Vlad made a covenant with the Devil, where he agreed to sell his soul. In return, the Devil committed to assisting the young Vlad in his rise to power. As part of their deal, Vlad was assigned a small collection of the Devil's minions to serve as his protectors.

The villagers referred to these protectors as fiară diavolului, Romanian for "Beasts of the Devil." Human in appearance only, they were said to be much closer to dybbuks, malicious spirits that possess human bodies. However, instead of possessing their victim's bodies, the Beasts fed off of their souls. It was this soul-sucking that would later be falsely reported as bloodsucking, and become the basis for all vampire lore.

The Beasts helped Vlad escape captivity and grow his forces. It took close to a decade, but eventually, Vlad seized the throne as Prince of Wallachia. Once in power, Vlad set out to fulfill part of his pact, helping wage the Devil's war on mankind.

While Vlad undertook his unholy war, his Beasts devoured the souls of anyone who stood in their way. They terrorized the lands for years until Vlad was finally defeated. Though there was no shortage of stories for how Vlad finally met his bloody end, some more fantastical than others, his exact demise was unknown. However, what was known was that almost immediately after Vlad was slain, the Beasts completely disappeared, retreating to wherever they came.

Many years after Vlad's death, the villagers claimed to have seen him from time to time, always at the side of someone else. They believed that he wasn't a ghost, but that he had become one of the Beasts. They said they could tell by his eyes, which were the only way to identify a Beast. His eyes were just like the others. They glowed like the embers of a campfire and had blue sparks that blazed across his corneas like shooting stars.

When Charlie heard the last part, he instantly thought of Cain's eyes. Even though he hadn't noticed anything that resembled a fire behind Cain's dark sunglasses, the image of the blue sparks—three of them, to be exact—was permanently seared in his brain.

While the story, combined with the realization that Terry's bodyguards were the same Beasts that the rabbi spoke of, had been enough to severely rattle Charlie, it was Rabbi

Klein's final disclosure, which came after Charlie had asked what became of the soulless bodies, that truly shook him to his core.

Rabbi Klein replied that, from what his grandmother had told him, a body without a soul behaved much like a body that had lost a significant amount of blood. This fact assisted in the perpetuation of the vampire myths. The victims of the Beasts would wander mindlessly for a short time, usually a matter of minutes, before coming to a most sudden end; however, that was just the beginning. They faced a fate much worse than death. Their souls remained trapped inside the Beast that had stolen them for as long as the Beast walked the Earth. With the stolen souls went all the memories of their lives, fading each passing day from minds of those they'd known until they were completely gone.

The revelation had caused the hair on Charlie's neck to stand straight up and every square inch of his skin to goose. The heart attacks that had killed his parents and Walter were just like the sudden deaths the rabbi had mentioned. His dream from the night before, where he still couldn't remember what his parents had said, seemed much like a memory that had faded away.

Charlie was certain that if both of those things were true, and he was woefully confident that they were, then his parents' and Walter's souls were the blue flashes that he'd seen. He was certain that they would be trapped in Cain forever. And as he sat on the floor of his bedroom, his head buried between his knees, he was certain that it was only a matter of time—minutes, or maybe even seconds—before he joined them.

CHAPTER
THIRTEEN

AFTER A HALF HOUR of silence, Charlie lifted his head from his lap. He opened his eyes and gazed expectantly at the stairway. He didn't anticipate his parents calling up to him; their former habit had been completely lost along with their words, and was no longer something that he even associated with them. Instead, he imagined the door to his room—of which only the top inch was visible to him—flying off of the hinges, the wood frame splintering as Terry's men busted through. He pictured a smirking Terry hovering over him while his bodyguards did the same thing to him that they'd done to his parents and Walter.

Charlie kept waiting, anticipating that it'd all go down.

Only it never did.

Another uneventful half hour passed before he finally concluded that Terry and his men might not be coming after all. All of the pent-up fear and anxiety that he'd bottled up began to release from his body. It created a void, one that he filled with anger.

Charlie went off on Walter. For sending him the drive. For thinking that he needed to know the truth. For thinking he could even do anything with the information.

After Walter, Charlie's parents caught his ire. Why did they have to get involved with Terry? Why did they have to do whatever they did, to make him decide to go after them? Why couldn't they have just given in to Terry's demands?

When he ran out of reasons to be upset with his parents, Charlie aimed his rage at Terry. After all, he was the one who had targeted his parents and Walter. He was the one who had taken them from him. And now he was the one who was taking his sweet time, toying with him. Why? Why play games? For his own sick pleasure? What had happened to the man who acted quickly, decisively, and frequently?

Charlie rose to his feet, empowered by his overflowing animosity. He yelled to Terry, as if he were in the room or might somehow hear him, "What are you waiting for? Just come and get me already!"

Charlie's chest heaved as he waited for a response. Seconds passed, and none came. It remained completely quiet, save for the gentle rustling of trees outside.

"I got an idea!" Charlie shouted, his rage reborn. "How's this? You let my parents and Walter go, and I'll sign your damn contract!" He was no longer speaking to Terry, nor had he thought his promise through. He hadn't thought at all. His temper had a firm hold of him; it was the one making the decisions.

Charlie went to grab the contract from his pocket, but his fingers met his Moleskine notebook first. Unlike every other time, he found no solace in his plan. It'd been rendered obsolete and did nothing but add to his aggression. He yanked the notebook from his pocket and began ripping the pages out and throwing them in the air. Once he had plucked every goal-filled page, he chucked what was left of the notebook across the room.

Charlie retrieved the contract from his pocket. He glared at the ancient words, then balled up the sheet and threw it in the same direction that he'd thrown his notebook. He dropped down on to the corner of his bed and buried his head in his hands.

Charlie's breaths became longer as his anger subsided. The ensuing adrenaline crash, combined with the lack of sleep from the night before, took its toll on his body. It wanted to shut down, but he refused to let it. He knew what was in store: more dreams and more lost memories of his parents.

Charlie's eyelids began a gradual descent. He realized what they were up to and caught them with his fingers, keeping them pried open. Unfortunately, his hands were no match for the rest of his body or mind. It was already eleven o'clock. He'd been awake for nearly twenty-two hours straight, and thirty-eight of the last forty. He was physically and emotionally exhausted. Even with his lids jimmied, his vision faded to black. His hands fell to his sides, and his body collapsed back onto his bed.

◆ ◆ ◆

Charlie's eyes shot open. He scanned the rest of his room from his bed, unsure if he was caught in a dream or if he'd actually woken up. He checked his clothes. They were the same as when he'd conked out. According to his cell phone, it was shortly after seven in the morning and a brand-new day.

Charlie had jumped through nightmares of his parents vanishing for the past eight hours, which qualified as the most continuous sleep he'd had in years, but this wasn't a dream. It was only a return to his harsh and uncertain reality. He did his best to recall the dreams he'd had during his deep slumber, but they'd mostly turned to lost memories. Only the last dream, the one he'd woken up in the middle of, left even the slightest trace. Most of it was fuzzy, but he vaguely remembered it involving a family dinner on the night that he'd faked playing in his first junior-varsity soccer game.

At the dinner, Charlie had not only told his parents that he'd started, but also that he'd scored the game-winning goal. In reality, he'd just stayed in the library and worked on his assignments. Throughout the rest of the meal, Charlie's parents couldn't stop talking about how proud they were of him. With each compliment, Charlie would grin and nod, but beneath his joyous exterior, his stomach twisted into tight knots as the guilt of accepting their unearned praise compounded.

Charlie had held onto his guilt ever since that night. But when his parents disappeared from the dream, so did any memories of their adulation, and so did his guilt. As he reflected on what he still remembered from the evening, his lies no longer bothered him.

Charlie swung his feet off of his bed and was about to get up when he noticed something on his nightstand that did bother him—so much so that it caused his heart to skip a beat. It wasn't what he saw that was particularly frightening, it was the fact that it hadn't been there when he passed out. At least, he was fairly certain that it hadn't been.

Charlie cautiously craned his head to get a better view. Maybe he was wrong. Maybe it'd been there the whole time. In which case, all of the other suspicions swirling in his head as to what exactly he was staring at and how it'd gotten there were unwarranted.

But as his eyes finished digesting what they were seeing, Charlie discovered that his concern was very much justified. This discovery sent a chill from the top of his spine all the way down to the tips of his already-tensed extremities: Resting on the nightstand was the contract.

No longer balled up in the corner where Charlie had tossed it, the contract had magically moved. But the physical location of the document wasn't the only thing that had inexplicably changed. The original Hebrew script was gone, replaced with English.

He grabbed the sheet and skimmed over the details as he lumbered to his desk. The language was almost identical to what the rabbi had told him. The only difference was an addendum at the bottom of the page. The addendum stated that in return for Charlie signing the contract and pledging his soul, his parents and Walter's souls would be set free.

Charlie swallowed hard. The Devil had heard him and agreed to his terms.

In the heat of the moment, Charlie would've signed the deal without hesitation. But that heat had long since cooled, and he was no longer buoyed by rage.

Charlie sunk into his desk chair. He laid the new contract out on the desktop and grabbed a pen from a souvenir glass that doubled as a penholder. He rapidly clicked the pen as he read the stipulations once more and tried to decide what to do.

There were only two options: He could sign the contract or not sign the contract. If he signed the contract, he'd be signing over his soul, but he'd be saving his parents and Walter, and he'd also probably get everything he ever wanted in his original plan. He'd be successful like Terry. If he chose not to sign the contract, he'd not only doom his parents and Walter for eternity, he'd almost certainly end up just like them when Terry finally came for him. And Terry would. Sooner or later, he'd find out what Charlie knew, and that would be the end of him.

With his options and outcomes clearly juxtaposed, there was no real choice for Charlie to make. He had to sign the contract. He clicked the pen once more, exposing the ballpoint, and lowered it to the paper. He was about to start the first letter in his signature when a faint voice inside his head told him to stop.

Charlie slowly peered up from the contract. The first thing his eyes met was the framed photo that sat on his desk next to his monitor. In the photo, a fourth-grade Charlie proudly displayed his first-place ribbon from his school's science fair. Alan and Mary stood at his side, both of them smiling.

Charlie unhooked the clasps on the back of the frame and removed the photo. On the back of the picture was a handwritten note from Mary. He read his mother's words: YOU'VE WORKED SO HARD. WE'RE SO PROUD OF YOU. AS LONG AS YOU GIVE YOUR BEST, WE'LL ALWAYS BE PROUD OF YOU. LOVE, MOM AND DAD.

Charlie read the note over and over. He focused on one part in particular: give your best. That's all he ever had to do to make his parents proud. Even if he didn't remember them saying that, he had it in writing. Give your best. He could hardly say that was what he was giving now. The truth of the matter was, he hadn't given anything at all and was in the process of giving in, giving up.

Charlie considered the contract once more, and then his eyes shifted back to the photo. He could see the looks of joy on his parents' faces. He knew that his parents wouldn't want him to agree to the Devil's pact, even if it meant saving them. He knew that they wouldn't want him to give up. They would want him to give his best. He also knew that there was a third option—he could fight.

It wouldn't be easy. Charlie was certain that it'd be the most challenging endeavor that he'd ever undertake. But he knew that he had to, for his parents and for himself. And so instead of submitting, Charlie clenched his fists, determined to put a stop to Terry and his men.

Charlie stashed the contract in his desk drawer. He crossed his room and retrieved his battered Moleskine. He turned to the first page and wrote with purpose: SAVE MY PARENTS AND WALTER.

Charlie knew that if he were going to stand any chance against Terry and his men, he'd need backup. He also knew that there had to be more kids out there who were just like him: kids who had lost their parents and all memories of their parents to the Beasts, kids who had nothing to lose and everything to gain. He just needed to find them. And so, he added to his notebook the first step toward executing his new plan: FIND MORE ORPHANS.

CHAPTER FOURTEEN

EDDIE HARPER WAITED in one of the padded wooden chairs that were positioned outside of the principal's office at St. Francis High School. He flipped his mess of blond hair away from his eyes and slumped down in his seat, increasingly upset with himself. It wasn't getting kicked out of class that had Eddie peeved—trips to the principal's office had become a daily staple of his education after his mother passed away—it was the fact that he'd gotten the boot from Miss McCallister's history class only seconds before the period ended. Because of his poor timing, he was stuck waiting for another one-on-one with Principal Daniels while the rest of his classmates were partaking in his favorite class: lunch.

Eddie's round belly rumbled, as if it were disappointed in him, too. "You growling at me?" he said to his stomach in his best Robert De Niro impression. He gave his stomach a pat. "Lucky for you, I always come prepared."

Eddie grabbed a Twinkie from the box in his backpack, tore it open, and stuffed it into his mouth whole. One Twinkie wasn't enough for Eddie or his stomach. He was still chewing the last of his first snack cake when he snagged a second package from his bag and scarfed it down in similar fashion.

His sugary cravings satisfied for the moment, Eddie retrieved his smartphone and snapped a picture of the principal's office door. He smirked as he uploaded it to all of his social media sites with the same caption: PRINCIPAL VISIT 2,125 #HARDWORKPAYSOFF #BLESSED.

Eddie was certain the picture would garner a lot of "likes"; all of his pictures did. Just like all of his little quips got laughs from the other students. Of course the teachers at his Fairfax, Virginia, Catholic school were a much tougher crowd. They would only tolerate his disruptions so much before sending him packing to Principal Daniels's office.

Eddie closed the social media app and opened his phone's web browser. He went to a popular Internet forum called themessagebored.com and clicked on the new posts.

On the top of the page, only a few seconds old, was a post that immediately caught Eddie's attention. He wasted no time clicking the link. He'd just finished reading the first sentence from the post when Principal Daniels poked his head out of his office.

Principal Daniels let out an exaggerated sigh when he saw Eddie. "I should have known it was you again."

Eddie didn't respond. He just sat in his chair with a thousand-yard stare. He was completely blown away by what he'd read so far and how it related to him.

It'd been a little over a year since Eddie's mother, Claire Harper, had passed away from cardiac failure, which the coroner reported was likely the result of an extreme lack of sleep and job-related stress. As an investigative journalist, Claire had committed her career to uncovering all forms of corruption. She considered herself an equal-opportunity exposer and despised others in her field who would sit on stories that "threatened" their personal and political interests.

On the last investigation before her death, Claire had been digging up dirt on government officials who had profited from the previous housing collapse and subsequent bailout. Her feature story never hit the presses—it didn't even make it to her editor's desk.

The night janitor at *The Washington Chronicle* discovered Claire slumped over on her own desk. The file for her feature was open on her computer. The Word document was as blank as the look on Eddie's face as he sat across from the frustrated principal. And much like Eddie's face, the document hadn't always been that way.

Principal Daniels noted Eddie's disconnected look and shook his head. He was painfully aware of Eddie's ADHD diagnosis. But of the many students in Eddie's boat, Eddie gave him the most trouble by far. "Well," Principal Daniels said, growing tired of waiting for Eddie's attention to shift, "are you gonna come in, or do I need to drag you myself?"

Eddie robotically got up, made his way into the office, and took a seat in his usual chair opposite the principal's desk.

Principal Daniels plucked the dismissal slip from Eddie's hand as he passed by, and then sat down in his desk chair.

He skimmed over the dismissal slip. "It looks like Miss McCallister thought you were being disruptive," Principal Daniels said, "which, of course, is nothing new." He laid the slip on his desk, grabbed a pen from his pen jar, and tapped it on his desk a couple times while trying to decide how to handle his wayward student. "I don't really see any point in reading you the riot act for the hundredth time, and I'm sure Maura Taylor is tired of hearing my voice."

Maura Taylor was the mother of Eddie's best friend. Eddie's father had never been in the picture, having walked out on Claire before Eddie was even born. When Eddie lost his mother, he lost everything he had. Fortunately, the Taylors took him in. If not for their kindness, Eddie would've spent his last year of legal childhood in foster care.

Principal Daniels waited for Eddie to offer an explanation for why he'd been acting up. Eddie always had a reason for his behavior, and it was always someone else's fault. But if he had an excuse, Eddie kept it to himself as he stared straight ahead.

"Are you even listening to me?" Principal Daniels asked.

Eddie nodded. Listening was one thing; actively paying attention was another. Eddie was trapped in his thoughts of what he'd read. His ADHD had cranked up to its highest gears.

"Great," Principal Daniels said, accepting the nod as confirmation. "Then what I want to talk to you about is your grades." He made a couple keystrokes on his computer and pulled up Eddie's records. "When I look at your transcript over the last year, I see nothing but Cs and Ds. Well, mostly Ds."

No surprises there. Eddie had never done particularly well in school or anything that involved a lot of thinking or concentrating. When he started forgetting things about his mother, Eddie just chalked it up to not being smart enough. Memories weren't something you could cheat on, unlike tests, which Eddie had attempted to cheat on after his mother passed. Of course, that just led to more visits with Principal Daniels.

"Do you know what that means?" Principal Daniels asked.

Eddie didn't say a word or move a muscle.

"Mr. Harper," Principal Daniels snapped, and then cleared his throat with the guttural force of an old garbage disposal.

Eddie finally jolted out of his trance.

"Straight Cs and Ds," Principal Daniels repeated. "Do you know what that means?"

Eddie put his previous thoughts on the backburner and took a moment consider the principal's question. "I'm not making honor roll?" he said.

Principal Daniels wiped his face with his hand and sucked in a deep breath to calm himself. "Yes. You are definitely right about that. Honor roll is not likely in your future. And there's a pretty good chance graduation isn't, either," he said. "If that happens, you can forget about even junior college, too. Is that what you want?"

"No."

"Then you need to start taking things seriously."

"You know what?" Eddie said, showing a sudden inspiration. "That's a great idea. I'll get started on that right now." He slapped the principal's desk for emphasis, and then popped out of his chair and strode toward the exit.

"Mr. Harper," Principal Daniels said, stopping Eddie in the doorway. "You're not getting off that easy." He scribbled something on a detention slip, got up from his desk, and handed it to Eddie. "Your presence will be required in detention for the next two periods. And I seriously hope you take my words to heart."

"I don't expect you to believe me, not at least until I prove myself, but I already have." He paused, and then added as heartfelt as humanly possible, "And thanks for not giving up on me. When just about everyone else did, you didn't. That means a lot."

Principal Daniels had never imagined that Eddie was capable of such sincerity. Flustered by it all, the principal replied, "Well, of course. I mean, it's my job."

Eddie gave Principal Daniels a pat on the back and then continued out of the office. He smiled back at the principal, waved, and then watched him close his office door. As soon as it was shut, Eddie balled up the detention slip and tossed it in the nearby garbage can. He chuckled to himself. Like usual, he'd played Principal Daniels like a piano.

Eddie retrieved his phone and reread the title of the post: LOOKING FOR ORPHANS. Eddie carefully perused the rest of the anonymously uploaded message. His awe increased with each sentence. All of the things mentioned in the post were identical to what he'd experienced in the year since his mother died. He wasn't sure if it was coincidence or if it could actually be real, but he was sure that he needed to find out more.

Without hesitation, he hit reply.

CHAPTER
FIFTEEN

"COME ON, SANCHEZ. Open the email already," insisted one of the offensive linemen from the Winchester Academy football team. He and a handful of the other varsity football players had gathered in the dorm room of their quarterback, JP Sanchez. That was what his teammates called him when they were feeling formal; however, most of the time they weren't, and opted for either JP or Sanchez.

JP was seated in his desk chair while the others were gathered behind him, jockeying for positions on all sides and peering over his perfectly spiked hair as they attempted to get a better view of his computer screen.

Like any great quarterback, JP had complete control of this huddle. "All right, all right, all right," he said. "Just calm the hell down."

The others heeded JP's direction and calmly got in formation so that they could bear witness as he opened the email.

All of their jaws promptly dropped as they gaped at the image before them.

"Man, I can't believe he actually sent that," the fullback chuckled. "I'm seeing it, and I still don't believe it."

"Yeah, well, believe it," JP said.

Earlier in the week, a freshman football player who was playing for the scout team picked off one of JP's passes. While the interception was enough to draw unwanted attention from JP and the other varsity players, it was what the freshman did after the interception that really rubbed them the wrong way. Instead of just handing the ball back, as was usually done in practice, the kid returned the pick for a touchdown and hot-dogged it in the end zone.

The varsity players, JP in particular, determined that there was no way they were going to let this cocky kid get away with such a brash display of disrespect. They decided that they needed to teach him a lesson.

JP came up with the plan. He sent the kid a message from a fake email account, using the name of a girl whom he'd dated the year before. It was a textbook catfish. And when the kid replied enthusiastically, JP knew he had him hooked. All he had to do was reel him in. He responded, attaching one of the suggestive cell phone pics that his ex-girlfriend had texted him. He told the frosh that he was a "cutie with manly muscles" and should return the favor.

The kid did exactly that and then some, sending a picture of himself in nothing but his tighty-whiteys, posing like he was competing in the lightest weight division of the worst bodybuilding contest ever.

"Look at him trying to flex," the wide receiver said. "What a scrawny punk."

The lineman laughed. "You don't have much room to talk. You're pretty scrawny yourself."

The comment started a shoving match.

"I'll show you scrawny," the wide receiver said. He tried and failed to get the upper hand in their little squabble.

"Keep it coming. You're doing a great job of it," the line-man chuckled before putting the much smaller wide receiver in a full nelson headlock.

JP easily broke up the petty quarrel. In spite of being built like the average quarterback, he was anything but that. In the beginning of the season, he'd tested out as the strongest and fastest player on the football team. It was something that would've been unimaginable only a couple years earlier.

"You guys are a bunch of clowns," JP said. "You both need to chill out. We gotta decide what we do next. We can't let something so amazing"—he gestured to the computer screen—"just go to waste."

"I say we make T-shirts," the fullback said, excited by his own idea. "We can have it say 'Mr. Puniverse' on the top and then give him a fake crown."

"I'd wear that every day," the wide receiver said, "and twice on Sunday."

"I like the T-shirt idea," the lineman said. "And I'm down to do that eventually, but right now, I think we gotta dream bigger. We gotta see how far he's willing to go."

JP's cell phone buzzed. He gave the message a quick once-over. By the time he finished reading, his enthusiasm for plotting their next move had noticeably waned. "I like both ideas," he said. "But we're gonna have to figure it out later."

"What?" the wide receiver shot back. "Why?"

"Yeah. What was the message?" the fullback asked.

"It was a reminder that I need to study for tomorrow's Physics test," JP said.

"You gotta be kidding me," the lineman groaned. "You don't need to study. You already know you're getting an A on it. If anything, I'm the one who should be studying."

"Yeah, you're right. You should be studying. Consider it a reminder for both of us," JP said with a grin. "Now all of you get the hell out of here." He gave his teammates friendly shoves out of the room. "And don't worry, the picture isn't going anywhere. Except to a custom T-shirt company."

"Yeah, yeah. Later, Sanchez," they all said as they exited.

As soon as they were all gone, JP shut the door to his dorm room. He sat back down at his computer and logged out of the fake email account. He retrieved his Physics book from his desk, rapped his fingers on the cover for a second, and then put the textbook down. His attention shifted back to his computer. He opened a new browser, went to The Message Bored website, and typed something into the search bar.

JP had a secret that none of his boarding school buddies knew. He was different. It had nothing to do with the fact that he wasn't from old Chicago money. Every student at the elite institution knew exactly how each other's families had made their fortunes, and their approximate net worth, rounded to the nearest million. The fact that he happened to be one of the only students on academic scholarship was as evident as his obvious physical differences. While there was no concealing his darker hair and skin tone, within those features was where his secret hid.

JP's secret, which he'd kept closely guarded for all of his teen life, was that he was an orphan.

JP hit enter on his keyboard. All of the popular posts with "orphan" in the title flashed on his screen. He scrolled through the results page. His eyes lit up when he read: LOOKING FOR ORPHANS. He clicked the link, digested the post, and then hit reply.

In his response, JP disclosed what he deemed to be the pertinent details from his background. How he'd been adopted just before his first birthday. How his adoptive parents had let him know the truth when he was in sixth grade. And how, during the summer before his sophomore year of high school, he'd tricked the adoption agency into releasing the names of his biological parents.

JP wrote that after searching for his parents online and coming up empty-handed, he'd set out to track them down. Armed with their names and the information from his birth certificate, he hopped a bus to the small South Texas town where he was born. There he discovered that his parents had both died of heart attacks shortly after he was born. Even more disturbing than the news of their deaths was the fact that everywhere he went, not one person could remember anything about his parents. All his information indicated that they'd spent their whole lives in this town, and yet it was almost as if they'd never existed.

Eventually, JP located his paternal grandmother. But even she hardly remembered that she ever had a son. The only thing she could remember was the terrible nightmares that she'd had about his father and mother right after their deaths. The nightmares sounded exactly like the ones that were mentioned in the post. The thought of such dreams still haunted him.

JP wrapped up his response: YOU'RE LOOKING FOR OR-PHANS, YOU'VE FOUND ONE. I'M ALL EARS. JP SANCHEZ.

CHAPTER SIXTEEN

THE AUTOMATIC DOORBELL at The Local Blend coffee shop and Internet cafe rang as sixteen-year-old Naomi Friedman entered. She stopped in the doorway and swept the room with her eyes. To the casual observer, it would've appeared as if she was just searching for a friend. In reality, she was making sure that there weren't any police officers or people who might recognize her. Over the past six months, she'd just about perfected this discreet surveillance tactic.

Naomi quickly determined that the coast was clear and approached the college-aged barista behind the counter. "Coffee. Black," she said before the barista could even say hello or ask for her order.

"Wow! Aggressive," he replied. "Can I get your name?"

"You need my name for a black coffee?"

"Sure. For that, too," he said with a flirtatious grin.

Naomi was accustomed to all kinds of unwanted advances. She'd expected them to stop when she went on the run, but they didn't. If anything, they picked up. It turned out that her well-worn clothes just made her seem more approachable. Additionally, her curly, dark brown hair had a way of hiding the fact that she hadn't showered for days, and her lack of makeup simply accentuated a natural beauty that only others could see. Naomi dismissed all of her suitors in similar fashion, with a simple but powerful rolling of her eyes.

Naomi used the same move on the barista, but he was too busy grabbing a cup and pen to notice her gesture. "So, what should I put?" he asked, the grin returning to his face.

Naomi rolled her eyes again, that time more for herself. "Roxanne," she replied. She never used her real name. Not since she'd first been on the run. Instead, she cycled through the alphabet like the World Meteorological Organization does with hurricanes. At her next stop, she might be Sarah or Sadie, but definitely not Samantha. She refused to use—much less say—the name Samantha.

"Roxanne. Nice," the barista said as he scribbled it on her cup. "Just so you know, you don't have to put on the red light."

Naomi glared at him. "Excuse me?"

The barista nervously stumbled over his words. "You know, like the song? By Sting? Well, really, The Police. I just assumed you got that a lot."

"That's actually the first time."

"Oh," the barista said, at a loss.

"I'm kidding," Naomi said after watching him squirm for long enough.

The barista's face went flush as he let go of all of his nervous energy. He smiled and shook his head. "You really had me going. That was a good one. You know, you got a toughness to you."

"Thanks, I think."

"Trust me, it's a compliment. I dig it." He winked and then grabbed her order. As he handed Naomi her cup of coffee, he added, "I don't know if you saw any of the posters, but we got an open mic here tonight."

Whatever the barista said next, Naomi tuned out. In the security mirror behind the counter, she'd spotted a bald, middle-aged man in a blue suit approaching from the back of the cafe and concentrated her attention on him. It wasn't his choice of suit or lack of hair that had put her on edge; it was the gold badge hanging from his belt and the protrusion on his right hip—most likely his government-issued firearm.

Naomi couldn't believe it. She'd seen the man during her earlier surveillance but had completely glossed over him. While she was adept at identifying police officers and social workers, she was still working on FBI agents, who were much better at blending in with the regular working stiffs.

Naomi's breath shortened as she watched him make his way in the mirror. Ten feet away. Nine feet. Eight feet. She felt the warmth of her coffee in her hand. It gave her an idea. Right before he was about to grab her, she'd heave her scalding hot coffee in his face and make a run for it. She wasn't excited about injuring a man who was merely doing his job, but she was more concerned with her own pain than with the pain of others.

Naomi hadn't been as lucky as Eddie Harper. When her parents passed away, there was nowhere for her to go. At the tender age of nine, she was placed into foster care.

The first three years couldn't have gone better. Her foster family was nurturing and supportive. They helped her get through the sudden loss of her parents as much as anyone could. They also taught her how to love and trust again, two skills she'd lost along with her parents.

Unfortunately, the recession hit her foster family harder than most. When Naomi's foster father lost his job, the family was unable to take care of her financially, and Naomi was thrown back into the system. The day she was taken from her foster family's home was the second saddest day of her life. Naomi felt like she'd lost her parents all over again.

If her first family was the epitome of how a foster family should be, her second was exactly how they shouldn't. Naomi's new foster parents, Carl and Samantha—hence her aversion to the name Samantha—seemed only to be in it for the paycheck. They'd taken in so many kids that they were living off the state money alone. It was like they were running a business, one that would've failed horribly if not for the steady stream of subsidies.

All of the children were underclothed and underfed. Even worse was the verbal abuse the children were forced to endure at the hands of their foster parents.

Naomi weathered the violent storm for as long as she could before deciding she had to escape. But her stay cost her more than just time. The open and loving little girl who had walked through the front door only four years earlier sneaked out of the second-story window in the middle of the night a hardened teenager. A shell of her former self. Never to return.

In her six months on the lam, Naomi had hopped from town to town in northern New Jersey, sleeping in residential construction sites and anywhere else she could find. It'd worked well for the summer and up to that point in the fall, but winter wasn't too far away. She'd need a new strategy. But she'd worry about that later. At that moment, her top priority was dealing with the advancing FBI agent.

Five feet. Four feet. Naomi's fingers tightened around the cup. The muscles in Naomi's arm contracted. She was like a tightly coiled spring, ready to release, to toss, to run.

Just as Naomi was about to jerk her arm over her shoulder, the FBI agent made a hard right for the exit. She watched him continue out the door. It wasn't until the store bell rang again that her muscles relaxed, and she heard the barista, who hadn't stopped talking.

"Yeah, I'm probably gonna play some of my original songs," the barista said.

"Huh?" Naomi said, forgetting where they'd left off.

"At the open mic. My stuff is kinda like boy band pop, but with a hard rock edge to it."

"Cool. Good luck with that."

"That was actually my way of inviting you."

"I know," Naomi said. She slapped exact change for the coffee on the counter, and then started for the wall of computers. She watched through the store window as the FBI agent hopped in his car and drove off.

The barista called after Naomi, "If you come, I'll buy you another black coffee. Maybe even one of our tasty scones."

"I'll think about it," she said without looking back, but there was no way she was going to attend the open mic. Even if she wanted to, which she didn't, she couldn't take that risk. She rarely went to the same place twice, and definitely not in the same day. That would be asking to get caught, asking to be returned to her evil foster parents.

Naomi continued to the computer stations and took the first open seat. While she wanted to get out of there as soon as possible, just in case the FBI agent came back, there was something she needed to do before she left.

Naomi had a ritual she performed once a week. First, she'd do an Internet search of her name, just to make sure that there were no new stories or missing persons reports about her. There weren't. For the most part, they'd stopped after the first couple weeks, but it never hurt to check. Next, she'd do an Internet search of her parents. It was the only way she could remember their faces and anything about them.

Howard and Amy Friedman had run a small, privately funded medical research lab. They focused their efforts on cures for what they considered to be two of the most debilitating and demoralizing diseases: Alzheimer's and Amyotrophic Lateral Sclerosis, also known as ALS, or Lou Gehrig's disease.

Naomi's favorite article about her parents was a touching, in-depth interview that not only talked about how they were weeks away from trials on their Alzheimer's cure, but also told the story of how they met and fell in love at Johns Hopkins Medical School, and how blessed they were to have such a darling, precocious daughter. Naomi smiled every time she read it. It was usually the only time during any given week that she'd smile.

Listed just below her favorite article in the search results was Naomi's least favorite article: Howard and Amy's double obituary. Naomi never clicked the link. The short synopsis was reminder enough. They'd both died from heart attacks. The publishing dates on the two articles were just a few days apart. They were also only a few days, plus seven years, from that particular day's date.

The anniversary of her parents' deaths was always a tough time of year for Naomi, especially since she'd left her first foster home. She needed someone to talk to, but not just anyone. And definitely not the barista. She needed someone who could relate to what she'd been through.

Naomi went to The Message Bored homepage and did a search for teens whose parents had died of heart attacks. She scrolled through three pages of results before she came across the post that—just like her—was seeking orphans.

After her initial shock dissipated, Naomi hit reply.

CHAPTER
SEVENTEEN

ANTONY WILLIAMS FLIPPED through his small wad of cash as he strode down Crenshaw Boulevard in South Central Los Angeles. Two hundred eleven bucks was the final tally. Antony grinned at the irony of his sum. Two-eleven was the police code for robbery, and that's basically what he'd just pulled off, selling a couple in-the-box DVD players and an old mountain bike for top dollar. His cousin, Maurice, would be proud. He'd only expected Antony to rake in a hundred seventy-five at the most, but Antony had used his wits to drive up the price.

Not only did Antony work for his cousin, he also lived with him. He'd moved in right after his father passed away two and a half years earlier. Less than a month after moving in with Maurice, Antony dropped out of Frederick Douglass High School—where he would've been a junior if he had stuck around—and joined his cousin in the family business.

Maurice liked to think of himself as the neighborhood pawnshop. However, unlike like pawnshops, he didn't buy and sell; he only sold. Most of his merchandise fell into the category of "found goods." Almost all the time, he was the one who "found" them. On any given morning, Antony would wake up to discover boxes stacked all over the living room, where he slept. As random as it was, Antony never asked questions. He didn't care about the answers. All he cared about was making his cut.

Antony had made more than his cut that day. He continued down the street until he reached the next intersection. The traffic light was green and the pedestrian signal had yet to even turn to the flashing hand and twenty-second countdown, but he stopped at the crosswalk, anyway. He stared at the small corner store on the other side of the crossing and waited for the light to turn red.

After the light had changed, Antony jogged to the point of the intersection kitty-corner to the store and waited again for the light to flash green before continuing up Crenshaw. As he made his way up the block, he glanced back at the corner store, and the sidewalk in front of it one last time. It was in that very spot, fifteen years earlier, that his mother had taken her last breaths.

Loretta Williams had gone to the store to pick up baby food for her one-year-old son. If she'd only left the store a couple seconds earlier or stayed inside a couple seconds longer, she would've been spared. But unfortunately, she hadn't done either. Consequently, Loretta was hit by the stray bullets from a drive-by shooting, collateral damage in the senseless and seemingly never-ending gang warfare that had long since overtaken the neighborhood.

All of the witnesses to the shooting refused to talk to the police. Some out of fear. Others out of distrust. Whatever their reasons, the shooter was never caught. Justice was never served. And Antony made sure to never cross the slab of concrete where his mother's chalk-lined body had laid.

Antony was only a couple blocks away from his cousin's house when he spotted three goons, former classmates of his who used to pound on him back in their elementary school days, hanging out on the stoop up ahead.

All three goons stopped what they were doing and grinned when they caught sight of Antony.

Antony put his head down and acted like he hadn't noticed their smirks. Running wasn't an option. While he was probably faster than all of them, he knew that running only made things worse. All he could do was keep heading toward them, and cross his fingers that they'd leave him alone.

Any thoughts of an uneventful passing were erased when Antony got within ten feet of the goons. They lined up on the sidewalk, shoulder to shoulder, blocking his way.

"If it ain't our old friend Urkel," one of the goons said.

That's what all the kids in elementary school used to call Antony. Not only had he been the most studious of all of his classmates, but he'd also had the misfortune of needing glasses at an early age. He had those glasses broken so many times by bullies, including the three goons, that eventually he stopped wearing them to school and only wore them at home.

Antony's dad, Darnell Williams, always told him to just turn the other cheek. He preached nonviolence, encouraging Antony to read the words of Jesus, Henry David Thoreau, and Martin Luther King Jr., as well as many Eastern philosophers. While Antony remembered all of the things he'd learned from those books, he'd forgotten exactly why he'd read them. He'd also forgotten his father's passion; not just for nonviolence, but for education.

"Education is the great equalizer," Darnell would say, quoting Horace Mann. That would be Antony's ticket out of the neighborhood and the violence that had claimed Antony's mother. Without a proper education, Darnell knew that Antony would fall through the cracks that everyone else in the neighborhood seemed to fall through. The cracks that at times seemed as wide as the Grand Canyon. The same ones that he himself had fallen through.

A high school football star with a promising future, Darnell's career was derailed by a knee injury he suffered his senior year. Having never put even the slightest emphasis on academics, when his knee went, so did all of the acceptance letters and scholarship offers. That had been his mistake. He owned it. But he wouldn't let his son follow the same path. He owed it to Loretta, and to Antony, to make sure that Antony didn't suffer a similar fate. And so, he fought tooth and nail to make sure his son had the best chance possible.

Darnell pushed to get education reform in the schools. So that parents would have more choices. So that failing schools would be held accountable. So that all children, not just Antony, would have access to a quality education. It seemed to be working, too. Other parents started getting involved and demanding options. Even the administrators began to listen, and Darnell was given the opportunity to speak before the board for the Los Angeles Unified School District.

The night prior to his big meeting with the school district, Darnell went out for a jog. Antony didn't remember his father coming home that night. He didn't remember the blank look in his father's eyes, or that he went straight to his room without saying a word. He only slightly remembered finding his father in his bed the next morning, dead from a heart attack, but even that memory was fuzzy.

When Darnell's voice went silent, so did all of the others. Nothing changed. The status quo remained, and all of the children suffered for it.

Antony stayed silent as the three goons looked him up and down, intent on making him suffer.

"I almost didn't recognize you, Urkel," said another of the goons as he jabbed his fingers into Antony's sternum. "You wearing contacts or something?" When Antony didn't respond, the goon continued, "Yeah, you gotta be. You must be making good money, too, aren't you?"

Antony knew where this was going. Next they would ask for—no, demand—any money that he had on him. If he said his pockets were empty, they'd find out for themselves. Even if he gave them everything he had, they'd still try to beat him down like they had back in grade school.

With his father's teachings of nonviolence having long escaped his mind, replaced with boxing lessons from his cousin, Antony employed what Maurice liked to call "Protect your neck and my money." He didn't say a word or wait for any of the goons to ask him how much he was holding. Instead, he spoke with a closed fist. He threw a right cross, cracking the goon closest to him in the jaw and dropping him like a sandbag.

Antony wasted no time tending to the next-closest goon. He struck him in the chest. The blow was so forceful that it knocked the wind out of the would-be perpetrator, who stumbled backwards onto the grass of the nearby yard.

The last goon standing went for his knife, but he picked the wrong pocket and retrieved his cell phone on accident. He tossed the device and went back for his blade.

Antony didn't give the goon a chance to make good on his error. Using the speed and strength that he'd inherited from his father, Antony swept the goon's leg, sending him falling to the ground, his head smacking the sidewalk. Antony kicked the goon's weapon away and was in the process of appropriating the discarded cell phone—a fifty-dollar bill for him— when he heard the whooping call of a patrolling police siren.

Without hesitation, Antony took off for the nearest alley. He knew the police wouldn't care that the goons had been the instigators. Facts and evidence weren't even second thoughts to many of the boys in blue who combed those streets. On top of that, the legal dropout age had been bumped to eighteen, and they would almost certainly pop Antony for truancy.

The goons attempted to flee as well, but they were slowed by the flashing stars that they were still seeing. Lucky for Antony, the police opted to focus on plucking the low-hanging, and badly bruised, fruit.

Even with the cops seemingly off his tail, Antony still sprinted the rest of the way to his cousin's dilapidated bungalow-style home.

Once he was safe inside, Antony took a moment to reclaim his breath, and then he retrieved the phone he'd lifted and inspected the condition. He was pleasantly surprised to find that he was wrong about it being a fifty-dollar phone. It was even nicer than he'd initially thought. There was a chance he could get a hundred bucks for it, assuming it worked. He swiped the screen to wake up the phone. Everything was in order. There was even a browser already open. The goon who owned the phone had been flipping through posts on The Message Bored.

The top link was titled: LOOKING FOR LOVE. Antony read the heading and chuckled. His eyes barely grazed the next post as he went to close the phone's browser. But before he could cancel the app, he was stopped by a sudden and overwhelming impulse. Antony lifted his thumb and read the subject line: LOOKING FOR ORPHANS..

With all of the Eastern philosophy that he'd studied, Antony was familiar with the idea of the universe, or God, pointing you in the right direction. While he'd subscribed to the belief in the past, it'd been years since he'd even thought to acknowledge any of the signs as they presented themselves. Even so, Antony couldn't overlook the one that was currently in front of him and calling for him to act.

With his head saying "no" and his heart screaming "yes," Antony clicked on the link to open the post.

CHAPTER
EIGHTEEN

CHARLIE DIDN'T REVEAL much in his responses to the other orphans. He simply told them that if they were interested in hearing more, he'd wire them money to pay for their flights to San Francisco so they could talk in person. Looking for answers, or at the very least, a free trip, almost all of the orphans immediately accepted the invitation. Only Naomi, who refused to fly, declined. A flight would require her to show some form of ID. That would be too much of a gamble. Charlie suggested that she take a train instead. He'd ridden trains a couple times with his parents, and they'd never been asked for identification. After thinking it over, Naomi tepidly agreed to make the cross-country trek by rail.

In the days that preceded the orphans' arrivals, Charlie's nightmares subsided. But it was hardly cause for celebration, as they didn't fully cease until he'd forgotten nearly every memory of his parents and Walter. All Charlie had left was the note on the back of the science fair picture, which he carried with him, tucked in the pages of his Moleskine.

Charlie wasn't sure if Terry and his Beasts were keeping tabs on him, but he knew it was of the utmost importance not to do anything that would raise their suspicions or tip them off, just in case they were. So Charlie kept up the guise of business as usual, still attending school and doing everything else that he normally would. He even emailed Terry about the internship, like Terry had told him to, and was in the process of crafting his second counter offer when the other orphans began to arrive.

Charlie had arranged it so that all of the orphans would get in at about the same time; however, a snowstorm in Colorado had delayed Naomi's train by an hour. During that time, the others waited in Charlie's room, mostly silent except for when JP and Eddie would urge Charlie to just tell them what was going on. But Charlie was adamant that they had to wait until everyone was there. After groans, they'd return to their silence until they decided to take another shot at changing Charlie's mind.

◆ ◆ ◆

"She's here," Charlie said as he finally spotted Naomi's taxi pull up through the small, diamond-shaped window in his bedroom.

JP and Eddie sighed. "It was about time," Eddie said.

Charlie left the others in his room and went outside to pay for Naomi's ride.

"Uh. Hi," Charlie stammered when Naomi climbed out of the taxi. "Naomi, right? Yeah. You're obviously Naomi.

There's only one girl." He hadn't anticipated her being so attractive. Now that he knew she was, it was all he could think about. Neither Naomi's exhaustion nor her eye-rolling was enough to throw cold water on the fire building inside Charlie's chest.

"So ... are you gonna pay the guy," Naomi said, "or are you just gonna stare at me like a creep?"

"Yeah," Charlie said as he mindlessly nodded his head.

"Yeah, what?" she asked impatiently.

Charlie snapped out of his daze. "I mean, I'm gonna pay him." Charlie paid the driver and then turned back to Naomi. "Okay, well, I guess you can follow me." He started up the driveway toward his house. "Everyone else is already here, so we can get finally started."

"Wait a second," Naomi said, yet to leave the curb. She hadn't been sure if she could trust Charlie when he emailed her back, and she still hadn't decided what to think of him after meeting him. "There aren't any cops inside, are there?"

Charlie stopped halfway up the driveway. "No. Not that I know of."

"Then who else is up there?"

"The other orphans."

Naomi considered her options. After a moment, she nodded to the cabbie, releasing him, and then started up the concrete driveway.

◆ ◆ ◆

Charlie returned to his bedroom with Naomi to find Antony still sitting respectfully on the bed. Meanwhile, JP had moved to Charlie's desk and was messing around on the

123

computer, and Eddie was in the middle of rifling through Charlie's dresser drawers.

"Hey, guys," Charlie said, getting their attention. "This is Naomi."

"It's about time we got a girl," JP said. "I was starting to think this was gonna be a sausage party."

"Speaking of sausage," Eddie said, "you got any snacks? I can't find anything."

"That's because we keep them in the kitchen," Charlie said.

"What do you do when you get hungry at night?"

"I go downstairs."

"That seems inconvenient." Eddie stuffed Charlie's clothes back inside the dresser but didn't bother to close the drawer.

"He probably doesn't want to attract rats," Naomi said, grimacing as she scanned the area. "This room is a dump. I'd rather sleep on the street than in here." She hesitantly touched the bed before taking a seat on the other corner.

"I don't have rats," Charlie said, getting defensive. "And I just moved up here a little while ago, so I'm still getting situated. But that's not important. Now that everyone's here, I can tell you why I invited you."

Everyone immediately went quiet. Eddie forgot about his hunger, and Naomi forgot about her disgust for Charlie's dilapidated bedroom.

Charlie took a deep breath before breaking the same news to the others that Walter had broken to him. "Your parents didn't die. They were killed."

The other orphans stared at Charlie, unsure what to make of his bold and unexpected revelation.

After a moment, Antony spoke up. "What's going on? Is this some kind of joke?"

"If it is," Eddie said, "it definitely isn't a good one."

"It's not a joke," Charlie said. "I'm serious."

"Seriously messed up in the head," JP said, and then looked to the rest of the orphans, who nodded in agreement.

"No, I'm not," Charlie shot back. He told them about everything that he'd uncovered about his own parents. He told them about the contract and the contact list. He also retold the rabbi's story about the soul-stealing Beasts.

"Just think about it," Charlie continued. "All of us have had at least one parent that died of a heart attack, some of us, two. And all of us have had our memories of them disappear from our dreams. That's not normal. I've known other people who passed away—three of my grandparents did—and that never happened. I still remember them."

"I agree that all the stuff that happened is mad weird," Antony said, "but I don't see how that proves that our parents were killed, or anything else about your whole crazy story."

"I saw the spark in one of the Beast's eyes," Charlie said. "It was so bright that it even shined through his sunglasses."

"Dude," Eddie said, "It was probably just a reflection."

"He's got a point," JP agreed. "That's pretty thin evidence. Thin enough that you definitely could've just said it over email and saved us all a lot of time."

"No kidding," Naomi said. "Do you even realize how long that train ride was?"

"You really should've flown," Eddie said. "They gave me extra cookies, soda, and I even got free Wi-Fi."

Charlie shook his head. This wasn't going like he'd planned at all. He hadn't expected so much resistance. He'd assumed that they'd all be grateful that he'd discovered the truth behind their parents' deaths, and that they'd be eager to hear his plan. Instead, they were pushing him to the brink. Charlie was close to snapping when he came up with the perfect way to silence their doubt.

"I have a printed copy of the contract," he said. "This will prove to you that it's all real." He retrieved the contract from the top drawer in his desk, along with a set of matches. He struck a match and held the flame to the paper.

Just like before in the rabbi's office, the letters on the contract caught fire but the paper did not.

Naomi and Antony watched in utter disbelief. JP wasn't quite sure what to make of it, but Eddie was, and confidently disregarded the display.

"Bravo," Eddie said as he gave a sarcastic slow clap. "That was a great trick. If I was David Blaine, I'd totally be looking over my shoulder for you."

"That wasn't a trick," Charlie said. He blew the smoke away from the sheet, making sure all of the flames were out, and then offered it to Eddie. "Try to tear it."

"That's obviously just part two of the trick," Eddie said. "I'm not falling for it."

"I'll give you a thousand dollars if you can tear it even the tiniest bit."

"I told you, I'm not falling for it."

Never one to turn down a chance for easy money, Antony snatched the paper from Charlie. "Hell, I'll fall for it," he said.

"Same deal?"

"Of course," Charlie said.

"You're on. But just so you know, I only take straight cash, homie." Antony used every muscle in his upper body as he tried to tear the sheet of paper, but it was no use.

"Give it here," JP demanded.

"Good luck," Antony said and then handed over the sheet.

JP nodded to Charlie. "When I shred this, you better pay up. Except I don't want one grand, I want ten."

Unfazed, Charlie countered, "I'll give you twenty."

"Rich kids," JP said and shook his head. He huffed and puffed as he pulled in every direction, but he couldn't tear the sheet either. He gave up in a fit, crumpled the paper, and chucked it across the room. "Eddie's right. That's a scam."

Naomi retrieved the balled-up sheet. It unfolded in her hand on its own. "What the hell is this?"

"I already told you," Charlie said. "It's a contract with the Devil. And it was printed on regular old printer paper."

This time, there were no wisecracks or criticisms. They simply waited for Charlie to explain further. He finally had their attention.

"I'm pretty sure all of the people in the contact spreadsheet signed it," Charlie said. "And I'd bet the people who killed your parents and stole their souls are on that list, too."

The others considered this reality for a moment.

"Let's say you're right," Eddie said. "So what? What do you want us to do?"

Before Charlie could respond, Antony answered for him. "You want us to team up and kill theses Beasts, don't you?"

127

Charlie nodded. "Exactly."

With that, Charlie lost the room all over again.

"That's insane!" JP erupted. "You are completely insane!"

"I totally agree," Eddie said. "I don't even believe in God, but the whole idea of taking on the Devil—that's just nuts. Plain and simple."

"I don't want anything to do with any of this," Naomi announced. "Thanks for the ticket, Charlie. It was great meeting you guys and seeing the West Coast for the first time, but I prefer the East. There are way less weirdos. I'm out of here." Naomi started for the stairs.

"Wait! Don't leave. Please," Charlie begged. He grabbed Naomi's arm. "Stay. For your parents."

Charlie's words didn't sway Naomi, they only made her more determined to leave. "You don't know anything about my parents," she snapped. "And you definitely don't know anything about me." She was about to yank her arm free when the doorbell rang.

Charlie's eyes went wide. He loosened his grip, dropping hold of Naomi's arm.

"What's going on?" Naomi asked. "Who is that?"

The doorbell rang again, this time twice.

"I thought you said we were all here," JP said.

Everyone *was* there, at least everyone that Charlie had been expecting. While he wasn't 100 percent sure who was at the door, he'd already made his best educated guess, and he couldn't help but assume the worst.

CHAPTER
NINETEEN

CHARLIE SCANNED THE STREET from his bedroom window. He'd expected to find Terry's Bentley waiting out front; however, he didn't. In fact, he didn't spot any cars, including the blacked-out suv that was still parked a couple houses down and out of view.

The slight relief that Charlie gained from the absence of the Bentley was quickly negated by the uncertainty that it left in its wake, as well as the realization that it could very well still be Terry and his men, hoping to surprise them.

"Just wait here for a second," Charlie said to Naomi. "At least let me make sure it's safe."

"Fine," Naomi reluctantly agreed.

Charlie slipped off his shoes and crept down the stairs in his socks, careful to not make even the slightest sound. He didn't want whoever was waiting at the door to know that he was coming.

Charlie had made it down the stairs from his bedroom and was halfway down the flight that led to the foyer when the doorbell rang four times fast. As jarring as the rapid-fire ringing was, it was the sound that he heard next that set his nerves off like Fourth of July fireworks.

Charlie had detected a faint and foreign chatter as he passed by his grandfather's second-floor bedroom. He recognized the racket as one of the many Korean game shows the old man watched on a daily basis and thought nothing of it. He immediately regretted his indifference right after the doorbell stopped ringing, when the muffled chatter unexpectedly jumped what felt like a hundred decibels. Charlie's eyes shot up toward his grandfather's room, where the door was now wide open, and Grandpa Kim was already halfway into the hall. Charlie emphatically swatted the air, trying to get his grandfather to go back into his room.

"You get the door, then! You get it," Grandpa Kim demanded as he waved back at Charlie.

Charlie bit his lip, squinched his face, and shook his head, suppressing all of the things that he wanted to scream at his grandfather. Instead, he gave Grandpa Kim one last firm shoo.

Grandpa Kim finally obliged and returned to his room and closed the door. The noise was once again muffled, but the damage was done.

Charlie turned back to the front door. He was certain that his cover was blown; whoever was at the front door had heard the commotion his grandfather had caused. The more he thought about it, the more his heart raced. By the time he'd reached the front door, his heart was pounding so hard that he not only heard it in his ears but also felt the throbbing beats in his fingertips.

Charlie took one last nervous gulp of air, held his breath, and then lifted himself up onto his tiptoes to peek through the peephole. He never could've guessed whom he'd spy through the fisheye lens, in part because he'd never seen her before.

Waiting outside was a young girl with long black hair and dark brown skin, her head impatiently oscillating back and forth between the door and the street.

Charlie estimated that she couldn't have been much older than eleven, if that, even. Regardless of her age, the fact that it wasn't Terry instantly put Charlie at ease. He exhaled every last molecule of oxygen that he'd been holding in his lungs. Figuring the little girl was probably just a neighbor selling Girl Scout cookies or something for school, he undid the locks. He intended just to tell her to come back later, but as soon as he opened the door the slightest crack, it burst all the way open, and the tiny girl barreled through like a tiny battering ram. Charlie was sent slipping backwards on his socks before coming to a tumbling stop.

"Sorry about that," the little sparkplug of a girl said as she looked down at Charlie on the wooden floor, "but we need to hurry." She didn't say another word; she just sprinted toward the living room and disappeared inside.

"Slow down," Charlie said as he picked himself off of the ground. "What the hell are you talking about? And who the hell are you?"

"Malika Prakash," she replied as she scurried out of the living room and went straight for the dining room without otherwise acknowledging Charlie.

"Well, Malika, I don't know what makes you think you can just barge into people's houses like you own the place. But you need to leave."

After a brief moment, Malika popped out of the hallway next to the stairs and back into the foyer. "That is exactly what I was intending to do. Where are the others?"

"They're upstairs," Charlie said reflexively.

"In your bedroom?"

"Yeah."

Malika immediately took off up the steps.

"What are you doing?" Charlie called after her.

Malika didn't respond. She just kept flying up the stairway.

Charlie watched her from the foyer. He was completely caught off-guard by the audacity of the preteen. But even more disconcerting than her brazen behavior was his realization that she'd specifically mentioned "the others." How did she know that anyone else was there? Had she been watching them? Still pondering the answers to his questions, Charlie halfheartedly called to the girl once more, "Hey, I told you to leave."

Even if Charlie had screamed at the top of his lungs, Malika wouldn't have heard him. She'd already passed through the door to his bedroom and was more than halfway up the stairs.

Charlie shook his head. "This doesn't make any sense," he said to himself, and then raced after her.

Charlie made it to his room just after Malika had finished informing the other orphans that they had to leave.

Eddie looked to Charlie for answers. "Do you know this crazy little girl?"

"No," Charlie said as he struggled to stuff his feet back into his tied sneakers. "She just stormed in here."

"As far as I'm concerned, she can storm back out," JP said. "There's no way some short-stack is gonna boss me around."

"It is for your own safety," Malika said, "so I would learn to get over it."

"I like her already," Naomi said with grin.

Antony was the only one who had seriously heeded Malika's warning. "What's going on?" he asked her. "Why do we need to leave?"

"Terry and his men are on their way," Malika said.

Upon hearing this news, Charlie went catatonic. If Malika mentioning "the others" had been a jab that stunned him, her very utterance of Terry's name was the equivalent of ten knockout punches. There was no logical explanation as to how this little girl could possibly know about Terry, or that he was on his way.

Naomi noted the look on Charlie's face. "Who's Terry?"

"I'm gonna go out on a limb," Antony said, "and guess he's the guy that killed Charlie's parents."

Charlie nodded. He turned to Malika, equal parts confused and suspicious. "How do you know he's coming?"

"Because I've been watching them," she said. "I've been watching them ever since they came to your house."

"Who are you?"

"I do not have time to explain. Terry and his men will be here any second. You must trust me. None of you are safe. We really need to hurry."

There was an honesty in Malika's eyes that Charlie couldn't deny. While he still had plenty of questions for this mysterious child, he no longer questioned whether or not they should accept the validity of her urgency. He looked to the others. "We need to listen to her. We need to—"

Charlie was cut off by the sound of screeching tires just outside of the house.

Naomi rushed to the bedroom window and gazed out onto the street. "This Terry guy doesn't happen to drive a sick blacked-out Bentley, does he?"

"Yeah," Charlie said.

"Then he's already here."

Charlie joined Naomi at the window. The others huddled behind them. Out on the street, Terry, Cain, and Max were already out of their car and storming for the house. Three additional Beasts that Charlie had never seen before—but at the same time looked strangely familiar—cut across the yard diagonally as they hurried to join Terry and his bodyguards.

All of the new Beasts were of medium height and build; however, they carried themselves as if they were much larger. They each had their own distinct features, too. The one leading the way sported a jet-black pompadour with a bushy mustache to match, the Beast just behind appeared to be of Southeast Asian descent, while the last—and clearly the oldest of the group—had snow-white hair and a long beard, and looked like Santa Claus might if he'd recently won a reality weight-loss show.

"Looks like we won't be leaving out the front door," JP said as he peered over Charlie's head. "Or probably any other door on the first floor, for that matter."

"Does this stupid window even open?" Naomi said as she searched for some kind of latch.

"No," Charlie said.

"It's too small, anyway," Antony said.

"Great," Eddie groaned as he threw his hands in the air. "We're trapped up here, and those Blues Brothers wannabe thugs are about to come get us. This is awesome."

"There's gotta be a way out of here," Naomi said.

"Over there," Antony said, noticing the floor-to-ceiling curtains that blended in with the wall at the back of the room. He dashed to the curtains, tore them open, and then tried to do the same to the French doors that had been hidden behind them, but they weren't so quick to budge. It'd been years since they'd been opened, and the wood had warped significantly in that time. Antony steadied his foot on the wall and used all of his leverage to rip the doors free.

Naomi joined Antony in peering over the railing of the Juliet balcony. It was a straight, twenty-five-foot drop down to a brick patio. "We jump, we probably break our ankles," Naomi said. "They get us anyway."

Antony turned back to the others, shaking his head. "She's right," he agreed. "We're trapped."

Eddie paced the room. "Well, this is fan-freaking-tastic. We're dead. And I didn't even get to enjoy a last meal."

135

"Enough," Malika ordered. "I did not want to take matters into my own hands, but it appears that I must."

"Little girl," JP said condescendingly, "I doubt your cuteness is gonna stop them from—"

JP stopped short when he saw Malika's shoulder blades beginning to bulge from her upper back. They moved violently as they pushed against her skin, like two tiny dogs caught under the bed sheets, trying to get out, until the bones finally broke free, tearing through the skin.

"Oh. My. God," Naomi said as she covered her mouth with her hand. "That's disgusting."

The protruding bones unraveled like the supports to a camping tent before locking into place. At their full width, they spanned eight feet, almost twice Malika's height. Golden feathers bloomed from them and glistened in the light from the window.

All of the orphans were paralyzed by what they saw. Surely their eyes were deceiving them. There was no way that this tiny eleven-year-old girl had just grown wings.

CHAPTER TWENTY

CHARLIE AND THE OTHER ORPHANS watched with their mouths agape as Malika's wings fluttered two times fast, shaking off their rust from being cooped up. Along with her wings, there was a bright, circular aura of gold that hovered over Malika's head. A halo.

It was obvious to all of the orphans that this girl who had stormed into their world was not a girl at all—she was an angel. Eddie slowly reached into his pocket, retrieved his cell phone, and snapped a picture of the little winged wonder.

The click of the camera caught Naomi's attention. She scowled at Eddie. "What the hell are you doing?"

"Probably making my last post," Eddie said, still working his phone. "Quick, someone come up with a hashtag."

"Screw hashtags."

"That's kinda funny, but I think we can do better than that. What else do you got?"

Naomi shook her head. "That wasn't a suggestion."

"There is no time for this," Malika insisted. "Which two of you are first?"

"First for what?" JP said.

"I am going to fly all of you out of here. Who is first?"

All of the orphans shook their heads in unison. None of them wanted to be the first to take flight with this little angel.

"Fine," Malika said. "I will choose." She turned to JP and Eddie, who happened to be the closest to her, and yanked them up by their belts, lifting them with surprising ease.

In the process of getting hoisted, Eddie dropped his cell. "My phone," he groaned as he reached for the device.

But it was too late. Malika was already sprinting toward the balcony with the guys in tow. Antony and Naomi parted just before Malika blew past them. She vaulted over the railing and took flight. She and the guys shot straight up into the sky, over a hundred feet above the house, cutting through some low-hanging pockets of fog.

"You better make sure someone grabs my phone," Eddie said. "My whole life is on that."

"Do not worry about that," Malika said. "Just keep quiet."

Eddie peeked down at the world below. He immediately regretted his decision and slammed his eyes shut.

JP looked at Eddie and chuckled. "Don't tell me you're actually afraid of heights."

Eddie opened his eyes just enough to glare at JP. "On a plane or in a building? No," he said. "But when it's an eleven-year-old girl with wings? Yes! I'm very much afraid of heights. And I'm not afraid to admit it!"

"Remain calm and quiet," Malika said. "And both of you will want to close your eyes for what I am about to do."

She didn't have to tell Eddie twice. He quickly followed orders. JP, on the other hand, refused to heed her advice. Big mistake.

Malika ceased flapping her wings. The three began to plunge back to the earth. Malika used her wings as rudders to flip them around. Now falling headfirst, she gave one last whip of her wings, to give them a little more speed, and then tucked them as they made their tailspinning nosedive.

JP's eyes went wide, both from his own reaction to the rapid descent and from the rush of wind smacking his face. He quickly swallowed his pride and attempted to shut his eyes, but that was easier said than done. The gushing wind, combined with the dryness it caused, was too much for his eyelids to overcome. He tried to use his arms to help them shut, but the force of the descent had effectively glued his limbs to his body. He had no choice. He was forced to watch as they spiraled toward the rooftop of the James's mansion.

At what seemed like the last second to JP, Malika spread her wings and let loose a powerful flap. The three touched down gently on the mansion roof.

The guys immediately fell to the floor, ecstatic to be back on something solid. "I don't wanna do that, or anything like that, ever again," JP said.

"Me either," Eddie agreed. "And I'm pretty sure I need a new pair of underwear."

Malika did a quick survey of Charlie's house. Through one of the front windows, she spotted Terry and the five Beasts making their way up the stairs to the second floor. Through another window, she saw the door to Charlie's room, which was closed. "Stay down," she said.

"Works for me," Eddie said, still hugging the concrete roof.

"And stay quiet, too." Malika crouched on one knee, lifted her head, and shot back into the sky.

The return flight only took a couple of seconds, since she was able to travel at her full speed. Doing so with human cargo would've made them extremely ill, or worse.

Malika landed softly on the balcony railing. In her absence, Charlie and the remaining orphans had debated which two of them would go next, but failed to come to a conclusion.

"Just go," Antony ordered Charlie. "I can hold my own."

"That's crazy," Charlie said. "There's no way you can. Besides, it's my house. I have to stay."

Naomi tried to add her two cents. "I—"

"Enough," Malika snapped, cutting Naomi off. She hoisted Antony and Naomi and prepared for takeoff.

"Hold up!" Antony said as he tugged Malika's arm.

Malika paused. "What?"

Antony looked to Charlie. "Don't forget the flash drive."

"Good call," Charlie said. He darted to his computer, removed the drive, and threw it to Antony.

Malika lifted Antony up so he could catch the errant toss.

"Why are you giving it to me?" Antony said.

"Just in case," Charlie said.

"I will hurry back," Malika said. "Just be ready."

Charlie nodded.

Malika jetted out the balcony doors with Naomi and Antony. She followed the same flight path as before, rapid descent and all. Both Naomi and Antony listened to her orders and kept their eyes closed for the full flight.

Malika dropped the pair off on the rooftop near JP and Eddie. Her gaze immediately returned to the Kim residence. "Oh, no," she said as she spotted something unsettling.

"What?" Antony said, turning his head up toward Malika. But it was too late. She'd already shot back into the sky.

Eddie crawled over to Antony and Naomi. "Please tell me one of you grabbed my phone."

"You're unbelievable," Antony said. He dug the device from his pocket and then handed it over to Eddie. "Here's your damn phone."

Eddie accepted the phone like he'd been handed a newborn baby. "Thank you. I owe you big time."

Antony peeked over the ledge of the roof and scanned the windows of Charlie's house. It didn't take him long to identify what had caused Malika concern. While he was easily able to place Terry, Max, and the three unidentified Beasts on the second floor, he couldn't pinpoint the location of the last Beast, Cain. However, he didn't need a confirmation to know where Cain was. He could clearly see that the door leading to Charlie's room, which he distinctly remembered hearing Charlie slam shut, was now open.

CHAPTER TWENTY-ONE

CHARLIE DANGLED ABOVE the backyard patio, his fingers tightly wrapped around the lowest rung on the balcony railing as he held on for dear life.

As soon as he'd heard the bedroom door creaking open, he'd hopped the railing, carefully closed the French doors, and then lowered himself down so that only the tops of his hands were visible from the bedroom. While it'd put him in an incredibly vulnerable position, it'd also bought him time that he desperately needed, and was much better than the alternative.

Charlie searched the sky for Malika. She was nowhere to be seen. He cursed under his breath. He could hear Cain ransacking his bedroom, foraging for any clues that might tip off their whereabouts. The clangor increased as Cain got closer and closer. Charlie knew that it was only a matter of time before Cain noticed him hanging there. By the same token, he also knew that there was only so much longer that he could actually support himself. What he didn't know was which unpleasant scenario would occur first.

The answer came much sooner than Charlie would've liked, as he realized that his body was already starting to give out. It started with his hands. The muscles burned like they were holding onto hot coals and not the metal railing. Then, the searing sensation travelled down his arms, over his shoulders, and across his back. He fought to hang on, but the blaze became too much. He lessened his grip to allow fresh blood to flow to his fingers and hopefully ease the pain, but, in doing so, he lost hold of the rail. Once his fingers started to slip, there was no turning back, only going down.

Charlie's arms and legs flailed as he plummeted to the ground. He prepared for the pain he expected after his legs broke. He'd broken a leg in third grade after falling from the monkey bars. It'd hurt so bad that he cried for most of an hour afterwards. He expected this to hurt much worse.

Charlie was so close to colliding with the ground that his mind had already begun to manifest the impending pain when Malika swooped in and caught him. The tips of his feet skidded across the patio brick as she hauled him away.

Malika and Charlie landed on the James's roof, reuniting with the others. With all of the orphans safe from Terry and his men, Malika folded her wings like a Swiss Army knife and then retracted them into her back. Her open skin closed over the exit points, healing instantly, and the sparkling halo faded from her head.

Eddie hesitantly ran his fingers across Malika's smooth shoulder blades so that his hands could confirm what his eyes had seen. "Yep," he marveled. "That just happened."

"After that, and everything else," Naomi said, "I'm a little more inclined to believe the whole Devil and Beasts stuff."

"Same here," Antony agreed. "I'm also inclined to believe that Charlie was right about our parents, too. They were killed." He turned to Malika. "I'm gonna go out on a limb and guess that you might even know why."

"I do," Malika said, "but we do not have time for that. We need to keep moving." She went to leave, but stopped when she realized that her footsteps were the only sound and the orphans weren't following her.

"None of us are going anywhere," JP announced, his arms extended to hold the others back, "until you at least tell us who you really are. You're obviously some kind of angel, but who are you?"

"Yeah," Charlie agreed. "If you want, you can keep it brief. But you need to tell us who you are."

Malika took a deep breath and sighed. She approached Charlie, grabbed his hands, and held them in hers. "I am your guardian angel. That is why I was watching you. That is why I came to protect you." She gave Charlie's hand a gentle squeeze and then let it go.

"Where are the rest of our guardian angels?" Eddie asked.

"For real," Antony said. "Where are they?"

"I promise to answer all of your questions in due time," Malika said. "But right now, my main objective is to keep all of you safe. Okay?"

The orphans said nothing, showing compliance in silence.

"Great," Malika said. "Now follow me."

The orphans did just that, taking off after Malika as she raced for the fire escape off of the back of the house.

Halfway across the rooftop, Charlie came to a sudden halt. There was something that didn't sit right with him. He searched his mind, trying to figure out exactly what it was. As soon as he found it, he turned around and sprinted back toward the street side of the roof.

Eddie was about to take his first step down the fire escape ladder when he noticed Charlie bolting back across the rooftop. "Where's he going?"

"I don't know," Naomi said, "but he's almost at the edge. They're gonna be able to see him from there."

"What are you doing?" Antony called as he led the charge after Charlie, who had already made it to the edge of the rooftop and didn't so much as flinch at Antony's instruction. "They're gonna see—" Antony's words and feet stopped as he made it close enough to Charlie to match his gaze.

The others did the same, coming to a sudden halt. Through one of the Kims' second floor windows, they observed what had absorbed Charlie's attention: Max was forcing Charlie's grandfather out of his bedroom. Max wrenched Grandpa Kim's arm behind his back as he pushed him toward Terry, Cain, and the three unnamed Beasts.

"Noooo!" Charlie screamed.

Antony restrained Charlie, covering Charlie's mouth with his hand to muffle his screams. "Stop it!" he ordered through gritted teeth. "You're gonna get us busted."

145

When Antony sensed that Charlie had given up fighting him, he removed his hand from Charlie's mouth, but kept hold of Charlie's arm to keep him close.

"They're gonna kill him," Charlie said.

"No, they will not," Malika said. "He is old and of no use to them. Most likely, they will just let him go."

Malika was right. No more than a couple seconds later, Max released Charlie's grandfather with one last shove, and then he and the others started to leave.

Unfortunately, while Malika had correctly predicted Terry's response, she failed to anticipate how Grandpa Kim would react. The prideful war veteran that he was, Grandpa Kim was not satisfied with just letting Terry and his men go without a proper retaliation.

The orphans watched as Charlie's grandfather gave everything he had left in his aged body and attacked Max.

Max just laughed off the old man's weak blows. He waited for Grandpa Kim to tire himself out. After a few more harmless swings, the punches slowed to a complete stop. Max grabbed both of Grandpa Kim's clenched fists and spun him around.

Cain flipped his sunglasses onto the top of his head and approached Grandpa Kim.

Even from all the way across the street, the orphans could clearly make out the flames forming in Cain's eyes. The bright orange and red blaze throbbed.

"W ... T ... F ... " Eddie said in complete awe.

While he and the others were unable to discern the way that Grandpa Kim's eyes swelled with each pulse of Cain's, the tortuous pain it inflicted was more than evident to the group as they witnessed Grandpa Kim's body convulsing in spastic fits.

Charlie ripped his arm free from Antony. "We need to help him," he pleaded. For all of their differences and disagreements, his grandfather was still family, and he couldn't stand to let him suffer. "We need to do something."

"There's nothing you can do," Malika said.

"Then you do something. Fight them."

"I am not able to."

"Well, we can't just let them have their way with him," Charlie said, tears forming in the corners of his eyes.

"We do not have any other choice," Malika said. She put a comforting hand on Charlie's back. "I am sorry."

Charlie brushed Malika's hand away. He wiped his tears and returned his attention to his grandfather. He could only watch as Grandpa Kim's body turned rigid.

A thin, clear gel began to secrete from the old man's bulging oculars. Blue sparks of electricity snapped and crackled as they circled around the mysterious ooze, which stretched through the air toward Cain, gradually closing the distance between the two men before latching on to Cain's fiery orbs.

CHAPTER
TWENTY-TWO

THE STRANGE FLUID continued to flow from Grandpa Kim to Cain, the flames in Cain's eyes growing brighter and brighter as they absorbed the liquid. Grandpa Kim's body went limp as Cain consumed the last drop with a blinding flash, like a star that went supernova before imploding directly into his eyes.

Max released Grandpa Kim. His body fell flat on the floor.

Cain lifted the old man's head, smirked, said something to him, and then let his head drop back to the ground.

Max pulled Grandpa Kim up to his feet, turned him around, steadied him, and then gave him a little nudge.

Grandpa Kim stumbled back to his bedroom, took a seat on his bed, and stared blankly at the wall.

The orphans' expressions were just as vacant as they monitored the old man, waiting for what they knew would happen next.

"He's gonna have a heart attack, isn't he?" Antony asked.

Malika nodded. "Yes. In the next thirty minutes or less."

"Talk about an underrated movie," Eddie said.

Antony shook his head at Eddie.

"What?" Eddie said. "*30 Minutes or Less* was hilarious."

Before Antony could respond, Naomi spotted Terry and his men exiting the Charlie's house. "Get down!" she barked as she pulled JP and Eddie to the ground with her.

Charlie, Antony, and Malika quickly followed suit, barely avoiding detection.

They all stayed sprawled on the asphalt rooftop until the sound of the Bentley's peeling tires, as well as those of a second squealing car, had completely disappeared.

One by one, the orphans returned to their feet. Their attention returned to Grandpa Kim, who was still in the same position as before.

"It would be best to let him be," Malika said. "Besides, we should really get somewhere safe as soon as possible." She started for the fire escape. The orphans immediately followed her, in too much shock from what they'd just witnessed to put up any resistance like they had before.

As they crossed the rooftop, Antony noticed Charlie was lagging behind and slowed down to meet up with him. "Hey, I'm really sorry about your grandpa."

Charlie didn't respond. He just kept staring at his feet.

After a second, Antony continued, "The way I see it, it's just one more reason to take them down. Not that you needed another one."

Charlie lifted his head and sniffled. "Yeah. You're right."

Antony dug into his pocket and retrieved the flash drive. "Here," he said as he handed it to Charlie. "It's yours. You might as well hold onto it. Now that you actually made it."

"Thanks." Charlie let out a half smile and then pocketed the drive.

"Hurry up, you two," Malika called to them.

"Let's go," Antony said. He threw his arm around Charlie and they both picked up their pace to catch up with the rest of the crew.

◆ ◆ ◆

Malika led the orphans down alleyways and other sparsely used streets until they finally reached their destination.

"This isn't exactly what I was picturing when you said somewhere safe," Eddie said as he inspected the rusty chain-link fence before him, which surrounded an old junkyard in a seedy section of East Palo Alto.

Malika and the rest of the orphans waited on the other side of the fence, having already crawled under. "This is only a temporary stop," she said.

"Just hurry up already," Naomi said.

"Fine," Eddie said. "But if I get tetanus, it's on your heads."

Eddie crawled military-style under the same small opening that the others had passed through. He got up and rubbed his hands on his jeans to wipe the dirt off.

"We need to find a car," Malika said. She looked at their numbers. "Preferably a van."

"Where are we going?" JP said.

"Far enough that we need to drive."

"That's all you're gonna tell us?" Naomi said.

"That is all you need to know," Malika said.

"For how long?" Eddie asked.

"Until all of you are ready."

"Are we talking a couple days or a couple weeks?"

"However long it takes."

"But I have three tests and a paper due next week," Charlie said, still thinking like his old self with his old plan.

"Not anymore," Malika said, "If you go back to school, they will be waiting for you." She turned to the rest of the orphans. "The safest assumption is that they know who all of you are and that they will come for you."

The orphans slowly came to terms with the reality of their situation.

"I guess there's no going back to our old lives," Antony said.

"There is never going back," Malika said, "only moving forward. If you need to call your families or friends and tell them that you are okay and that you will be going away for a while, feel free. But after that, we must focus on finding a vehicle so we can get on the road as fast as possible."

Eddie and JP went off on their own to make calls to their respective guardians while everyone else stayed back.

Antony nodded to Naomi. "You don't have anyone you need to call?" he asked.

"I'm kind of in between places," Naomi said. "What about you? No family or friends?"

"Just my cousin. But if called him and told him I was gonna be gone, he'd probably just get pissed at me for costing him money. I'd rather just keep him in the dark."

"That's probably the smart move."

151

With everyone else preoccupied, Charlie grabbed a seat on the mangled hood of a totaled Toyota. He retrieved his Moleskine and studied his original list of goals. He was still coming to terms with the fact that he wouldn't be returning to school for the foreseeable future, if ever. That hadn't been part of his plan at all. He'd planned on keeping their mission as clandestine as possible so that he could still maintain his regular life and keep working toward everything he'd outlined for himself.

While their current situation had been caused by no real fault of his own, Charlie didn't see things that way. As far as he was concerned, he'd failed himself, the group, and his grandfather. He flipped to the back of his notebook and added this much to his list. He then skimmed over the rest of his failures, hoping to glean some desperately needed motivation.

After a minute of skimming, Charlie pocketed his notebook and approached Malika. "So what's next when we get to where we're going?"

"If we do not focus on what we have to do now, there will be no next," Malika said. She checked her pink digital watch and then shouted to JP and Eddie, "Time is up, guys."

JP finished his phone call and rejoined the crew.

Eddie wrapped up his call but took his time returning. He was busy tapping away on his phone.

"Hurry up, Eddie," Malika said.

"Sorry," Eddie said, not looking up from his phone. "I just had a great idea for a status."

"Let me see," Malika said as Eddie returned to the group.

"Fine, but I don't think you're gonna get the reference," Eddie said as he handed over the phone.

Malika tossed the cell and raised her foot.

Eddie's eyes went wide. "Whoa! What are you—" Before he could finish, Malika smashed his phone with the heel of her pink Velcro shoe. "Are you kidding me?" Eddie groaned. "I didn't even post it. Why the hell did you do that?"

"Everyone needs to destroy their phones," Malika said. "They can track you with them, if they have not already."

"She's right," Naomi agreed. "That's why I never use them."

"Mine's just a burner, anyway," Antony said. He dropped his phone on the ground and heel-stomped it to pieces.

Charlie was a little more hesitant than Antony but did the same, anyway.

"This sucks," Eddie whined. "How am I gonna take pics or update my status now?"

"You aren't," Naomi said.

"I know," Eddie said. "That's what's killing me."

"How's this?" Antony said. "Anytime you have a funny status, you can just tell me."

"Do you promise you'll like it?" Eddie said. "You know, give it a thumbs up."

"Yeah, sure," Antony said as he rolled his eyes.

"You gotta be more enthusiastic than that."

"Yeah!" Antony flashed two thumbs and every tooth in his mouth.

"That's more like it. Still not the same, though."

All eyes turned to JP, who flipped his phone in his hand.

"What?" JP snapped in response to their stares. "I'm not doing it. I just paid two hundred bucks for this phone. I'll turn it off, but I'm not breaking it."

"That is not good enough," Malika said. "I would have had all of you destroy your phones earlier, but I knew that it would receive this kind of reaction. We did not have the time to argue then, and we barely have it now."

"I don't care," JP said. "And you know what? I'm really tired of being bossed around by a little girl. I don't care if you are an angel."

"Little girl?" Malika said. "I was a little girl many thousands of years ago. I only picked this form because I assumed it would be less intimidating. But if you would rather see me in my true angelic form, I can change."

"Honestly, I don't know that I wanna see you in any form."

"The choice is yours. While I am here for your protection, I cannot force you to accept it. Nor can I force you to join us. All I can do is insist that if you choose to come with us, you follow a few rules so that the others are not put in jeopardy."

"Well, then, maybe I won't come with you."

"Like I said, the choice is yours."

Naomi could tell that JP was actually considering making good on his threat. She grabbed him by the arm. "You can't seriously be thinking about leaving so you can keep your phone. You can't go home. Where would you go?"

"Come on," Charlie urged. "You won't stand a chance on your own. None of us do. You just need to trust her."

JP chewed on the corner of his lip like it was a piece of gum as he eyeballed Malika, still trying to decide where he stood: Should he stay or should he go?

CHAPTER
TWENTY-THREE

JP CONTINUED TO flip his phone in his hand and chew on his lip while the others waited with bated breath for him to make up his mind.

Malika was over waiting. She knew that the orphans were anything but safe and needed to keep moving. "Whatever your decision is," Malika said, "you must decide right now."

JP said nothing. Whether he was serious or just seeing how far he could push Malika, none of the other orphans could tell.

Malika didn't care. Her main focus was protecting Charlie and those who welcomed her protection. "I will take that as a no," she said, and then turned to the others. "It is—"

"Fine!" JP blurted, cutting her off. "I'll stay, but only for everyone else, not you. And for the record, I'm still not happy about this."

"I did not ask you to be," Malika said.

"Clearly," JP said. He laid his phone on the pavement, rested his heel on the device, and pushed down with a crunch. "Are we good?"

As soon as JP lifted his foot off of the cracked device, Malika gave it an extra stomp for good measure. "Now we are."

"Thanks," JP said sarcastically. He picked up the inoperable phone. "I'm gonna keep it just in case this is covered under the warranty. Although I'd probably have better odds playing the water-damage card."

"New status," Eddie announced. "Off the grid for barely a minute. Hashtag sucks already."

"Wow, I feel bad for everyone on social media that missed out on that gem," Naomi said, and then rolled her eyes.

Eddie turned to Antony. "How do you feel?"

"Like," Antony said. He gave two thumbs up for effect.

"Newer status," Malika said. "It is time to find our van."

The orphans and Malika split up and hastily scoured the aisles of the scrapyard. Most of the cars were in varying stages of disrepair, but there were a few serviceable vehicles scattered about. It wasn't long before Charlie found a decently maintained Volkswagen van, which closely resembled the Scooby Doo Mystery Machine, and called to the others to join him.

When Naomi opened the van's sliding side door, she was hit by the stench that had been trapped in there for who knows how long. "Oh my God," she said as she fanned her face. "It smells like it was the tour bus for some hippie jam band."

"Probably was," Eddie said. He held up a tie-dyed shirt and drumstick he'd retrieved from the van. "It's also pretty obvious why they call these places junkyards."

"As long as it starts," Malika said, "it will be sufficient."

JP climbed into the front seat. He searched the steering column for the keys. "I don't know that we're gonna find out," he said. "Unless someone here knows how to hotwire a car?"

"I don't," Eddie said. "But I'm sure one of us has to." He turned to Antony.

"Why the hell did you look at me after you said that?" Antony said. "It better not be 'cause I'm black."

"No, man," Eddie replied, shaken. "It was because you're standing next to me. I was actually trying to look at Charlie."

"Good."

They both looked to Charlie.

"Well?" Eddie said. "You know how to boost cars?"

"Sorry," Charlie said. "I don't know cars, just computers."

Everyone turned to Naomi, the only one yet to respond.

"I don't know cars or computers," Naomi said.

"Can't you do something?" Charlie asked Malika.

"There are only a few things I am able to do on Earth," Malika said. "Unfortunately, starting cars is not one of them."

"I guess we need to find another ride," JP said as he climbed out of the van. "If there even is one. I know I didn't see anything."

"All right! Fine," Antony said as he threw his hands up in defeat. "I might know how to hotwire the car."

"Seriously?" Eddie said. "Why'd you get so mad at me?"

"Because you just assumed I knew how to do it. And I'm not some stereotype. Besides, I've never actually done it myself. I've just seen my cousin do it a bunch of times. It's how he starts his car."

"Are you sure it's actually 'his' car?"

"If you ever meet him, you can ask him. He's about your weight, but all muscle."

"You know what? I'm gonna pass and just assume it's his."

Antony hopped in the driver's seat and got to work removing the steering column and detangling wires. The others swiftly cleared all of the garbage out of the vehicle, keeping their noses plugged the whole time. The cleaners finished first and then waited for Antony.

"One more second," he said as he put the final touches on his hotwiring job. "That's all she wrote. Time for the moment of truth."

The others crossed their fingers and held their breath as Antony tapped the wires together. Sparks flew, and the engine sputtered for a couple seconds before turning over. They all congratulated Antony with high-fives and slaps on the back.

"All right, where to?" Antony said.

"I will drive," Malika said.

"I don't know what the driving age is in Heaven," Eddie said, "but it's sixteen on Earth. And you don't exactly look sixteen. We'll get pulled over in seconds."

"I had no intention of driving like this." Malika brought her hands together at her chest as if she were praying. In a sudden burst of white light, she transformed, gaining twenty years in age and beauty. While her wings stayed hidden, her halo returned, along with a bright golden aura that pulsed around the outside of her body.

JP and Charlie's jaws dropped, but neither fell as far as Eddie's, which practically hit the soiled floor of the old van.

"What's, uh ... how did you ... wow," Eddie babbled.

"I think what he's trying to say is that that's gotta be the true angelic self you mentioned, right?" Antony said.

"It is," Malika said as her aura and halo faded away.

"I take back what I said about not wanting to see you in any form," JP said.

The guys weren't the only ones affected by Malika's beauty; so was Naomi, whose eyes focused on Malika's figure and all of its curves. Naomi instantly became self-conscious, pulling her flannel shirt tight to cover her own body. She elbowed JP and Eddie to rouse them from their stupor. "You guys are like a pack of dogs."

"Woof," Eddie said, still staring at Malika. "I can't wait to go to sleep. I'm gonna have some good dreams tonight."

"That is a fantastic idea," Malika said. "All of you could use some rest. It has been a very hectic day."

"No! No! No! I said tonight, not now."

"Now is always the best time for anything. Resting will help your body and mind."

"But I'm not even close to tired."

"Me either," JP agreed.

"Do not worry," Malika said, "I can take care of that." She brought her hands together at her chest and mumbled a couple words to herself.

Eddie reached out to stop her, "Wait—"

But before he could finish, his arm fell to his side, and he slunk in his seat. The same happened to the rest of the orphans, whose bodies went slack like volunteers in a hypnotist's show.

Malika smiled to herself. It'd been a long time since she'd cast a sleep prayer, one of the few powers that she was able to exercise on Earth. She made sure everyone was buckled into their seats, and then threw the car into gear and hit the gas.

The van's tires spat rocks as the vehicle picked up steam on the gravel road before barreling through the locked front gates and disappearing off into the distance.

◆ ◆ ◆

No more than five minutes later, Terry's Bentley passed through the wrecked junkyard entrance, followed by the blacked-out suv that had been stationed near Charlie's.

The cars parked, and Terry and his men got out. Cain, Max, and the three other Beasts immediately set off combing the lot, while Terry stayed next to the car, his eyes doing all of the work.

Terry noted the twisted metal that was the front gates as well as the tire marks on the road, and put two and two together. "We missed them," he called to his men. He scanned the rest of the junkyard. He spotted the busted cell phones about thirty feet away, walked over, and picked them up. He checked each of the phones. None of them worked.

"Is it possible they're getting help?" Terry asked Cain as he and the other Beasts rejoined him.

"It's possible, but not likely," Cain said.

"There's at least one phone missing. We'll have to keep our trace open in case it draws a signal." Terry chucked the last broken phone. It skidded across the dirt until it hit against the concrete wall of a small office building and shattered to pieces. He took a step toward his car, and then stopped.

Terry turned back to the office building. His gaze traveled up the side until it reached the corner roof. Underneath was a tiny security camera, which was pointed in the direction of the busted gate. "Looks like they're right about God," he quipped. "When he shuts one door, he really does open another. Now, speaking of opening doors." He gestured to the door to the main office.

Cain and Max wasted no time executing Terry's orders. They kicked down the door, splintering it at the hinges, and then entered the building.

Terry strolled in just behind his men. He went straight for the closet in the corner that was marked "Security." Cain lifted his leg, preparing to kick it in, but Terry stopped him. "Let's try the handle first." He jiggled the door handle. "What do you know?" With a twist, he opened the door.

Inside the closet-sized room was an equally small setup: a couple recording devices and a thirteen-inch black-and-white TV resting on a flimsy metal cart.

Terry rewound the security footage until he reached the part where the van rammed through the front gate. He rewound a couple seconds more and paused the video. Through the shotgun window, Malika was clearly visible. "Did anyone see this girl enter the house?" he asked as he pointed to her on the TV screen.

Two of the three new additions shook their heads.

The last Beast spoke up, "There was a girl that had similar features, but she was much younger. At least twenty years."

Terry turned to Cain and shook his head.

"I was wrong," Cain said. "They might be getting help."

"It appears so," Terry said. He pressed play on the recorder and let the video play until the back of the van was in full view. He grabbed a Post-it note from a nearby desk, took down the license plate, and handed the Post-it note to Cain.

"Do you want me to work with our people in the police department and put out an APB?" Cain asked.

"No," Terry said. "I don't think that's best. I would rather this be handled discreetly, through back channels. Sift through all of the government surveillance feeds that we have access to, and find where they are going yourself."

"Of course. We'll get on it right away."

Terry stared at the van on the tiny TV screen. "One more thing first. Destroy any evidence that we were ever here."

Cain nodded. Then, with one sweeping hammer-fist, he turned the TV and recording devices into a smoking heap of electronic rubble.

"Good," Terry said with a smirk. "Now find them."

CHAPTER TWENTY-FOUR

MALIKA SAT IN the driver's seat of the parked van, watching through the windshield as the sun started to rise from behind the pine-covered mountains just ahead. The sun's rays crept across her face. She squinted her eyes and smiled.

After soaking up the sun for a few more seconds, Malika bowed her head and recited a short chant to herself. Tiny sparks of gold began to explode from her skin like air bubbles bursting from a freshly poured glass of champagne as she transformed back to her younger self. Once the process was complete, she snapped her fingers. "We're here," she said to the sleeping orphans in the back of the van.

Charlie and the others slowly came to.

Eddie looked to the driver's seat where the now-young Malika was smiling at them. "I had the weirdest dream last night," he said as he let out a full body yawn. "I dreamt that you were way older and smoking hot."

"That wasn't a dream," Antony said. "That really happened."

Eddie shot up in his seat, suddenly alert. "Seriously? Why did you change back?"

"Probably because of the way that you all acted," Naomi said. "Not to mention the way you're acting now."

"Naomi is correct," Malika said. "You are too easily distracted. In time, you might be able to see me in my true form, but that time is not now."

"That's not true," Eddie said. "I can totally handle it. I think we should vote on it, right?" He looked to the others for support.

"Of course," JP agreed as he nodded a little too excitedly. "That would obviously be the democratic thing to do. Last time I checked, this is America."

"What do you think, Charlie?"

Before Charlie could pick a side, Naomi emphatically cleared her throat to get his attention. Charlie swallowed hard as he took in her steely eyes, which he found to be both intimidating and, at the same time, unbelievably captivating.

Naomi shook her head as if to say, "Don't even think about saying yes."

Eddie took exception to Naomi's attempt to influence Charlie. "Don't look at her," he said. "Look at us. Bros before—"

Naomi turned her glare toward Eddie. "Before what?"

"Beautiful, intelligent women, of course."

"Uh … " Charlie stuttered, still undecided if he should listen to his head or his heart.

"Enough," Malika said. "There will be no vote. Everybody out." She hopped out of the van.

"Nice one," JP said to Charlie as they and the rest of the orphans climbed out of the van's sliding door.

Charlie didn't respond. He was too embarrassed. He just glanced at Naomi, who was taking in their new surroundings.

"So where are we?" Naomi said.

"It looks like *The Little House on the Prairie*," Eddie said. "You know what a prairie is, right?"

Save for the small clearing about the size of a soccer field where they were standing, there was nothing around them that even remotely resembled a prairie. It was a mountainous sea of evergreens that extended in every direction as far as the eye could see.

"Yeah. I was mostly talking about the little house part," Eddie said, pointing to the rickety one-story building with a gable roof and tiny steeple that faced the clearing.

"I'm pretty sure it's a church," Antony said, checking it out.

"It is St. Michael's Church, and we are about fifteen miles north of Lake Tahoe," Malika said. "It was built shortly after the gold rush, but has been abandoned for close to fifty years."

"Please tell me we don't have to go to mass," Eddie joked.

"You do not. The church will serve as your new home."

"Good. 'Cause I already did my time in Catholic school."

Malika started for the church. Charlie and the other orphans followed her inside the neglected house of worship.

The interior of the church had held up only slightly better than the exterior. There were ten rows of pews that looked like they could be knocked over by a stiff breeze. They faced a tiny altar and stained-glass window that was missing half of its panels.

"Are you sure this place wasn't abandoned more than fifty years ago?" Naomi said. She ran her finger across the top of a pew and picked up a Swiffer sheet's worth of dust. "This looks more like a hundred years' worth of dust."

"I am sure of it," Malika said.

"At least it has a bathroom," Charlie said as he opened a door in the back. He immediately began to gag from the dank stench that he'd accidentally unleashed. He slammed the door shut and let out a couple more coughs. "Never mind. That's just a hole. We definitely want to keep that closed."

"Great," JP said. "It looks like we get to go to the bathroom in the woods."

"I've always liked peeing outside," Eddie said.

"That doesn't surprise me."

"I guess we'll get to find out if Henry David Thoreau was right," Antony said.

"Why?" Eddie said. "What did the guy that shot Lincoln say?"

Antony shook his head in disbelief. "He didn't shoot Lincoln. That was John Wilkes Booth."

"Oh, yeah, you're right. He shot Kennedy."

"That was Lee Harvey Oswald," Charlie said.

"Thank you," Antony said.

"Then who did that Henry guy shoot?" Eddie asked.

"He didn't shoot anyone. He was an author, philosopher, and abolitionist. He wrote the book *Walden*."

"Are you positive he didn't shoot a guy named Walden, too? 'Cause only crazy shooters and serial killers get three names."

"Yes, I'm positive. Anyway, my point was that Henry David Thoreau said that most of the luxuries, and many of the so-called comforts of life, are not only not indispensable, but positive hindrances to the elevation of mankind. So we'll get to see if that's true or not."

The other orphans didn't respond. They just looked at Antony curiously.

"What?" Antony said.

"Are you sure you're from South Central?" Naomi said. "'Cause you could've fooled me."

"Me, too," Charlie agreed.

Antony chuckled at their questioning his street cred. "Yeah, I'm from South Central. I just used to read a lot. Like I said before, I'm not some stereotype."

"I don't think any of us are," JP said. "And while that was a fantastic quote and all, I can't imagine that toilets actually prevent the elevation of mankind. And even if they did, I'd rather hold humanity back than crap in the woods."

"I realize this place is not perfect," Malika said, "but it will be perfect for us. No one will think to look for you here, and the holy ground will provide protection from the Beasts."

"Does that mean we're finally safe?" Naomi asked.

"It does."

"So you can tell us what the hell is going on."

Malika nodded. "You all might as well have a seat."

The orphans wiped the dust off of the pews up front before grabbing seats. Charlie went to sit by Naomi, but JP beat him to it. He settled for a seat across the aisle next to Antony and Eddie.

"Are any of you familiar with The Great War?" Malika asked as she took to the altar.

"Are you talking about World War I or II?" Charlie said.

"Neither."

"I doubt you're talking about *World War Z*," Eddie said, "because it was really good, but I wouldn't say it was great."

Naomi rolled her eyes at Eddie. "Can you not turn it off?"

"Not that I know of."

"You're talking about the war in Heaven, right?"

"Yes, I am," Malika said. "The final battle of which is actually depicted on the mural behind me." She pointed to the stained-glass window. Even with much of the glass missing, it was still possible to make out the image of Saint Michael defeating the Devil. "The Great War was the first war, and it forever changed both Heaven and Earth." The heaviness in Malika's voice and the weight of her words silenced the orphans, who remained rapt as she revealed the history of The Great War.

Malika explained that the seeds of the war were planted when Lucifer, one of God's highest-ranking—and also most prideful—angels, first took exception to God's unwavering love for mankind. What started out as petty jealousy grew like a weed in fertile soil to become complete resentment for all human life.

Lucifer detested the fact that the angels were tasked with protecting what he saw as such inferior beings. Eventually, he became so disillusioned with God and the kingdom of Heaven that he set forth to stage a rebellion. He was able to recruit many angels who sided with him.

One Sabbath morning, Lucifer and his army launched their attack. The war pitted friend against friend, brother against brother. The battles waged for years.

In the end, Lucifer and his army were defeated and banished from Heaven. Lucifer was so furious after his defeat that he slaughtered all of those who had willingly followed him.

"I'm confused," Naomi said after Malika finished explaining Lucifer's massacre. "Angels can die?"

"In heaven? No," Malika said. "On Earth? Yes, they can. However, not in the same way that you have been taught to think of death. All things born of God are divine. And that which is divine never truly dies. It merely changes form, or starts anew."

"Can you repeat that in English, please?" Eddie said.

"They are reborn as new souls. And eventually humans, to work their way back to the highest levels."

"Close enough," Eddie said with a shrug. "Continue."

"After killing his army, Lucifer set out to build a new legion of followers. No longer bound by the laws of Heaven, he exploited his angelic powers to gain his soldiers, offering his assistance for their sworn obedience. His first recruit was actually someone that all of you are familiar with, especially you, Charlie."

"Cain," Charlie said softly.

"Yes. While Charlie's house was most likely the first time the rest of you have seen him, you most likely heard about Cain from the Old Testament."

"No way," Naomi said. "The son of Adam? The one who killed his younger brother Abel?"

The other orphans shot Naomi the same confused looks that they'd shot Antony.

Naomi shrugged them off. "Antony isn't the only one who used to read. I did a couple years of Hebrew school back in the day."

Malika continued, "Lucifer found Cain wandering in the desert. He had the mark of God on his face. It would look like an N to all of you, but it is really an aleph. The first letter of the Hebrew alphabet. God gave it to Cain to force him to live with what he'd done, and to let everyone know he was the first—firstborn, and first to kill. But the scar isn't his only mark. Lucifer gave him a branding of his own. The mark of the beast: three sixes over his heart. It was the number of angels who had failed him. It is a mark that he gives to all who join him. To remind them of what happens if they fail."

"Sounds like a pretty crazy guy," Eddie said. "I mean, obviously, he's crazy."

"After his army had grown sufficiently," Malika said, "Lucifer retreated to the underworld. He left his army of Beasts to grow on their own, recruit new members, and do his bidding."

"That still doesn't explain why they came after our parents," Charlie said. Even with everything that he'd learned in the past week, the answer to his next question still evaded him. "What did they have to do with any of that?"

"The answer is twofold," Malika said. "There are angels, like myself, who were part of the genesis of Heaven. But since the original creation of angels, all new angels were elevated through their works, through their lives on Earth, with only the strongest of souls ascending to the rank of guardian."

"So our parents were on their way to becoming angels?" Naomi said, in awe of this revelation.

"That is most likely the reason they were targeted," Malika said. "Not only do the Beasts gain strength from the power of the souls they collect, but in doing so, they prevent the potential creation of an angel. In addition, the lost memories that vanish with every stolen soul also weaken the collective spirit of mankind. This compounding effect decreases the likelihood of any future angels even more, which serves to expedite their ultimate objective."

"And their ultimate objective is?" Eddie asked.

While Eddie needed hand-holding, Charlie had already filled in the pieces to the puzzle. "To launch another attack on Heaven," he said.

Malika nodded.

The orphans shook their heads in disbelief.

"Awesome," JP said. "A second Great War. Do you at least have any idea when it's coming?"

"Unfortunately, we do not," Malika said. "All that is known is that the collective spirit has never been so weak, and Heaven has never been so vulnerable."

"So in theory, it could come any minute," Antony said.

"Yes, it could," Malika said. "The likelihood only increases with each second that passes."

"Well, that's really reassuring," Eddie said sarcastically, and then buried his head in his hands.

"I would encourage all of you to focus on that which is reassuring instead of that which is not."

"What, exactly, should we be reassured by?" Charlie said.

"By the fact that there is something you can do about it," Malika said. "When you succeed in destroying the Beasts and freeing your parents' souls, you will not only save all of the other souls that are trapped inside and create new angels, you will also weaken Lucifer's army and delay their attack. The more Beasts you destroy, the longer the delay."

"What if we don't delay their attack in time?" Charlie said. "What if they strike before we can save our parents? Then what happens to them?"

"You will still have the ability to save them. However, the task will become exponentially more challenging."

"Hold on a second," Naomi said. "You keep saying 'you.' What about 'we'? When are the rest of our guardian angels, and all the other angels, for that matter, coming to help us?"

"Yeah," Eddie said, ditching his doldrums and getting pumped up. "They need to swoop down here and kick some serious Devil ass!"

The other orphans excitedly agreed with Eddie. All of their spirits were lifted by the thought of assistance from the army of angels. It made everything that Malika had told them much more palatable.

"When are they planning on joining us?" Charlie asked.

"There are no such plans," Malika said, matter-of-factly.

All of the wind was instantly knocked out of Charlie and the other orphans' lungs. They didn't consider Malika's disclosure to be the minor detail that she treated it as. No, this wasn't the kind of information that was just slipped in the back section of the daily paper. This was front-page news—and terrible news, at that.

"It is much too risky," Malika added. "Because of the work of Lucifer and his army, there has not been an angel created in over one hundred years. Any meaningful loss suffered would only tip the scales in the balance of good and evil even further, and ensure that Lucifer would be victorious when he eventually attacks. It was for this reason that Michael the Archangel barred any angels from coming to Earth."

Antony was the first to get his breath and voice back. "I don't get it," he said. "If angels are barred from coming to Earth, how did you get here?"

"I broke the rules to save all of you. I will face severe punishment upon my return, and possible expulsion. It was a choice that I made, but I do not expect any of my brethren to do the same."

"So what are you saying?" Charlie said, choking on his words as he struggled to get the clarification that they all needed. "That all the other angels are just gonna sit this one out. That, besides you, we're on our own."

Malika didn't say a word; she simply nodded.

CHAPTER
TWENTY-FIVE

THE ORPHANS WERE SPEECHLESS. None of them could believe that they were expected to take on Lucifer's army alone. That more than just the fate of their parents was depending on them. That potentially, the weight of the world and the heavens above rested firmly on their shoulders. It was unfathomable. It was unrealistic. It was—

"Bullshit!" JP snapped. "This is bullshit!"

"Yeah," Eddie said.

Charlie was about to agree when JP chimed in again.

"I didn't sign up for this," JP griped.

"Me, either," Naomi added.

Charlie zipped his lips. He knew that if he spoke, the attention would shift to him, and most likely so would the anger. After all, he was the one who had gotten them into this situation. It was his post that had brought the orphans together. He was the one who deserved their vitriol and blame, not Malika.

Charlie couldn't blame the others for being upset, either. None of them had officially agreed to his proposal before they were forced from his house. And even Charlie wasn't sure if he would've agreed to the mission if he'd known then everything that he knew at that moment. A large part of him regretted ever making the post and reaching out to the others. He wished he could just take it all back.

"You realize we don't stand a chance, right?" JP said.

"You are correct," Malika said. "If you believe you do not stand a chance, you most certainly will not stand a chance."

"Great pep talk," Eddie said, clapping his hands. "You're a regular Vince Lombardi."

"I am not giving you a pep talk. I am merely giving you the truth."

"Well, for future reference, in situations like this, most people prefer pep talks."

"What makes you think we can even do this?" Naomi asked.

"I have seen it done," Malika said.

"So there were other kids like us?"

"Not kids, and many years ago, but yes."

"So they were older than us and they still lost, right?" JP said. "Obviously, they had to—otherwise we wouldn't be here right now, and our parents would still be alive."

"Their past holds no bearing on your present or your future," Malika said. "I will teach you everything you need to know to rescue your parents' souls. I will teach you to believe."

"This is crazy," JP said. "We should just quit while we're ahead. Or at least before we get even further behind."

"No," Antony said, finally jumping into the conversation with authority. "We should let Malika finish explaining. I don't like this any more than you guys, but she was right about what she said before, there is no going back. So we might as well go forward and at least hear what she has to say."

JP, Eddie, and Naomi quieted.

Charlie sighed inwardly, relieved that the tension seemed to be subsiding and that the finger-pointing hadn't made it in his direction.

Antony nodded for Malika to continue.

"Thank you," Malika said. "Each and every one of you has the potential to unleash unlimited powers that will allow you not only to battle Lucifer's Beasts, but to be victorious."

"Let me guess," Eddie said flippantly, "everything we need is inside us, right?"

"Actually, it is. There is no better way to doom someone to failure than to convince them that they do not have control over their success. The world you live in has done this many times over. However, the reality is that you are the most important factor in determining your success. When you come to accept this much as fact and truly believe in yourself, it creates the opportunity for unlimited potential, and you can do wonders." Malika surveyed the orphans' faces, all of which showed varying degrees of uncertainty and skepticism. "Right now, the path as you see it may appear to be unnavigable. But I implore you to focus on the first step that you must take and not the last. For the road ahead is anything but static and will most certainly change course many times along the way."

"What's the first step?" Naomi said.

"Accepting the challenge. You must willingly choose to follow your path."

"We can't go home," Eddie said. "And the other angels are in Heaven picking their butts. So it looks like we don't have much of a choice, do we?"

"Yes, you do," Malika said. "You always have a choice."

"Well, not a good one."

"That is a matter of perception, which in itself is also a choice. There is only one way for all of you to succeed at this, or at anything that you truly desire to accomplish in your lifetimes: You must be 100 percent committed, and you must be willing to put in the necessary work."

"I've already made up my mind," Antony said. "I'm gonna save my dad. I'll put in the work. I'm 100 percent."

One by one, the others mustered up the resolve to commit to the challenge before them. First Naomi, then Charlie, and then JP. Eddie was last.

"I'm 100 percent with all you guys," he said. "I just—" He was interrupted by a low rumbling. He looked down to his belly, the source of the noise, and gave it a couple pats. "I just think my stomach has some thoughts of his own. There isn't any chance we could grab some food before we get started?"

All of the others agreed. It'd been a long time since any of them had eaten even so much as a snack.

"There's gotta be a town with a little shop or something somewhere down the road that we can go to," JP said.

Malika grinned. "There is something that is much better and much closer."

"It can't be a McDonald's," Eddie said. "My nose can usually pick up any fries within a five-mile radius."

Malika led the group out of the church. "There," she said as she gestured to vast wilderness before them.

Charlie scratched his head and then looked to the others, who were equally perplexed. "Uh, you realize you're just pointing at the woods, right?"

"Yes, I do."

"And how's that better?"

"Anything you can take from the land is infinitely better than that which you can buy from a store," Malika said.

"Seriously?" Naomi said.

"Yeah," JP said. "We really gotta pick our food?"

"Pick, hunt, forage, whatever you must do," Malika said. "Few things boost your belief of self more than the knowledge that you can provide with your own two hands."

"I definitely agree with you," Eddie said. "But I think the reason everyone else might be struggling to digest your sage-like advice is because you look like a third-grader. I just think that maybe if you were, I don't know, thirties-ish and super sexy, it'd probably help them see the bigger picture."

Naomi rolled her eyes. "Come on," she said as she yanked Eddie by his shirt collar and started for the woods.

"Just think about it," Eddie shouted back to Malika as he was dragged away.

◆ ◆ ◆

Twigs snapped and dried-out pine needles crackled with every step as the orphans trekked through the mountainous terrain. They didn't hear the sounds they made or even the birds chirping in the trees. All of their attention was concentrated on the grumbling in their own stomachs and their shared annoyance of having to search for their own food.

"I can't believe there could be an attack any second and we're roaming the freaking forest," JP complained.

"Does anyone even know what the heck we're looking for?" Naomi said.

"I'm looking for a Doritos tree," Eddie said, dead serious. "Preferably Cool Ranch, but I'll settle for Nacho Cheesier."

Charlie couldn't tell if he was actually kidding or not. "You know chips don't grow on trees, right?" he said.

"Of course," Eddie said. "I'm just trying to be optimistic. Didn't Malika say something about believing in stuff? Well, I choose to believe that Doritos and bear claw pastries naturally occur in the wild."

"Good luck with that," Naomi said.

"I was actually a Cub Scout back in the day," Antony said. "We never left the city, but we learned a little about surviving in the wild, how to find edible wild plants and whatnot."

"Perfect," JP said. "How about you Webelos go look for berries and nuts, and Naomi and I will go find some meat."

"Webelos, like we blow," Eddie said. "Good one."

JP smirked.

"You guys don't think we should stick together?" Charlie said. "What if we get lost?"

"The church is just at the top of that hill," JP said. "If you can get lost, we've got bigger problems than finding food. Besides, we'll be more efficient if we split up."

"He's right," Antony said.

179

"Okay," Charlie reluctantly agreed. He watched Naomi and JP as they started down the slope, focusing on Naomi as they continued on their descent.

Antony scanned the forest. "We need to find a spot that gets good light and is close to a water source. That's gonna be our best bet." He turned his gaze to the sky, traced the sun's path, and then headed in the opposite direction of JP and Naomi.

Eddie followed Antony.

After a moment, Charlie tagged along, too.

"Now that it's just us guys," Eddie said, "can we talk about how hot Malika is?"

Antony shot Eddie a disturbed sidelong glance.

"I meant the older her," Eddie quickly corrected himself. "Not the younger her, obviously. You're messed up for even going there." He nodded to Charlie. "What do you think?"

"I agree," Charlie said. "She's really pretty."

"Really pretty?" Eddie said, taken aback. It wasn't a quarter of the enthusiasm he'd been expecting. "On a ten-point scale, she's a twenty. Status update: You guys are certifiably crazy."

"Dislike," Antony said.

"You can't dislike stuff. That wasn't the deal. And it's not even an option online." Eddie turned back to Charlie. "And your vote doesn't count, anyway. You're obviously biased."

"What are you talking about?" Charlie said.

"Don't act like you don't have a thing for Naomi."

Charlie throat cinched, and his heart fluttered from the accusation. It was the first time he'd ever been called out for liking anyone. Did he have feelings for Naomi? Of course he did. But his instincts quickly took over and told him to deny it. "What? No, I don't."

"Sure you don't. And the Pope's a Protestant." Eddie shook his head. "It's cool. She's pretty, in that angry, tough girl that probably likes to punch guys kind of way."

"I, uh, don't know what you're talking about," Charlie stammered.

"That she likes to punch guys, or that you like her?"

"Both."

"Dude, I just saw you watch her leave," Eddie said. "Not to mention the way you totally froze up earlier in the van. Plus, you're way too defensive right now. It's a dead giveaway."

Charlie said nothing. He didn't have a comeback.

"I'll take your silence as an admission of guilt," Eddie said. "All right, Antony, you get to break the tie. What do you think? Malika, and by that I mean older Malika, or Naomi?"

"I think we need to focus our attention on finding food," Antony said.

"I can multitask," Eddie joked. He waited for a response that never came. "Fine. I'll count that as a non-vote. And I'm not gonna bother asking JP 'cause it seems like he has a thing for Naomi, too. Which I guess breaks the tie. Naomi wins." Eddie considered the results and shrugged. "But hey, that actually works better for me, less competition. I doubt I could compete with JP, anyway." He patted Charlie on the shoulder. "But good luck with that, buddy."

"Thanks," Charlie said.

Eddie grinned. "Look at that, he admits it!" He playfully shook Charlie by his shoulders.

Charlie smiled. He'd never admitted to liking anyone, either directly or indirectly. His thoughts drifted to Naomi. A rush of warmth started in his chest and expanded outward. But his sense of elation was quickly dashed, replaced by an aching tightness in his stomach, as he considered the questions that arose from this admission. Did Naomi know? What did she think? Was he really competing with JP? If so, did he even stand a chance?

"Enough messing around," Antony said, getting the others back on track. "Let's focus on finding food."

The three continued deep into the woods, traversing over a mile before they found what they were searching for: a large clearing in the trees. In the clearing, were vines upon vines of wild grapes and bushes filled with all sorts of ripe berries. They plucked what they could as fast as they could, with much of their early pickings conveniently finding their way into their open mouths. Once they'd harvested all that their arms could carry, they began their hike back to the church.

◆ ◆ ◆

Charlie and the guys were the first to return. Antony had the idea of removing the van's bench seats so they would have somewhere to lounge. They situated the seats around a small fire pit that they built.

JP and Naomi arrived not long after the guys had finished setting up. With them, they carried fifteen squirrels. JP had used rocks and his cannon of an arm to hunt the little critters.

They all pitched in to prep the squirrels, which they roasted over the open fire with skewers. When they were fully cooked, no one wanted to take the first bite.

JP jokingly volunteered Malika, who informed the group that angels didn't require human food for sustenance.

"Screw it," Eddie said. "I'm too hungry, and I can't eat any more fruit." He bit the bullet and took the first taste.

The others waited for his reaction.

Eddie finished chewing the meat and considered it for a second. "Status update," he said. "Does everything taste like chicken, or does chicken just taste like everything?" He turned to Antony.

"Does it really taste like chicken, or are you just saying that?" Antony said.

"It did to me. Not KFC, but regular grilled chicken."

"Then like." Antony flashed two thumbs up, and then grabbed a skewer and took a bite. "You're right. It's not bad," he agreed as he finished chewing.

After the others got past their psychological hang-ups, they, too, found the meat to be more than tolerable. Chewy, but tolerable. All in all, it made for a more than satisfactory meal, and they made quick work of the skewers.

"How do you feel?" Malika asked the orphans as they wrapped up their squirrel brunch.

"Full," Charlie said, finishing his last morsel of meat.

All of the other orphans agreed.

"You might not notice any difference just yet," Malika said, "but in time, you will all feel a stronger sense of self-reliance. And that is not the only benefit you will receive. Much of the food you purchase in stores is highly processed and inflammatory. It prevents your body from absorbing any of the nutrients you ingest, which negatively impacts your physical energy and mental clarity. Cleaning your diet will help clean your body and mind, and allow both to operate more efficiently."

"I don't know what you're talking about," Eddie said. "My body is already a well-oiled machine." He flexed his arms like a bodybuilder and then gave each of his biceps a kiss.

Naomi pointed to the sweat accumulating on Eddie's forehead. "I'd go with a greasy machine over well-oiled."

"Same difference."

"We shall see soon enough," Malika said. "Each of you is about to change in ways that you could never imagine. And it starts right now, with your first lesson."

CHAPTER
TWENTY-SIX

MALIKA RETRIEVED ONE of the discarded skewers that was lying on the ground and stuck the tip into the fire. Once it caught, she removed the skewer and blew on the lit end. The tiny ember pulsed and expanded spherically, the hue shifting from a reddish-orange to a bright yellow. She continued to blow on the bright bulb. With each subsequent breath, the flame grew in magnitude, while the glow progressed up the thermal spectrum. After the last exhalation, the incandescent orb had reached the size of a softball and was as blue as the blaze from a butane torch. Malika swirled her newly formed fire wand with a quick flick of the wrist.

The orphans watched in awe as a matching flame sparked up from the ground like burners on an old gas stove. The flames were no more than a couple inches high and encircled their little camp. The ring of fire seemed to come at the expense of their campfire, which went completely dark.

Malika whipped both of her arms high above her head as if she were conducting an orchestra. The previously restrained circle of flames shot upwards, arching above the orphans and creating a radiant cobalt dome.

"We're gonna get cooked alive!" JP shouted as he dove from his seat.

The other orphans, reacting equally to the enclosing inferno and to JP's screams, tucked their heads in between their legs and covered the backs of their heads with their hands.

"Do not worry," Malika said. "The flames are harmless."

The orphans tentatively lifted their heads from their laps.

Still skeptical, Charlie slowly raised his hand toward the flickering wall of flame that enclosed them. Any lingering fears of a fiery death that he still held faded the closer his hand got. "They're not hot at all," he said, surprised. If anything, it was the most neutral temperature he'd ever experienced. "I don't even feel anything."

"That is the point," Malika said. "Because of the many years of conditioning that each of you has been subjected to, you are all too easily distracted. The chamber I have created eliminates any potential interference from the outside world. Within this sacred space, there is no sound, no sight, no smell, no touch, and no taste."

"Apparently, there are no warnings, either," JP grumbled as he picked himself up off of the ground. "You could've told us it was coming first."

"Your displeasure is duly noted," Malika said.

JP dusted off his clothes and then retook his seat.

"Eventually," Malika said, "you will be able to block out any distractions on your own when it is called for. But for now, this will help you focus for your first lesson, which is the foundation of your development. Much as you cannot walk before you crawl, if you are to truly believe in yourself, you must first learn to love yourself."

"I already got that one down," Eddie said. "If anything, I might love myself too much. If you know what I mean." He made a gesture like he was shaking dice; however, he was referring to shaking something much more inappropriate.

"Pretty sure she didn't mean that," Naomi said. "But thanks for the visual, you perv."

Malika continued, undeterred by Eddie's joking. "But in order to cultivate an unconditional love of yourself, you must first get to know your divine self."

"What's our divine self?" Charlie asked.

"It is all of your intrinsic desires, unencumbered by any learned judgments," Malika said. "It is your truest self, your spirit. The stronger the connection between mind and spirit, the stronger you are. In complete harmony, the Beasts will be unable to overpower you. But all it takes is the slightest crack in your armor, your belief of self, and you will be susceptible."

"So, how do we achieve this harmony?" Antony said.

"Awareness. You must bring awareness to all of the doubt that is stored deep inside of you. This acknowledgement, combined with the understanding that you have created these thoughts, empowers you to release them by consciously letting them go," Malika said. "In the absence of negativity, positivity will prosper."

JP was skeptical. "That's it?" he said.

Malika nodded. "Yes, but to even become aware of the self-doubt that you harbor, first you must have a conversation with yourself and afford your divine self the opportunity to speak. You must ask yourself to reveal the biggest block, or impediment, to loving all that you are."

"So I just ask myself what my biggest block is," Eddie said, "and my divine self will be like, 'Hey, Eddie, this is what's wrong with you, you big weirdo.' Sounds easy enough."

"Do not underestimate the difficulty of this task," Malika said. "Identifying the problem is often the most difficult part of finding a solution. Rarely will your mind be so honest. It has been conditioned to conceal its true thoughts and conform to society's constructs. Most likely, you will need to ask yourself more than once. You may have to ask yourself one thousand times, and receive one thousand different answers, before you attain the correct one. But until you uncover your biggest block and let it go, you will not be able to truly let the rest of your pent-up negativity go and free your divine self from society's shackles."

The orphans didn't respond.

Malika could tell by the looks on their faces that they'd already begun trying to have the conversations with themselves. "I will give you as much time as you need," she said. "I encourage you to close your eyes to help eliminate any potential visual distractions from within the chamber."

The orphans obliged, closing their eyes.

Malika continued, "And keep in mind that your block can manifest itself in a multitude of ways. It may appear as anger, fear, or just about any other negative emotion. All you need to do is relax, center your thoughts, and let your divine self speak."

The orphans sat in silence.

Ten minutes passed. Then twenty.

After thirty minutes, Antony opened his eyes. Malika greeted him with a smile. He gave his own half-smile back.

One by one, the other orphans followed, all of them greeted with the same smile from Malika. Charlie was the last to open his eyes. Once he did, Malika retook the floor.

"While awareness begins the process of letting go of your mental block," she said, "sharing that block and really admitting it to others is integral to accelerating its expulsion. With that in mind, who would like to share first? Antony, you were the first to open your eyes."

"I still need to think about it more," Antony said.

"That is fine," Malika said. "Anyone else?"

A couple seconds passed without a volunteer. Then, finally, Naomi stepped up. "I guess I can," she said. "But mine is stupid."

"All negative thoughts are, especially if you give them power over you."

"Yeah, I don't disagree," Naomi said. "I'd have to say my biggest block has always been my body."

"That's crazy," Charlie blurted out. Naomi narrowed her eyes at him. "I meant that in a good way," he said, trying to recover. "You have a great—"

"That is enough, Charlie," Malika said, holding her hand up to stop him. "Your validation is unnecessary." She faced

Naomi. "One's physical appearance is an incredibly common source of negativity and doubt. And while that is especially true for women your age, it is also true that everyone here suffers from it to varying degrees."

"She's right," Eddie agreed. "I was actually just kidding about all that well-oiled machine stuff. That's not how I feel at all."

"I was just kidding about the greasy stuff," Naomi apologized.

"I know." Eddie said with a half-smile.

Malika continued, "Here is a little piece of history: Since the creation of mankind, the so-called measures of beauty have changed many times over. In fact, at one point or another, all qualities have been considered ideal. Do not think that Lucifer did not play a role in that. His footprints can be found every step of the way. Most of his work is conducted off of the battlefield and is concentrated on weakening the human spirit. His objective was to make sure that everyone could conceivably question their own beauty. But true beauty is not a moving target. It is something that exists abundantly inside everyone and appears in every smile."

Encouraged by Malika's words, Naomi couldn't help but let loose a toothy grin.

"That is exactly what I speak of," Malika said. "Instead of emphasizing your appearance, you must remember that your physical body is merely a vessel. The only concern you should have for it is that you maintain it through good health. Now tell me something you love about yourself, unrelated to your physical appearance."

"Uh, okay," Naomi said and then considered her options for a few seconds. "I guess I love how sharp my memory is. It's almost photographic." Her smile crept back across her face. "I'm also great writer," she exclaimed. "I really love that. And I can always tell a song on the radio right after it starts to play."

"Perfect," Malika said.

"There are more things I like, too," Naomi said excitedly. "They're all just popping into my head."

Naomi's enthusiasm was infectious. Charlie soaked up her energy and the glow created by her grin, which made her even more alluring.

"Of course they are," Malika said. "By choosing to focus on those things you love about yourself, you begin to view yourself in a whole new light. Eventually, you will only find things to love. But first, you must completely release your block. Tell yourself that you are free to let go of the belief that your body should be any other way than how it is right now. Repeat it as many times as you need to hear it."

The others waited while Naomi closed her eyes and did as she'd been told. A minute later, she slowly reopened her eyes. "Thank you," she said to Malika with a newfound calmness in her voice.

"Thank yourself," Malika said. "And if your negative thoughts ever resurface, simply release them again and replace them with two positive thoughts." She spoke to the group, "That technique is something that all of you can benefit from. Who's next? JP?"

"Why not?" JP said. "But I feel like I need to say that mine is stupid, too."

"Say what you must," Malika said.

"It's stupid because he doesn't have problems," Eddie said.

"I wish that was true," JP said. "I've got my fair share. But I'd have to say my biggest block is"—he hung his head, peered at his feet, took a deep breath, and sighed it out before picking his head back up—"well, I've just been hurt so many times in my life. I guess that I've kind of convinced myself that maybe they're hurting me because of me. That maybe I somehow deserve it. That maybe I'm the one that's flawed. That maybe I'm not meant to be loved."

JP's words clearly struck a chord with Naomi.

Charlie watched as she put her hand on his leg.

"No one deserves to be hurt," Malika said. "No one deserves pain. But you are allowing yourself to be hurt by determining your own value based on the opinions and actions of other people."

"It's hard not to," JP said.

"That does not alter the fact that the opinions of others should never dictate your own sense of self. The only sustainable belief comes from within. No one should ever believe in you more than you believe in yourself. Conversely, you should never believe in anyone else more than you believe in yourself. Know that you have value and love yourself unconditionally, and you will attract more love than you could ever imagine, and it will be directed toward the true you."

JP smiled. He put his hand on top of Naomi's, which was still on his thigh, and gave it a gentle squeeze.

Charlie immediately felt jealous. An overwhelming desire to have the attention—particularly Naomi's attention—

on him swelled deep inside. "I'll go next," he exclaimed, with more enthusiasm than he intended. His excitement quickly faded as all eyes turned to him.

"Let JP finish first," Malika said.

"I'm actually done." JP said.

"Not yet," Malika said and then reminded JP that he still had to release his feelings that he didn't deserve to be loved. After he had, Malika turned to Charlie. "Now you may go."

"Okay. Well, um, I don't actually know where to start." Charlie paused for a moment. "I've never liked my body. I've always wished I was taller and stronger and a lot of other things. And sometimes I wonder if I'll ever really find love." He glanced at Naomi to see if she was still looking at him. She wasn't. He continued, "I guess I—"

"Need to focus harder," Malika said, cutting Charlie off before he rambled any further. "You are overlooking the one block that is bigger than the others. Close your eyes and ask yourself once more what your strongest negative emotion is."

Charlie nodded, and then closed his eyes. After a couple seconds, he slowly reopened them. "It's fear," he said with a seriousness that had been lacking before. "Fear of failure."

"To unlearn such a fear, you must first establish the meaning of success. What do you consider to be success?"

"Saving my parents," Charlie said without hesitation.

"Of course. But this fear has been with you for longer than your parents have not. How else do you define success?"

Charlie shrugged. "I don't know. The same way everyone does ... Money."

"Do you all share this feeling?" Malika asked the rest of the orphans. They all nodded in agreement. She turned back to Charlie. "What if you amassed a sizable fortune, and then one day, the markets crashed and you lost most of your money? Would you still consider yourself successful?"

Charlie wasn't quite sure how to answer the question.

"Of course," JP said, jumping in. "Because even if he lost his money, he'd still have some assets, like a sick mansion and maybe a yacht. And at the end of the day, he'd still have relatively more than everyone else."

"I see," Malika said. "So money is not just a means to transact, it is a means for comparison, and success is a comparison as well. You versus everyone else, right?"

"Yeah."

"Do you agree, Charlie?"

"Sure," Charlie said.

"Then imagine that the whole world is turned back to zero. Everything you have earned is gone, by no mistake of your own, and you now have the same monetary worth as everyone else. Would you still consider yourself successful?"

"Uh, I don't know."

"Anyone else care to answer?"

The other orphans contemplated Malika's question for a moment before Naomi broke the silence. "I guess it depends," she said. "Is he happy?"

Malika nodded, pleased. "That is the correct question to ask. Without that answer, it is impossible to determine whether he is successful or not. For happiness is the only legitimate gauge of success. The beauty of true happiness is that it does not require comparison, nor does it come at the expense of others. Either you are happy or you are not. If you can find happiness in every moment of your life, you are successful. So I ask you, Charlie Kim: Are you successful? Do you live happiness?"

Charlie didn't need long to think about it. He was happy at times, like when he achieved one of the goals in his plan, but he couldn't say that he was happy in every moment, or even most moments, of his life. "No," he said.

"Why not?"

"I don't know. Because a lot of the stuff I do doesn't make me happy. I guess I've always figured that I'll have time to be happy later on, after I have everything I want."

"Stop wanting. Stop delaying joy. Start finding happiness, from this moment forward. Everything that gets in the way of that, let it go." Malika paused for a second to let her words sink in and then spoke to the group. "All of you must let go of your notions of success or failure. Think only of happiness, and find it in every moment."

The others nodded in agreement, taking more from Malika's message than Charlie had.

"Let it go, Charlie," Malika instructed him.

"Okay," Charlie said, but it was apparent that he wasn't completely sold. In spite of his hang-up, he closed his eyes, and did as he'd been told.

A minute later, Charlie reopened his eyes, but he was even less satisfied than before he'd closed them. While Malika's advice seemed so helpful to Naomi and JP, it hadn't brought him the sense of relief he'd hoped for or expected.

Malika noted Charlie's discontented look. "That might not be enough for you now," she said, "but in time, you will fully grasp the power of those words and their meaning. All right, who is next?

Eddie turned to Antony; it was between the two of them.

"It's all you," Antony said.

"Fine. I'll go," Eddie said. "I guess what keeps me from loving myself is that … I don't know." He chuckled to himself. "It's kinda funny, I just said I don't know."

"Why is that?"

"Well, I guess I feel dumb sometimes, or a lot of the time. Actually, all of the time."

"And what makes you feel that way?"

"School. Other people. Pretty much anything that could. I feel like it's harder for me to remember things, or learn stuff, or even pay attention."

"And have you ever committed yourself to learning?"

"A little bit, yeah. I've tried to."

"You have tried, but you chose to quit instead of truly committing. You have resorted to jokes and pretended that you do not care, but in reality, you care very much."

"Well … yeah. You pretty much nailed it." Eddie chewed the corner of his lip and nodded.

"Your intelligence has never been your limitation," Malika said. "It is your feelings of doubt that hold you back. No one's intelligence is fixed. In fact, the human brain grows most when you fail and continue to persevere. But you must embrace the challenges instead of shying away from them. You must push through instead of succumbing."

Eddie nodded with resolve.

Malika continued, "Know that anything you truly want to learn, you can. It might not come as fast as it does to others, but do not worry about that. It will come if you truly desire it and are committed to doing the necessary work."

Eddie closed his eyes and let go of his long-held feelings of inadequacy.

"And one more thing," Malika added after Eddie opened his eyes. "Humor can be a great medicine, but it is a terrible mask."

"I'll file that one away," Eddie said with a smirk as he tapped his temple.

All eyes turned to Antony, the last to go. He averted their gaze, took a deep breath, exhaled, and prepared to tell them his biggest obstacle to loving himself. It was something that he'd never told another person, something that he always knew in the back of his head, something that he'd never even fully admitted to himself.

CHAPTER
TWENTY-SEVEN

THE OTHER ORPHANS took some time to digest what Antony had told them. None of them had expected him to reveal what he had.

After a moment, Eddie broke the silence. "I should've known," he said. "That's obviously why you're so jacked."

"What are you talking about?" Charlie said.

"I can't be the only person that knows that all gay people are ripped."

"All gay people aren't anything," Naomi said.

"They're all gay, aren't they?" Eddie said.

"Well, besides that."

"Will everyone just be quiet?" Antony said. The heaviness in his voice made it clear that he was still very much struggling to accept his own admission. "I don't know for sure if I actually am gay or not."

"Is this true?" Malika said.

Antony shook his head and sighed in frustration. "No. I mean, I know I am. I've known since as long I can remember. I just don't want to be. I never have."

"Why is that?"

"I don't know," Antony said. "I guess it's 'cause, like, everybody always wants to put people into different buckets, you know? The last thing I want is another bucket to be thrown in. I just want to be my own person."

"The two are not mutually exclusive," Malika said. "You are and always will be your own person. While your sexuality is a part of that person, it plays no more of a role in defining you than the color of your skin, your gender, or any other inherited trait that the human world attempts to divide you with. That is to say, it plays no role unless you make the choice to let it define you. Others will surely make that mistake, but it means nothing unless you choose to do the same."

"I guess you're right," Antony said, slowly coming around.

"Yes, I am." Malika turned to the rest of the group. "This holds true for all of you: nothing about who you are, at your core, should ever be a source of shame. Each of you was made in God's image. Therefore, any rejection of yourself is a rejection of God."

"I definitely wasn't trying to do that."

"Then don't. Accept and love yourself for who you are."

"I will," Antony said with a smile. He closed his eyes, let go of his denial, and took the first giant step toward loving his divine self.

"You have all moved in the direction of believing in yourselves, but that was only just the beginning," Malika said.

She flicked her wand and swept her hands downward. The flaming dome vanished instantly, while the blaze that had disappeared from the campfire returned in a flash of light and smoke. "Like an iceberg, most of it still lies beneath. Now that you have identified the tip, you must uncover the rest. You must go out into the woods on your own, and search deep inside yourself to find every last negative emotion and judgment that is holding you back, and one by one, let them go. Until they are all gone."

All of the orphans began their march into different corners of the woods. All except for Charlie, who held back from the rest of the group.

"What's next?" Charlie asked Malika as soon as everyone else was out of earshot. "Like, after this, what do we do for step three?"

"Do not concern yourself with what is next," Malika said. She rested her hand on his shoulder. "Focus on what is. When what is next becomes what is, then you can focus on it."

It wasn't the answer Charlie had wanted, but he knew that it was all that he was going to get. Instead of pushing her further, he simply nodded, then chose the direction that none of the other orphans were heading in and began his journey into the forest.

◆ ◆ ◆

Charlie wandered deep into the woods for well over a half hour before he found an old incense cedar that had fallen and split to make the perfect seat and backrest. He parked himself on the cinnamon-colored tree trunk and leaned back to get comfortable.

Charlie didn't take even a second to consider the picturesque view of the expansive valley just beyond the trees or the sparkling river that cut through it. He didn't have the time to waste. He needed to get right to work. He retrieved his notebook from his pocket and skimmed his list of failures. None of his listed failures had a particular monetary value attached to them, and they all had made him unhappy, so he figured that they were still suitable to be used for their motivational purposes.

After reading over his list a couple times, Charlie flipped to the front of his notebook and added his new goal: find happiness.

"Find happiness," he said to himself. He echoed the words a handful of times, hoping it'd help them settle into his consciousness, build his confidence in their power, and magically alter his perspective; however, it didn't. It only had the opposite effect. The more he repeated the words, the more unreasonable they sounded, and the more his thoughts drifted away from his intention of finding happiness toward something else.

Charlie didn't doubt that Malika knew what she was talking about and agreed that her words sounded great in theory. But even so, he couldn't fathom how he could possibly be happy. Focusing on what was, and not what was next, like Malika had encouraged him to do, didn't help, either. It only made him think of everything he was up against. At that very moment, his parents' souls were trapped in some Beast, Terry and his men were most likely scouring everywhere for them, and an attack on Heaven was possible at any second.

That was what was. How was he supposed to find happiness in that? It was completely unrealistic.

As if all of his issues weren't enough to keep him from finding happiness, Charlie recalled how he hadn't received half of the attention he'd hoped to get from Naomi. All that he'd received was the knowledge that if there was going to be any competition for Naomi's affection, JP appeared to have a significant head start.

Charlie shook his head and pocketed his notebook. He scraped chunks of bark from the tree trunk with the heels of his shoes as his frustrations compounded. "Find happiness," he repeated with each thrust.

◆ ◆ ◆

Hours later, all of the orphans returned to the church with high spirits and empty bellies—save for Charlie, who only had the empty belly and had to fake his enthusiasm.

With food on everyone's minds, Eddie offered to go hunting with Charlie. Of course, he had ulterior motives. He'd informed Charlie of his scheme just before attempting to execute it. His plan was to invite Naomi and Malika to join them. Then, once they were in the woods, he'd suggest that they split up like they had that morning, only with their preferred pairings. Partial to plans, and this plan in particular, Charlie eagerly agreed.

Unfortunately for the two would-be Casanovas, both Malika and Naomi declined the invitations.

"You miss almost all of the shots you don't take," Eddie joked to Charlie as they, along with Antony, who volunteered in the girls' place, ventured back into the forest.

◆ ◆ ◆

After an uneventful dinner, Malika encouraged all of the orphans to get as much sleep as possible. Worn out from their day, they all eagerly retreated inside the church.

"Wow," Naomi said as she entered the surprisingly pristine chapel. "It looks way nicer."

"I did a little cleaning when you were gone," Malika said.

Really, Malika had just opened the front and back doors to the church. With a couple heavy flaps of her wings, she'd sent all of the dust twirling out of the church in a massive gust of wind. She'd also found a trunk filled with a bunch of old cloth alter covers in one of the closets.

Antony commented that the smell reminded him of his grandmother's closet, and not in a good way. But it was all they had to work with. They made their own beds on the pews, using the alter covers as sheets.

"What are you doing?" JP asked Eddie, who had finished with the bed and was in the process of wiggling out of his T-shirt.

"Uh, getting ready for bed," Eddie replied, his shirt stuck around his shoulders.

"Don't you think you should keep your clothes on? You know, given the company."

"It's cool. I talked to Antony. He said I'm not his type."

"I heard that," Antony said from across the room, where he was putting the finishing touches on his bed. "And what I said was I don't really have a type yet."

"Close enough," Eddie said.

"I was talking about Naomi, anyway," JP said.

"Thank you," Naomi said to JP. "He's right, Eddie. You can keep your clothes on."

"Fine," Eddie said as he pulled his shirt back over his head, "but if I lose any of my leg hair from the chafing, I don't wanna hear any comments about it."

Antony finished making his bed and noticed that Charlie had already laid down a couple pews ahead of his. He'd also noted that Charlie had been mostly quiet since halfway through their hunt. He sidled up to Charlie's pew. "Hey, don't worry about what happened tonight. You'll get them next time."

While Antony had had no problem picking off the squirrels during their hunt, both Eddie and Charlie had struggled. After a while, Eddie finally found his groove; however, Charlie never did. The more opportunities they gave him to get his first squirrel, the worse he did. Eventually, he just faked a stiff shoulder and let the others take over.

"I know," Charlie sighed. His errant throws during their hunt were only one of the things on his mind, but there was much more than that bothering him.

Antony could sense that his issues were deeper. "Are you still having the nightmares?"

"No."

"Good," Antony said. "Although sometimes, I'd almost take a nightmare if it meant I could hear my dad's voice again."

"Yeah."

"But once we take care of the Beasts that killed our parents, I'm sure all that will come back." He put his hand on Charlie's shoulder.

"Uh huh," Charlie said as he rolled onto his side away from Antony. That was the plan: to save their parents. But Charlie had already begun to doubt whether or not it was something that he could even accomplish.

"All right," Antony said. "Well, goodnight."

"Goodnight," Charlie replied.

"Lights out," Eddie shouted just before the room went dark.

All of the orphans tucked themselves into their beds.

In a few short minutes, they were all asleep—except for Charlie. He just stared at the moonlight passing through the stained-glass mural. As he absorbed the image of Saint Michael battling the Devil, he engaged in a battle of his own. He fought with his own mind, trying to suppress the swelling doubt and trying desperately to find happiness. But with each waking minute, his mind only advanced its position.

◆ ◆ ◆

A couple days passed, during which the orphans followed the same routine: breakfast and then into the woods; lunch and then back into the woods; dinner and then rest.

When Malika was satisfied with how the orphans seemed to be progressing, she surprised them. She didn't send them off after breakfast as she had the days before. Instead, she told them to wait where they were.

"Why?" Eddie asked.

"It is time for your first test," Malika said, and then headed for the woods by herself.

CHAPTER TWENTY-EIGHT

"WHERE'S SHE GOING?" Naomi asked the others as Malika disappeared into the thicket of trees.

"I have no idea," Charlie said. He wasn't as concerned about where she was going as he was about the test. He was keenly aware of how much the other orphans seemed to be improving, and how far behind he was. Naomi had lost much of her edge, Eddie was much more attentive, and both JP and Antony exuded a confidence that Charlie had never seen before. Charlie had done his best to put up a façade as he pretended to keep up with everyone. But he knew that his façade was built with weak bricks and wouldn't withstand even the slightest inspection.

After a minute or so, Malika reemerged from the woods, but she wasn't alone. She carried with her a four-foot mountain garter snake. The snake had a black head, a light yellow belly, and two thick strips of black that ran down the length of the body, separated by a thin white dorsal stripe at the crest of its spine. It slithered back and forth between her hands as it let out a gentle hiss.

"Whoa!" Eddie shouted as he jumped back behind the others. "You never said anything about snakes."

"You're really that afraid of snakes?" JP said with a chuckle. "Who are you, Indiana Jones?"

"You kidding me? No one likes snakes," Eddie said. "Except for maybe crazy people. That's about it."

"You will all learn to be comfortable with snakes," Malika said. "For they are not only essential for testing your sense of self, they are also what you shall use to slay the Beasts."

"How?" Antony said. "That snake is barely venomous. It can't even hurt a human."

"That is very true. In this form, it is mostly harmless. But all it takes is a little positivity and belief." She clenched her fingers around the snake and raised her hand high.

The orphans watched with amazement as gold sparks began to fizzle away from Malika's hand, extending in both directions. By the time the glittery flashes simultaneously reached the head and the tail of the reptile, the snake had transformed into a wooden staff. The staff was twice the original length and circumference of the snake.

"And it can become very powerful," Malika continued. She swung the staff down to ground, crushing a small rock and turning it to rubble in the process.

"That was sick!" JP said. "What is that?"

Charlie was equally enthralled and curious; however, his thoughts and worries of the test kept him quiet.

"Have any of you heard of the rod of God?" Malika asked.

"Yeah," Eddie said. "Everyone knows about Rod Stewart."

The others just shook their heads.

"That wasn't a joke," Eddie said. "Nobody rocks like Rod."

"You're talking about the staff Moses had, right?" Naomi said. "The one he used to part the Red Sea, cause the plagues, and win the Battle of Rephidim."

"That is the one," Malika said.

"I can thank Hebrew school for that nugget."

"Many believed that Moses transformed his staff into a cobra when his brother, Aaron, threw the staff before the Pharaoh's feet," Malika said. "However, in reality, it was the opposite. The staff had been a cobra all along."

Malika tossed the staff on the ground. It immediately turned back into a snake. She retrieved the snake before it could slither away. It turned back into a staff in a flash.

"Does that work with all snakes?" Antony said.

"Yes," Malika said.

"So anyone can do that to like a viper or mamba?" JP said.

"Not just anyone," Malika said. "It takes a very connected spirit. The more venomous and deadly the serpent, the more powerful your sense of belief must be to exert your will over it. And consequently, the more powerful the staff will be. But there are risks with using such deadly snakes. As is true with the Beasts, all it takes is the smallest seed of doubt"—she used her power to show what happens when doubt is present; the snake fluctuated between snake and staff forms—"and it returns to its reptilian state. That is why it is such a useful instrument for measuring one's strength of spirit."

"Awesome," JP said. "Well, I'm ready to give it a shot."

Malika let the staff return to its snake form and then handed it to him.

"What do I gotta do?" JP said.

"Eliminate all negativity and doubt," Malika said. "Allow positivity to flow through you and fuel your belief of self. Everything else will handle itself. Close your eyes if you need to." She turned to the others. "Remain quiet so he can concentrate."

JP closed his eyes. After a second, the same golden sparks began to burst away from his hand, growing brighter and brighter. When his eyes finally opened, so did his mouth. The snake had completely transformed.

"Very good," Malika said.

"Who wants next?" JP said as he twirled the staff in his hands like a well-trained martial artist.

"Right here," Naomi said, raising her hand.

JP tossed the staff to Naomi. It turned back into a snake in midair, and wrapped around her arm as she caught it.

Naomi closed her eyes and concentrated. Small flicks of glitter sputtered from her hands. Very slowly, the snake started to transform. The specks reached a point about a foot from her hand in each direction but couldn't push through the invisible barrier that seemed to hold them back.

"You are still holding on to something," Malika said. "You do not need it anymore. Find it and let it go."

Naomi took a deep breath and exhaled. The golden flecks fluttered to the tips of the snake. She opened her eyes and smiled ear to ear, somewhat surprised by her success.

"Very good," Malika said. "You must keep reminding your-self to recognize negativity any time it appears in your mind and let it go. Never let it burrow in your brain. Who is next?"

Naomi looked to Charlie. His stomach immediately dropped. After all the times when he had actually wanted her attention, this was the one time he'd been hoping to avoid it. He quickly averted her eyes and turned to Eddie, hoping to deflect the challenge.

"Why not," Eddie said. He took the staff from Naomi. It turned back to a serpent the second she let go. Eddie cringed, turning his head away. "Ugh, this feels so gross."

"Do not focus on how it feels," Malika said. "Focus on your thoughts."

"All right," Eddie said. He closed his eyes and focused. Just as had happened with Naomi, he seemed to reach an invisible barrier that he couldn't break through. Malika went to speak, but Eddie stopped her. "I got this," he said. He squinched his eyes even tighter and clenched his jaw. It worked. The trans-formation continued the length of the snake. He opened his eyes and grinned. "Boom goes the dynamite," he shouted. He tried to twirl the staff like JP had, but dropped it in the pro-cess. "Whoops."

"I guess it's my turn," Antony said as he picked up the snake. He narrowed his eyes but kept them open.

"You need to close your eyes," JP said.

"He only needs to do whatever feels right for him," Ma-lika said.

Antony concentrated his focus. He rid himself of all neg-ative thoughts and doubts, and let positivity fill his mind. He reinforced his belief in himself and his ability to transform the snake, as well as his belief that he could accomplish anything he wanted if he put his mind to it.

The snake exploded a cloud of golden sparkles and enveloped Antony. The other orphans instinctively dove, taking cover from the blast. When they picked their heads up, they found Antony standing with the transformed staff.

"What the hell was that?" Naomi said.

"A very strong belief in self," Malika said.

"You think?" Eddie said facetiously.

Charlie was less surprised than the others, who had clearly only been focusing on themselves like Malika had instructed them to, and not on Antony. Or maybe they hadn't noticed his growth like Charlie had because he wasn't as vocal about his improvement as JP was. Changing the staff in such an impressive fashion didn't change that fact, either. Antony didn't gloat. He just respectfully handed the staff back to Malika.

Malika let it turn back into a snake. "Your turn," she said as she held it out to Charlie.

Charlie stared at the snake. Its unblinking eyes. Its split red tongue, with a tiny black tip that slipped rapidly in and out of its mouth. Charlie swallowed hard. "This is probably a waste of time," he said. "Everyone else has done it. No reason I won't pass, either. We can just move on to the next step."

"What they have accomplished has nothing to do with you," Malika said as she put the snake in Charlie's hand.

Charlie sighed. He reluctantly tightened his grip, took possession of the snake, and closed his eyes. He could feel the snake sliding through his hand, its tongue tickling his wrist.

He tried his best to block out those sensations and to remind himself to find happiness and let go of any fear of failure. He kept repeating the words in his head. But as with all of the times in the woods before, the words proved to be more destructive than helpful. Each time after he said them, he thought of a counterargument. He had nothing to be happy about. He'd never get things right. He was a failure.

Charlie opened his eyes. He didn't need to look at the snake; he could still feel its scales with his fingers. Plus, the faces of the other orphans told him everything he needed to know. The snake hadn't changed at all. Not even one tiny fizzle. Charlie slumped and dropped the snake to the ground.

"Hey, maybe it's broken," Eddie said. "I meant the snake. Not you, Charlie."

"No," Malika said. "Excuses are only a means to resist accountability. He must accept that it is not the snake, it is him. It is his mind. He must accept that he needs to work harder."

"You will," Antony said as he patted Charlie on the back. "You'll get it next time."

"Yeah, I guess," Charlie said.

Malika yanked Charlie by the shoulders so that he was forced to stand up straight. It was an unexpected jolt of power from the tiny girl. "This is not a guessing game," she said. "You have to know. Right now, they still believe in you more than you believe in yourself."

"I don't know about that," JP said with a chuckle.

The others shot JP disapproving looks.

"Excuse me," JP said, defiantly, "I didn't realize Eddie owned the market on jokes."

"That didn't sound like a joke," Antony said.

"Well, I meant it as a joke."

Malika continued her instructions to Charlie. "You must return to the woods. Concentrate on finding happiness in everything, including what has just happened, and on letting go of your fear of failing. Do not even consider dealing with your other negative judgments until you have resolved that much first. Focus on what is."

Charlie headed for his spot in the woods. The others watched him disappear into the brush. However, he didn't continue any further, he merely took cover behind a massive redwood on the fringe of the forest and peeked one eye around the trunk as he eavesdropped on the others.

"So," JP said, "are we learning to fight now?"

"No," Malika said. "First, you must learn to be present."

From behind the tree, Charlie shared the same look of confusion as the other orphans.

"What are you talking about?" Eddie said. "We're all here, aren't we?" He raised his hand like any good student when their teacher takes attendance. "Present."

"Physically, you are all here," Malika said. "But mentally? I am less certain of that. Right now, you are still incredibly susceptible to distractions of the mind. Some of these distracting thoughts may even be positive in nature, but they are still thoughts that exist outside of the present. You need to learn to be present at all times."

"What do you mean?" Antony said.

Charlie listened carefully as Malika gave several examples of not being present, many of which involved the increasing attachment to recent technologies and the distractions they created. He could relate to all of the instances she gave, particularly the one about needing to frequently check your cell phone, even in the company of others. His parents had often chided him for it. "No phones at the dinner table," they would say on a nightly basis. Charlie always argued his way out of it, claiming it had to do with school, even when it clearly didn't.

Malika explained that being out of the moment not only opened the door to negative emotions, which were more often than not a result of thinking forward or backward, it also weakened the connection to one's divine self and created noise that had a dulling effect on all of one's senses. She stated that the latter was of the utmost importance due to the fact that when they eventually took on the Beasts, the Beasts wouldn't be burdened by this noise. The Beasts would have nothing on their minds besides the task at hand, and the orphans would need to be able to bring the same focus and clarity.

"If you do," Malika said, "your senses will work together in a collective and heightened state. One that you have never come close to experiencing."

"Status update," Eddie said.

Naomi rolled her eyes.

"Let me finish," Eddie said. "I'm deactivating my account."

"Like," all the other orphans said while giving two emphatic thumbs up.

"How do we learn to be present?" Antony said.

"You practice mindfulness," Malika said. "When you go into the woods, start by releasing any negativity from your mind, as you have done before. Then focus on your breath.

Start with three deep breaths, and then return to your normal breath, counting each inhalation and exhalation."

"For how long?" JP said.

"There is no set limit, no goals. It is a practice, one that you will continue to grow with the more time you spend doing it," Malika said. "Be aware that thoughts will surely pop into your head at one point or another, just acknowledge them and then return to your breath."

"What if we lose count of our breath?" Naomi asked.

"Then you have lost focus and are not being mindful. Do not become disappointed with yourself, simply start over." Malika finished with a short blessing and then sent the orphans into the woods to get to work.

Charlie waited until the others had been gone for a while before he crawled out from his hiding spot and returned to his place in the woods. He sunk into his tree seat. His shoes slipped as he attempted to rest his feet on the trunk, which, after days of frustration, his heels had stripped bare.

Charlie began by focusing on finding happiness and letting go of failure, but he couldn't help but think about what the other orphans were doing and how badly he needed to catch up to them. He attempted to do the mindfulness exercise that Malika had just taught, but he didn't get past the fifth breath before his mind began wandering. His thoughts jumped from how he'd failed to transform the snake to how he'd failed with the squirrels, then to how he was currently failing to let go of failure, which led him back to his Language Arts grade. With everything else going on in his world, all of his troubles, that damn grade still bothered him.

A while passed before Charlie realized how badly he'd lost count and focus. After a couple minutes of venting his frustrations, he gave it another shot, only to have the same exact thing happen all over again. But this time, when he realized he had lost focus, he didn't try a third time. He just kept venting about everything in his life. After an hour or so, his forehead began to throb, the very familiar pain, and he called it a day.

◆ ◆ ◆

Over the next three days, each morning began with breakfast and Charlie's test. After he was unable to control the snake, Charlie would reclaim his hiding spot in the woods and spy on the others while Malika gave the next lesson.

The first morning, Malika educated the orphans on the importance of being mindful of their own bodies. She instructed them to focus on each of their five senses, one at a time, to heighten their awareness of them.

The second morning, Malika taught the orphans how to practice walking meditation by using their breathing and heightened senses while interacting with the world. She stressed that during the meditation, they should never be doing anything—even something as minor as taking a single step—without consciously putting forth the effort.

The third morning, there was no lesson, only the announcement that they were ready to begin sparring. Charlie didn't watch from his nook. He couldn't bear to. He trudged to his spot in the woods and plopped down on his tree seat.

Charlie felt a slight sense of relief that day. Unlike the days before, there was no new lesson for him to attempt and fail miserably at. But his relief faded quickly as he realized that meant that there was nothing to save him from his rut, other than the things that he'd already learned. All that he knew was all that he could turn to. With that in mind, he reluctantly returned to square one.

"Find happiness," Charlie said to himself. But with those words, came a memory from the night before that gave him the exact opposite emotional response. It filled him with jealousy and other undesirable emotions.

The night before, Charlie had gone off into the woods to go to the bathroom. As he was making his way back to the church, he overheard Naomi and JP talking in the woods. Charlie wished that they had just kept talking. They didn't. He watched as they embraced, their arms wrapping around each other, bodies touching from their toes all the way to their lips. Desperately wanting to do something to break them up, Charlie grabbed the closest rock he could find and bounced it off of a nearby tree. His distraction worked, immediately putting an end to the make-out session. But the end was only temporary. While JP and Naomi stopped for a second to look around, they quickly returned to their lip-locking after deciding everything was all right.

Now, as Charlie sat in his tree chair, he imagined how it might feel for his chapped lips to meet Naomi's. The thought had consumed him and kept him up the night before. Would it be like two pieces of sandpaper rubbing together? Or would there be a surprising softness? Only JP would ever know.

The envy in Charlie swelled. How could he have been so foolish? How could he have thought he had a chance? After all, Naomi would've been the first girl to take an interest in him. Why should she be any different than everyone else?

Find happiness, he tried to remind himself over and over again. But the words were even more useless than ever before and only caused jolts of pain to shoot across his forehead.

Charlie attempted to change gears, to move on from Naomi, and to focus on letting go of his fear of failure. But instead of letting go of his fear, he could only draw attention to his failures. Each failure that crossed his mind was accompanied by another stinging jolt. He abandoned that plan and turned to the mindfulness exercises, his last resort. Unfortunately, they only threw more fuel on the burning fire in his brain. His head pulsed harder than ever before. The pain was unbearable.

Charlie rolled off of his tree stump and down to the dirt ground. He clutched the back of his head in his hands as he knelt in a fetal position. He shot up to his knees and screamed in agony. He screamed even louder as he repeatedly pounded the earth, tiny shards of rock and pine needles embedding in the skin of his knuckles with each blow. He slammed both fists to the ground in one final violent thrust.

Charlie's chest expanded and collapsed spastically as he huffed and puffed. Tears began to stream from his eyes. He'd reached his edge. He'd broken. It was done. He was done. But while Charlie had already decided to give up, someone else he knew was just getting started.

CHAPTER
TWENTY-NINE

DR. HUANG LISTENED INTENTLY to the voice on the other end of his cell phone as he paced about the lab room at the San Mateo Coroner's Office. He'd spent most of the morning calling all of his colleagues, trying to find anyone who may have heard of any new types of drugs that could induce sudden cardiac failure. After more than a dozen calls, he'd finally found someone who knew of such a drug.

Dr. Huang's first call that day hadn't been to any of his associates. The first number he dialed was Charlie's cell phone, which he'd found on the teen's social media page. Dr. Huang's call went straight to voice mail. The second number he tried was for the Kim residence. Predictably, it also went to voice mail. Dr. Huang hadn't expected to get an answer for either call. He knew as well as anyone about Grandpa Kim's death and Charlie's sudden disappearance. He'd seriously contemplated reopening Alan and Mary's file the day he heard that

Charlie had gone missing, but he held off. He'd made a promise to the teen and was determined to honor it.

To that end, Dr. Huang waited the full fourteen days that he'd agreed to wait so that Charlie could do what he needed to do. Dr. Huang had even held off reporting his findings from Grandpa Kim's autopsy, which included a troponin measurement—not from a rapid test, but from a more exact testing—that was the highest he'd ever recorded, because he knew the results would likely cause a stir. But now that his and Charlie's negotiated time had passed and he still hadn't heard from him, Dr. Huang had done what he needed to do. He'd reopened Alan and Mary's files and put in a request to exhume their bodies for further examination, and then he started making his calls.

Dr. Huang took notes as his friend relayed what he knew about a diabetes drug that had been banned during FDA trials because of its tendency to cause heart palpitations. His friend explained that the drug occasionally caused blood sugar levels to free-fall and in larger doses was believed to be fatal. The good news was that the presence of the drug was easy to identify. All that was required was a simple glucose test. It was yet another analysis that Dr. Huang hadn't considered conducting—with good reason, given that none of the victims were known to have any diabetic history.

Dr. Huang thanked his friend, and then hung up the phone and got right to work. He readied rapid tests for Alan, Mary, and Grandpa Kim. There was no doubt in his mind that whatever had led to Alan and Mary's death had also contributed to Grandpa Kim's. But he was right and wrong at the same time: right about their connected cause of death, and wrong for thinking that he'd actually found his break. All of the test strips came back negative. The glucose levels were normal.

Dr. Huang let out a heavy sigh. He was out of options for calls to make. He'd have to wait until Alan and Mary's bodies were exhumed before he could confirm what he had with Grandpa Kim's full examination. None of the old man's internal indicators had been consistent with myocardial infarction. There wasn't even one area, let alone a speck, of black on his heart, a sign of dead tissue. Nor were there any hardened walls of plaque or the strawberry-colored clots that a medical examiner would expect to find. Grandpa Kim's heart wasn't just healthy for someone his age, it would've been considered healthy for someone twenty years younger. The findings heavily supported the fact that drugs and foul play had to be involved. But Dr. Huang still didn't know what, how, or who.

Dr. Huang was trying to decide on his next course of action when his cell phone chirped. He had a new email. He hoped it was a positive response to one of the messages he'd left earlier, maybe another drug lead or just anything he could work with. It wasn't. The email was a form response that let him know that his request to exhume the bodies of Alan and Mary Kim had been denied, with no specific reason given.

Dr. Huang shook his head. It didn't make any sense. He'd never had a single request rejected without a detailed explanation of the reasons for denial. He pocketed his phone, and then grabbed a seat at the lab computer station. He opened the Kims' file. Much to his surprise, their file had been switched back to closed. He clicked the toggle button to reopen the file, but all that he got was a pop-up that told him he was unable to execute the change. The file was permanently locked. He attempted to put in another request to exhume the bodies, but that was also disabled.

"What the hell is going on?" Dr. Huang said to himself, his confusion turning into anger. "I'll get to the bottom of this." He hopped up from his seat and stormed out of the lab.

Dr. Huang went straight for Coroner Stevens's office, which was in the wing on the opposite side of the building from his. He pounded on the Coroner's door. "Why'd you lock me out of the Kim file? Answer me," he demanded as he continued to beat on the door.

But there was no response.

After a minute, Dr. Huang marched to the receptionist's desk at the front of the building. "Where the hell is Coroner Stevens?" he angrily asked.

"Is everything okay?" the startled receptionist replied.

"No. Where is he?"

"He stepped out a half an hour ago. He said he had a meeting. It sounded important. Apparently, a private donor is interested in giving money to help upgrade some of your equipment. You should be happy."

"I'll be happy after I talk to him," Dr. Huang said. "As soon as he gets back, make sure to tell him to see me. I'll be in my office."

"I will. But he said it might be a while."

Dr. Huang didn't respond. He just started for his office. He had an idea, a new angle. He had a decent relationship with the head of tech support. He figured his friend might be able to help him get back into the file or maybe even override the request altogether.

Dr. Huang strode down the hall and into his office, shut the door behind him, and took a seat at his desk. He'd been so focused on what he needed to do that it wasn't until he heard the grating racket of someone forcefully clearing their throat that he realized he wasn't alone.

Dr. Huang looked up to find three men, all in black suits, in his office. Two of them wore dark sunglasses and faced him. The third had his back to the medical examiner and appeared to be admiring his framed diploma.

"Johns Hopkins," the man said as he slowly began to turn around. "That's really impressive."

Dr. Huang recognized the man as soon as he saw his face. It was Terry Heins. Dr. Huang immediately put two and two together. Charlie had said that a very powerful man was behind his parents' deaths. Terry Heins was an incredibly powerful man. "It was you," he said, his voiced slowed by shock.

Terry chuckled. "I really expected you to be a little smarter, with your degrees and all. I thought there might be some kind of back and forth, maybe a denial. But you just came out and told me everything I needed to know. He did come to see you."

Dr. Huang immediately regretted not playing his cards right. He should've tried to bluff, but instead he'd totally showed his hand. He'd sealed his fate. He was next—that is, unless he did something about it.

Dr. Huang did his best to maintain his composure while his stomach turned itself into a balloon animal and his toes curled tightly in his shoes, a necessary, even if only nominal, release of all of the tension that was building in his body. His eyes shifted to the closed office door. But before he could even decide if it was worth the shot, if there was any way he might make it, Max slid in front and blocked the exit. He wouldn't be leaving.

Dr. Huang knew that he could try screaming. But he also knew that given where his office was, it was highly likely that no one would hear him. That meant he only had one option: a literal call for help. He reached for his desk phone. His fingers barely had a chance to wrap around the receiver before Cain's fingers latched onto his wrist and squeezed with a force stronger than Dr. Huang had ever felt or imagined was humanly possible. He couldn't help but let go of the phone as an overwhelming pain shot up his arm.

Max moved from the door, slipping behind Dr. Huang. He restrained the medical examiner, gripping him by his arms, and pulled him out from behind his desk.

"I applaud your effort," Terry said.

"You're not gonna get away with any of this," Dr. Huang said as he struggled against Max's grasp.

"You might be surprised," Terry said, "but you aren't exactly the first person to tell me that. I will get away with this, and so much more."

"You can buy off Coroner Stevens," Dr. Huang said, "but you can't buy off everyone."

Terry found Dr. Huang's words to be particularly funny. "Buy off Coroner Stevens?" Terry said as he tried to contain his laughter. "I couldn't think of a bigger waste of money. No, all I did was get him out of the way for an hour or two. See, I understand people. And he's just like every other elected official. All they really care about is donations. You dangle a carrot, and the donkey comes wagging his tail." He checked his watch. "I actually have a few more carrots to dangle. So, if you don't mind, we're going to wrap this up quickly."

Dr. Huang was resigned to his fate. He knew there was no way he could save his life short of cooperating, which his morals would never let him do. But there was one thing he needed to know. "Just tell me how you do it. What drug do you use?"

"Of course you want to know. It's your job. You'll be disappointed to find out that no drugs are involved. Just my handy associates. Of course, that's only where the disappointment begins." Terry patted Cain on the back, letting him know he was free to begin.

Cain smirked and flipped his glasses on top of his head.

Dr. Huang's legs gave out as he caught sight of Cain's eyes, which glowed like two hot coals. Tiny blue flashes ricocheted across the flames in his jet-black pupils. Dr. Huang's eyes darted nervously from Cain to Terry as Cain approached. "What the hell is he? What's he gonna do?"

Terry's only response was a menacing grin.

Dr. Huang craned his head, attempting to avert his gaze as Cain drew even closer. Cain grabbed the doctor's head and squeezed his temples in a vise grip.

Dr. Huang let out a weak moan.

Cain wrenched Dr. Huang's head straight and stared deep into his eyes. The bright orange flames pulsed.

Dr. Huang was overcome by a piercing pain in the center of his brow. He could feel his corneas bulging to the point of bursting. He went to scream, but Max silenced the doctor, covering his mouth with his hand.

Less than a minute later, Cain had completely absorbed the doctor's spirit with a blinding flash. Max helped the now-docile doctor back into his desk chair.

Terry retrieved his phone and dialed his secretary. "Do me a favor and tell Coroner Stevens that I'm sorry, but I'm going to have to cancel. Tell him that I can't—hold on a second. I have another call." Terry checked his phone's caller id, and then switched lines. "I only want to hear news if it's good." He listened for a moment. "I'd say that qualifies as good, now make it great. Find them and deal with them." Terry grinned, switched back to his secretary, and continued. "Change of plans. I'm feeling generous. Tell Coroner Stevens that I've decided to give him the money." He hung up his phone and slipped it back in his suit pocket.

"They've confirmed the location of the van?" Cain said.

"Close enough," Terry said. "It was last seen exiting the freeway near the California-Nevada border. They've called in some additional support and are about to begin combing the area. It shouldn't be long before they find them."

"I'll put together a list of all of the abandoned churches within a twenty-mile radius and get it to them. I have no doubt that she has the pests holed up in some place like that. Angels like her are nothing if not predictable."

"Perfect. Soon enough, she and the little thorns in my side will all be removed."

CHAPTER
THIRTY

DEEP IN THE WOODS, Charlie wandered aimlessly. He had wanted to head back long before, but decided it wasn't a good idea. He knew that if he showed up too early for lunch, the others would likely figure out that he'd given up. Even though he wasn't sure what he was going to do next or what his options even were, he didn't want his quitting to be known and reasoned that it was best to keep up appearances, no matter how minor they were.

After a few more hours, Charlie determined that enough time had passed and began his trek back to the church and the other orphans. He was almost to the edge of the clearing when he heard Naomi yell, "Behind you!"

Charlie froze. He hadn't heard that kind of urgency in her voice since they'd escaped from his house. He didn't know what to make of it. He quickly gathered his wits and took cover behind a tree. "Nice save," he heard Eddie shout back.

"Switch!" Antony ordered.

Charlie waited a moment before mustering the courage to crawl out from the safety of the tree. He stealthily crept toward the voices, staying as low and quiet as he could until he reached his old hiding spot.

When Charlie finally caught sight of the action, he couldn't believe what he saw. His eyes fluttered, as if they were trying to erase what he was witnessing: All of the other orphans were engaged in a fierce battle with a group of five Beasts.

Charlie didn't recognize any of the Beasts—not only were Cain and Max not with them, neither were the three Beasts that had been at his house—but it was obvious what they were. They were all sporting the same black suits and matching sunglasses as Terry's men. Charlie knew that it could only mean one thing: in his absence, they'd been discovered.

Charlie ducked down behind his hiding spot. His hands gripped his legs so tightly that his nails dug into his skin even through his jeans. His heart raced. His breath joined it, trying to keep up. A mad dash to a frightful finish line. He struggled to conceal every inch of his body. This wasn't like the times before, when he simply hoped that he wouldn't be seen. Now he couldn't be seen. His life depended on it.

But what about his friends? What about their lives? Charlie wanted to help them, but his fear and doubt wouldn't let him. He knew that he wouldn't stand a chance. He couldn't fight. All he could possibly do was absorb a couple blows. That wouldn't do any of them any good, especially him.

"Suck on that," Charlie heard JP yell, followed by a strange sound that resembled a sheet of flash paper going up in flames, except for the fact that it was much louder, like a whole stack of flash paper had been lit at once. His own curiosity, combined with the confidence he heard in JP's voice, gave him the little bit of courage that he needed to lift his head and check back in on the other orphans.

Much to Charlie's surprise and excitement, the fight was down to four on four, an even match-up. The sound he heard had been the extermination of one of the Beasts. Charlie felt some of the weight in his chest lifting. What also eased his anxiety was the realization that besides the better odds, all of the orphans seemed to have things perfectly under control.

Charlie gazed in absolute amazement as each of the orphans battled back and forth with their own Beast. He couldn't believe how fast his friends were maneuvering and how high they were leaping to avoid the strikes from the Beasts. It was like their legs had been replaced by pogo sticks. Charlie had never seen anything so fluid, and at the same time so lethal, in real life. It was something he'd only seen in movies. They all had an acrobatic grace to their movement, even Eddie, who had never given off the impression of possessing any athletic abilities.

Charlie watched as Antony leapt high into the air and drove his staff into his foe's forehead. The skin around the puncture in the Beast's brow began to crack. Bright, burning molten lava filled the fractures, which continued to spread and break off, creating new fault lines. The Beast went up in a spontaneous volcanic burst, followed by the same sound that Charlie had heard before. All that remained was a small pile of carbon ash that was quickly taken away by the wind.

"Whoa," Charlie said under his breath.

Just beyond Antony, Charlie saw JP make quick work of his Beast, then turn his attention to Naomi. He rushed to her side. "You need any help?"

"Don't worry about me. I got this," Naomi said with a confident grin.

Even with all of the fear, excitement, and other emotions fighting for attention in Charlie's body, as he watched JP and Naomi's interaction, he found some room for jealousy.

Four on two became four on one when Naomi used a deke to dispatch her opponent. The orphans took measured steps as they moved to surround the Beast that Eddie had been tussling with.

"You need any backup?" Antony said.

"Nah, but I wouldn't mind a lift," Eddie said, and then made a gesture with his eyes that let Antony know exactly what he was thinking.

"Good idea."

Antony clasped his hands in a cup by his waist. Eddie sprinted toward Antony and leapt, landing his foot in Antony's joined hands. Antony heaved Eddie at the same time as Eddie sprung upwards.

Eddie twisted his body one hundred eighty degrees and laid out in a near perfect reverse swan dive as he floated above the outstretched arms of the Beast. He kicked his legs over his head so that he was facing the ground, and drove his staff into the center of the Beast's brow.

By the time Eddie crashed to the earth, all that remained of the Beast was the pile of ash. Eddie tumbled for about ten feet before coming to a stop. He got up and threw his arms in the air like an Olympic gymnast finishing their routine.

"I'll give you a seven for degree of difficulty," JP said. "Would've been an eight if you stuck the landing."

"You must be the Russian judge," Eddie said.

Charlie couldn't believe that they'd just defeated the five Beasts. He wanted to congratulate his friends. He stood up, ready to rush to their sides and get in on high-fives, but stopped. He knew his timely presence would only raise questions. Like how had he seen the whole fight? And why had he stayed in the woods? He knew it would be better to just wait for a moment. And so, he watched as Malika rejoined the group from somewhere out of his view.

"Very good," Malika said. "I think you are ready for the next challenge: two vessels at a time."

Challenge? Vessels? Charlie quickly put it all together, realizing that what he'd just witnessed was not an actual battle, but merely sparring. Regardless, he was no less impressed. He was, however, incredibly relieved to learn that they hadn't actually been discovered.

"I think we're ready for more than that," JP said, "I think we're ready to take on the real thing. No more of these vessels, we need to start kicking real Beast butt."

"The sparring vessels are no different than the Beasts," Malika said.

"Yeah. Except for the fact that we aren't saving any of our parents' souls when we destroy them. I know we're all ready to take on the Beasts." JP stopped, corrected himself, "Well, at least all of us except for Charlie are."

Upon hearing this, Charlie slinked back behind his little hiding spot. He had an uneasy feeling about the direction that the conversation appeared to be heading.

"We're a team," Antony said. "If one of us isn't ready, then none of us are ready."

"I know we're a team," JP said. "But every team has a weak link. That's just how it is. The Ninja Turtles had Raphael, the Power Rangers had the Yellow Ranger, and we have Charlie."

"Hey," Eddie said, "I liked Raphael and the Yellow Ranger. She had some great moves."

"And I like Charlie," JP said. "But that's not the point."

"What is the point?" Antony said. "You brought it up."

"I don't know. I guess all I'm saying is that maybe we need to accept the fact that Charlie might never be ready. He might never pass the first step. Maybe the only thing he'll ever do is keep holding us back."

"If it wasn't for Charlie, none of us would be here."

"I couldn't agree more," JP said. "Of course, I have a different way of looking at it. The way I see it, it's his fault we can't go back to our old lives. It's his fault those Beasts want to kill us. And now it's his fault that we'll probably be stuck out in the woods forever, when we should be out there actually doing something."

What Charlie had feared since they fled from his home had finally come true. The blame had found its way back to him. He was certain the others had to have at least considered what JP had said. He knew that JP wasn't misguided in holding him responsible. He waited for the others to join in and pile on, but they never got the chance.

"Enough," Malika said, finally chiming in after purposely letting them go. "Do not worry about Charlie. Worry about yourselves. Your attention to others and perception of being stuck are proof that you are still susceptible to distractions and letting your emotions take over, and that you must work harder to remain present. Now take a deep breath, acknowledge that your emotions are there, and let them both go."

The orphans followed Malika's instructions.

"All I wanna know is if we could take out the Beasts?" JP asked Malika after he finished letting go of his emotions.

"Yes," Malika said with a nod. "There is no denying that you could hold your own with a Beast or two. That is true for all of you, but there is still much room for each of you to grow. For starters, each of you must learn to not focus your energy and efforts on the third eye center. While piercing it may be the only way to vanquish a Beast, the more attention that you give it, the more they will defend it. Therefore, you must learn to respond to their movements, while concurrently using all of your senses, a skill that can only be acquired through practice."

"Fine," JP said. "Then we might as well get back to practicing. Hook me up with a couple vessels to tango with."

Malika scooped up two fistfuls of loose soil from the ground. She blew the dirt from her palms. It swirled in the air, creating a miniature tornado that then split into two, each of which left behind a hulking, sparring vessel. The little remnants left were swept away with the wind.

Charlie stayed slumped behind his little hiding spot while each of the orphans took turns going toe-to-toe with two sparring vessels. He didn't watch any of their victories or listen to their cheers. He kept his thoughts and attention inside, replaying JP's words while contemplating his new plan.

◆ ◆ ◆

Charlie waited an extra twenty minutes after the training session had ended before he pulled himself off the ground, brushed off all of the dirt and leaves his clothes had picked up, and joined the group for lunch.

Charlie didn't speak a word the whole meal. He just kept to himself, nodding yes or no when asked any questions, which was only a of couple times, and then headed back into the woods.

Charlie didn't speak after he came back from his afternoon trek or during their dinner, either. He simply finished his meal and went straight to bed, only he didn't fall asleep. That was never his intention. He merely wanted to appear to be asleep. He kept his eyes shut tight as one by one, the other orphans called it a night.

After everyone else had fallen asleep, Charlie discreetly slid out of his bed, and then quietly gathered the few things that he had with him. He didn't bother writing a goodbye letter. All he left behind was the flash drive, which he slipped inside Antony's shoe.

Charlie looked at the sleeping orphans one last time. It wasn't how he'd wanted it to end, but it was better for him, and it was definitely better for them. He wouldn't hold them back anymore. He said goodbye in his mind, and then tiptoed out of the church and into the night.

CHAPTER
THIRTY-ONE

CHARLIE WALKED CLOSE to a mile down the gravel road that led away from the church before he came to a fork. One direction went right, the other went left, and both were the same combination of dirt and rock. "Great," he said to himself, unsure of which road to choose or where either path led.

Charlie turned his head toward the night sky. He knew if he could locate the North Star, he could use that to determine if either of the roads pointed west, or some western variation. That was the direction he was headed. Unfortunately, the sky was so clear and full of stars that they all looked the same. He couldn't make out Orion's belt or either of the dippers in the overcrowded celestial light show.

Charlie was debating his options when he felt a soft breeze on the back of his neck and heard a gentle rustling of gravel. He whipped around to find Malika, who had just touched down and was in the process of retracting her wings. Charlie shook his head and sighed. "I guess I probably should've assumed my guardian angel would be watching me."

"Yes, probably," Malika said.

"So, are you gonna make me go back?

"I cannot make you do anything."

"Right," Charlie said, not completely believing her. He started toward the road on the left. Malika made no effort to prevent him from continuing. Charlie stopped himself. "You really aren't gonna make me go back?"

"There is no point," Malika said. "If you do not want to be there, what good would forcing you to stay do?"

"It's not that I want to leave," Charlie said, trying to defend his actions. "I have to. I haven't been able to even get past the first step in the training. I haven't been able to find happiness in anything, either. I've only gotten worse and lost any confidence that I thought I had. Besides, I think it's pretty obvious that I'm just holding everyone back."

Malika realized part of the motivation behind Charlie's exit. "You were watching today, were you not?" she said.

"Yeah," Charlie said as he nodded. "And JP was right. Not just about me holding them back, but that it's my fault they're all here. I got everyone into this mess."

"There is no one person at fault. You made choices that led to your current situation, and they made choices as well. But the only person who can really hold them back is themselves, not you. You do not have that power."

"Yeah, 'cause I don't have any power."

"That is very far from the truth. But if that is what you believe, then that is what it is."

"Like I said, I've only gotten less confident." He looked down at his shoes and gave the gravel a couple kicks.

"Where will you go?" Malika asked.

"Home."

"You know that they will come for you, right?"

"That's what I'm banking on. I'm just hoping I can figure out a way to take Cain out before they get me. At least that's my plan."

"And if your plan does not work?"

"Well, assuming I don't die, I guess I'll come up with a new plan."

"Have you ever considered that instead of coming up with new plans, maybe it is time for you to move on from plans altogether?"

"What are you talking about?" Charlie said, confused. His reaction made it very clear that he had never contemplated the option, not even for a second.

"I am talking about the true reason for your struggles," Malika said. "They have not come because you do not have any power or are less capable than the others. Your struggles persist because you are unique. They persist because you actually have two blocks that prevent your divine self from shining through. It is a testament to the strength of your mind, which, if harnessed properly, is capable of anything you can envision."

"I don't understand," Charlie said. "Why didn't you tell me I had two blocks earlier?"

"You were not ready to hear it," Malika said. "Even the most powerful message can be rendered meaningless if it falls on deaf ears. Because of your uniqueness, you needed to reach your very bottom before you could begin your ascent."

"Yeah, well, I'm pretty sure I hit it today. My ears are as open as they'll ever be. I'll do anything."

"All you must do is let go of all of your plans. They have done nothing but give you a false sense of direction and cause many more problems."

"That doesn't make any sense," Charlie said. "Everyone that's ever been successful has had a plan."

Malika smirked. "I can see that your own plans have continued to force you to look at success through an improper lens. When you define success as happiness, as I encouraged you to do, those with rigid plans are rarely successful. The more detailed the plan, the more this is true. A plan is nothing more than an attempt to control something that is uncontrollable. The truth is that the more you try to control your plan, the more it controls you. Let me ask you this, how many times have you compromised your integrity, your divine self, to preserve your plan?"

Charlie thought about the numerous times that he'd done things he wasn't proud of to maintain his plan. While he'd lost the guilt from the deceptions that he'd pulled on his parents, he hadn't forgotten the lies that he'd told others. The recent incident where he'd attempted to sway his teacher by using his parents' deaths jumped to the top of his mind. "A lot," he said, his voice full of regret.

"Your plans have also prevented you from finding happiness in each moment and closed you off to opportunities that fall outside of your predetermined path," Malika said.

"You must let go of your second block, your desire to control everything and achieve perfection. You must accept that you cannot control the universe, that the past has already happened, that the future is no guarantee, and that the only thing you can truly control is what you do in the present."

Malika gave Charlie time to let her words resonate. The last three points cycled through his mind. The past already happened. The future is not a guarantee. The only thing you can truly control is what you do in the present. His thoughts returned to his Language Arts class. But it wasn't his talk with his teacher or his bad grade that flooded his mind, it was his unwritten assignment, the one that he'd struggled with and never cracked. "Now," he said, finally realizing the answer. "That's the most important moment in my life."

"Yes, it is," Malika said. "It always has been, whether you realized it or not."

"If I'm not supposed to have a plan, what am I supposed to do, nothing?"

"Not at all," Malika said. "Do whatever the moment calls for. Allow your divine self to guide the way, knowing that it will lead you in the right direction. It will always follow the proper path."

Charlie nodded, accepting Malika's instruction.

"Have you ever heard the Serenity Prayer?" Malika asked.

"I don't think so," Charlie said.

"It is a great reminder to only focus on that which you can control, or change. It goes: God, grant me the serenity to accept the things I cannot change, the courage to change the things I can, and the wisdom to know the difference."

"I really like that."

"As do I," Malika said. "However, I have found that it can be even more impactful in reverse. Instead of serenity, courage, and wisdom, it is optimal to consider wisdom and courage as a means to serenity. If you use your wisdom to determine whether you are dealing with something that you can or cannot change, the knowledge gained will grant you acceptance of the situation. If it is not something you can change, there is nothing to do but let it go. It is out of your control. If it is something that you can change, you will find the courage to execute the appropriate action by focusing only on controlling the moment. Knowing that you are doing something, and that you are following your divine self, will supply you with all the serenity you could ever need to find peace and happiness."

"Wisdom. Courage. Serenity," Charlie said to himself.

"Use those three words as your serenity mantra. If you ever find yourself in a rut you cannot escape, simply identify the source of your troubles, repeat the mantra while determining where your issue lies, and then respond accordingly."

Charlie repeated the serenity mantra. Unlike the times before, when he'd simply told himself to find happiness, the words left an imprint on him. Even after saying it just a couple times, he could feel the weight of his burdens lifted. He finally experienced the rush of positive feelings that others had received the day they surrounded the campfire and revealed their biggest blocks.

Malika noticed the difference in Charlie's eyes. No longer wide and lost, they had narrowed. There was a determination behind them. However, Malika could still sense a slight lingering doubt. "Is there something that still constrains you?"

"It doesn't have to do with me, really," Charlie said. "Well, it kind of does. I know I won't have a problem taking care of Cain and saving my parents. But when it comes to Terry, I don't know if I could actually go through with it."

"Do not be concerned about that. It will resolve itself," Malika said, and then explained something to Charlie that helped assuage his doubts and put them to rest.

◆ ◆ ◆

Charlie sneaked back inside the church. He carefully retrieved his usb drive from Antony's shoe, slid it in his pocket, and then climbed into his bed. As he stared at the stained-glass mural, he was no longer filled with the fear and doubt that had plagued him before. His negative feelings had been replaced by an excitement that rushed through his veins. He felt like a kid on Christmas Eve, full of joy and anticipation for what the next morning held.

Charlie reminded himself to stay focused on what was, not what was next. He knew that at that moment, the thing he needed most was rest. He'd have plenty of time to do everything that he wanted to do tomorrow. He repeated his serenity mantra a few times. It helped clear his mind and ease his anticipation. Shortly afterwards, he was able to fall asleep.

Charlie woke up before the sun and the other orphans. While he hadn't slept terribly long, it'd been a deep sleep, and he felt completely rejuvenated. He sneaked out of the church for a second time, and then ventured through the sparse dawn light until he arrived at his spot in the forest.

Charlie noticed his knuckle prints were still in the dirt. He wiped them over, erasing any memory of his frustration from the day before with the prints. There was no point holding on to the negative reminder of a past he couldn't change.

Charlie used two sticks and one of his shoelaces to make a bow drill, something he'd seen Antony do. With his contraption, he was able to create a spark and ignite a little tuft of dead grass that he'd balled up tightly for kindling. Once he had a small tepee fire going, he took his Moleskine notebook from his pocket, removed his picture with his parents, and then tossed the notebook into the flames. He watched the pages—and all of his old plans—turn to ash. After the fire had died down enough, he stomped out the remaining embers, and then hopped into his seat on the tree trunk.

Charlie considered all of the issues that had weighed on him before: his parents, Terry, the impending attack on Heaven, and even Naomi. He repeated the words from the serenity mantra and was able to find peace in all of his problems by accepting what he could and couldn't control, and reminding himself that he was working toward changing the things that he could. It gave him the peace of mind that he needed so that he could finally find happiness in his life.

With his fear of failure behind him and no attachment to any plan, the floodgates opened, and Charlie was able to liberate himself from every negative opinion that he'd ever held. On a superficial level, he appeared to be no different. Same hair. Same eyes. Same height. But on the inside, he was a completely new person.

Charlie smiled as he stared out into the seemingly endless wilderness; the positive energy that had been restrained by negativity was now flowing free. He felt a connection to the world, which he was finally able to see for what it truly was and appreciate all the beauty before him. He took it all in. The sun that had just begun to peak over the mountains and was casting a bright orange hue on the valley before him. The trees that had taken many human lifetimes to grow to their heights and were like nature's skyscrapers. The birds that flocked in complex coordination and softly cawed to one another as they flew from perch to perch. The clouds that hung in the sky like large, fluffy pillows as they floated across the fresh mountain air that filled his lungs and gave him life.

Charlie felt compelled to capture its beauty in some way, shape, or form so that he could share it with others. So that they could experience all that he had, and share in his appreciation and gratitude. But while he had a strong desire to express himself, his internal desire to continue building on his achievement was even stronger. He had only succeeded in step one. He had much further to go.

Charlie closed his eyes, centered his thoughts, and began to count his breaths. One, two, three, four, five. He kept going, making it to one thousand breaths before consciously breaking his attention.

He spent the next couple hours after that increasing his body awareness and spending time focusing on all of his senses. In just that short time, he noticed his own reflexes speeding up.

Around noon, his stomach let him know that it was approaching lunchtime. Charlie set off into the woods, on a walking mediation and in search of nourishment to appease his demanding stomach. He knew that he'd find what he was looking for; he'd provide for himself. But what he didn't know, was that the wild animals he was in search of weren't the only things roaming the nearby mountains.

CHAPTER
THIRTY-TWO

"ANY IDEA WHEN Charlie's gonna get back?" JP asked Malika as he checked his watch. He and the orphans had just wrapped up another simulated battle where they took turns scrapping with three Beasts at once. "I feel like he should be back by now."

"Do not worry about Charlie," Malika said, already in the process of spawning more vessels for their next challenge. "He will return whenever he feels he is ready."

"I was only asking 'cause I'm getting hungry," JP said.

"Me, too," added Naomi.

Eddie and Antony agreed as well.

"If you would prefer to break for lunch right now, that is fine," Malika said. "Afterwards, each of you will get a chance to battle with five vessels at once." She tossed the loose dirt that was left in her hands, and then took a massive inhale as she swept her puckered lips down the line of sparring vessels.

Each of the vessels instantly dissolved, turning back to dirt that was wisped away by the wind.

"I guess I can make the trip to the grocery store," JP said as he gestured toward the woods. "Anyone wanna join me?"

Antony and Eddie turned to Naomi, expecting her to volunteer. To their surprise, she didn't. "I'll pass," she said.

"Eddie?" JP said.

"Why not?" Eddie said with shrugged. "Let's do this." He and JP set off into the woods to find their lunch.

◆ ◆ ◆

"I honestly don't think I've ever felt this good," Eddie said as he and JP stocked up on hunting rocks half a mile into the forest. "I've already dropped two holes on my belt. That's just in a week. If this keeps up, by the time I get home, I'm gonna need a whole new wardrobe."

JP chuckled. "Yeah, well, you've been looking good in the training, too. Forget five vessels, I bet you could take on ten Beasts at a time, no problem."

"Thanks."

"Like Malika says, thank yourself."

Eddie grinned. "Yeah, right. Thank you, me."

JP grinned back. "I'll grab a couple more rocks and then we should have more than enough ammunition." He knelt down to grab another rock and froze. His eyes intently swiveled in all directions.

Eddie picked up JP's concern. "What's wrong?"

"Did you hear that?" JP asked.

Eddie listened for a moment. All he heard was the rustling of pine needles in the light wind. "I don't think so … "

"Listen closer."

Eddie concentrated his hearing. Through the soft whispers of the trees, he heard what JP was referring to: a gentle rattling. He froze, too. His eyes scanned the woods, unable to locate the source or even its general direction. He had a feeling what it was, but tried to convince himself otherwise. "What are the odds that's the rhythm section for the quietest mariachi band ever?"

"Slim to none," JP said.

"I'm assuming it probably isn't a lost baby, either."

"Doubt it."

Less than a second later, JP and Eddie's guessing game came to an end. Just to the right of where JP was knelt, a three-foot Great Basin rattlesnake, its body suited with nature's version of desert camouflage, slid out from under a fallen tree. It shook its rattle fiercely, a stern warning to ward off any would-be challengers.

"Stay still," Eddie whispered through gritted teeth. "It'll just go away."

Eddie was correct in assuming that. That was what most snakes would do. However, this snake was of its own breed. Instead of retreating, the rattler took one look at JP and slithered even closer, moving dangerously close to its striking distance. The snake coiled up, methodically lifted its head, and let out a harsh, combative hiss.

"Change of plans," Eddie said. "Just slowly get up and back away."

JP didn't move a muscle. "That's not gonna work," he said out the side of his mouth.

"Then I'll hit it with a rock." Eddie wrapped his fingers around one of the rocks in his pocket.

The snake's head swayed side to side like a metronome as it hissed even more violently.

"If you miss, I'm screwed," JP said. "I have a better idea. I'm gonna catch it."

"That sounds like a terrible idea. That's definitely a worse idea."

"Just be quiet." JP was done debating. He didn't need Eddie's approval. It was his butt on the line.

Eddie stood perfectly still. He knew that any sudden movement he or JP made would cause the already defensive serpent to strike.

The rattler hissed as JP carefully let go of the rock in his hand. JP took a deep breath, focused his thoughts, and readied for what he was about to do. But before he even had a chance to make his move, the rattler sprung from its tight coil and launched itself at JP.

With his view obstructed by JP's positioning, all Eddie could do was focus on his own breath and staying present while he watched JP react to the attack.

"Ahhh!" JP screamed as he lunged his body toward the snake, falling on top of it like he was jumping on a grenade. He remained motionless for a couple seconds.

Eddie couldn't help but let a little bit of worry get past his guard. "Are you okay? Did it bite you?"

JP said nothing. He slowly picked himself up from the ground. When he turned to face Eddie, he was grinning as wide as his face would allow. In his hand was the snake, only it was no longer a snake. It'd transformed into a staff.

The resulting staff was noticeably different from the ones that they were accustomed to. It was broader, appeared sturdier, and had a dark, reddish aura that shined around the tip, just like the wand Malika had made from the campfire.

"How cool is this?" JP said. He waved the staff back and forth a couple times. Tiny, ruby-colored sparks danced from the glowing tip as it swung in the wind.

"Seriously cool," Eddie said.

JP twirled the staff in his hands, noticing that the faster he swung the staff, the larger the sparks were. "And Malika wasn't kidding when she said the more powerful the snake, the more powerful the staff. I think it has some kind of power of its own."

"What do you mean?"

"I'm not totally sure. But we're about to find out." JP whirled the staff in a circular fashion, like a lacrosse player cradling a ball. A small fireball appeared in the center of the swirl. As soon as he stopped, the fireball disappeared.

"Whoa," Eddie said. "I got an idea! Make one of those fireball things and then fling it."

JP swirled the staff to create another fireball, then cast the staff like a fishing rod. The ball of fire zipped through the woods before making an explosive collision with a tree trunk, leaving behind a charred black crater in the bark.

"That. Is. Freaking. Awesome!" Eddie said.

"Screw rocks," JP said. He held up his new toy. "We're hunting with this."

◆ ◆ ◆

Naomi and Antony forgot about their empty stomachs almost immediately when JP and Eddie returned. They couldn't care less about the six squirrels that came precooked and ready to serve. They were too enthralled by JP's new staff.

"What is that?" Naomi said.

"Only one of the most poisonous rattlesnakes in the country," JP said with a smirk.

"No way," Antony said.

"Way," Eddie said. "And it shoots fireballs."

Malika didn't share the others' excitement. "You should not have taken that," she said. "You are not ready."

"Doesn't the fact that I was able to control it," JP said, "kinda prove that I am ready?"

"There is more than just control," Malika said. "There is the personal restraint that comes with such power. You have yet to learn the very important practice of humility."

"Then teach us how to practice humility," JP said, "after I'm done practicing with this." He twirled his staff and shot off a small fireball into the sky.

"That is not how it works," Malika said.

"Come on," JP said. "Make some vessels. I wanna see how many I can take down."

"No," Malika said firmly. "You need to slow down. You are not—"

JP didn't let her finish. "Enough of the 'I'm not ready.' You should be happy I can do this," he said. "If anything, it just shows how great of a teacher you are."

Malika was about to respond, but stopped when she heard screaming off in the distance. It sounded like someone was launching an attack. She and the orphans stiffened as they tried to place the yelling, which grew louder and louder.

"What is that?" Naomi said.

"I have no idea," JP said.

"I think it's Charlie?" Antony said.

"What the heck is he doing?" Eddie said.

Seconds later, Charlie burst through the woods and into the clearing, his face beaming. He stopped, let out a primal howl, and pounded his chest like Tarzan.

The other orphans knew better than to let Charlie's energetic arrival surprise them—surprise was nothing more than your thoughts removing you from the moment—but they were still young trainees and couldn't help but be somewhat shocked by the confidence he exuded. It was such a stark contrast to the Charlie they'd last seen, the Charlie they'd come to know.

Charlie continued his sprint to the group. "Toss me a staff," he said as he came to a stop.

The other orphans just stood there, still in awe.

Charlie looked to JP and Antony, the only ones holding staffs. "Come on. Toss it!" he demanded. JP and Antony instinctively flung their staffs at the same time. Charlie wasn't the least bit fazed when both staffs transformed into snakes as they floated through the air in his direction. The same couldn't be said for the others. Their jaws bottomed out as they watched Charlie reach his hands to receive the snakes.

Charlie was so determined that he didn't notice their reactions. Nor did he hear Antony shout, "No!" Charlie just kept his eyes focused on the snakes as they landed in each of his palms and, in bright explosions of golden and ruby-colored light, transformed into staff form. He raised the staffs high, like Moses splitting the Red Sea, and looked up to the heavens. He closed his eyes and inhaled deeply, calming his excitement and pulling himself closer to the present moment.

It didn't take heightened senses for Charlie to figure out that something was amiss. While he hadn't anticipated any particular reaction to his feat, the silence was more than unexpected. He slowly opened his eyes to find anxious looks on the faces of the other orphans. He glared back. "What?"

They didn't respond, afraid their voices might trigger something. Afraid that they might cause Charlie to lose focus.

Charlie studied their faces. Their concern had no effect on him; his will and belief were too strong. That is, until he saw Naomi. The panicked look in her eyes was enough to plant the smallest seed of doubt in his mind. That was all it took. He lost control of his breath and his mind wandered. Almost immediately, he felt one of the staffs turn back into a slick and scaly snake.

Naomi's eyes went even wider. "Watch out!" she shouted.

Charlie heard Naomi's warning, followed by a soft rattling. He turned his attention toward the snake in his raised hand. The rattler let out a vicious hiss, its razor-sharp fangs exposed and dripping with venom, before sinking them into his wrist.

The staff in Charlie's other hand transformed back into a garter snake. His arms fell to his sides, and his hands unclenched, releasing both of the serpents.

The garter dropped to the ground, while the rattler hung on, determined to infuse Charlie with as much poison as possible. The rattler didn't let up until it sensed the orphans moving in to assist their friend. It quickly retracted its fangs, freeing itself, and stealthily slithered away just as soon as it touched down on the grass.

Charlie swayed as the venom began to take hold of him.

"Are you all right?" Antony said as he steadied Charlie, grabbing him by the shoulders.

Charlie's eyes rolled into the back of his head. His body went limp, slipped through Antony's grasp, and crashed to the earth in a heap.

CHAPTER
THIRTY-THREE

"FIND THE RATTLESNAKE!" Malika shouted. "We need it to save him." She knelt down to tend to Charlie while the rest of the orphans scattered about the clearing, searching for the rattlesnake that had disappeared as soon as it hit the grass.

"I got it!" Eddie exclaimed as he held up a staff.

Only there was no red aura.

"That's just the garter," Naomi said.

"Dammit," Eddie said, and then tossed the staff.

"Keep searching," Malika said.

Antony scanned the area. He got a visual of the snake's rattler just before it disappeared into some brush on the edge of the woods. "Over there!" he said, simultaneously pointing and breaking into a sprint in the direction of the snake.

When Antony got to the brush where the snake had vanished, it wasn't anywhere to be seen. Naomi, Eddie, and JP quickly joined him, huffing and puffing.

"Where'd it go?" Eddie asked.

"I don't know," Antony said. "We need to flush it out."

The orphans furiously overturned rocks and logs in a desperate attempt to startle the snake from its hiding spot.

"Be mindful," Antony reminded the crew. "We gotta use all of our senses."

The others followed Antony's recommendation, searching with as much haste and attention as possible. Naomi was about to flip over another log when she was greeted with a hiss. But she knew right away that the snake wasn't hiding under the log. She could tell by the ensuing rattle that it was directly behind her. "I think I found it," she said. "Or it found me."

The others stopped what they were doing. They spotted the snake just a few feet behind Naomi. It had her cornered in a cluster of trees and was well within its striking distance.

"Don't move," Antony said. He grabbed two sticks and slapped them together to get the rattlesnake's attention.

The snake craned its head toward Antony. It flicked its tongue and whipped its rattle. A faint smile crossed the serpent's mouth, as if to say it relished the challenge. The snake made no noise to tip off its assault; it simply shot off toward Antony, and launched itself toward his leg.

Antony swiped his hand down to block the attack like a hockey goalie protecting the five-hole. The snake went up a golden explosion as it turned into a staff. Antony went to the ground with the weapon in hand and screaming in pain, "Ah!"

"Are you all right?" Eddie asked. "Did it get you?"

Antony winced as he examined himself. There were two fang holes in his jeans, but his leg was completely fine, aside from the quickly growing welt. "No, I'm good," Antony said, shaking off the discomfort. "The damn thing just nailed me in the shin."

"Well, then get up and let's go!" Naomi said.

Antony nodded, hopped to his feet, and then led the charge with a limp as they made a mad dash back toward the clearing and Charlie.

By the time they returned, Charlie was drenched in sweat. His hand and wrist had doubled in size and continued to swell with each passing second.

"What do I do?" Antony asked Malika.

"You must use the staff to suck out the poison," she said.

"How do I do that?"

"Believe that you can do it, and it will become reality."

Antony held the staff over the raw puncture marks on Charlie's wrist. He took a deep breath in, exhaled even deeper, and focused his mind.

The tip of the staff transformed into a wooden likeness of the snake's head, with its mouth stretched wide and fangs extended. Tiny waves began to roll down Charlie's arm like a helicopter was landing on his skin. The ripples came from both ends of his arm. Starting at his shoulder and fingertips, they grew in size as they came to a head at the bite. The skin around the bite tugged away from the bone until it released two golf-ball-sized globs of venom, one from each of the incision marks. The orbs floated from the wound for a second before being absorbed by the staff.

Eddie patted Antony on the back. "Great job, brother."

Antony nodded.

"Now you must cauterize the wound to prevent infection," Malika said.

"Same instructions as before, just believe?" Antony asked.

"Yes. It should not take much effort, either."

Antony kept the staff away from Charlie, just to be safe. As he imagined making a fire, the ruby tip of the staff began to pulse, brighter and brighter, like a fire iron that had been left in the flames too long.

"Scale it back a little," Malika said.

"That's what I was thinking," Antony said. He narrowed his eyes. The pulses dimmed and slowed.

"Perfect."

Antony held the flame to Charlie's wrist. The others cringed as Charlie's skin sizzled like bacon on a hot stove. A couple seconds later, the crackling faded and Antony removed the staff. Charlie's wound had been replaced by a large black scab that covered all of his wrist and most of the back of his hand.

"That looks even worse than before," Antony said.

"And it's still pretty swollen," Eddie said.

"There was an incredibly large volume of venom," Malika said. "It will most likely take a day for all of the swelling to go down. And then a couple more days before he fully recovers. But it all depends how quickly he can recover mentally."

"But he's gonna be okay, right?" Naomi said.

"Yes. Right now he just needs rest." Malika hoisted Charlie up on her own and carried him inside the church.

The rest of the orphans remained outside in the clearing.

"Now that Charlie's okay," JP said, "we should probably eat

quick and then get back to training. Antony, you wanna hook me up with my staff so I can I can give it a run?"

"Are you kidding me?" Antony said.

"No. Why?"

Antony shook his head. "Malika said we aren't ready for it. And what just happened made that pretty damn clear." He heaved the staff like a javelin. It flew through the clearing and well into the woods.

"Don't you think that was a little unnecessary?" JP said.

"Not at all. Unnecessary was giving the rattlesnake to Charlie. You almost killed him."

"That was an accident," JP said, taking issue with the accusation. "The only reason I tossed it to him was 'cause he told me to. He came in all screaming. I was caught off-guard."

"We were all caught off-guard," Naomi said.

"What do you think, Eddie?" JP asked.

Eddie tilted his head and shrugged in agreement. It was true.

JP continued, "I obviously wouldn't have given it to him if I was thinking and had remembered it was a rattlesnake."

Antony didn't say a word. He just stared at JP.

"What? You don't believe me?" JP said, growing even more agitated.

Antony kept his mouth shut.

JP threw his hands in the air. "You know what? I don't care if you don't. It was an accident."

"Breathe," Malika said as she exited the church and attempted to throw cold water on the argument that had escalated in her absence and quickly become a heated exchange.

"No," JP said. "This is ridiculous. I'd rather consciously not calm down right now. I'm genuinely sorry that Charlie got hurt, but the only thing clear to me is that he's still way behind the rest of us. Now it's gonna take him a week to get better and who knows how long to catch up. It'll probably take him at least two weeks to be ready. That's at a minimum. In that time, who knows what could happen. The Beasts could steal the souls of hundreds of other kids' parents, or even worse, launch their attack on Heaven. We can either start saving our parents and the world, or we can just keep waiting here."

"We're not just waiting," Antony said, "we're growing."

"And how much more do you actually think we need to grow? Because it almost seems to me like you're trying to keep us here. Why? Don't you wanna save your dad?"

"Don't even go there," Antony said, getting in JP's face.

"Seriously," JP said, not backing down. "Do you have some other agenda? 'Cause all I wanna do is save my parents."

Eddie slid in between JP and Antony, separating them. "That's all any of us want," Eddie said.

"I'm not convinced," JP said.

"If Malika says we aren't ready," Antony said, "then we aren't ready."

"She doesn't know everything," JP said. "She doesn't even know when the Beasts are gonna attack."

"He's right," Naomi said. "We know we can kill them now. We're just wasting time."

"I say we draw straws and see whose parents we save first," JP said. "When Charlie is ready, he and Malika can join us. What do you think, Eddie?"

"I don't know," Eddie said. "I mean, it's not a bad idea."

"No, it's not a bad idea," Antony said. "It's a terrible idea."

"Why don't you at least wait until you draw before you make up your mind?" JP said. He plucked four long blades of grass from the ground and then split the bottom of one of the pieces. "Split grass wins. Who wants to go first?"

Naomi turned to Eddie and Antony, gauging their interest. Neither of them moved a muscle, and neither did she.

"Fine," JP said, "I will." He grabbed one of the blades and held it up. The bottom was intact. "Looks like it's not my parents. Antony?" He offered his hand for Antony to draw from.

"I'm not drawing anything," Antony said.

"Fine," JP said, "I'll draw for you." He pulled another blade. The bottom was intact. "I guess it's not Antony's dad, either. We're down to a fifty-fifty shot. Who wants to make the pick? Eddie? You know you do."

"Ladies first," Eddie said.

Naomi looked to Eddie and Antony, then to the two blades of grass protruding from JP's clenched fist, and then back to Antony and Eddie.

"We're stronger when we stick together," Antony said.

"I know," Naomi said. "I'm hoping we stick together." She grabbed a piece of grass and held up her selection. The bottom of the blade was still intact.

JP opened his hand so that the last remaining piece fell into his palm and displayed the tiny tear at the bottom for all to see. "Looks like you were right, Eddie. Ladies will be first," he said with a smirk. "Assuming you're down, we'll start by saving your mother. What do you say?"

CHAPTER
THIRTY-FOUR

"THIS IS BULLSHIT," Eddie said. "It shouldn't be like this."
He and Antony sat on the church steps, watching as JP and
Naomi moved one of the bench seats from the campfire and
back into the van.

"I know," Antony agreed.

After Eddie had turned down the offer to save his mother, in part because Antony held firm that he wouldn't leave
without Charlie, Naomi and JP redrew, with Naomi selecting the winning blade of grass. None of Eddie's pleading had
been able to convince them to stay.

Malika exited the church, a couple medium-sized cloth
pouches in tow, and stood next to Eddie and Antony. "Both
Charlie's pulse and temperature are down. It appears he may
have turned a corner."

"Finally, some good news," Antony said.

"I get the whole free-will thing," Eddie said to Malika,

"but you don't have to make their decision easier by driving them to the train station."

"It would make no difference if I drove them or if I did not," Malika said. "They have made up their minds. They have made their choice and decided to leave."

"Yeah, but still," Eddie said.

"But still, nothing," Malika said. "The both of you must let go of any feelings of disappointment you harbor. Acknowledge them and release them."

Antony and Eddie took deep breaths and exhaled. While it was obvious that much, if not all, of Eddie's weight was lifted, Antony appeared to hold onto his. He remained silent as JP and Naomi joined them at the church steps.

"I think we're good to go," JP said.

"Before we leave," Malika said, "I found these inside." She handed both JP and Naomi their own pouches. "They shall work perfectly for carrying your serpents."

Naomi hefted her pouch. The contents wriggled around. "I'm assuming there's a garter already in there."

"Yes, there is," Malika said. "And if you should deem it necessary to carry rattlesnakes or anything equally venomous, which I do not doubt that you will, I would recommend using something sturdier than cloth, preferably leather."

"Thanks. I definitely will," JP said. He looked to Naomi. "I guess that's it, right?"

"Yeah," Naomi said. "Although, I feel like I should say goodbye to Charlie first."

"He just fell back asleep," Malika said. "It would be best to leave him as such."

"I don't need to wake him. I'm pretty sure I saw some loose-leaf paper inside. I can just write him a note. It's at least better than nothing."

"That should be fine." Malika stepped aside.

Naomi cut in between Antony and Eddie and disappeared inside the church. All of the others stayed back.

An awkwardly quiet minute passed before Eddie finally attempted to defuse the tension.

"You know, it's not too late for you guys to change your minds," he said.

"It's funny you mention that. Because I was just about to say the same thing to you guys," JP said. He chuckled, laughing at his own joke.

"Fair enough," Eddie said. "So, how should we get a hold of you guys when we're ready?"

"Since none of us have phones, email is probably the easiest," JP said, and then gave them his address, which was just his name and a few numbers. "Hopefully, it doesn't take you guys too long to get out of the woods. Otherwise, I might have to save your parents for you." He looked at Antony while he said the last part.

Antony stood up from the steps. "Yeah, well, hopefully you guys don't end up in over your heads," he said. "And then we have to come save you."

"Ha!" JP said, feigning laughter. "Now, that'll be the day. I'd bet it's more likely you guys never even leave here."

"We'll just have to wait and see."

Naomi exited the church, her return interrupting the escalation. She nodded solemnly to Malika. "You were right," she said. "He was out pretty hard."

"Sleep is his best medicine," Malika said.

"Hopefully, it starts kicking in soon."

"It will. But his full recovery will take time."

"Speaking of time," JP said, "we might as well get going. I'd be willing to bet the trains don't run that late around here." He gestured to Naomi. "Are you good to go now?"

Naomi nodded.

They all said their goodbyes, some more genuine than others, and then continued to the van as a group. JP and Naomi climbed into the van and shut the door.

"The train station is about a half hour away," Malika said to Antony and Eddie, "but I think it would be best if I wait there with them, so it might be a couple hours before I return. However, I will leave you with a little something to keep you occupied while I am gone." She scooped two large mounds of dirt and blew them into the wind. A slew of miniature tornadoes swept across the clearing, depositing sparring vessels in their wake. When it was all said and done, the vessels stood in a tight formation, six per row and ten rows deep, like some imposing IRS agent versions of the terra-cotta warriors.

"Those dudes look like they're here to party," Eddie said. "I can't wait to show them a good time."

Malika grinned, and then started for van. As she made her way, she transformed into her angelic self.

"On second thought," Eddie shouted to her, "I could always ride along with you. You know, to keep you company. The vessels will always be here when we get back."

"Thank you for the offer," Malika said, "but I will be more

than fine." She hopped in the driver's seat, shut the door, and fired up the engine. Before pulling away, she lowered the window and reminded Antony to acknowledge and release one last time.

Antony nodded in acceptance. His nod turned to a shake as he watched the van drive off.

Eddie patted him on the back. "They're gone. Nothing you can do now except just listening to what Malika said."

Antony let out a heavy sigh, closed his eyes, and cycled through a handful of inhales and exhales.

Eddie continued his thought, "Of course, I wish Malika would've said she needed company. I'd be lost in those eyes right now, but that's another story."

Antony was just beginning to exhale and exploded with laughter. "You are completely ridiculous." He smiled, no longer burdened by his feelings.

"No. I'm the tortoise. Slow and steady wins the race."

Antony cut to the campfire. "You're gonna have to shed your tortoise ways if we're gonna get through those guys," he said as he retrieved a snake from an old steel barrel they'd found behind the church and were using to house the serpents, and then tossed it to Eddie.

"Don't worry," Eddie said as he caught the snake. "I can turn it on and off." He transformed the snake into a staff.

"Good." Antony pulled two snakes from the barrel and transformed them both. "Because right now, it's time for some action." He twirled the staffs with his wrist before catching them under his armpits. He swept his staffs across the first row of vessels, challenging them.

"Let's do this," Eddie said with a grin as he and Antony stepped toward the center of the clearing and the six vessels that were on their way to meet them.

◆ ◆ ◆

A couple hours later, Antony and Eddie had battled their way through nearly fifty of the sixty vessels, including the five that they were currently engaged with, which had been whittled down from ten.

"Where is everyone?" Antony heard from an unexpected voice. The question caught him by surprise. He turned his head for a split second to find Charlie leaning against the railing as he struggled to make his way down the church steps. He was about to respond to Charlie's question when he picked up a whooshing sound, the same sound a very large fist makes when it flies through the air. Rightfully so, the fist took priority.

Using the sound of the fist to estimate its location and trajectory, Antony flipped his head backwards to avoid contact. The vessel's knuckles barely grazed the crest of his forehead as its fist flew by.

"Give us a minute," Antony shouted back to Charlie as he popped his head back up. He nimbly sidestepped and swung both of his staffs, one low and the other high. The low shot was just a fake. The high shot was a bull's-eye, or more accurately, third eye. His staff pierced the vessel's forehead, turning his opponent to dust.

After some acrobatics and swift strikes from both Eddie and Antony, they'd worked their way down to the last remaining vessel. With the two-on-one advantage, they closed in from opposite angles.

"Wanna wrap this up with a little *Karate Kid* action?" Eddie said to Antony.

"Sure," Antony said. "I'll be Johnny."

"Then I guess I'll be Daniel-san." Eddie raised both of his arms and one leg as if he were about to pull off a crane kick.

The vessel's head swung back and forth, unsure which of the two teens to focus on.

"Over here," Antony said, getting the vessel's attention. He swung high on the vessel. But this time, high was the fake. When the vessel blocked the staff with his arm, he dropped to his knee and spun around, swinging his other staff and sweeping the vessel's legs.

Eddie moved quickly on the grounded vessel, planting his staff in the vessel's head. "There's your body bag," he said as the vessel combusted. He withdrew his staff and twirled it expertly.

"Nice work," Charlie said, attempting to clap and keep himself steady at the same time. He quickly discovered that his legs weren't quite strong enough and began to sway.

Antony rushed to the church steps and grabbed hold of Charlie's arm, catching him just as he was about to go down.

"Thanks," Charlie said.

"Of course," Antony said.

Charlie examined his injured wrist. "What happened?"

"You don't remember? Eddie said.

"I remember turning the snakes to staffs, but that's it."

Eddie explained to Charlie how he and JP had found the rattlesnake in the woods, how JP had accidentally tossed it to him, and how it'd turned back and bitten him.

"You need to get your rest," Antony added. "Malika said that rest and your mind-set will be the biggest determining factors in how fast you recover."

"Don't worry about me," Charlie said. "My mind-set has never been stronger. You guys saw that I controlled both snakes, right?"

"Of course," Antony said. "Everyone saw it."

"Yeah," Eddie chimed in, "I was freaking out partly because I knew it was a rattlesnake, but mostly because you totally owned it."

Charlie smiled. Bite and all, his belief in himself hadn't wavered one bit. "I knew I could do it," he said. "I just had a split second of doubt when I saw the look on Naomi's face. But like Malika said, that's all it takes."

"Yeah," Eddie agreed. "That's all it takes."

"Speaking of Naomi and Malika, where are they? And JP, too? Did they go out into the woods or something?"

Antony and Eddie shared a look. Antony shrugged and then broke the news about how Naomi and JP had left to save Naomi's parents.

Charlie nodded. "That stinks, but I understand why they would wanna do that. We all want to save our parents."

"Yeah," Antony agreed. "Well, we're glad you're feeling better, but you really need to get more rest and heal up. We need you at full strength as soon as possible."

"Fine," Charlie said. "Just let me see one of your staffs."

"You might be too weak still," Antony said. "I don't want you to get down on yourself."

"Don't worry about me. Just let me see it." Charlie extended his hand.

The glare in Charlie's eyes made it clear that he wouldn't be backing down. Antony reluctantly handed over his staff, which instantly turned back into a snake as soon as it settled in Charlie's grasp.

Charlie narrowed his eyes, concentrating his focus. But it appeared to be no use. The snake continued to wrap itself around his good wrist.

"You're still really tired," Antony said, trying to keep Charlie from letting even more doubt enter his mind.

"Yeah," Eddie agreed. "Your energy has to be affected or something."

"No excuses. It is what it is," Charlie said. "Maybe I'm not as strong as I thought I was"—a slight grin began to cross his face—"or maybe I'm just messing with you guys."

The snake flipped back into staff form in a flash, startling Antony and Eddie. Antony shook his head as the smirking Charlie handed the staff back to him. "You're a clown," he said. "You know that, right? Now go get some rest."

"Okay," Charlie said, still chuckling to himself. "Just make sure to leave some of those guys for me. I don't want you two to have all the fun."

"Don't worry about them. There's plenty more where they came from."

"Yeah, and in no time, you'll be all healed up," Eddie said. "And we'll be back with Naomi and JP, taking on the real thing and saving our parents."

"For sure," Charlie said with a grin. He started for the church door, got a couple feet, and then stopped. "Wait a second," he said, the wheels in his mind still turning. "How are JP and Naomi gonna find the Beast that took her parents' souls? They don't even know who to look for."

"Naomi seemed pretty confident," Antony said. "She must have some clue."

"When she first emailed me, she said she had no idea," Charlie said. "The only way they could find who was responsible is if they cross-referenced her parents' associations with the contact spreadsheet."

"But you still have the USB drive, right?" Eddie said.

"Yeah. Of course. It's in my pocket." Charlie patted his pants pocket for confirmation. He got a confirmation, but not the one he expected. His faced dropped.

"What's wrong?" Eddie said.

"It's not in my pocket," Charlie said. "It's gone."

Antony and Eddie shared in Charlie's worry.

"Maybe it fell out when Malika was carrying you inside," Antony said. "It could be by your bed."

Charlie hobbled, as fast as he could, back into the church. Antony and Eddie followed.

Charlie dropped to his knees by the pew where he'd been sleeping. He scoured the surrounding area. "It's not here," he said. "It's not freaking here!"

"Well, where could it be?" Eddie said. "When was the last time you had it?"

"I don't know. I know for a fact that I had it right before I came back from the woods today."

"I bet JP took it," Antony said. "It had to have been him."

"It couldn't have been him," Eddie said. "He never had a chance. We were with him the whole—" Eddie stopped short, a realization dawning on his face. He knew exactly where it was. "Naomi has it. Remember? She came in here by herself."

"You're right," Antony agreed. "She said she was gonna leave Charlie a goodbye note."

They searched every inch of the church for the note, hoping that the letter would contain some much needed answers. But just like the flash drive, Naomi's note was nowhere to be found. It'd merely been a lie, an excuse to be alone with Charlie so that she could take possession of the USB drive.

CHAPTER
THIRTY-FIVE

JP GLANCED AT NAOMI as they sat in the backseat of the parked van. He shot her an uneasy look. Naomi responded by narrowing her eyes and aiming them in Malika's direction.

Malika caught a glimpse of the two of them in the rearview mirror; their heads immediately darted in opposite directions. She kept her focus on Naomi for a few more seconds before returning her gaze to the otherwise empty parking lot for the Truckee Train Station.

Truckee, an old frontier tourist destination that was currently in the middle of its post-summer and pre-winter lull, had been made famous by the Donner Party. The town's log cabin look-alike train station—located just a few miles from where much of the party had tragically met their fate—ran just two trains a day: one westbound train in the early morning, and one eastbound train in the afternoon that continued all the way to Chicago.

While JP had never been there before, it wasn't Naomi's first time waiting at the station. She'd actually passed through on her way out to San Francisco. She recalled it being the only stop where no passengers had gotten on or off of the train. The small stretch of downtown had reminded her of something out of a Western movie, the kind of place where two angry cowboys might settle their poker debts in the street. That is, if the town even had enough people to play a game of poker.

The surrounding area had appeared just as dead from Naomi's train window as it had when they pulled up in the van a little more than an hour before. Most of that following hour, minus the few minutes it'd taken to purchase their tickets from the electronic kiosk, had been spent inside the van, in an uncomfortable silence, as they waited for their train to arrive.

After a minute or so, Naomi finally spoke up. "I, uh, need to go to the bathroom," she said as she started to get up from her seat.

"Yeah," JP said, following her lead. "And I should probably try to get ahold of my parents one more time."

They both climbed out of the van.

"You know, it's not a big deal if you wanna head back," JP said to Malika as he stood in the van's sliding doorway. "The train will be here pretty soon. We should be fine."

"It is no trouble," Malika said. "And I would prefer to stay and make sure that everything is all right."

"Suit yourself," JP said with a shrug. He closed the door, and then he and Naomi headed in their respective directions.

◆ ◆ ◆

Naomi finished washing her hands in the bathroom sink. She dried them with a paper towel and then retrieved the flash drive from her pocket. She stared at the drive as she held it in her palm. She glanced at herself in the bathroom mirror, sighed, and then turned back to the drive.

Things hadn't gone how she'd expected them to go, but there was nothing she could do about it now. What was done was done, and she had no regrets. She knew that she needed the drive and the information it contained if she was going to save her parents. And that was all that she was concerned with. While Malika's lessons had taught her a lot, the last seven years had taught her just as much. The most important lesson being that she needed to look out for herself above anyone else. She and JP seemed to share that same mentality, which was a big reason why they'd hit it off so well, and why she'd finally decided to let her guard down and let him in.

A knock at the door rattled Naomi from her thoughts. She quickly pocketed the drive before responding, "Who is it?"

"It's me," JP said from the other side of the bathroom door. "Is it okay to come in?"

"Yeah."

JP entered. He scanned the facilities. "This is a lot dumpier than I'd imagined a women's bathroom to be. Aside from the lack of urinals, it's basically the same as the men's room."

"This bathroom is more of the exception than the rule. It's usually all flowers and potpourri," Naomi said with a smirk. "So, did you get ahold of your adoptive parents this time?"

"Yeah. They were freaking out when they answered. And just as a word of caution, they don't really like when people call them that."

"Oh, sorry about that."

"Don't worry. It doesn't bother me. That's what they are. But maybe don't say it when you meet them." He smiled to put her at ease.

"I won't," Naomi said and returned the smile.

JP and Naomi's plan was to take the train to Chicago. There they would stay with his parents for a night or two before continuing on to New Jersey. What they did there would depend on what they were able to discover from on the drive.

Naomi's eyes shifted back to the bathroom door. "I wish Malika would just leave already."

"Tell me about it," JP said. "I told her she can go like a hundred times, but she keeps refusing."

"I feel like she's watching us." Naomi lowered her voice. "Do you think she knows anything about, you know?" She pointed to her pocket, indicating the drive.

"No. She would've said something if she did"

"You're probably right," Naomi sighed. "This all would've been easier if everyone would've just come with us."

"I worked on Eddie as hard as I could," JP said. "He was close. I thought I had him convinced."

"I thought you did, too," Naomi said. "And I did my best with Antony. He just wouldn't budge. It seriously seemed like he was trying to keep us there for some reason. I don't know."

"He acted like we were safer there, but we weren't. We were just sitting ducks."

"Yeah," Naomi agreed. She checked her watch. "Well, at least the train will be here in eighteen minutes. Once we're on it, we should be in the clear. Until then, I say we sit in the van, play it safe, and just keep quiet."

JP nodded. "We could always hang out here a little longer, too. If that's cool with you. I'm pretty sure we can have a lot more fun here than waiting in the van with Malika." He grabbed Naomi by the hips and pulled her close, their eyes locking.

Naomi blinked rapidly, unable to conceal her startle. She knew exactly what he was implying. "Are you serious? You really wanna make out in this bathroom?"

"It'd obviously be better if it had the potpourri smell to help set the mood, but I'll make out anywhere I can." He ran his tongue over his lips to wet them and then grinned.

Naomi subconsciously licked her lips and smiled back. She was starting to close her eyes when she caught what sounded like several sets of tires screeching to a stop. Her eyes shot open. "What was that?" she said as she quickly broke away from JP.

"I have no idea," he said, completely caught off-guard.

Naomi retrieved her snake from the pouch Malika had given her and transformed it into a staff. Before JP could get a word out, Naomi took off. He readied his staff and then rushed out of the bathroom door after her.

JP caught up with Naomi just as they rounded the corner for the front porch of the train station. They both spotted Malika, her wings beginning to unravel from her back as she sprinted up the steps toward them.

Naomi looked to the street, where six blacked-out suvs were parked with open doors, suited and sunglassed Beasts spilling out of each of them. There were at least thirty in total, three of which she recognized as the second team from Charlie's house. The three were charging toward Malika, and gaining fast. Just as he had at Charlie's house, the Beast with the bushy mustache led the pack, with the other two just a step behind.

Naomi's eyes darted to their only other exit option, but it already had its own cadre of Beasts covering it. There was nowhere to run. They were effectively surrounded, with the swarm of Beasts converging from all angles.

Naomi turned to JP, who looked surprisingly unprepared, like he was trapped in some kind of daze and his thoughts were back in the bathroom. "Snap out of it!" she ordered, elbowing him in the stomach for an added jolt.

"Sorry," JP said, his mind still noticeably distracted.

"We're gonna have to fight our way out of this," Naomi said, getting into a warrior's stance.

JP followed suit.

The Beasts were only a couple arms' lengths from Malika when she finally finished unleashing her wings. She flapped her angelic appendages to give herself an added burst of speed and create distance from her pursuers. With another flap, she achieved liftoff and pulled even further away from the Beasts. She coasted toward JP and Naomi and grabbed them by their shirts.

"What are you doing?" Naomi said. "We can take them."

"It is too risky," Malika said. "Hold on!"

JP and Naomi each grabbed Malika's wrists with their free hands while still holding their staffs with their other hands.

Malika gave her wings a powerful flap, and the trio shot up and away from the porch just as they were about to be met by the storming Beasts.

The mustachioed Beast made a diving attempt to catch them but was only able to get a hold of the heel of Naomi's shoe, causing her Vans slip-on to slide off.

"I'll be back for that and more," Naomi shouted to the Beast, watching as he tossed her shoe. She then glanced up at Malika as they flew away, keeping a consistent altitude of twenty feet above the main street. "Thanks," she said with a grin, grateful for the fact that Malika had insisted on staying to watch them and, in turn, saved them.

Malika looked down at Naomi and started to smile back, but her mouth never reached even half of its full upright turn before she was forced to trade her smile for a much less joyous expression. The muscles and veins in her neck protruded in pained constriction.

All of the excitement instantly vanished from Naomi's face. She watched with dread as Malika's skin began to crack open like dried-out clay, a blinding white light escaping from the spreading fault lines. Malika's eyes turned into two tiny headlights set on high beam; Naomi was forced to close hers.

Naomi didn't witness what happened next, but the only logical conclusion she could make was that it was some kind of explosion. The light Malika emitted grew even more intense and rendered Naomi's eyelids completely useless. It was followed by a violent force, which reminded Naomi of a warm hurricane wind, and only served to accelerate her and JP's rapid free-falls back to Earth.

JP and Naomi crashed to the ground with heavy thuds. Their bodies skidded across the gravel pavement, tumbling many times over down the main street before finally coming to an exhausting stop more than a hundred yards beyond the train station.

When Naomi reopened her eyes, all she could see were white spots. With her clothes ripped and body scratched like an old DVD, she struggled to pick herself up off of the ground. She wasn't sure what, exactly, had caused Malika to go up in a brilliant flash. But she was regrettably certain that Malika was gone. Whatever the Beasts had done, they'd killed Malika. No sooner did this realization shoot across her mind than she also noticed that her staff had turned back into a snake. She attempted to will it back into staff form, but the serpent simply refused, and continued wrapping itself around her wrist.

CHAPTER
THIRTY-SIX

NAOMI KNEW THAT she couldn't let her emotions take over, especially not at that moment. She had more immediate issues: the thirty Beasts that would be on her and JP any second, and the flash blindness that was still causing her eyes to go in and out of focus. She took a deep breath to calm herself, acknowledged her thoughts, and released them. Almost immediately after her attention returned to the present, her snake transformed back into a staff.

"Are you okay, JP?" Naomi called out as she simultaneously wielded her staff to fend off any approaching attackers and attempted to blink away her clouded vision. The only response she received was wounded laughter. "JP? Is that you?" she said, blinking harder. As her eyes finally focused, she discovered JP standing ten feet in front of her. His face was bloodied and his body was scraped; however, none of his ailments seemed to damper his mood. He looked downright giddy.

"Yeah," JP said, still chuckling. "It's me. And I've never been better."

Naomi didn't have time to question how JP could be so content given their situation. Her eyes and attention had moved on to the three familiar Beasts who were now creeping up behind JP, seemingly unbeknownst to him.

"Behind you!" Naomi shouted as she swung her staff, launching an attack on the mustachioed Beast.

Much to Naomi's surprise, JP blocked her strike, swung her staff around in a full circle, and pinned it to the ground. "That won't be necessary," he said.

"What's going on?" Naomi said. "What are you doing?"

"Do I really need to spell it out for you?" JP noticed the bewilderment in her eyes and shook his head. "These gentlemen, and all of their friends, are with me."

As the reality of the situation set in, there was nothing Naomi could do to prevent the shock and confusion from running wild in her mind. It was even more damaging than Malika's death, but with a similar effect, causing her staff to return to snake form. Before she could even hope to remind herself to remain present, JP took advantage of his opportunity and cracked her across the wrist. A sharp pain shot up her arm; she reflexively opened her hand. Her snake fell to the ground and quickly slithered away.

The bearded Beast behind JP immediately moved in and restrained Naomi. "You used me," she screamed at JP, her wonder turning to rage. "You killed Malika! You bastard!"

"Breathe," JP said with a smirk. "Isn't that what she'd tell you if she were still here?"

"What about your parents?" The words barely left Naomi's mouth when she realized the answer to her own question. "You were lying. They aren't dead, are they?"

"To be honest," JP said, "I have no idea. My birth parents were just a couple careless teenagers that got pregnant. My adoptive parents are still alive. But they're just regular old nobodies. So was I, until I signed that contract. And guess what? I haven't regretted it for one second."

"You will now," Naomi said as she furiously attempted to free herself from her captor's clutches.

"She's a feisty one," the mustachioed Beast said in a thick Russian accent. "But not for much longer." His eyes began to burn through his dark sunglass lenses as he took a step toward Naomi.

JP swung his staff, stopping it inches away from the Beast's chest and keeping him at bay. "Not so fast. We might still need her. Were you able to complete the trace?"

The mustachioed Beast shook his head.

"Then it looks like she stays alive," JP said. "You can't set a good trap unless you have a little bait. And live bait is always better."

"Agreed," the mustachioed Beast said.

"Did you bring my other cell phone?"

The mustachioed Beast dug in his pocket, produced a cell phone, and handed it to JP.

JP dialed a number and then waited for the call to connect. He smiled as he listened to the voice on the other end. "It's great to hear your voice, too, Mr. Heins," he replied. "It took longer than I had hoped, but I had to wait for the right time to make my move. Where are you right now? I keep hearing a humming." He paced while he listened to Terry, an impish grin spread across his face. "Then I understand why you couldn't make it. I'm almost tempted to share the news with our friends. I'm sure they'd be excited to hear it."

Naomi wriggled one of her hands free and reached for JP. All she was able to get was a fistful of his shirt. She yanked it, ripping it open, before the bearded Beast subdued her again.

JP continued his conversation, unfazed. He listened for another moment before responding, "Of course. If you think that's best, I can try. And I'll let you know as soon as they are all taken care of." He hung up his phone. He turned his attention to re-buttoning his shirt, speaking to Naomi without looking at her. "That was an interesting call. I got some really big news, but I should probably save it for later." Not getting the reaction he'd desired or any reaction at all, JP stopped, his shirt still mostly open, and looked directly at Naomi.

Naomi had barely heard a word that JP had said. She was too busy staring at his exposed chest and the thick, branded scar directly over his heart. It was the same scar Malika had told them about: three sixes in a row. The mark of the Beast.

JP traced Naomi's gaze. "Pretty cool, right?" he said, sneering as he ran his fingers across the raised flesh.

Naomi said nothing. She just shot daggers with her eyes.

"Now you know the real reason I wanted to take things slow," JP said as he finished re-buttoning his shirt. "Oh, and before I forget." He reached into Naomi's pocket and retrieved the flash drive. He tossed it into the air and caught it with a cocky grin. "Thank you so much," he said, his voice full of false sincerity. "I couldn't have done this without your help. I really mean that."

"Screw you!" Naomi screamed.

"Maybe later," JP said, and then gestured to the Beast restraining Naomi.

The Beast gripped the muscle connecting her neck and shoulder and squeezed. The intense pain was so immediate that Naomi didn't even get the chance to scream before blacking out.

◆ ◆ ◆

"Come on, buddy. Wake up," Eddie said as he tapped Charlie on the cheek. Both he and Antony had been trying to rouse their friend for the past fifteen minutes to no avail. Eddie gave Charlie a few more gentle taps. They seemed to do the trick. Charlie's eyelids finally fluttered open.

Charlie's eyes wandered as he regained his bearings. He squinched his lids tightly to help wake himself up. "What happened?" he moaned.

"You passed out," Antony said. He helped Charlie sit up. "We were trying to figure out why Naomi would steal the drive, and then you just went down all of a sudden."

Charlie massaged his sternum.

"Are you okay?" Eddie said.

"I don't know," Charlie said, still rubbing his rib cage. "Something feels off. My chest is really tight, but at the same time, almost empty."

"I'm not a doctor, so I can't really help you there."

"You probably just need more rest," Antony said. "We'll help you back to your bed."

Antony and Eddie supported Charlie as he limped back to his pew. They were nearly there when they heard an unexpected buzzing and stopped.

"What is that?" Eddie said.

"I don't know," Charlie said.

Antony thought about it for a second, trying to place the familiar rattling, until he finally realized: "It's a phone." He left Charlie with Eddie and searched for the source while the buzzing continued.

Antony located the vibrating phone under the pew where JP had slept. He hesitantly swiped his finger across the shattered screen, uncertain if it would even answer the call or who was on the other end. The call connected and automatically went to speakerphone.

"Hello?" Antony said.

"Why, hello there," JP said over the speakerphone, with a smugness in his voice. "For a minute, I was worried this wasn't gonna work. I spent hours putting that phone back together in the woods, but I still wasn't able to use it to make any outgoing calls."

"Yeah, well, it worked. Congratulations. Now do us a favor and ask Naomi why she took the flash drive."

"She's actually indisposed at the moment, but I don't need to ask her. She took it because I told her to."

"You know, if you would've just asked," Eddie said as he helped Charlie down the aisle so that they could both join in the conversation, "we could've found a way to share the information. You guys didn't have to go behind our backs."

"Thanks for the kind offer, Edward, but I didn't actually

want the information. I just wanted to make sure that none of you had it. That's all. Now I have the drive and Naomi, too."

JP's words caught all of the others by surprise. They'd spent so much time speculating the details behind the missing drive. Was it Naomi's idea? Was it JP's? Were they working together? They'd asked themselves all those questions and many more; however, at no point during their spitballing did any of them suspect that JP had been actively working against them. And yet, it was now clear that he had been the whole time.

"Why?" Eddie said, still trying to process the answer that had eluded them.

Charlie asked himself the same question that Eddie had raised. Why? Why would JP sabotage them? Why would JP kidnap Naomi? JP. JP. JP. The name bounced around his head. Ever since he received JP's email, Charlie had accepted JP Sanchez to be his actual name, never considering that it might just be a nickname or trying to guess what the abbreviated initials stood for even once. But now that he knew JP had been playing them, he rightfully questioned everything JP had ever told him. It didn't take long for the truth to hit him. "James Podesky," he blurted out. "His real name is James Podesky. He's one of them."

"Bravo," JP said, clapping arrogantly for effect. "It looks like I might have underestimated you, Charlie. Of course, only by very little."

While JP was mildly impressed, Antony and Eddie were more confused than anything else. "How did you know that was his name?" Antony asked Charlie.

"I saw it on the contact list," Charlie said. "The only reason I remembered the name was because of his age. I should've seen it coming."

"No looking back, guys," JP said with a chuckle. "Remember, that's what Malika taught us."

"Where is she?" Eddie said. "Do you have her, too?"

"No. I don't. And I actually have no idea where she is. The last time I saw her, she was blowing up like a Fourth of July fireworks show. It was something to see. An angel's death is really quite beautiful."

The bomb that JP dropped left the others staring aimlessly in its aftermath. He'd done much more than just betray them; he'd severed their lifeline.

When the dust finally settled, Eddie was overcome with anger. "You son of a bitch!" he screamed into the phone. "I'm gonna kill you!"

JP burst into an uncontrollable fit of laughter.

"You won't be laughing much longer!" Eddie said.

Antony locked eyes with Eddie and put his hand on Eddie's chest to calm him down. Antony returned his attention to JP. "You said you still have Naomi," he said into the phone.

"I do," JP said.

"What do you want with her?"

"I want all of you to come save her. At the very least, I want you to try. I'll make it worth your while. If you're successful, I'll even throw in the flash drive, too."

"How do we know you haven't already killed her and destroyed the drive?" Charlie said.

"Look at you using the old bean. Good job, Charlie," JP said. "How's this? I'll let you talk to her."

Charlie, Antony, and Eddie listened over the phone as JP instructed one of his henchmen to get Naomi. They could hear her put up a fight. At first, she refused to speak. She opened up when JP informed her who was on the line.

"Don't trust him!" Naomi shouted. "It's—" Her voice was muted to a mumble, most likely by one of the Beast's hands.

"Well," JP said, jumping back on the line, "I bet you're all wondering what she was gonna say. Of course, some things are just better left unsaid. You got your proof of life. As for the flash drive, you'll just have to trust me when I say that I'd much rather have you see me destroy it in person. That way, I can watch all of the optimism disappear from your bodies. Then, one by one, your souls will follow."

"You're sick," Eddie said.

JP chuckled maniacally. "Well, that's just your opinion." After a second, his giggling petered out, and he continued in a most serious tone, "We're at the Truckee Train Station. You have until six o'clock tomorrow morning. If you're not here by then, you lose the drive and Naomi loses her soul."

"Wait," Charlie urged, just in case JP was about to hang up on them. "We might need more time. We don't have any idea how far away that is. It could be thirty miles or more."

"Yeah. And Charlie's still really banged up, it's gonna slow us down," Eddie added, hoping fact would aid their negotiation.

"Well, isn't that funny?" JP said. "That's what I've been telling you guys all along. Unfortunately, that's all the time you get. And you should consider yourselves lucky that you even get that. I was actually planning on surprising you, but the GPS receiver on the phone was broken, and these damn mountains made triangulating your location impossible. If not for that, I'd be coming to you instead of having you come to me."

"Don't worry about doing us any more favors," Antony said. "We'll be there."

"I'm glad to hear that, Antony. Because I have a friend with me who's just dying to meet you. Or maybe I should say you'll be dying to meet him. He said that after he takes your soul, you'll have all the time in the world to catch up with your father."

Antony's face froze from the news. He knew that it could only mean one thing. The Beast who had killed his father was with JP and would be waiting for them.

Before Antony could recover or even get a word out, JP cheerfully added, "Great chatting with you guys. Hopefully see you soon," and then hung up.

CHAPTER
THIRTY-SEVEN

THE INSIDE OF THE CHURCH was so quiet that it could've passed for outer space. Eddie and Charlie had shared a look to let each other know to remain silent and let Antony decide when he was ready to speak.

After a minute that felt more like an hour, Antony tossed the phone back onto the pew. "We gotta get moving," he said.

"Are you sure you wanna do this?" Eddie asked. "I mean, you realize it's just a trap, right?"

"It's not a trap. It's a challenge. We know there's gonna be a bunch of them, and not a lot of us."

"Yeah, by my count, I got two," Eddie said. He looked to Charlie and shrugged. "Sorry about that, but you don't exactly count right now."

"I'll be ready," Charlie said as he stood upright without the aid of the pew railing; however, his weakened body begged to differ and quickly gave way.

"Save your energy," Antony said. "We've most likely got a long walk ahead of us."

Charlie swallowed his pride and sat back down.

"Do you really trust JP to hold up his end of the bargain?" Eddie said. "He killed Malika."

"No," Antony said. "I don't trust him at all. I'm sure he has something up his sleeve. But if we don't go, Naomi dies for sure, and we'll definitely lose the drive." He took a deep breath, continued, "I might never get a better chance to save my dad. I need to take it. Even if the odds are against us, which they definitely are. I believe in myself."

"The odds have always been against us," Charlie said, "but we can't control the odds, only our actions."

Charlie explained the serenity mantra to the guys. He had them repeat it so that they could truly focus on just the things that they could control. He also relayed the secret that Malika had told him, which helped give Eddie the little boost he needed to regain his full confidence that they could conquer the task before them.

"All right, I'm in," Eddie said. "I believe in myself."

"I do, too," Charlie said. "I believe in myself, and I'll support you guys any way that I can."

"I know you will," Antony said. "Now let's bring it in." He put his hand in for a cheer to break their little huddle.

Charlie laid his hand on top of Antony's, and then Eddie added his to the pile. "So, what exactly are we cheering to?" Eddie asked. "And don't say team. We're better than that."

They all thought about it for a brief moment.

"The Orphans?" Charlie suggested with a shrug.

Antony and Eddie considered the name.

"I dig it," Antony said, nodding his head.

"That is exactly what we are," Eddie added.

"All right, then. Here we go, Orphans on three."

They all recited the cheer, and then threw up their hands.

◆ ◆ ◆

The clock was ticking, but Antony and Eddie knew that they couldn't concentrate on their dwindling amount of time. They had to remain mindful, focused on the moment. There were plenty of matters that they needed to address before they could even set off on their way.

Their first order of business was dealing with the leftover vessels. While the vessels had shown themselves to be rather harmless on their own, waiting patiently in the clearing in Antony and Eddie's absence, the guys knew that they couldn't risk just leaving them there for someone or something else to stumble upon. Better to tie up their loose ends.

"A little extra practice never hurt anyone," Antony said as they challenged all of the remaining vessels at once.

"Tell that to Mariano Rivera," Eddie jokingly replied.

After they'd made quick work of the vessels, they rounded up a couple squirrels, and then the three orphans indulged in a quick meal to make sure they were well nourished and to minimize any potential internal distractions.

With their bellies adequately full, there was only one thing left for them to do before beginning their trek. They all took five minutes to bring awareness to any negative thoughts that had entered their minds following the most recent and unfortunate events, from JP's betrayal to Malika's passing. They knew that such thoughts would only serve to distract them, and so they released them with each conscious breath.

Feeling rejuvenated, they cleaned up their camp, dousing what was left of the fire. They each grabbed their own cloth pouches from inside the church to carry their snakes—Charlie grabbed a few extra snakes and pocketed JP's cell phone, just in case he tried to call them again—and then the three began their journey down the long gravel road.

The setting sun proved to be a useful beacon when they came to the same fork where Charlie had previously struggled. It was clear that the paved road to the left led west, while the similar option to the right would take them east. Going only off of what Malika had told them about their location, that they were north of Lake Tahoe, Antony figured that they would need to follow some combination of west and south to reach Truckee. So left was the direction they headed.

They continued in that direction long after the sun had disappeared beyond the horizon, traveling for miles and miles as they made their way up and down the winding mountainous road. Antony and Eddie took turns serving as a crutch for Charlie, who, much to the surprise of Antony and Eddie, only seemed to get stronger with each mile.

◆ ◆ ◆

It was shortly after two in the morning when the orphans finally encountered their first sign of civilization: a gas station. Once they were within a hundred yards, they went off the road, slipping into the woods. They carefully surveyed the surrounding area as they crept closer to the sole source of light in the otherwise pitch-black wilderness.

The flickering neon sign in the front window indicated that they were open for business; however, at that hour, business appeared to be worse than bad. An overweight, middle-aged attendant, who was relaxing with his feet up on the counter while he read a magazine, was the only person inside the main building, which also served as a minimart. The parking lot was empty, save for a late '70s Chevy Chevette, almost certainly the attendant's, which was parked off to the side and out of view.

"You think you can hotwire that car?" Charlie whispered.

"Usually, the older the car, the easier it is," Antony said.

"Then that piece of crap should be a piece of cake," Eddie said. "It's a crap cake."

"I was with you up until the last part," Antony said.

"You can't win them all," Eddie said with a shrug.

"We should probably distract that guy," Charlie said.

"I'll handle that," Eddie said. He nodded to Antony. "How much time do you need?"

"At least five minutes," Antony said.

"I'll get you six, just to be safe. Hoot like an owl when you're ready." Eddie started to make his move.

"Wait," Charlie said, stopping Eddie. "Get a map and some waters. Maybe a couple snacks, too."

"Good thinking. I'm on it." Eddie crawled out of the woods and crossed the street for the gas station.

The attendant couldn't have been more surprised when Eddie opened the door. The sudden ringing of the welcome bell made him flinch so violently, he threw his magazine in the air and his body almost went flying out of his chair with it.

"Jesus Christ!" the attendant said as he steadied himself. He picked his periodical off of the floor. "I didn't hear you coming. You drive one of those electric cars or something?" He scanned the parking lot, looking for Eddie's ride.

"No," Eddie said. "I walked. I'm just staying down the road." He pointed in the direction from where they came.

The attendant stared at Eddie, instantly suspicious. "There ain't nothing down that road for just about eight miles," he said. "You mean to tell me you walked all that way? At this hour?" He kept his eyes on Eddie while he slowly moved his hand from the counter to just below.

Eddie noticed his own reflection in the one of the mirrors and was reminded how he hadn't showered or shaved in about a week. He didn't exactly look like the most upstanding citizen. The attendant clearly thought he was up to no good, but a much different no good than he was actually up to.

"Whoa, whoa, whoa," Eddie said, quickly covering. "Wait a second. Did I say down the road?"

The attendant nodded, leaving his hand hidden beneath the counter and steady.

Eddie chuckled to himself, trying to deflate the tension. "I meant up. Up the road." He pointed in the other direction. "Up, down, left, right, I always get it confused. I'm just visiting for the week. I still don't know my way around."

"Okay," said the still-hesitant attendant. He had only partially bought Eddie's story. Just enough that he stopped reaching for whatever was concealed below the counter.

"Speaking of figuring out my way around," Eddie said. "You don't happen to have any maps of the area, do you?"

"Over there." The attendant gestured to the far side of the front counter. On the lowest rack was a small selection of cheap folding maps.

"Thanks," Eddie said. As he made his way to the end of the counter, he sneaked a peek out the front window, catching a glimpse of Antony and Charlie hobbling across the street, perfectly lit in the exterior light.

The leery attendant, whose eyes had never wavered from Eddie, started to crane his head to match Eddie's gaze.

Eddie caught him out of the corner of his eye. "Hey!" he shouted, catching the attention of the attendant, who jerked his head back just before he could spot the others. "Were you talking about these maps?" He grabbed one of the maps and held it up.

"Do you see any other maps?" the attendant said, glaring at Eddie, clearly annoyed.

Eddie watched over the attendant's shoulder as Antony and Charlie disappeared into the darkness. He smiled. "Nope. Just making sure." He tapped the window on the roller grill, which rested on the counter just above the maps. "How new are these hot dogs?"

The answer was obvious. They looked like they'd been on the grill since the turn of the century, and not the most recent one. But Eddie had to kill time, and that meant small talk.

"They're new to you," the attendant said.

"Good one," Eddie said with a grin. He whistled Rod Stewart's "Do You Think I'm Sexy" as he casually made his way to the beverage fridge in the back and grabbed three waters. He kept his whistling going while he completed a loop around the store and back to the checkout. "Name that tune," he said as he laid his drinks and map on the counter.

The attendant silently rang up Eddie's things.

"Come on. You gotta know it," Eddie said. "'Do You Think I'm Sexy.' And that wasn't a question. That's the song."

The attendant bagged Eddie's stuff without a word.

Eddie continued, "This is kinda on-topic, but how are the ladies in the area? I imagine they're pretty low-maintenance."

The attendant didn't acknowledge Eddie's newest question. He had no interest in small talk. He just wanted Eddie gone so he could get back to his reading. "Is that it?" he said.

"Actually, I'll also have three bananas and three apples," Eddie said, pointing to the fruit basket on top of the small black-and-white TV that displayed the in-store security feed.

But just as Eddie finished asking for the fruit, the feed on the TV switched to an outdoor shot that showed Antony crawling into the car while Charlie waited next to him.

"Never mind!" Eddie blurted out.

The attendant was halfway turned around when Eddie's scream startled him. His body shot upright, stiff as a board. He took a second to calm his jolted nerves, and then scowled at Eddie even stronger than before. "What the hell is wrong with you, kid?"

Eddie watched the TV out of the corner of his eye as the feed switched to a third camera angle. "Nothing. I just realized it's too late for fruit. It has more sugar than you think."

"It's too late for a lot of things. Like putting up with all of your crap. You can pay for your map and drinks, and then you need to leave."

"Sure," Eddie said, pretending to be perfectly agreeable as he handed over a couple bills. But he'd already determined that he couldn't leave just yet. The guys had come up on the security feed again while the attendant was getting his change, and it was apparent that he still needed to buy more time. At least a couple minutes.

"There you go," the attendant said as he handed Eddie his money. "And now you go."

"Okay," Eddie said, but he didn't move.

"Hit the road."

Eddie just stood there, racking his brain. There were many things he was uncertain of, like how far the nearest police station was, or if the attendant really had a gun and was willing to use it. But he knew for certain that he needed an excuse. He knew that if he were forced to leave, it would only be a matter of seconds before they'd all be caught, and he'd have the answers to more questions than he cared to know.

The attendant cleared his throat. "Do I need to help you? 'Cause I can." He started to reach below the counter.

Eddie's eyes made a last-ditch scan for a play and found one. "Ho Hos," he said, finger-gun pointing to the half-eaten package next to the register.

The annoyed attendant paused. "What about them?"

"That's just a very good call. A dessert novice might go with the Swiss Rolls. But if you're picking between the two, the Ho Ho is by far the superior choice."

The attendant stared at Eddie for a second before easing up. He raised his hand above the counter. "You know, my ex-wife thought they were the same."

"I can see why she's your ex. They couldn't be more different. The Ho Ho wins on all three counts: creamy filling, consistency of the cake, and the chocolate exterior."

"I can tell you're obviously not a novice."

"Guilty as charged," Eddie said, raising his hands as if he'd been busted by the police. A slight grin crossed the attendant's face. Eddie smiled back and lowered his hands. He knew he was in. He could talk for hours about his old favorite snacks. While the cravings were long gone, the knowledge remained. "I'll tell you what," he said. "If you ever really wanna treat yourself, you need try a Bergers cookie."

"Are you kidding me?" the attendant said, his eyes lighting up. "They're my favorite. I got a cousin who lives in Baltimore. He sends me them for Christmas."

"You know what I call that? A great cousin."

"Me, too. He's always been my—"

The attendant was cut off by an unexpected clangor from outside. It wasn't the hooting that Eddie had hoped for. It was a harsh, metallic cough. A short-lived sputter, no more than half a second long. But the sound was unmistakable: It was an old engine struggling to turn over. And both the attendant and Eddie immediately knew exactly where it came from.

All of Eddie's goodwill was gone in a flash.

The attendant turned to Eddie, his eyes filled with rage. "You," he said through gritted teeth. "I knew you were up to something." His hand shot under the counter, going for his gun. This time, without the slightest hesitation.

CHAPTER
THIRTY-EIGHT

LACK OF INDECISION on the part of the attendant not-withstanding, Eddie was still much quicker on the draw. In one swift motion, he retrieved the snake from his pouch— the serpent turning into a staff in a rapid burst—and wielded his newly formed weapon, meeting the attendant's shotgun while it was still on its upswing.

The weapons collided with a loud crunch.

"You're dead," the attendant yelled as he recovered his handle of the gun, only to fail in his attempts to pump the shell into the chamber. His eyes examined the weapon, searching for a solution. But his problem required more than a simple fix. The shotgun barrel was now bent like a boomer-ang. Fear washed over his face. "Who the hell are you?"

"I'm, uh," Eddie said, pausing to give himself time to come up with an explanation that would lead to the least amount of pushback. "From the future!" he said. "I'm from the future."

The attendant's eyes went wide, his jaw slack. His hands fell to his side, and the shotgun fell to the floor.

It was more than apparent to Eddie that the attendant had completely bought his story, and Eddie was perfectly happy to run with it. "You've seen *Terminator*, right?" he said.

"Of course, like a thousand times," the attendant said, nodding emphatically. He stopped abruptly, his eyes going even wider, as a realization dawned on him. "You're here to save me so that I can save the world, aren't you?"

"No. I'm actually here to save the world by myself." Eddie let his staff return to snake form and slipped it back into his pouch. "Well, I'm doing it with other people, too. But not you."

"Oh." The attendant slumped, disappointed.

"But you never know," Eddie said, attempting to lift the attendant's spirits. "That doesn't mean you won't do something great after I save the world. If you believe in yourself, you can do whatever you want. Trust me on that."

"I do," the attendant said, a smile returning to his face.

"Good. I need you to do me a favor."

"Anything."

"First off, you can't let anyone know I was here. Also, I'm gonna need to steal your car, like the Terminator would do."

"Don't worry. I won't tell anyone. And you can just borrow the 'vette." He reached into his pocket for the keys.

"I have a feeling we're probably past that point. But I actually will take the bananas and apples."

"Here you go," the attendant said, grabbing the fruit and handing it over. "Good luck with everything."

"Thanks," Eddie said. He hurried to the door, stopping in the exit. "One more thing. All those desserts are good, but you might wanna cut back. Everything is better in moderation. Your future self will thank you."

"Totally. I won't eat the other Ho. Unless you think it's alright and I shouldn't let it go to waste."

"Go with your heart," Eddie said. He nodded and then continued out of the front door.

Eddie only made it a couple feet outside before he spun back around and re-entered the store, where the attendant was already halfway finished with the Ho Ho.

"My heart said to eat it," the attendant said, guiltily.

"Hey, I'm not here to judge. I just need one last favor. Can you show me where we are? Believe it or not, they still haven't perfected time travel. They just drop you off wherever."

"I can only imagine." The attendant popped the last Ho Ho half into his mouth and took the map from Eddie. He spread it out on the counter and scanned the map with his finger. "We're right ... here."

"Thanks." Eddie marked their location with a pen.

"Can you do me a solid, Futureman?" the attendant asked, somewhat timidly. "I don't want to screw up the space-time continuum or anything, but can you tell me who wins the World Series next year?"

◆ ◆ ◆

The orphans sped down the winding two-lane road that had been carved into the towering Ponderosa pine forest in their newly acquired Chevette.

Antony shook his head as he drove. "I can't believe you

told him the Nationals were gonna win the World Series."

"They might," Eddie said defensively. "They have a better shot than anyone else, assuming they don't blow it. And I can't believe you touched the wires. Accident or not, you almost got me shot."

"Like I said, I'm not a pro."

"Yeah, well, for future reference, the whole future thing actually worked really well. You might want to try it."

"Hopefully I won't need to, but I'll remember that."

"I think this guy is an amateur ornithologist," Charlie said as he finished digging through the glove box.

"I don't know anything about that kinda stuff," Eddie said. "But whatever he's into on his own free time is not any of my business."

"I think you're confusing ornithology with something else," Antony said. "It's bird watching."

"Yeah, I was way off."

"He has all sorts of bird books," Charlie said. "And a really nice pair of binoculars." He held up the binoculars.

Eddie grabbed the binoculars and gave them a once-over. "Wow. I bet these are worth more than the car."

"They're probably not the best in this light," Antony said. "But they might help us scope out the area before we roll up."

"We'll find out soon enough," Charlie said, pointing at the sign on the road just ahead that indicated that Truckee was only five miles away.

They all went silent. The realization that their destination was so close, and that their mission had now become the moment, had forged a firm determination that swept over the car.

A few minutes later, they made a right onto Donner Pass Road. They crossed over the interstate and continued downhill, making a slight bend. At the end of the curve, everything opened up, revealing the sparsely lit downtown area of Truckee, which sat at the bottom of the small valley, just a little under a mile ahead.

"Cut the lights," Charlie said.

Antony immediately turned off the headlights. "I'm gonna kill the engine, too." He put the car in neutral and shut down the engine.

They quietly coasted for a quarter mile before coming to a stop near a small hill that was positioned just before where the residential section of town began. Antony disabled the interior lights so that they wouldn't turn on when they opened the doors, and then the orphans slipped out of the car.

Eddie led the charge, weaving through trees on his way to the summit of the hilltop, while Antony assisted Charlie just behind him.

Once they reached the crest, they peered through the gaps in the thick tree trunks, searching for any signs of JP and his Beasts.

They found nothing. All of the houses and businesses in the area were completely dark. The only light in the town came from the handful of streetlamps that lined the main strip and the full moon that hung in the sky above.

"Are we sure we're in the right place?" Eddie said.

"It has to be," Antony said. He used the binoculars to scan the downtown area. He didn't spot JP or any signs of life, nor did he see the blacked-out suvs, which had been moved.

However, Antony did confirm that they were exactly where they were supposed to be. "This is it. I found the train station. It's around ten blocks away. And our van is parked right out front." He handed Eddie the binoculars.

Eddie had a look for himself. "You're right."

"They're probably hiding, waiting for us before they show themselves. Just like Malika taught us, we can't allow ourselves to be surprised. We can't assume anything. We can only mindfully react to everything."

Eddie nodded in agreement, and then all three of the orphans closed their eyes, focusing on their breaths and clearing their minds, one last time. They ended their session by holding hands and taking turns reciting the serenity mantra.

"We'll be back soon," Antony said as he patted Charlie on the shoulder, and then he and Eddie started down the slope.

"Wait," Charlie said, struggling to follow. "I'm coming with you."

"You can't," Antony said.

"I feel a lot better."

"You're still not well enough to take them on."

"You said that Malika told you my mental state would be the most important factor in my recovery," Charlie said. "Well, I've never felt mentally stronger."

"I don't doubt that," Antony said, "but your body is still too far behind your mind."

"Antony's right," Eddie said. "At this moment, you definitely wouldn't stand a chance. If your mind's right, then just focus on your body. Give it the chance catch up."

Charlie went to argue, "I—"

But Eddie stopped him before he could get going. "I got an idea," he said. "I'll just throw a punch. If you can stop it, you're ready. If not, you're not."

"Okay," Charlie said. "Whenever you're—"

Eddie didn't give Charlie the chance to finish, throwing his punch before Charlie could say "ready." The objective wasn't to determine if Charlie was able to stop something that he knew was coming. The objective was to determine if he could protect himself.

It wasn't even Charlie's reaction to the punch that silenced him, either. It was Eddie's fist pressing against his lips. The punch had landed as softly as a hummingbird before Charlie's hands had even left his sides. Charlie sighed; he knew had only proven Eddie and Antony's point.

"Sorry," Antony said. "We know you wanna help, and we appreciate it, but you just aren't ready. The best thing you could do is what Eddie said: Focus on your body, and give it the chance to catch up."

Charlie couldn't argue with the results. They were right. "I'll focus on my body," he said.

"And we'll be back soon," Eddie said.

"I know," Charlie said. He couldn't help but be a little disappointed. However, he didn't let the frustration fester in him. As soon as he felt it cross his mind, he acknowledged it and then let it go with his breath.

◆ ◆ ◆

Antony and Eddie finished making their way down the wooded slope. It led them through the Truckee Cemetery before dropping them off in a small development of wooden cabin vacation homes. They both kept their eyes peeled and voices low as they cautiously treaded down the street.

"I don't see anything." Antony whispered.

"Me either," Eddie whispered back. "Just a lot of empty driveways. It's like everyone left town."

They continued down the road, slipping through the shadows and down the backstreets before popping out of a small alleyway just in front of the train station. Everything was even quieter and more still than it'd appeared from the top of the hill. Antony and Eddie kept their heads on swivels, spinning themselves in circles as they crept to the center of the street. They stood back to back, still searching for any signs of the Beasts or JP.

"I feel like we should be doing this at high noon, not four in the morning," Eddie said.

"Yeah," Antony agreed. "This does feel like a showdown."

"All that's missing is the bad guys. We might as well bring the rats out of their holes."

"Might as well."

Eddie began to whistle the theme song from *The Good, the Bad and the Ugly.*

Antony added the "wah, wah, wah."

Silhouettes lurked in the shadows ahead of Eddie like a black cloud that slowly drifted into the faint light. "I've got ten guys at my twelve o'clock looking to party," he said.

"Me, too," Antony said, taking stock of the Beasts he was facing. He heard swinging doors and glanced to his right out of the corner of his eye. He spotted five more Beasts exiting the nearby shops. "And we have some more on your left."

"Same goes for your left." Eddie watched yet another grouping of Beasts exit the train station and spread out.

All of the Beasts that had revealed themselves simultaneously removed their sunglasses. If there was any doubt whether the Beasts had Antony and Eddie surrounded, their fiery eyes, which pulsed in unison and created an ominous ring of bright orange dots in the darkness, put those doubts firmly to rest.

"I've got about thirty of them, by my count," Antony said. "Give or take a few."

"This will definitely be a first," Eddie said. "But you know what they say about first times."

"I do. And I expect this to be a charm, too."

"Me, too." Eddie said as he slipped his hand in his pouch. "These punks must be feeling pretty lucky." He retrieved his snake and turned it into staff form in explosive fashion.

Antony did the same, except he retrieved two snakes. "They won't be feeling anything pretty soon," he said with a smirk as he twirled his two staffs.

"Except for pain."

Antony and Eddie got into their fighting stances, spreading their legs and bending their knees to keep their muscles loose. "What are you waiting for?" Eddie shouted as he pointed his staff at the Beasts before him. "Come and get it!"

The Beasts were more than happy to oblige, charging at the orphans from all directions at once.

CHAPTER
THIRTY-NINE

ANTONY WAS THE FIRST to land a lethal blow, taking out the lead Beast with a swift strike from his staff. When the Beast went up, it was unlike anything Antony had ever witnessed while practicing on the vessels. There was the usual cracking skin that spread like seeping lava, followed by a spontaneous combustion and the Beast turning into a heap of ash. However, the freeing of the trapped spirits, which occurred in between those two familiar actions, added an unforeseen and most awe-inducing element.

As soon as Antony removed his staff from the Beast's forehead, a bright white beam burst out from the entry point. The Beast's shoulders shot back and its chest and head arched up to the sky. The burst from the Beast shined straight to the heavens like a spotlight with one hundred million candlepower, and was followed by tornadic swirls of electric blue that corkscrewed around the luminance like strips of a DNA strand as they ascended upwards. The whole cosmic fireworks show lasted less than five seconds, and then the light and the Beast expired together.

Even though Antony had almost immediately slammed his eyelids shut, he still hadn't closed them fast enough. Against the darkness, the very brief encounter with the powerful radiance was exponentially more blinding than it would've been otherwise, and caused his eyes to lose their lock on his other attackers.

While the Beasts had quickly shuffled to the side to give their fallen compatriot space, they didn't afford Antony any time to recover. They just kept coming for him.

Thanks to his training, Antony's other senses picked up the slack for his momentarily hindered vision. He utilized his heightened hearing, feeling, and smell—along with his staffs—to block the flurry of jabs that flew at him from every possible angle.

"Watch out for the released souls when you kill the Beasts," Antony shouted to Eddie as he diverted another onslaught of strikes. "The light they give off is strong as hell and will mess up your vision."

Eddie was still busy trying to keep the five Beasts assaulting him at once at bay. "I'll cross that bridge when I come to it," he yelled back.

"You do that," Antony said, and then swiped away another combination of punches.

After a few seconds and countless stymied strikes, Antony's eyes finally readjusted to the darkness. He now had a chance to do more than just defend. He delivered a debilitating shot to another Beast. This time, he made sure to tilt the Beast's head away from him when he withdrew his staff so that he wouldn't get blinded by the escaping flash and could keep up his offensive, which he did, landing another incapacitating shot.

Shortly thereafter, Eddie came to his aforementioned bridge. One of the Beasts went to throw a punch and leaned right into his rising staff. Eddie expertly removed his staff and whacked the Beast across the cheek with the backside of the weapon in one fluid motion.

The Beast went stumbling sideways.

All of the other Beasts nearby leapt out of the way of the disintegrating Beast, as if he were carrying some incurable disease that might possibly infect them.

Eddie quickly discovered why.

One of the Beasts made a wrong move and ended up getting caught in the glare of the dying Beast. The beam swiped across the unlucky Beast's leg at the thigh, cutting through it like it was warm butter. The now-one-legged Beast was sent falling to the asphalt. His face contorted as he screamed in excruciating pain. A black tar oozed from the wound where his leg had been. The fire in his eyes flickered as the ooze molded back into a functional leg.

"Nasty," Eddie said to himself as watched the Beast during his brief break before another Beast attacked.

Eddie dispatched the new aggressor, sending him tumbling in a similar fashion, and then informed Antony of what he'd discovered while keeping up his defense. "The light hurts them! It won't kill them, but it messes them up and slows them down."

"Then we gotta use it to our advantage," Antony shouted back, and then did just that. He fired off a quick double hit like Eddie had executed.

The dying Beast barreled into the crowd, taking out two other Beasts at once like a perfectly executed bowling split.

Unfortunately for Antony and Eddie, even with their newly uncovered weapon, there were still plenty of Beasts that were more than willing and able to join the fight. For every Beast that perished or was temporarily taken out, a new one just stepped forward and took its place on the frontlines. Antony and Eddie didn't let this seemingly unending onslaught distract or discourage them. They simply moved on to the new target.

Blocks and blows were levied in bunches. Antony and Eddie made the most of the opportunities that presented themselves. They made sure to never overreach, only taking what they could, as they gradually chipped away at their opponents' numbers.

Four more Beasts had perished, their legion almost cut in a third, when Antony encountered another barrage of fists. He successfully intercepted all of the strikes; however, in the process of protecting himself, he unintentionally rerouted one of the fists right into the back of Eddie's head.

The punch not only caught Eddie off-guard, it sent him tumbling through the narrow gap in between his attackers. He somersaulted head over feet.

The Beasts broke off into two new groups like cellular division, with half of the circle staying with Antony and the other half forming a new barrier around Eddie.

The first thing Eddie realized when he came to a stop on his back was that he'd lost his staff. The second thing he realized was that one of the Beasts was already taking advantage of his being disarmed and had leapt into the air, pouncing for him.

Eddie detected a faint hiss off to his side. His hand shot toward the sound, and he snagged his snake just as it was about to slither away. He turned the snake into staff form only milliseconds before the Beast was set to land on him. The rod pierced the Beast's skull, poking clean out the back.

The same fate was met for a second Beast, which had also gone airborne for the pile-on. Both Beasts stuck to Eddie's staff like a kebabs on a skewer.

Eddie gave a powerful push, sliding the Beasts off his staff like two chunks of meat and depositing each on opposite sides of him. He used his weapon to manipulate one of the Beast's heads and aim the beams shooting from its forehead.

The rays sent the Beasts around Eddie diving for cover.

Once the dying Beast had expired to ash, Eddie did a kip-up to get back to his feet. "You getting lonely over there?" he called to Antony.

"A little bit," Antony shouted back as he blocked a fist. He dropped to his knee, swung low with his second staff, and took out the Beast's legs. He popped up and pierced the Beast before him. He followed the blow with another vicious hit. However, instead of striking the Beast on the side and into his comrades, like he'd been doing, Antony struck him square in the forehead, knocking the Beast flat on his back.

The Beasts nearby scurried out of the way, creating a gap.

Antony blocked the unrelenting attacks while counting in his head. After one last defense, he closed his eyes and leapt, perfectly timing his jump so that he crossed over the dying Beast just after it finished expiring. He bolted by a couple of the scattered Beasts, who were still recovering from Eddie's assault, and grinned as he rejoined his friend. "It's a pleasure seeing you again."

Eddie smiled and tapped staffs with Antony. "Please, the pleasure is all mine."

The Beasts returned to one large mass, but their numbers were noticeably lighter. They were down to just under half of their initial force. They closed in, tightening their boundary around the guys.

"This seems a lot more manageable," Antony said.

"I almost feel bad for them," Eddie said. "If not for—"

Eddie was cut off by a cry for help.

"Help me," the voice screamed, again. The exact location of the source was not quite clear, but the source itself was unmistakable. It was Naomi.

Eddie swung his staff furiously, beating back the Beasts and buying himself a second to search for Naomi.

"Help!" Naomi shouted once more.

Eddie picked up the direction of the calls. He spotted Naomi a couple hundred yards away on the train tracks. While most of her features were hidden in the darkness, the large curls in her hair were apparent. She struggled to break free from the bondage that held her to the chair.

"She's on the tracks," Eddie said before blocking an incoming assault at the last second.

"Is JP with her?" Antony asked while thwarting a few shots of his own.

"I didn't see him," Eddie said. He took out the Beast between himself and Naomi, and then struck him square in the head, as Antony had. "But I'm gonna go save her."

Just finishing an attack of his own, Antony went to tell Eddie otherwise. But before he got a word out, Eddie had already hopped over his fallen opponent and was racing for the tracks and Naomi. Not even a single Beast followed Eddie. Instead, they all opted to focus their collective efforts on Antony. "Great," he said to himself as he shook his head.

The Beasts took a step forward. Then another.

Antony knew that with one more step, he'd be in their striking range. Even so, he let them take that step. As soon as they did, he faked a double strike forward, and then threw his arms and staffs backwards, planting them into the foreheads of two of the Beasts behind him. He wasted no time utilizing the leverage and using his staffs like poles in a pole vault to launch himself out of the middle of group with a back flip. He landed on one knee about thirty feet away.

"Sorry," Antony said with a shrug to the Beasts as they turned around to reengage. "But I've never been one for being the center of attention." He leveled his staffs, ready to meet the Beasts head on.

The enraged Beasts' eyes burned brighter and brighter, to the point that the flames appeared to be spilling out. One of the Beasts let out a savage scream. The others followed suit. And then they all charged toward Antony, full steam.

◆ ◆ ◆

Eddie had made it to the far end of the parking lot and was sprinting toward the train tracks. He kept his eyes peeled for JP, who was nowhere to be seen. "I'm coming," he called out as Naomi continued to cry for assistance. He slowed to a stop about ten feet away and did a quick 360-degree scan of the area. There was still no sign of JP, or any of the Beasts.

"Help," Naomi whined.

"It's okay," Eddie reassured her. "Everything is gonna be okay. I'm gonna untie you." He knelt down to loosen the rope. As he went to grab the bulk of the knot, his fingers grazed Naomi's hands. He immediately knew that something wasn't right. Not only was the temperature of the hands cooler than expected, the texture was off. It didn't feel like skin. It felt like rubber.

Before Eddie could do anything, Naomi—or more accurately, the figure he'd presumed to be Naomi—sprung from the chair, leaving the fake limbs tied to the back of the seat. The figure struck Eddie on the wrist, disarming him and knocking him onto his back.

Eddie scurried on his hands and knees to catch up to his snake as it slithered away. He reached out to grab it, but quickly pulled back when he saw out of the corner of his eye that his opponent had produced a large fireball with its staff.

The figure hurled the fireball, blowing up what was Eddie's snake and leaving a charred crater in the ground.

Eddie turned back to the figure, which was in the process of shedding its wig. The figure's face reflected in the faint glow of the staff, but Eddie didn't need to see its face to know who it was. It was JP. He had tricked Eddie, and now he stood over him with a satisfied smirk.

"Help!" Naomi's voice screamed once more. By now it was clear that the scream wasn't actually coming from Naomi. It was from the recording device in JP's pocket.

"Well, that's getting a little annoying," JP said. He retrieved his phone and stopped the recording. "Much better." He looked at Eddie. "So, would you like to go easy, or should we see how you can handle yourself without a staff?"

"No way I'm going easy," Eddie said, returning to his feet. "And I don't need my staff. I'll beat you with my two hands." He lunged toward JP.

JP delivered three lightning-quick strikes. The first one blocked Eddie's attempted assault. The second tripped up Eddie's legs and sent him stumbling. And the third was a crack to the base of Eddie's neck, which was intended to both impair him and speed up his fall.

Eddie smacked the ground, face first, landing hard on his jaw. The blow and ensuing collision didn't knock him out, but it dazed him enough that he wasn't able to put up anything that resembled a fight when the Beast with the bushy mustache went to restrain him.

"You were saying?" JP said, tauntingly.

Eddie mumbled as the Beast dragged him away.

JP stalked across the parking lot back to the main street, where Antony had whittled his opponents to just two remaining Beasts. "Enough!" he shouted. He shook his head at the Beasts. "You've all failed me, and you've failed Lucifer. I'll handle this myself."

The Beasts backed away, giving Antony and JP space.

Antony and JP stood fifty feet apart. They both slid side to side in a circle, matching each other's steps as they sized one another up.

"So you're finally gonna try to do your own dirty work?" Antony said as he slid to his right.

"Try?" JP said with a chuckle. "I don't have to try. The only reason you even think you stand a chance with me is because I was holding back during our training."

"The only reason you even have anything to hold back is because you sold your soul to get it," Antony said. "Everything you have was given to you. That just means it isn't even yours and can be taken away, which is exactly what I plan on doing."

JP fumed, Antony's dig clearly having gotten under his skin. He took two more steps, which Antony mimicked, and then stopped. "Even if that were the case," he said as his scowl was replaced by a grin, which then turned to a full-blown smile, "it doesn't really matter. None of this does."

Antony realized that just because JP said he'd handle it himself didn't mean he had any intention of actually fighting him. JP had something else planned. Antony's eyes darted, searching for the two remaining Beasts. Were they part of the plan? Antony found them almost immediately. They hadn't moved an inch, only he and JP had.

It dawned on Antony that he'd literally walked right into JP's trap. They'd both shuffled halfway around their imaginary circle, and he was now standing where JP had stood when they started. He remembered watching JP as they began their little dance, and he knew that no more than twenty feet behind him was an old fashioned gas station and a handful of fuel pumps.

The grin on JP's face grew along with the fireball on the tip of his staff, the flames reflecting off of his eager eyes.

Antony dove out of the way as the fireball shot from JP's staff and whizzed past him.

The fireball collided with one of the fuel pumps. The explosion sent gasoline-charged flames shooting a hundred feet into the air, and sent Antony flying ten times further than his legs had been able to.

Antony's body skidded down the street, coming to a stop just before JP's feet. "Well, that was fun," JP said with a smile. He nodded to the Beast with the gray beard. "Tie him up with the others."

CHAPTER
FORTY

"NAOMI, NAOMI, NAOMI," JP said as he clutched her jaw in his hand, controlling her gaze to keep it locked on him.

Naomi remained silently defiant. She, Eddie, and Antony were each bound to their own metal support beams, which collectively held up the small porch roof that covered the loading platform of the train station.

Standing ten feet from the orphans were JP's three most trusted Beasts, each of them paired up, while the last two holdover Beasts waited off to the side, further behind them.

"Leave her alone," Antony ordered.

"Quiet," JP said, glaring at Antony, who was all the way at the other end. "You aren't in a position to be making demands. But don't worry, I'll get to you shortly." He turned back to Naomi, running the back of his free hand down her cheek as she fought to crane her head. "We could've had something special, but I was just too afraid you'd hurt me."

He shook his head and chuckled. "I can't believe you actually fell for that routine. You really are damaged goods. I could tell that within a minute of meeting you. Unfortunately for you, history only repeated itself. I'd apologize for ruining you for other guys if it wasn't for the fact that no other guy will even get the chance."

Naomi didn't respond verbally. She just cleared all the saliva from the back of her throat and hocked it on JP, nailing him in the forehead.

"No!" JP screamed, staggering backwards with his hand blocking his face. "You got me in the third eye." He snickered as he steadied himself and lowered his hand. He wiped his head with his sleeve, and then sidled up next to the Beast of Southeast Asian descent, who was standing opposite Naomi. "As much as I may have hurt you, Naomi, I promise that my friend Saloth"—JP smirked as he patted the Beast on the back—"is gonna make that seem like nothing."

Naomi fought against her restraints.

Saloth's mouth lifted at the corners, and his eyebrows rose above his sunglasses. It was evident that he was taking the utmost pleasure in watching Naomi struggle.

JP smirked as he moved on to his next captive. "Eddie."

Eddie said nothing.

"You're so quiet all of a sudden," JP said. "This isn't like you at all. Don't you wanna tell me how you're gonna kill me? I swore that's what you said you were gonna do?"

Eddie remained silent.

"I don't know if this interests you," JP said, "but you're not very far from where Malika was when she died."

Eddie had to bite his lip to keep from screaming.

JP noted the gesture and nodded to himself. He could tell he was getting to Eddie, he just needed to push a little harder. He patted the mustachioed Beast on the back. The Beast's face was as stern as they come. He exuded much more power than his 5'8" frame should.

"This is Joseph," JP said. "He's really been like a father to me. And since you never had a father, I figured the two of you might get along."

JP's dig hit deep enough that Eddie was no longer able to control himself. "Screw you!" Eddie shouted, his face turning beet-red as his swelling emotions took over.

JP smiled from ear to ear.

"Breathe," Antony reminded Eddie. He knew exactly what was going on and what JP was up to. "He's just trying to get you angry. He needs you to doubt yourself. Repeat the serenity mantra."

JP clapped his hands together and then held them to his lips in feigned excitement. He tiptoed toward Antony. "Serenity mantra? That sounds so interesting. I didn't know I missed a lesson. Maybe one of you can teach me."

Antony didn't respond.

"No? You're not gonna teach me?" JP said. "I guess I probably don't need it, anyway. I also don't need to get you to doubt yourselves. You do already. Sticking with the father theme"—JP put both of his hands on the bearded Beast's shoulders and gave them a couple firm squeezes—"this is my friend Leopold. He's the one that I told you about. He's best buddies with your father."

"He says hi," Leopold said with a half smirk to go along with his deep Belgian accent.

Antony didn't react to either of their words or Leopold's devious grin. He wasn't going to give them the satisfaction or the power to alter his mind. Instead, he concentrated on everything he'd learned. He reminded himself to stay present and to release any negativity and doubt as it entered his mind, and then he recited the serenity mantra in his head.

"Well, I'd be lying if I said I wasn't hoping to get more out of you," JP sighed. "But I guess I'll have to settle for that. Of course, we're still short one person before we can destroy the drive." He retrieved the drive from his pocket and twirled it in his fingers. "Do any of you happen to know where our good friend Charlie is? We can't start without him."

The orphans said nothing.

"Are you guys giving me the silent treatment?" JP said. He paced in front of the orphans as he tossed the flash drive to himself. "Don't you all think that's a little immature?" He stopped and studied the looks on the orphans' faces. "If you guys aren't gonna talk, I guess I'll just have to see if I can reach him myself. I'm sure he's not too far away."

◆ ◆ ◆

Charlie hadn't moved from his perch on the hilltop. He'd spent his first few minutes of solitude considering ways to speed up his healing process. Years ago, while doing research for a paper, he'd read about people who had successfully healed themselves using only their minds, curing ailments as minor as common colds and as major as cancer. He was certain that he could do the same. He could cure himself.

After all, the placebo effect was proof of this phenomenon. He wasn't positive how he'd pull it off or how long it might take, but he figured his best bet would be using all of the lessons that he'd learned to strengthen his mind and applying them to his body.

Charlie had been in the middle of attempting to release his physical pain and envisioning his wounds healing when he was distracted by the sudden bursts of light exploding from the tiny downtown. At first, he had no idea what he was witnessing, but with each successive eruption, he grew more and more confident that they were a good thing. One, two, all the way to twenty-eight, he'd counted. And then the flares came to an abrupt stop.

Ten minutes had passed. Charlie knew that, assuming they'd been successful, his friends should have returned already. With each fleeting second, he couldn't help but begin to worry. He repeated the serenity mantra to calm himself. He exhaled deeply and returned his attention to healing his body, only to be interrupted seconds later by a vibration in his pocket.

Charlie retrieved JP's cell phone from his pocket and hesitantly swiped the cracked screen, answering the call, which went straight to speakerphone.

"Charlie, buddy, where are you?" JP said. "I thought we had a deal."

Charlie frantically fumbled to turn down the volume, knowing that the sound could easily carry at this time of night and not wanting to give up his location. He whispered back, "I'm not gonna tell you where I am."

"Why the hell are you so quiet? I can barely hear you."

Charlie wasn't about to answer JP's question, but that didn't stop JP from figuring it out, anyway.

"Ohhh," JP chortled. "You must be really close, then. That's good. Why don't you come join us? We can get the whole band back together."

Going off of JP's words and cockiness, Charlie already knew the answer to his next question, but he had to ask it, anyway. "You have Antony and Eddie?"

"Of course I do. You guys couldn't have actually thought your plan, or lack thereof, was really gonna work, did you?"

Charlie had, and now he didn't know what to say.

JP continued, "Don't worry. It's not all bad news for you. I'll be honest with you, Charlie, I think you're completely worthless."

"Thanks for the honesty," Charlie replied sarcastically.

"You're very welcome. But that's not the good news. The good news for you is that my opinion matters much less than my superiors' right now, and I have to defer to them. One of these people in particular, for one reason or another, happens to be your biggest fan. Apparently, he sees a lot of himself in you. I don't, but he does."

Charlie knew JP was referring to Terry.

"Anyway," JP sighed, "he'd prefer to make a deal with you."

"What kind of deal?" Charlie said.

"You remember the revised contract, right?"

"Yeah."

"All you gotta do is sign it. That's it. Plain and simple."

"I don't believe you. It's just another trap."

"Don't flatter yourself, Charlie. I wouldn't need any kind of trap to take you down. I'd just do it. But like I said, I have to defer. Which is why I have the contract in my pocket. The only thing it's missing is your signature."

"If I sign it, my parents' souls will be freed?"

"Walter's, too. That's what it says."

Charlie took a moment to consider all of his options and their likely outcomes. The answer should've been easy. He couldn't sign it. He'd decided that the first time he was faced with this decision; however, he was in a much worse position than the first time. That time, only his life was on the line; now there were three more lives hanging in the balance.

Charlie heard Antony scream over the phone, "Don't do it!" Next came a loud thud, like a boxing glove pounding a heavy bag, followed by Antony moaning in extreme agony.

"Don't listen to him," JP said. "You're a big boy. You can make your own big boy decisions."

"What happens to the others?" Charlie asked.

"You saw what happened to your grandfather, right? Well, pretty much the same thing."

"The only way I'll sign it is if you let all of them go, too," Charlie said. He didn't want to sign the contract, but if it saved his parents and his friends, he'd have to. He'd gotten them into this mess, and it was his responsibility to get them out of it.

"No!" Naomi screamed before being silenced.

"That's not part of the deal," JP said.

"Then make it part of the deal," Charlie demanded.

"Whoa! Somebody ring the tough guy alarm," JP said. "Unfortunately, it's non-negotiable."

"Then there's no way I'm signing it."

"Good. Very good," JP said, genuinely content. "That's exactly what I was hoping to hear. You've just made your bed, which happens to be a coffin. And now I can't wait to watch you lie in it."

The line went dead.

Charlie's mind raced. He hadn't expected the negotiations to end so abruptly. Had he played his cards wrong, and in doing so, doomed himself, his parents, and his friends? There was no way to know for sure, and no way of going back. All he knew was that time was running out if he was going to save his friends and most likely himself. He wasn't dealing with minutes or hours. All he had was seconds.

Charlie reminded himself to try to control what he could control. He closed his eyes and took a deep breath. He let go of the doubt that had recently arisen, and then focused all of his thoughts on the present and on getting better. As he squeezed his eyes even harder, concentrating all of his energy, a faint golden light began to emanate around the outer edges of the scab on his wrist. The radiance grew and grew as it enveloped the wound.

◆ ◆ ◆

JP approached the two holdover Beasts. He pointed to a faint sparkle up on the hill where Charlie was holed up. "See that little light?" he said. "It's the cell phone. He's up there. Bring him to me alive. And don't screw it up this time."

The two Beasts took off.

JP clasped his hands behind his back and casually strolled over to the group. "And now the fun begins," he exclaimed. He nodded to Saloth, Joseph, and Leopold. "They're all yours. Bon appétit, my friends!"

The three Beasts removed their sunglasses in unison. Their eyes pulsed with bright orange flames. They slowly crept in on the tied-up orphans and dropped down to one knee, getting eye to eye.

"As long as you believe in yourself, they can't hurt you," Antony reminded the others. "Eliminate any doubt."

"That's great in theory," JP said, "but much harder in practice. I doubt"—he giggled as he stressed the word—"my friends will have a hard time finding yours."

Antony shook off JP's snide remark and stared right into Leopold's eyes, challenging him. He saw the sparks shooting across his corneas like cobalt solar flares exploding from the sun. He repeated the serenity mantra to himself to keep his mind calm.

Eddie craned his neck to avoid eye contact.

Joseph grasped Eddie by the temples and yanked his skull straight ahead. Their eyes locked.

Eddie smiled through the pain. "I'm not an optometrist," he said, "but you might wanna get that checked out. It could be astigmatism."

Joseph's eyes pulsed brighter, like a freshly stoked fire.

"Seriously," Eddie said. "It's not normal."

Chills shot down Naomi's back and goose bumps popped up on her arms and legs as Saloth ran his hand through her hair. She tried to remember everything she'd been taught, but all she could think about was that this was all her fault. If only she wouldn't have followed JP, they wouldn't be there. The regret and blame continued to swell up insider her before turning into anger. With one hole popped in the dam, many others soon followed.

Saloth grinned. He could see Naomi's anger morphing into doubt. He leaned closer and peered deep into her eyes.

Naomi felt a tinge of pain in the center of her brow. The more attention she gave the pain, the sharper it got. More pins added to the prick in bunches, until it became too much for her to take. She screamed in tortuous pain.

"One down, two to go," JP excitedly proclaimed.

CHAPTER
FORTY-ONE

"YOU'RE GONNA BE ALL RIGHT. Everything is gonna be all right," Eddie shouted to Naomi. "I promise. Just look at me." He turned to face her, intending to reassure her with his eyes in addition to his words, only to discover that the thin, clear gel had already begun secreting from her eyes and was floating toward Saloth with the blue sparks of electricity swirling circles around it.

Joseph was more than happy to let Eddie observe. He wanted him to watch. He knew that by witnessing his comrade's demise, Eddie would soon start to doubt himself as well. After he determined that Eddie had seen enough, he cranked Eddie's head back to face him. He sneered and then went to work on the rattled teen.

Antony kept his focus on Leopold. He watched the flames dance in the Beast's eyes, confident that he still had the upper hand. Unlike Eddie, Antony had consciously blocked out Naomi's screams. Not because he didn't care about her pain, but because he knew he couldn't at that moment. There was nothing he could do about it, and getting angry or sad wouldn't do either of them any favors.

While Antony had successfully suppressed the screams, he couldn't help but pick up the snapping and crackling in the background. Its unexpectedness allowed it to sneak into his eardrums. It reminded him of the shocks he used to get from walking on the shag carpet and then touching the basement doorknob at his childhood home. It sparked a strong curiosity in him, one that he tried to shake. He knew he needed to keep his focus on himself and nothing else.

"Ahhh!" Eddie wailed.

"And another one bites the dust," JP gloated.

The snapping and crackling doubled in intensity, and so did Antony's curiosity, which finally got the best of him. He turned to check on his friends. He saw Naomi's soul latch onto Saloth's eyes, while Eddie's was just beginning to drain. Antony jerked his head back to face forward and blinked his eyes hard, trying to forget what he'd just seen, trying to dig up that tiniest seed of doubt that had been planted in his brain.

JP was just as swift to act, attempting to add water to the seed to help it grow. He hovered behind Leopold, taunting Antony. "The pressure is all on you now," he said. "Can you do it? I don't think you can."

Leopold took a more direct approach. He forcefully twisted Antony's head to face him and gazed into his eyes.

Almost instantly, Antony felt a pinch in the center of his brow. At first, the pain was mild; however, it was still strong enough to distract Antony as he tried to clear his mind. And then the aching began to build, exponentially, like a snowball that started at the top of a mountain and soon became an avalanche. Antony could feel his corneas expanding from their sockets. The burning was unbearable. His body writhed. He howled in agony. His vision blurred as his soul began to seep from his body.

"Three for three," JP giddily exclaimed as he watched the orphans suffer. "All we need now is for Charlie to join the party." He shifted his attention to the hilltop, hoping to get some indication that his Beasts had fulfilled their duty. The smirk was instantly wiped from his face as he discovered that the speck of light that had helped him pinpoint Charlie's location hadn't disappeared—it'd grown.

No longer merely a flicker, it'd amplified into something significantly more substantial, about the size of an adult human, and continued to grow even still. When it appeared that it couldn't get any brighter, the bulb of light burst, sending rays and energy shock waves shooting in all directions. The trees shook, shutters rattled, and the train station's bell rang from the rippling aftershocks.

JP's skin goosed as he felt the warm breeze wrap around him. "What the hell was that?" he said. He didn't get more than a second to contemplate what he'd witnessed before he felt a second gust. His eyes turned up toward the source of the breeze and were met with a dark blur in the sky that was nose-diving in his direction.

JP leapt out of the way at the last second, tumbling across the platform. When he picked himself off of the ground, he found Charlie, with massive, white-feathered wings protruding from his back and his staff raised and ready to strike Leopold down from behind. "No!" he screamed.

Charlie planted his staff in the back of Leopold's head, driving it all the way through until it burst out from the Beast's forehead. The once-burning coals in Leopold's eyes extinguished immediately, turning jet-black.

Antony's head whipped back as his soul was shot back into his body.

Charlie ripped his staff from Leopold's skull, and the motion yanked the Beast's head back and up. The brilliant beam emitted from his brow lit up the night sky above. All of the spirits fled their confines, save for one. The stray solitary spark broke from the group and floated down in front of Antony, where it hovered for a split second before going supernova.

The explosion of light shook Antony from his haze. The world around him slowed to a near halt. In the cosmic glow that shined before him, he watched all of the lost memories of his father replay as they reentered his consciousness. He finally remembered his father's smile, his laugh, and his voice. He remembered how much his father cared for him, and how much he wanted him to be happy. He remembered every hug his father had ever given him, and every little piece of advice. He remembered how dedicated his father was to him, and how he fought to give him every opportunity he could. Antony remembered it all.

Its duty fulfilled, the supernatural energy collapsed on itself, returning to just a tiny electric spark. It rejoined the other lost souls that had been stolen by Leopold and shot up to the heavens.

Everything returned to normal speed for Antony. His eyes readjusted just as Leopold combusted into a pile of ash, leaving Charlie, a look of pure determination on his mug, standing in his place. Antony was overcome with extreme emotion. He began to tear up.

"Breathe," Charlie reminded Antony as he went to free him from his bind. "You need to focus."

"Right," Antony said. He took a deep breath and exhaled, regaining control of all of his senses just in time to spot JP putting the finishing touches on his biggest fireball yet. "Behind you!" he warned Charlie.

"Too late," JP snarled as he hurled a flame the size of a volleyball right at them.

Still on his knees, Charlie spun around to find the flame from JP's staff barreling right toward them like a Major League fastball. Charlie flexed his muscles and prepared to leap, but he knew simply diving out of the way wasn't an option. While it would save him, it would only expose Antony to a fiery end. There was really only time for one option, and Charlie wasn't even sure that it would work.

Charlie sprung to his feet, spread his wings, and flapped them with all of his might. The force it created was so powerful that it extinguished the flame mid-flight, and the continuing gust sent JP sliding backwards across the platform like a cable-news reporter caught in a hurricane.

Charlie quickly finished freeing Antony. "Here," he said as he retrieved two extra serpents from his hip pouch, and then handed them to Antony.

Antony took the snakes and turned them to staff form.

JP was beyond livid. "You can finish with those two later," he screamed to Joseph and Saloth, who were still in the process of absorbing Naomi and Eddie's souls.

Both of the Beasts' eyes flickered as they released their hold on Naomi and Eddie. The ooze snapped back into the teens' bodies. Naomi slumped, unconscious, her binding the only thing keeping her upright. Eddie's head rolled from side to side. He was awake, but in a daze.

JP shot off another fireball, right in between Antony and Charlie, who dove for cover in opposite directions. It was exactly what JP had intended, to separate them. "Get him!" he ordered as he pointed his staff at Antony. "You, too," he said, gesturing to the two holdover Beasts that had just returned.

"That's not fair," Charlie said as the four remaining Beasts moved in and surrounded Antony.

JP glared at Charlie. "I don't care," he said. "I want you all for myself." He grunted furiously, flexing every muscle in his body. His face went flush, and the veins in his neck bulged to the point that it looked like they might burst. However, the only burst came from behind him, when his scapulae broke free from his back. They tore through his skin and clothes, expanding nearly ten feet wide. Wings to match Charlie's. But there was one key distinction between them: his feathers were black like those of a raven, almost blending in with the surrounding darkness.

"Thanks for showing me this was even possible," JP gloated. "Without you, I would've never even imagined it."

He whipped his wings and took off toward Charlie like he was blasted out of a cannon.

Charlie flicked his wings and thrust himself upwards, letting JP whiz by. He fluttered his appendages, hovering ten feet off of the ground.

JP looked up toward Charlie with a devious grin. "It looks like we're gonna have to take this to the sky," he said, and then shot diagonally for Charlie.

Charlie avoided this second attack by zigging to JP's zag and climbing even higher in the air. They continued this game of cat and mouse, which almost resembled JP chasing Charlie up some invisible fire escape, while they made their rapid ascent. Eventually, they settled on the same plane, nearly one hundred feet in the air and about twenty feet apart.

"You're just delaying the inevitable?" JP snarled.

Charlie couldn't deny that he was delaying. He had every intention of stalling JP as long as he could while Antony battled the Beasts below. He glanced down to check in on his friend.

On the ground, Antony was doing more than holding his own. He defended a joint attack from Joseph and Saloth, slipped past them, and then delivered a lethal blow to one of the holdover Beasts. The luminous beam from the dying Beast blasted into the atmosphere, cutting right in between JP and Charlie.

The very second that the final flicker faded, JP charged through the air at Charlie. He unleashed a barrage of strikes.

Charlie blocked half of the blows with his staff; the other half were absorbed by his rib cage. While each direct hit sent a burning jolt down the corresponding side of his body, they did nothing to wound his confidence.

JP screamed like a samurai as he used both hands and a downward swing to unload his most powerful strike yet.

Charlie defended the blow, but there was such force behind JP's swing that it sent Charlie tumbling backwards through the sky. He righted himself just in time to thwart the first shot in JP's new wave of attacks. He smiled. He was feeling more and more comfortable with his staff and protecting himself against JP's blows with each passing second. Charlie countered the next five strikes before JP finally connected with one. But even the shot that landed was partially obstructed, and more of a graze than a clean hit.

JP took note of Charlie's rapidly advancing skills and was determined to do something about it. He attacked high, low, and everywhere in between. All in quick succession, each one right after the other.

But Charlie successfully blocked every attempted strike, not letting even a single shot slip past his defense.

JP huffed and puffed, his frustrations mounting. He raised his staff above his head with both hands, intending to register another powerful blow. But before he could begin his downswing, another beam of light flashed up from the ground. The rays clipped one of his wings, severing the tip. "Ah!" he screamed as he faltered, falling away from the light and from Charlie.

Charlie used JP's injury to quickly check in on Antony again: He was down to just Saloth and Joseph. Charlie turned his attention back to JP, who was just regaining his balance.

Charlie prepared to protect himself. He was sure another attack would be coming as soon as the brilliance disappeared.

But when the last little speck of light whizzed by, JP didn't charge at Charlie. He merely began to swirl around him with a wicked grin on his face, as if he had something else in mind. "Looks like you're not as worthless as I thought you were," he sneered. "Maybe you do have some of Terry in you."

"No, I don't," Charlie said.

"Well, even if you did, you wouldn't for much longer." JP jetted toward Charlie, this time opting to use his staff to engage his opponent instead of attacking him.

Their staffs locked as they tussled in the air, spinning around, with each of them taking turns trying to overpower the other.

"You're gonna need more than that," JP said with a shove.

"So are you," Charlie said, then gave a thrust of his own.

JP glimpsed at the ground where Antony was about to land a direct shot on Saloth. He turned back to Charlie. "Don't worry about me," he said with a smirk. "Worry about yourself." He made a sudden move, shoving Charlie while disengaging at the same time.

Charlie flew backwards, away from JP and right into the center of the tunnel of light as it exploded into the sky and enveloped his whole body.

CHAPTER
FORTY-TWO

CHARLIE'S BODY CONVULSED as it absorbed all of the celestial energy. The radiance illuminated his skin. His eyes turned into two white-hot orbs.

JP watched eagerly. The buildup was strikingly similar to the one he'd witnessed before Malika's explosion, and he intended to savor every second of it, especially the grand finale. "Bye, Charlie. It's been a blast," he said, emphasizing the last word and timing it so that it coincided with the final ray of light and what he expected to be the end of Charlie.

But much to JP's chagrin, Charlie didn't detonate like he'd hoped. While Charlie's whole body pulsed like it'd gone radioactive, it remained shockingly stable. "What the hell's going on?" JP grunted, a slight tremble in the tail end of his words. "That should've killed you."

"Sorry to disappoint you," Charlie said with a grin.

JP gritted his teeth, his determination resurfacing. "No disappointment. I'd rather end you myself, anyway," he said before bum-rushing Charlie.

Charlie effortlessly swept aside each of JP's strikes and then, for the first time, began to launch an attack of his own. JP's defense was no match for the new Charlie, who landed every strike he attempted. JP's arms, legs, and abdomen all felt the brunt of the blows. But no part of JP took the drubbing harder than his mind. As Antony had pointed out, JP was given what he had, and therefore it could be taken away. JP's evil enthusiasm was beaten from his body with each successive strike.

Charlie raised his weapon over his head and swung the staff downward with a firm two-hand grip, like a Norse god commanding his hammer.

JP absorbed the blow with his staff as each of his hands held opposite ends; however, in taking the hit, his arms and staff were both knocked to his sides. He was temporarily defenseless, leaving a clean path to his neck and what would be a deadly blow if Charlie took it.

Charlie gave every indication that he would. He quickly spun in the air and swung with all of his power.

JP closed his eyes, accepting what was to come.

And then there was nothing.

Another moment passed. More nothing.

JP reopened his eyes. He slowly glanced to his left, where Charlie's staff hovered centimeters from his neck. He turned his attention back to Charlie. Even with Charlie's glowing face, JP could read his expression like a book. "You can't do it," he scoffed. "You can't kill me."

Charlie said nothing.

JP slapped Charlie's staff away with his hand. "Malika was supposed to make you stronger," he said. "But when it's all said and done, you are what you are. You're as weak as you've always been. And there's only one way this ends: You die!"

JP went to launch another attack, but before he could finish his backswing, Charlie whirled his staff and struck JP on the wrist, disarming him.

"Wrong," Charlie said, his eyes burning even brighter as he spoke. "I don't need to kill you."

JP retrieved another serpent from his pouch and transformed it to staff form. "Yes, you do." He wielded his new weapon.

Charlie blocked the strike, keeping JP's staff at bay. "No, I don't," he said firmly, and then turned his gaze down below, where shimmers of light were beginning to escape from the forehead of Joseph, the last of the Beasts.

The rays shot into the sky, right toward Charlie and JP.

JP whipped his wings to avoid the beam.

"It's over," Charlie said.

"No, it's just getting started," JP said. "I don't need them. They clearly weren't much help to me, anyways. I'll just take you all on by myself. I'll—" He stopped short, his face contorting. He was overcome by an intense pressure building in between his temples. It was as if his head had been placed in a vise that kept screwing tighter. "What did you do to me?" he screamed in agony.

"Nothing," Charlie said. "You did this to yourself." He revealed the secret that Malika had told him, and that he had later told Antony and Eddie. He explained that when JP had signed his deal with Lucifer, Joseph didn't just become his protector, he also became the executor of their agreement. As executor, he was required to take collateral from JP: a piece of his soul. This meant the two of them would be forever tethered, and if Joseph went, so did JP.

"You're lying," JP growled.

"No," Charlie said, shaking his head. "You should've read the fine print."

JP cocked his staff over his head and readied to attack Charlie, but the pain had become too much for him. His arms fell back to his sides. His staff returned to snake form and was released from his grasp.

JP's body began to sway like a helicopter hit by enemy fire and struggling to keep from going down. Eventually, his wings stopped fluttering altogether, and he followed his serpent, falling back to the earth.

Charlie dove headfirst after JP. He whipped his wings to boost his acceleration and help him catch up to the free-falling JP. He intercepted JP just before he was about to collide with the pavement. They both landed softly on the asphalt in the train station parking lot.

As soon as they touched down, all of the celestial energy that Charlie had stored escaped through his eyes, shooting back up to the heavens. Once the last ray had faded, his wings neatly folded and disappeared into his back on their own, leaving behind no evidence of their existence except for the rips in the back of his shirt.

◆ ◆ ◆

Antony had already freed Eddie, who had regained his full faculties and was back to his regular self, and they were both finishing untying the still-unconscious Naomi when they spotted Charlie carrying the wounded and wingless JP toward them.

Charlie laid JP down on the platform pavement.

Eddie stormed toward JP, who moaned in agony. "Your pain is only gonna get worse," he said as he cocked his foot back, preparing to plant his boot in JP's ribs.

Charlie yanked Eddie's arm, pulling him back. "No!" he said. "You need to let it go. Let go of your anger. You know that's what Malika would've wanted. Besides, he's already in enough pain. And we won."

Eddie took a deep breath and exhaled. "You're right."

JP looked up at Charlie, Eddie, and Antony as they stood over him and scowled. "If you aren't gonna torture me, why'd you even bother saving me?" he groaned. "Why didn't you just let me die?"

"No one can really save you," Charlie said. "You only have a couple minutes left. But I don't believe that you're all bad. I think there's still some good in you."

"That's what you think?" JP said with a chuckle that was cut short because of the pain. He moaned some more.

"I do," Charlie said. "I think you can help us. I think you will help us, by telling us who killed Eddie and Naomi's parents. So we can find them."

JP's moaning morphed into a sick laughter. "Like I would ever tell you that. But even if I did, it wouldn't matter, anyway," he said, gloating even as he was in the grips of death.

"You'll never get a chance to save them."

"Why?" Eddie said. "Why not?"

"Why?" JP let out a maniacal laugh that sent chills down the others' spines before divulging something even more chilling. "Because it's already too late."

"What do you mean?" Antony said.

JP didn't respond, he just kept cackling harder and harder. Not even the pain it caused could stop him.

Eddie grabbed JP by the shoulders and shook him, asking again, "What the hell do you mean? What's too late?"

JP's fit sputtered to a stop. He let out one last snicker.

Eddie could feel JP's body go limp in his hands.

JP's eyes faded to black, like two ovals of onyx. Eddie quickly let go of JP. His head bounced off of the ground. A dark ooze that resembled motor oil poured from the corners of JP's eye sockets and dripped onto the platform pavement.

The guys jumped out of the way as the sludge beaded and rolled around the ground, as if searching for something. It eventually located cracks in the flooring and disappeared into the earth.

"That was weird," Charlie said.

"Yeah," Eddie agreed. "You think he's gonna go Mount Vesuvius on us?"

Before they could really consider the question, Antony had a realization. "The drive!" he shouted. "He still has it."

Charlie quickly dropped down on one knee and reached into JP's pocket. Nothing. He patted the other pocket. "I got it," he said as he retrieved the drive.

"That was close," Antony said.

They waited a moment to see if JP would turn to ash.

"Or not," Eddie said. "I could be wrong, but it doesn't look like anything is gonna happen."

"No, it doesn't," Charlie said. "What do you guys think he meant when he said we're already too late?"

"There's only one thing I can imagine that it means," Antony said. "The attack is gonna start soon. Real soon."

Charlie was about to respond, when a deep cough just behind the guys interrupted him.

It was Naomi. She was finally coming to.

Charlie and the others rushed to Naomi's side.

"Are you okay?" Charlie asked as he knelt down by her.

Naomi nodded and then quickly averted his gaze, looking down. "I'm so sorry I left you guys. I'm so sorry—"

Charlie gently lifted her head up by the chin. "Don't worry about it," he said. "We all make mistakes. We're just glad you're all right."

Naomi looked to Eddie and Antony, who nodded in agreement. "Thanks," she said and let out a faint smile. "I am now."

The guys helped Naomi to her feet.

"If there's any truth to what JP said, we should probably get a move on it," Charlie said.

"Yeah," Antony agreed. "Even though this area is pretty remote, there's no way someone didn't see all that action in the sky. It's only a matter of time before the cops roll up."

The orphans hurried to the van and piled inside. Antony took the driver's seat, Eddie claimed shotgun, and Naomi and Charlie slid in the bucket seats in back.

"Where are we going?" Eddie asked as he retrieved the gas station map from his pocket.

"Well," Antony said, "since we don't know how much time we have. And we really only have one guaranteed lead. I think it only makes sense we pay Terry Heins a little house visit." He fired up the engine, threw the van in gear, and peeled out of the train station parking lot.

CHAPTER
FORTY-THREE

THE ORPHANS HEADED WEST, back toward the Bay Area. As ready as they were to do battle with Terry's men, they still couldn't help but be somewhat rattled by JP's final words, which continued to dance in their heads.

"I was thinking about what JP said, and it doesn't really make any sense," Charlie said a half hour into their drive, breaking up the silence.

"Why not?" Eddie said.

"There are only two options," Charlie said. "Either we're too late to save our parents, or like Antony pointed out, we're too late to stop the attack on Heaven."

"But we can't be too late to save our parents," Antony said.

"Why?" Naomi said. "Because you already saved yours?"

"No," Antony said. "Because Malika said that even if they attacked first, it wouldn't stop us from saving them."

"That's right," Charlie agreed. "She said that we still could, but that it'd just be a lot more challenging."

"So it has to be that we're too late to stop the attack on Heaven, like Antony said," Eddie concluded.

"Except that doesn't make complete sense, either," Charlie said. "After all of the souls we freed, that should delay the attack at least a little. Not to mention, as far as I can tell, it doesn't seem like anything is going on just yet."

"It really doesn't," Antony said. "You'd think the skies would open up or something."

"It can't be too late if nothing has happened."

Eddie twisted the radio knobs, but all he got was static. "If only this thing worked, we could check the news."

"So what do we do?" Naomi said.

"The only thing we can do is keep our eyes peeled and be ready for anything that happens," Antony said. "Everything else is out of our control."

The orphans continued down the interstate in silence, their heads on swivels, searching for any signs from the outside world that the attack had begun.

◆ ◆ ◆

After a couple hours and not even the faintest hint of trouble, all of the orphans were starting to feel the effects of their sleepless night. The rising sun gave them temporary boosts of energy, but less than ten minutes after the light first crept up over the mountains behind them, those jolts were all spent.

Antony squinched his eyes a couple times in hopes that ocular exercise would correct his vision, and he'd stop seeing double. But the results were minimal. "Any chance someone else wants take a turn at the wheel?" he asked.

All of the others passed on the invitation. They were in no position to drive, either.

"Maybe we should just pull over," Charlie said.

"But we're only a couple hours away," Eddie said as he fought off a yawn.

Naomi yawned in reaction to Eddie's yawn. "We could get some food," she suggested. "That might help wake everyone up."

Eddie scanned the area around them. They were a couple miles outside of Davis, California. Both sides of the freeway were flat farmlands. "I don't know that we're gonna have much luck around here," he said. "Looks like mostly grains. Nothing we can just pick and eat."

"I was thinking we'd go to a restaurant," Naomi said.

"Oh, yeah. I forgot about that was even an option."

"I can treat," Charlie said.

"I never turn down a free meal."

Antony turned off at the next exit. He passed through a couple lights before pulling into the Dixon Diner. The orphans stumbled out of the van and plodded toward the '50s-style restaurant that resembled a large silver lunchbox.

"What happened to your shirt?" Naomi asked, noticing the tears down the back of Charlie's shirt. She poked through the hole with her finger.

"Oh, my wings must've ripped it," Charlie said.

"No way!" Eddie shouted, his eyes practically popping out of his head. "So you did grow wings?"

"Keep it down!" Antony said.

"I thought that was a dream," Eddie said, still worked up but opting for a more appropriate volume.

"You seriously grew wings?" Naomi asked Charlie. She was clearly as excited as Eddie, but did a much better job containing her emotions.

"Yeah," Charlie said, playing it off.

"You gotta teach us how you did that," Eddie said.

"I don't really know how I did it," Charlie said with a shrug. "I just did it."

"You 'just did it'? What are you, Nike?"

"No. I mean, that's just what I did. After I healed myself, I figured that I didn't have time to run down to the station to save you. So I just believed that I could fly, and before I knew it, I had wings."

"That's it?" Eddie said, skeptical.

"Yeah."

Eddie shook his head. He stopped in the parking lot while the others continued toward the diner. He closed his eyes and worked to focus all of his energy letting out a few grunts.

Antony turned to Eddie. "What the hell are you doing?"

"Isn't it obvious?" Eddie said, keeping his eyes shut. "I'm about to grow some dope wings."

"You might want to reconsider that."

"Why?"

"Let's just assume you're successful," Antony said. "Don't you think that might draw a little unwanted attention, maybe make some of the nice, small-town people around here freak out?"

Eddie finally opened his eyes and scanned the area. A handful of cars passed by; even without wings, the obvious out-of-towners were already drawing attention. "You might be on to something," he said.

"I think I am." Antony took off his coat and handed it to Charlie. "That'll cover the holes in your shirt, too. Might as well try keep any suspicions to a minimum."

"Thanks," Charlie said as he threw on the jacket.

They continued toward the restaurant and headed inside.

A hostess in her fifties waited at the stand by the entrance, watching a small TV that hung in the corner and was playing the news. "Four?" the hostess asked, holding up four fingers as the orphans entered.

"Yeah," Charlie said with a nod. He glanced at the TV—everything appeared to be normal—and then at the hostess's nametag. "Any big news today, Gillian?"

"Well, the Cowboys lost last night," Gillian said.

"Nice," Eddie said. He could tell by the scowl on Gillian's face that she didn't agree with his assessment. "Well, for me, at least. Go 'Skins!"

"Nothing else, though?" Antony said.

"Just the same old, same old," Gillian said.

"Nothing wrong with that," Charlie said. He shared a knowing glance with the others. Whatever JP had been talking about hadn't happened yet.

Gillian led them through the otherwise empty diner to a red-and-white faux-leather booth in the back. She handed them menus and silverware, ran down the daily specials, and then went to grab their waters.

"I'm so hungry, I could probably eat everything on this menu," Naomi said as she opened her menu.

"The old me would've really loved a lot of these options," Eddies said as he perused the options before him. "But I'll probably just get the garden omelet."

"I was thinking the same thing," Charlie said, putting his menu down. "I'm gonna need some coffee, too. A lot, actually."

"Totally," Naomi agreed. "If I don't get half a pot soon, I'll probably fall asleep in my food."

"I can go put that in right now. How do you like your coffee?" Charlie said as he started to get up from his seat. "Cream? Sugar? Anything?"

"Just black."

"Me, too," Charlie said. "I usually get a lot of crap for it."

"So do I," Naomi said and then smiled at Charlie.

Charlie smiled back.

"Whoa, whoa, whoa," Eddie said, breaking up their small moment. "Slow down. You guys aren't gonna do this now. Not with me and Antony right here."

"I don't know what you're talking about," Charlie said.

"Of course you don't," Eddie said, not buying what Charlie was selling. "We were all born yesterday and have no idea what's going on. And don't even get me started on the fact that Antony totally dropped the ball and should've said you guys like your coffee like you like your men."

"That joke is tired," Antony said. "No one uses it anymore."

"I do."

"Maybe your jokes need to be updated."

"That's irrelevant."

"What are you even talking about?" Naomi said.

"This whole little cutesy thing between you two," Eddie said, gesturing to Charlie and Naomi. "The numbers don't work anymore, and we saw how the last hookup ended. I say no dating or grouping up."

"Don't be so close-minded," Antony said as he rested his hand on Eddie's thigh.

Eddie chuckled. "Okay, that was actually funny. But I'm serious. There aren't enough of us. We can't have factions."

"I agree," Naomi said.

"Me, too," Charlie said, not wanting to concede but knowing that Eddie was right, they didn't need any distractions.

"See," Eddie said, "that's exactly what I'm talking about. Right there, you were just a little too quick to agree."

Charlie shook his head and sighed. "Whatever. We're all on the same page. I'm gonna go put in the order for the coffee, okay?" He made his way back down the narrow aisle to the front of the restaurant. "We're gonna have four coffees," he said to Gillian, who was back at her stand.

Gillian didn't respond.

"Excuse me?" Charlie said firmly, trying to get her attention, but Gillian remained silent. Charlie studied her face. It was frozen. Her eyes were completely glassed over and stuck on the tiny TV. He matched her gaze.

BREAKING NEWS flashed on the screen. A network anchor explained that they'd just confirmed that the president of the United States had passed away that morning from a heart attack. The co-anchor noted that he was the thirteenth world leader to succumb to a heart attack in the past two weeks.

"Guys," Charlie called to the others, "you're gonna want to see this."

The rest of the orphans joined Charlie in the front of the restaurant. They all shared in his shock as they read the details on the scrolling ticker. But that was only the beginning.

Seconds later, one of the reporters jumped in with another breaking story: the new president had already selected his vice-president. The reporter added that a confirmation hearing would be required before the newly appointed vice-president could officially take office, but that it wasn't believed to be a problem given the bipartisan popularity of the pick.

The news program cut to the White House press room. Camera flashes exploded from all angles, washing out the face of the new vice-president as he stepped to the podium. When the little bursts of light subsided and the cameras regained focus, the orphans were blown away by who they saw standing there. It was Terry Heins. As usual, Cain and Max were right at his side.

The orphans watched in stunned silence as Terry nodded solemnly to the crowd, and then delivered a generic speech, asking for prayers and thanking the recently deceased president for his service before moving on to the standard campaign platitudes. And then, as it all seemed to be winding down, Terry's message and tone took an unexpected turn.

"There is one last thing that the president asked me to address," Terry said. "And that is the fact that certain unnamed countries have felt the need to dock their nuclear submarines on the edge of our borders for far too long. Our leaders have repeatedly advised them to reposition their fleets, but they have refused to stand down. We view this to be a clear act of aggression. Now, I've learned a lot during my years in the corporate world, and the president and I agree that people, and countries, work better with deadlines. Which is why we have decided to give these unnamed nations until noon Eastern Standard Time to remove all of their submarines from our waters, or we will have to remove them by force. That is all. And again, prayers for the late President Griffin."

To the average viewer, Terry's closer would've appeared to be nothing more than the usual political posturing. Surely there would be no escalation. However, Charlie and the orphans knew better. They knew what Terry was capable of, and that his threats were anything but empty.

Terry's speech had answered all of the questions that JP's last words had raised. While there would undoubtedly be an attack on Heaven at some point, it wasn't the first target. The first strike would be against Earth.

Naomi turned to Charlie. "What are we gonna do?" she asked, the weight of her words worn heavily on her face.

"There's only one thing we can do," Charlie said as he narrowed his eyes, which remained aimed at the TV and the image of Terry Heins that it displayed. "Whatever it takes to stop them."

END OF BOOK ONE

ACKNOWLEDGMENTS

I'd like to thank everyone who took the time to read *The Orphans*. I really appreciate your support. Hopefully you were able to get as much joy from reading the book as I received writing it. If you have a second, please rate the book on Amazon, iTunes, or Goodreads. And if you have two seconds, write a short and honest review.

My deepest thanks to ...

My parents and siblings for their love and guidance. My wife for being my sounding board and biggest cheerleader. Brian Levy for helping shape my career. Zoe Sandler for making the book even better and believing in me as a writer. Kristie Minke for her amazing illustrations. Lauren Leibowitz for cleaning up my grammar and teaching me the difference between blonde and blond.

My beta readers (in alphabetical order) for helping make the book the best it could be: Daniel and Julia Descalso, Michael Diliberti, Christine Gamlen, Tod Gamlen, Chris Gauthier, Dave Hartung, Kristin Moak, Carrie Sullivan, John Sullivan, Joseph Sullivan, Maura Sullivan, Michelle Sullivan, and Dilshad Vadsaria.

And all of the members of the Sullivan Street Team (also in alphabetical order) for pounding the pavement and getting the word out: Isaiah Aguilar, Maggie Astolfi, Ron Babcock, Eric Barker, Maia Bentz, Amanda Bernal, Chad Bernal, Tim and Michelle Bower, Scott Bowser, Shawn Carlow, Jill Carter, Brian Clark, Tony Cortez, Brian Daniels, Paul Danke, Ray Dara, Raj Desai, Daniel and Julia Descalso, Steph Descalso,

Meg Dolny, Gretchen Domek, Eric and Ginny Dorflinger, Stephanie Dorsey, Tom Ebnet, Kate Ellingson, Casey Feigh, Ryan Feigh, Keith and Casey Florance, Bob Flury, Gina Forte, Marisa Forte, Tony Forte, Barbara Gamlen, Christine Gamlen, Marie-Jose Gamlen, Tod Gamlen, Victoria Gamlen, Andrew Gettens, Josh Goldenberg, Tia Gonsior, Sean Green, Ed Greer, Talin Gregorian, Danielle Guidry, Dave Hartung, Jared Hasbrouck, Jon Hofeller, Eugene Huang, Michael Huber, Kristian and Carmen Hughes, Khalid Itum, Chris and Dorothy Jackman, Adam Jacobs, Nandini Jayaprasad, Allison Johnston, Tim and JoAnn Johnston, Walton Jordan, Soo Kong, Mike Kong, Marcus Krause Beth and Greg Lewis, Katie Lochte, Garrett Logan, Chris Lutz, Scott Maciej, Katie Martin, Blair Marshall, James Mastroianna, Mollie McCurry, Ryan McKee, Mike and Amanda McQuigg, Aaron and Kristin Moak, Hormoz Moaven, Leonard Monfredo, Bryan Mosko, Jenna Pfannenstein, Evan Phillips, Jon Post, Sarah Potthoff, Dave Prakash, Neil and Laura Prakash, Kiera Reilly, Brent Salner, Andrew Schmidt, Natalie Seufferlein, Shawn Shaffie, Nick Straiter, Brendan and Sarah Sullivan, Dan and Erica Sullivan, John Sullivan, Joseph Sullivan, Lise Sullivan, Maura Sullivan, Michelle Sullivan, Mike and Carrie Sullivan, Brendan Taylor, Heather Taylor, Laura Taylor, Mary Clare Taylor, Mellany Walia, Trevor and Trish Wetterling, Caren Williams, Courtney Woods, Avi Yashchin, and Satra Zarghami.

Thanks!

ABOUT THE AUTHOR

According to his mother, Matthew showed signs of creativity at a very early age. Of course, that might just be a polite way of saying he was a little weird.

After graduating from The Johns Hopkins University, Matthew began working as an investment banker and was certain he had his whole life and career mapped out. He even had a twenty-year plan to prove it. But after a yearlong battle with cancer (he's been cured for over thirteen years now), Matthew realized that he needed to scrap his plans and focus on living in the moment. A few weeks later, he quit his job and began writing.

Since taking the leap, Matthew has written for film (*30 Minutes or Less*), television, and print, and loves crafting stories for all mediums and audiences. Matthew currently resides in Arlington, Virginia with his amazing wife. When he isn't writing, he enjoys spending time with his family and friends, and watching sports.

For more information on Matthew and his upcoming projects, including the second book in the *Orphans Trilogy*, please visit his website:

www.matthewsullivanwriter.com

36250608R00216

Made in the USA
Middletown, DE
27 October 2016